The Last Pilgrims

Book 1

by
Michael Bunker

The Last Pilgrims
© Copyright 2012 by Michael Bunker.

ISBN 978-0578088891

FIRST PRINTING

To keep up with the latest on The Last Pilgrims saga:
www.lastpilgrims.com

For information on Michael Bunker, or to read his blog:
www.michaelbunker.com

To contact Michael Bunker, please write to:

M. Bunker
1251 CR 132
Santa Anna, Texas 76878

The Last Pilgrims

Book 1

by
Michael Bunker

Acknowledgments

I hate to make this come across like an Academy Award speech, but this book required a lot of helpers, who all deserve mention. There is no way I will remember everyone, and that is to my shame. I want to thank all of the hundreds of readers, commenters, and reviewers who helped with their comments and advice in the earliest creative stages of *The Last Pilgrims*. More than anyone, I want to thank Stewart for all of his help, support, artistic input, and encouragement. I want to thank David S. for his advice, support, and leadership. I want to thank all of my editors: Danielle, Shannon, Carol, Stewart, David, Mihai, Billybob and Natasha. Special thanks go to Pat Tolbert, Chad McCarthy, and Kris Dahl for their support, and to the dozens of other loyal supporters on IndieGoGo.com for their donations to the project. Thanks to my friend Herrick Kimball for once again being willing to review the book for me, and to all of you other reviewers as well. To everyone in our Agrarian community here in Central Texas for your support and loyalty—you are the *real* Vallenses.

Special thanks to my family, for allowing me the freedom to spend the thousands of hours that go into this sort of endeavor; and especially to my wife Danielle for her never-ending patience and long-suffering with me. I love you all.

A shout-out to all of you *"Lasties"*, who believed in this project from the beginning and never failed to be enthusiastic about it. Thank you for staying along for the ride.

Table of Contents

"Do you fear God's wrath, Phillip?"

"I know that, if we let these people be slaughtered by Aztlan, I'd have every reason to fear it."

"Will the Vallenses fight now?"

Phillip shook his head. "No."

Prologue

In the two decades following the collapse of the imperial Western powers, and the destruction of the industrial system, much of the medieval system of monarchy and aristocracy had reasserted itself throughout the world.

The collapse of the unviable and unsustainable world system had watered the earth with blood in a way that very few could have imagined, and only 20 years later, most of those who had lived through the crash now wondered how that system had managed to last for over 200 years.

Across a massively depopulated continent, ancient superstitions and idolatries multiplied as the new monarchs adopted Napoleon's idea that a monolithic state religion, even if it were a false one, was necessary to the peace and security of the realm. The freedom to practice one's own religion, or to practice no formal religion at all, was rare, indeed, following the collapse. North America had come to resemble Old Europe in many ways.

Although the most ancient of motivations—greed, avarice, and covetousness—were behind most of the persecutions and genocides of this new era, these were almost exclusively carried out under the pretext of religion. The Bishops and Cardinals, much as they had done in Europe six centuries earlier, had multiplied like locusts across the land and served the more predacious monarchs as willingly as they did their own bellies.

Even though much of what was once the United States had been conquered, the land and people absorbed into the fiefdom of some newly formed kingdom or another, large areas of the country—usually the wildest and most inaccessible parts—were classified as "ungovernable". Many of these areas were still farmed by 'plain' peoples and sects. Akin to Amish or Mennonites of the past, these peoples universally rejected absorption into the realms of those regal idolaters who intended to force the practice of predominantly ceremonial religions, contrary to their own beliefs, upon them.

The *Vallenses*, one of the largest and most well-known of the 'plain' sects in the South, were branded as heretics by the religious authorities in order that the King of Aztlan, as he greatly hoped, could either subjugate them or remove them from his Kingdom. Due to the rather inhospitable climate, the relative inaccessibility of the region, and active militant or "insurgent" activity, the King had heretofore met with little success in bringing the Vallenses under his domination. For these reasons, most of Central Texas and the Hill Country were considered by the King of Aztlan to be in open rebellion against his rule, and persecutions and martyrdoms were not uncommon.

The Vallenses considered themselves humble and obedient servants and an exceedingly peaceful people. They only wished to farm their lands, raise and nurture their families, and serve one another in humility and meekness. Their 'crime' was that they desired to do these things outside of the predatory control of people with whom they had nothing in common.

The Bishops of New Rome had, over the intervening decades, sent missionaries and emissaries to the Vallenses in order to receive their voluntary submission to both the King of Aztlan, and the accepted religion of the realm. Though they met with no success, the missionaries were always treated well by the plain people, and they had been assured that the Vallenses desired no Kingdom in this world, and that they sought only to be helpful and productive citizens in the realm. However, they had no intention of abjuring their religion or the free practice of it.

Though some of the Vallenses' co-religionists from former urban areas and regions more easily controlled by New Rome had capitulated and had brought themselves and their parishioners under the umbrella of the capital, the Vallensian people of Central Texas and the Texas Hill Country had resisted any amalgamation into the Kingdom and religion of Aztlan.

Of late, the duty and obligation of the subjugation of the Vallenses had fallen to the Duke of El Paso, an ambitious man who had been a drug kingpin prior to the collapse. The Duke intended, by whatever means necessary, to foully and finally bring an end to any resistance in Central Texas.

The Vallenses, led for some 30 years by Elders, elected from among themselves, foresaw the evil that was coming—both the collapse and the global disasters that followed. They believed that the Providence of God had guided them to their lands and to a way of life that left them mostly unharmed and untainted by the collapse of what they called 'The World System.' They were thus largely unaffected by the fall of the system of commerce, industry, and society that ruled and reigned, they believed, via *mammon* prior to the collapse.

The Vallenses believed that the lamp of the apostolic faith continued to burn among them, and they did desire to be a light to the world in the darkest of the last days of the epoch.

And, the Vallenses were not the only ones who rejected the rule of Aztlan. Opposition to the King of Aztlan, who now reigned from his capital city of New Rome in the Sangre de Christo Mountains of what was once northern New Mexico, had united many militant bands of 'freemen' who, like the plain people, would not bow to either nearby prelates or distant kings.

Among the Vallensian low-rolling hills, valleys, and plains, there were free men of independent mind and action. Some of the militia groups in Texas actively traded with the Vallenses, and supported their freedom of lifestyle, worldview, and belief. New Rome considered the militias to be terrorists and branded them "insurgents."

The relationships between the pacifistic Vallenses and the militia were complex. The official position of the eldership of the Vallenses was that they did not condone or support militia activity—even in their own defense. Some of the Vallenses, though, openly traded with, and often materially supported, the freemen against the laws of New Rome and the desires of their own leaders. Thus, relationships were often tense and strained. The plain people desired peace and tranquility and rejected violence in pursuit of those aims. Most of the plain people believed that the violent actions of the militias, even if they were defensive and measured, brought more attention and persecution

12

upon all of the people of the region. Their own history provides ample evidence in support of this view.

Only a decade earlier, in the midst of the coldest days of a very cold post-collapse winter, a great tragedy befell the Vallensian people. Months prior to the tragic massacre, a handful of Vallensian traders were returning to their homes via the Old Comanche Road, when they were captured by a mounted unit of Atzlani soldiers under the command of Santos, a lieutenant in the service of the Duke of El Paso.

The Duke, answering a call from the King of Aztlan and the religious leaders of New Rome to purge the land of heretics and rebels, had sent out raiding parties in hopes of capturing Vallensian traders. New Rome hoped to gain from the captured men intelligence about the militias, after which the Vallenses would be executed as an example and warning to the rebels. The traders were dragged from their wagons, tied up, and hauled over 80 miles to San Angelo, now a frontier town amidst the vast and virtually ungovernable western expanse, where they were burned at the stake in the city square.

In response, a unit of militia riders stole into Santos' camp at night, taking the Aztlani commander hostage, and killing all of his entourage. Santos was carried back into San Angelo by night and left impaled on a pike not far from where the Vallensian traders had been burned.

The Duke of El Paso, offended and enraged (Santos had been his brother-in-law), and seeking to appease both the King and his own wife, had ordered a large army to march on a Vallensian colony to the East of San Angelo. This was an unprecedented attack, both in type and in scale. Prior to this event, the Aztlani leadership had been cautious and measured in their attacks, especially when those attacks called for them to move a large body of men across vast distances, traversing areas under nominal control of the freemen militias, without supply lines or pre-positioned material.

On their journey, the army was harried by freemen scouts and raiders who killed several of their troops. Nonetheless, the army arrived mostly intact and had stormed suddenly into the innocent Vallensian colony, hoping to kill every man, woman and child. Those Vallenses not killed in the initial attack fled eastward into the freezing night, carrying their young and their old with them.

The fleeing Vallenses—most without winter clothing—made it to the rolling hills and valleys of Central Texas, where many of them froze to death over the first few nights due to lack of food or shelter. Along the path of their flight, over 100 people—mostly children, the elderly, and the family members who would not abandon them—were found lying on the ground, dead from hypothermia, babies in the frozen clutches of their mothers, and aged couples dead in icy embraces. This massacre had a polarizing effect on many of the free people of the region. Most Vallenses believed that the royal reprisal, though monstrous and murderous, was the result of the rash actions of the militant freemen. Others, including free traders, believed that the colonists had suffered because of their unwillingness to defend themselves. They had made targets of themselves, and they had suffered for it. In the years that followed the Winter Massacre, the Vallenses had attempted to persuade the militiamen with whom they had contact to be more cautious and circumspect in their responses to Aztlani tyranny. "We do not want to pay for the vengeful notions of freemen honor," they would say.

The free militias, on the other hand, increased their numbers, their training, and their intelligence gathering. Keeping the memory of the Winter Massacre alive in the minds of innocent people became one of their greatest recruiting tools.

There were other incidents and, as time passed, tensions grew.

The King of Aztlan, from the moment he had assumed power, desired absolutely to rid himself and his realm of all heretics and insurgents. He had on many occasions requested, even *demanded*, his underlings and bannermen to sweep the Vallenses and all of the free militias from Texas soil.

The king's decrees did not have the desired effect for a number of reasons. First, the Vallenses lived in areas over which it was very difficult to impose rules or laws from outside. Furthermore, following the collapse, the roads had degraded (some naturally, others by the willful acts of both rebels and

14

saints), making travel difficult and unpredictable; and because most remote villages were hostile to Aztlan, it would have been nearly impossible to maintain a full-time fort or base so far away from Aztlani-controlled areas.

Second, the freemen militias patrolled most of the areas of Central and West Texas that were not directly and effectively under the active control of Aztlan.

Third, local leaders were not keen to incur a loss to themselves and their own people. The Vallenses were the most fruitful producers of food and goods in all of Texas, thus a ruler was more likely to be immediately concerned with meeting the needs of his people than obeying a distant King. Oftentimes the belly trumps the heart.

In many ways, the world had returned to what most people had once believed were the idyllic and romantic days of kings and knights. However, once it became real, the romance was harder to appreciate. Still, many saw it as an act of God, who had hewn down the weeds and brambles (the deceitfulness of riches and the cares of the world) that choked out the Word and the way God would have men live.

Some of the same people who had once programmed computers, sold cars, or built shopping malls now plowed fields, picked cotton, and hand-dug their own root cellars.

So much of the old world had been an edifice built on shifting sand. Like an onion, technology had been layered upon technology until only a handful of people actually knew how anything really worked. People made their lives increasingly dependent on a structure that was less and less reliable and destined to crash. The amount of raw materials needed to maintain the most critical technologies on which the entirety of the advanced world balanced so dangerously was mind-boggling.

Prior to the collapse, the whole world could be shaken by what were, by historical standards, relatively minor natural (or unnatural) disasters. In their ignorance, people shut their eyes to the perilous condition of the entire system, ignoring the signs of the impending systemic collapse.

Like Rome and Ancient Greece before it, the Western lifestyle, coveted by the entire world, had created a very productive system (one that was both enviable and unviable). The system was unsustainable, as it was reliant on an increasing number of consumers, while a very small and ever shrinking number of people, using ever more advanced (and therefore tenuous) technology and machines, provided for most of the means of life, living, and survival.

New wonderments, gadgets and entertainment devices appeared daily, as if by magic, to keep the people stupefied and working mindlessly at highly specialized tasks in order to be able to afford a "dream" concocted for them in the boardrooms of large corporations and in the advertising offices of Madison Avenue. The world had become a cult of dependency, and the deception was so complete and so overwhelming that to question it was considered de-facto proof of insanity.

In the end of the old world, nobody was responsible, yet everyone was complicit. The collapse was as inevitable as the arrival of a new morning. Almost everybody died.

Part One

Chapter 1 - Jonathan

Jonathan handed the sealed letter to the post rider, knowing that it could take anywhere from a few weeks to several months to travel from Central Texas to the King of the South States—that is, if it ever got there at all. It was a typical Texas summer morning, and it had never really cooled down overnight so that the heat was on them early as they stood under a sky as blue and as immense as any artist could have ever conjured.

Communications had degraded significantly in the 20 years following the collapse, and although many people, even Jonathan, clearly remembered the days of instant messaging and cellular text service, those short-lived aberrations in the pattern and method of communicating had long since come to an inauspicious end. Post riders were, considering all of the dangers and obstacles they faced, remarkably effective and efficient at delivering important communications over long distances, especially when traveling east—away from the dangers of Aztlan. This was no Pony Express; nonetheless, he was hopeful that, at some point in the future, the King of the South States might be reading his letter.

One beneficial result of the collapse was that it had balanced out the slow nature of long-distance communications... everything else moved slower too. Armies took weeks to travel distances they used to cover in just hours or days, or sometimes even in minutes. Without automated transport, helicopters, airplanes, and tanks, the world had once again become a much bigger place.

He and several Vallensian friends had hiked out to meet the post rider down south of the Bethany Pass just off the Old Comanche road, about a quarter-mile south of Bethany. The summer hadn't been a particularly wet one, but the buffalo grass—where it grew—was still green, waving softly in the warm morning breezes.

Rumors of war were rampant—even more so than normal—so he had decided to meet the rider out on the road in order to keep all speculation, concern, and gossip in Bethany to a minimum. Even as he handed the letter over to the rider, he hoped he was doing the right thing for his people. For a pacifist, a plea for help and defense from a foreign King may not be over the line, but it certainly was tiptoeing near to it.

"May the Lord keep you well and safe on your journey," he said, holding the reins for the post rider as he mounted his horse.

There was no time for a reply because, just as the last words slipped from his mouth, an arrow sliced the air between them, burying itself in the gnarled bark of an ancient oak tree behind them. Jonathan reflexively, almost instinctively, reached up and pulled the rider by the collar from his horse and down to the ground. They both began to crawl towards a small, brush-covered hillock just off the road, in the hope that it might afford them some protection.

The men of Jonathan's party swarmed around noisily, shouting to one another as each tried to identify the direction from which the arrow had come. Several of the men came and surrounded Jonathan and the post rider, creating a protective wall around them.

After a few moments, they began to make their way slowly over the hill back towards the pass and in the direction of Bethany. Almost immediately, and before they were able to react or even run, eight mounted men who seemed to appear out of nowhere surrounded them. All were dressed in the garb of freemen militia, heavily armed with what once would have been called 'primitive' weapons.

These were warriors, and young, and only two could have even been born before the collapse. With the exception of the two *oldlings*, these men had experienced none of the comforting and corrupting influences of the pre-crash world. Stern of face and confident, they were evidently born to battle.

Several of the freemen had longbows in addition to the swords and knives they all carried.

Jonathan stood upright and examined the faces of the men, looking for some clue as to their intentions, when the familiarity of one of them struck him. *Phillip.* As sure as anything in the world could be, he recognized his old friend, who now looked back at him and smiled stiffly. "I suppose that arrow was a gift from you, old friend?" Jonathan asked.

"It was not ours," Phillip responded stiffly. "If it had been, you'd be dead. I reckon it was fired by an assassin... here to kill you. He most likely snuck between our lines overnight." Phillip looked Jonathan in the eye, and the faintest hint of sorrow entered into his voice. "I apologize for our failure, Jonathan."

The two men looked around in uncomfortable silence for a few seconds, before Jonathan looked back at Phillip and replied. "I accept that it wasn't your arrow, Phillip. However, I do not believe that I was its intended target either. From its trajectory and direction, I would say that it was aimed at the post rider."

Phillip's eyes widened and he grinned almost imperceptibly. Turning to the man on his right he whispered a command and the man nodded obediently and rode off to the south. "Ten of my men are out there, already searching for the shooter. I issued my orders as soon as I knew that you were unharmed. We will make sure that they keep him alive when he is captured. We'll need to talk to him. If he has been sent to kill a post rider, there might be more that we need to know."

Phillip rode over to the oak tree and pulled the arrow from it. He examined it for a moment, and then rode back to the company. "This is an Aztlani arrow. The wood used to make it is unlike any found around here, and the fletching is helical, rather than straight. I've pulled plenty of these from the bodies of friends. I have no doubt about its origin."

Jonathan gestured to the post rider, and with a slight nod, the rider galloped eastward carrying the letter to the King of the South States.

"It seems as if no time at all has passed since I saw you last, Phillip," he said, after a brief pause, "but we both know that it has."

Phillip looked up from examining the arrow. "Yes, It has."

"It's good to see you alive and well after all these years. Of course, we had heard word that you were out there... fighting. But," Jonathan rubbed his beard, "it is hard to know anything for sure these days." He looked his old friend in the eye. "Whether you believe it or not, I am happy to finally see you. It's been way too long. Let's go into Bethany and get something to drink. It's hot and..." he smiled at Phillip affectionately, "...I feel as if I have seen a ghost."

He knew that the "ghost" line was a throw-off one, since *The Ghost* was what people already called Phillip, but Jonathan, indeed, felt as if he were in the presence of a ghost. Or a myth. Or maybe a legend. Still, there was no mistaking his old friend. Phillip was only a few years younger than him, but the militia leader was a hard, leathery man, muscled and firm—a man of war and of action. His eyes were piercing, blue, and deep.

Phillip beckoned to his men, and they responded instantly, moving in an immediate, well-coordinated response. "We have some business to attend to here first. We've had a mission failure, and there will need to be... an inquiry. Please go on back to Bethany. I know where to find you, and I'll be along in good time." Without another word, Phillip turned and rode back over the hill, followed by his entourage. In seconds, they were gone.

Jonathan and his men made it back to the village in good time. Although somewhat shaken by the turn of events, he really was glad to see Phillip. Phillip had once been his closest friend, and for many years since then, Jonathan had heard the stories, the legends of *The Ghost* and of Phillip's War against Aztlan. For some time now—maybe since the collapse—Phillip and his Ghost militia had been patrolling a buffer zone around the community of Vallenses, and, more particularly, around Jonathan. While the two men had not spoken in decades, it was widely speculated that the militia had some vested interest in protecting the Vallenses and their leader. This new situation—the two leaders actually meeting together—if it became widely known in Aztlan, could cause troubles for Jonathan and his people.

The village that the Vallenses called Bethany was still a small one, but it had grown significantly in the last 10 years. Very few people lived in the town proper, but several stores and small shops lined the main street and many of those who worked in the shops lived in small homes of adobe or stone construction in the town. For anyone with knowledge of history, Bethany looked as a small village in England or France might have looked only a few hundred years ago... with some Old American West exceptions. There was the blacksmith shop that flew the banner of Grayson the Smithy, and a General Store not unlike many that dotted the West during the first European expansion into those lands. The town of Bethany now had a Cooper, a Wheelwright, a Thatcher, a Cobbler, a Brewer, and a small grist mill powered by mules and human muscle and sweat.

Bethany was neat and ordered, like the homes and lands of all of the Vallenses, and it may have been most notable for what it lacked. Owing to what had happened to the world over the last few decades, there were no 'poor', no beggars, no thieves, and no highwaymen in the town. Some attributed this fact to the presence in Central Texas of the militias, but it could not be denied that everything seemed to have a meaning and purpose, and the town gave off an essence of safety and security, of peace and of contentment.

Jonathan and his men entered the public house, which offered all that its name implied, and a little bit more. It was a pub, but it also was the primary meeting place and conference center in Bethany. Jonathan glanced at the oaken walls, decorated with postings and notices—advertisements or requests for anything from barter labor, to ratting dogs, to cattle. The pub was constructed of thick old post oaks, drawn up by oxen from along the Colorado River and hauled north where they were hewn and placed by hand. The structure was one of the few buildings in Bethany made entirely of wood.

The Elders and the men of the town who were present in the pub gathered around and Jonathan related what had happened south of the pass. He had started the day wanting to keep the business with the letter and the post-rider as a closely held secret, but he knew that after the attack—with Phillip coming into Bethany—there was no way secrecy was possible. The men listened with fascination and not without some trepidation. "The *Ghost* is coming here?" they whispered to one another, in childlike awe. Jonathan was amused.

"Phillip is a friend and not a phantom. He will have information we need, and we can hardly be inhospitable to him and his men. However, meeting with him could be... problematic... if word of it gets to the Duke or the King," he explained. "We'll have to accept the risks, and probably much more than that. We are neither at war with Aztlan, nor in alliance with the militia. We speak freely to both sides, and the King will just have to accept that."

"The King will accept no such thing." It was David, his 25-year-old son, who interjected. "Aztlan is not in the business of *understanding* our situation," he said, with respect, but not without a hint of sarcasm. "You give them too much credit, Father. Aztlan wants us destroyed and out of their way. They will use any pretext for war against us, as you well know, and meeting with the leader of the resistance will be interpreted by them as an act of war. Not that I oppose it, because I don't, but you know it is true."

"Agreed," Jonathan replied, looking his son in the eye. "But our actions are not dictated by New Rome or El Paso. We do not answer to commanders of freeman base camps hidden on the Colorado, or in the desert, or up on Guadalupe Peak. Our actions are dictated by what is right and good—what is honorable."

David smiled, "I'm glad to hear you say that, Father. Then let us join forces with Phillip, have war with Aztlan, and be done with it!" Restrained laughter filled the room, as Elders and laymen alike watched the son jovially jab his father.

Although pacifism was the official position of the Vallenses, and had been from the beginning, not everyone was in agreement with it—at least not in the present situation. David, the pastor's own son, was among those who, though non-violent by nature and up-bringing, believed that the time had come, and was now long past, for armed resistance, or, at the very least, active material support of the freemen militias.

The light-hearted dispute among the men in the pub devolved into a more general discussion of current events, Aztlan's belligerence and genocidal intentions, and the state of the world as they knew it. Eventually, the conversation drifted back to Phillip and his Ghost militia, and to the speculation as to his reasons for actively defending Bethany and protecting Jonathan.

After an hour or so, Phillip and several of his men rode up to the public house. Jonathan watched through the large, open, glassless windows as Phillip's men silently took up defensive positions throughout the village. Everyone assumed that a larger force of militia were out there, posted outside of the town, primarily to the west and south.

When Phillip entered the pub, a palpable silence settled on the room. Jonathan heard only the occasional whisper as Vallensian men examined Phillip the Ghost and looked around at one another in awe—resulting from both fear and simple curiosity.

There was not a man present who hadn't heard of Phillip and his exploits at the helm of his tiny army. Some of the Elders looked suspiciously at the militia leader. They vividly recalled the events and aftermath of the Winter Massacre, the names and frozen faces of the dead imprinted in their memory forever. A few admired Phillip, and secretly (or in some cases, not so secretly) hoped that the Vallenses would decide to help the freemen in their war against Aztlani tyranny and aggression. It was a room divided by passions, policy, and principles.

Phillip nodded to the assembled Vallenses and greeted them individually as he made his way through the gathered throng to where Jonathan had risen from his seat. Phillip and the Vallensian pastor embraced as old friends ought, and Jonathan clasped Phillip's arm and back as he guided his guest into a seat of honor at the head of a long trestle table carved exquisitely by Vallensian hand out of the reddest Mesquite wood.

"Welcome Phillip, and may God's grace, mercy and protection be upon you and your people," Jonathan intoned, almost sadly.

"And upon you all," Phillip replied. "It was not our plan to disturb you today, or to interfere with your business in any way. However, it seems that the attack on the post rider—if that is indeed what it was—has altered our plans."

"It was God's will." Jonathan stated plainly, and all of the Vallenses nodded their agreement.

"Then it seems that God has also willed that you face your attacker, because my men caught up with the Aztlani assassin. He had not fled very far. He was captured as he stopped to rest by Mud Creek and was taken into custody." Phillip dropped his head and fiddled with his hat, which he had removed upon entering the pub. "If this had been merely an assassination attempt upon your person, Jonathan, we would have already dealt with him according to our own justice. He'd be dead, and we'd be gone. But it seems that an attack on a simple post rider, when the leader of the Vallensian people is only steps away, requires that we spend some time questioning the man." Phillip glanced around the room before adding, almost as an afterthought, "He surrendered peacefully enough."

"Where is he?" Jonathan asked.

"My men are holding him just outside of the village. We wanted your permission to bring him in, since he is bound and in our custody."

"If he is not armed, will you untie him and bring him here?"

"No, brother," Phillip replied seriously, "we will allow you to *assist us* in questioning him, but only if he remains bound. If you don't agree, we will take our leave and deal with him in our own way."

Jonathan looked up into the dark oaken rafters before closing his eyes in thought. After a pause, he nodded to Phillip. "Given that you leave me no choice, I request that you bring him," Jonathan sighed, shaking his head, "with the understanding that the man may not be killed or harmed while he is on our soil." The Vallensian men whispered among themselves, some indicating disagreement, while others nodded solemnly.

Phillip nodded to one of his men who was standing outside the open window watching the proceedings. The man signaled to an unseen compatriot and, moments later, the assassin appeared at the door of the pub, in the very effective control of three of Phillip's armed soldiers.

A rush of activity ensued. Tables were moved, chairs were stacked along the walls to provide the observers a better view, and an area for questioning was cleared near the center of the pub. David Wall provided a chair for the Aztlani prisoner, and, for the longest time, there was silence, as the men in the room quietly debated how to conduct the proceedings. After much shuffling and whispering, Jonathan rose and approached the bound man.

"I am Jonathan Wall, Pastor to the Vallenses. We welcome you, in these unhappy circumstances, to our village. We pray that no harm comes to you here." Jonathan paused to collect his thoughts. "We would like to know of your mission, and of your intentions. We would like to know why you have attacked us, as we are a peaceful people, and why your government seeks to do us evil when we strive only towards good." Jonathan paused again before continuing, "But let me tell you a bit about the situation you face, so you do not try to deceive us." Jonathan approached the prisoner and crouched down before him, "We have not bound you. These soldiers are not with us. They are not part of us. They don't care for your life or your soul. It is most probable that, barring some divine intervention, you *will* die today. If you lie to me, we will all know it, and your fate will be sealed by your own hand. Know also that it will be an act of suicide, which we do not believe God forgives. If, however, you are killed today by these men, against our will and your own, after you have dealt honestly with us and have provided us with the answers we seek," Jonathan paused a moment for effect, looking over to Phillip then back to the assassin, "your death will be a murder, and will be on the head of

26

another. I desire to help you, not hurt you, regardless of your aims or intentions."

With that, Jonathan stood up and began to pace back and forth before the prisoner. "Here is where I am confused, so perhaps you can help me... First, you are a single assassin, and clearly very capable. You infiltrated many miles behind the military lines of very able and wary militiamen. You are obviously skilled and trusted by those who sent you. Yet, your shot missed the target as if by intent. It was evidently not blocked or deflected in any way. My fourteen-year-old daughter could have made that shot, and successfully too. I cannot fathom how an assassin could have missed that shot." Jonathan stopped for a minute, and then scratched his head. "Second. Given that you were able to sneak through the lines of the freemen militia, it is incomprehensible that you would not use the same precautions on your return journey. Instead, you took your sweet time, and were captured out in the open, resting by a creek. That makes it seem, at least to me, that you wanted to get caught. Why?"

The men in the pub began to whisper to each other excitedly. Obviously, these were the factors that most of them—even the men who had been there during the attack—had not considered. Jonathan continued...

"Third. Your arrow was obviously that of Aztlani military. It was readily identifiable. If your intention was to kill either the post rider, or me, by using an Aztlani arrow, you would have openly announced the belligerent intentions of New Rome to deal murderously with us. Such a foolish action could prompt many neutral people, and even some among ourselves, to join the likes of Phillip in their fight against the Aztlani army." Jonathan looked around the room, silently indicating that he recognized that many of them privately hoped to join the battle against Aztlan. "Your actions betray you, my friend, and they make me wonder what your true intentions are. Come now! Intentionally missed shot? Using an Aztlani arrow? Then you just saunter on down to the creek and wait there to be captured? Tell us! What's your game?"

"He is a spy, sent here to infiltrate us!" David exclaimed, pulling on the sleeve of his father.

"Let's ask him. If he is as smart as he appears to be, he will not lie to us, given the implications I outlined for him," Jonathan retorted calmly. "Are you a spy, sir? Are you here to infiltrate our peaceful people? What did you hope to learn?"

The assassin was clearly nervous, but not to the extent that would be expected under the circumstances. It seemed to Jonathan that all of his actions had led their captive to this moment. He knew what he was doing. He was a short man, but athletic and strong. His black curly hair was in stark and ironic contrast to the very short, almost military hairstyle of the pacifistic Vallensian men. All of the men, both militia and Vallensian, wore beards. The time when men spent hours grooming and shaving their faces and bodies had long passed. He was young, probably a *middling* like David, who was born five years before the collapse; and the Assassin had obviously been trained in military tactics, probably in some Aztlani school. His voice was steady as he addressed Jonathan. "I am not a spy, but I have been trained as an assassin. I did miss on purpose, and I did use the Aztlani arrow intentionally to signal that purpose to you, sir. My target, at least by orders given to me by my superiors in El Paso, was the post rider and not yourself. The Duke, and the King for that matter, would never assassinate you, Mr. Wall, at least not based on the current situation. You are as safe against Aztlani violence as any man could be. The Duke ordered that the post rider be killed, and preferably in your presence. Your letter was never to reach the King of the South States."

The fact that the Duke, over 500 miles away in El Paso, knew of his letter disturbed him not a little, but it was not time to go on a mole hunt.

"You were to kill the post rider, but it is evident that you missed on purpose." Jonathan asked.

"I did"

"Why is that?"

"To warn you, sir," the assassin replied, his eyes staring intently at the Vallensian leader.

"To warn me of what?"

"Of war, sir."

As the word slipped out of his mouth, a blood-curdling scream froze everyone in the room. The tension had been so thick that it had the men—Vallensian and non-Vallensian alike—hanging on every word. The scream came from the throat of one of the Vallensian men, a farmer, and seemed to paralyze all who were present, including Phillip's guards, which seemed to be its intent. As the man moved forward, he brought forth a dagger that had been hidden in his belt, covered by his Vallensian vest. In a split second, he struck the bound assassin.

Almost instantaneously, the sword of Phillip the Ghost flew from its sheath, the finely honed blade slicing soundlessly through the neck of the farmer Ronald Getz. Getz fell to the floor, bleeding profusely from the gaping wound in his throat. He bled out in seconds.

Jonathan, who had barely had time to flinch, stared at the still twitching Vallensian farmer whose blood soaked into the plank floor. His glance then followed slowly upward until it settled on the Aztlani assassin. The farmer's dagger had missed its mark and the hilt of the knife stuck out of the man's shoulder. He was clearly in pain, and appeared shocked, gasping for air, as Vallensian men and Phillip's soldiers alike rushed to him.

The eyes of Jonathan the Pastor and Phillip the warrior met as blood dripped from the tip of the sword of the Ghost.

Chapter 2 - Gareth

Gareth stirred in his large Vallensian bed. It was an unattractive but comfortable one, consisting of a hand-stuffed mattress of rough woven cotton, amply filled with goose down, and possibly cotton, wool, or whatever else was soft and near at hand. The bed frame was made of tall, gnarled, hand-hewn mesquite posts, serviceably fitted together with oaken pegs. The bed stood quite high off the ground to take advantage of any cool breeze that might flow in through the windows. Handmade mosquito netting hung over the posts at the head of the bed, ready to be draped over all four posts at night, when the windows were all opened to let in the June night air. The mattress rested on ropes drawn very tightly through holes drilled through the frame. Overall, it was a nice bed, Gareth thought.

The heat was constant, but bearable. Jonathan Wall had designed his house to remain as cool as possible throughout the summer. This part of the house was built mostly below ground level, with only 3 or 4 feet extending above the ground where windows brought in breezes and carried out the heat. In portions of the house—according to Wally the cook—underground "pipes" hundreds of feet long brought in cool air, just like air-conditioning, only without any electrical power. Even in blistering heat, the Wall house remained quite comfortable. Still, for the 25-year-old Gareth, raised at nearly 7,000 feet in the mountains of Aztlan, terms like 'hot' and 'cool' were certainly relative.

Outside the window, the ground fell sharply and he could see that the fields on the other side of the drive were ripe for harvest. He watched as the wind made waves in the golden wheat that flowed on for several thousand yards before crashing uneventfully into a pecan orchard. The sky was as blue as any he had ever seen, even in the clear air of the mountains, and unspotted by any clouds whatsoever.

A sharp pain shot through his body as he tried to twist his torso so he could get a better look out of the window. The wound to his shoulder was healing slowly, but he knew that it would take time before the pain subsided. The injury had been severe, but non-lethal. The infection that set in after only a day in custody was what had nearly killed him.

Jonathan and his family attacked Gareth's infection very aggressively, using dozens of anti-bacterial and anti-viral herbal remedies, including large doses of fresh, spicy garlic, ginger, goldenseal, echinacea, sage, peppermint, thyme, cayenne, and aloe.

The most effective cure, though, to his delight, was copious amounts of beer brewed according to the most ancient traditions. Wally informed him that beer, when brewed naturally—according to the recipes used by the ancient Nubians, Hebrews, and Egyptians—created *tetracycline* in the human body—a powerful broad-spectrum antibiotic. This fact was discovered in the last decade of the 20th century when archeologists and scientists detected tetracycline in the bones of mummies dating back 3,000 years, and concluded after much investigation that the tetracycline was a byproduct of natural beer production. Subsequently, many historians and scientists concluded that naturally fermented beer was likely responsible for halting many of the plagues that devastated Europe during and after the Middle Ages.

It seems that when Europeans stopped drinking the infected water from filthy rivers, which were infested with deadly bacteria, and started drinking naturally fermented beer, the plagues were stayed and the populations of Europe stopped decreasing. Even babies and children were given beer instead of water and their mortality rates plummeted. In this way, beer had likely saved the world. As for Gareth—he was mainly just glad that beer had saved *him*. Jonathan had promised him that after he had recuperated sufficiently, if it were possible, he would show him how beer was brewed at the Wall's ranch.

Gareth had been brought to the Wall homestead after the farmer—actually an Aztlani spy named Ronald Getz—had attacked him in the pub. Getz's bloody death during an attempt to stop him from reporting the pending attack on the Vallenses, had shocked the community, and it was still the main topic of conversation among the Vallensian people.

He was still not sure exactly where he stood among these plain people, but he was glad to be alive, and to be able to move forward with his personal mission.

"Good afternoon, Assassin," Phillip greeted him jokingly.

When exactly Phillip had entered the room, Gareth could not say. *I hate it when he does that!*

"Peace be unto you, Ghost," Gareth responded, showing exaggerated irritation with Phillip's manner of entry by spitting out the word 'ghost' with emphatic, but almost playful derision. He knew that Phillip hated the name 'ghost' as much as he himself hated being called 'assassin'.

"One day, perhaps when you deign to get out of your invalid's bed, you and I can work out our nicknames in the yard, with swords, like peaceful gentlemen," Phillip retorted, smiling.

"I would never fight you, Phillip. I'm told that you never lose a fight, you can walk between the raindrops, you never leave footprints, and you cannot be killed. Only a fool would engage in swordplay with a spectre."

"I'm afraid," Phillip said, rolling his eyes, "that both my prowess and my constitution are highly exaggerated."

"They say the infection got into my blood, which is why my recovery has been a bit delayed," Gareth changed the subject, "but I can tell you that there are worse places and worse ways to spend a summer. The Vallensian peasant food is fabulous, and the beer mugs are bottomless. Who would have known? I've gained twenty pounds while almost dying of an infection from a knife wound."

"A scratch, really—nothing to cause a grown man to spend a week in bed," Phillip replied.

The militia leader was obviously enjoying himself, so he continued. "I've had at least two dozen such nicks and I cannot recall a single one that even made me sleepy. You are a strong young man; you should have bounced back in no time at all."

"Well, Ghost, I am clearly not the man you are, but then, neither are you. Still, they do tell me that I'm healing and getting stronger."

Gareth prodded the knife wound gingerly, testing the area with his fingertips. He noticed that, almost imperceptibly, Phillip showed some satisfaction that he was improving. He sensed from his many conversations with the militia leader over the past week that Phillip was somehow ashamed or angry with himself that he had not moved fast enough to prevent his prisoner from being harmed while in his custody. Maybe that was why he visited so often.

"If Vallensian hospitality and food have anything to do with it, I'll be fit enough for hanging in no time."

"Sadly, they'd not have you hang. They'd have you as a pet dog, curled up on the hearth, nibbling at their dainties from a bowl. They are pacifists, remember." Phillip stroked his long, graying beard, looking out of the window as if in deep thought. "As for me, Assassin, I cannot decide whether I would rather see you hanged, run through with a sword, impaled on a pike, or made into a eunuch so you can fetch me beer and apples."

"I can tell that you are growing fond of me, Ghost."

"Maybe I am. Now, enough fun. We need to talk."

Gareth had become accustomed to daily sparring with Phillip. Sometimes Phillip would spend most of the day with him. Still, he knew that the battle of tongues was just a prelude and that the militia leader inevitably wanted more intelligence from him about Aztlan, El Paso, and the Duke.All light jesting aside, he knew that his future would be decided as soon as he was well enough to walk. There were those who still did not believe him. They didn't believe that he wasn't a spy, and that he had actually come to warn them and encourage them to defend themselves. Some folk saw his manner and means of arrival as suspicious, and he really couldn't blame them for those suspicions. They rightfully wondered why he had not just walked up and announced that he was a traitor to Aztlan, and that he had critical information for the militia and Jonathan.

It is true, Gareth thought, that any number of things in his seemingly complicated plan could have ruined his opportunity to warn Jonathan and the Vallenses. He could have been captured or killed by the Ghost's militia as he made his way toward Bethany. Confident in his abilities and training, Gareth did not see this as likely as some apparently did.

Some Vallensian folks said that his stunt with the arrow could easily have been missed altogether or mistaken by Jonathan. If Jonathan had not decoded the message in his mind fast enough; if the pastor had not indicated to Phillip that the post rider was the real target; if Phillip had not noticed that the arrow was from an Aztlani quiver, then the militiamen men might have immediately killed him when they caught up with him as he waited for them by the creek. *True*, Gareth thought. *Any of those things might have happened.* But what alternative was there? His goal was not just to warn the enemies of Aztlan. His goal was not even to be believed by Jonathan. His goal was *to be trusted*, because that was the only way that he was ever going to accomplish his own private objectives.

To ride up to the Ghost's militiamen and claim to be a traitor to Aztlan would just as likely have gotten him killed. In Aztlan, it was said that Phillip's ghostmen generally shot first and asked questions later. The militias were suspicious and paranoid, and—according to some—that is what keeps them alive. The militia might trust information that they extracted from a captured enemy, but they were very unlikely to trust information freely given by an Aztlani traitor.

So... what if he had snuck through the militia lines, and had gotten to Jonathan without being intercepted? That certainly seemed like the most obvious option; in fact, it was the one he had pondered the most, as he rode over the many hundreds of miles eastward from El Paso. Maybe Jonathan and the Vallensian people would have believed him. They might even have heeded his warning, but they would never trust him, and he would never have gotten to meet Phillip at all. Aztlani refugees didn't get an audience with the Ghost merely by calling for it.

Certainly, he never would have gotten Jonathan and Phillip in the same room, which had been the real coup, considering his goal. Phillip would have reckoned it as a trap. Many Aztlani refugees had found a home among the Vallenses, but building trust with the plain people of Central Texas took time. His assailant, the spy Ronald Getz, had apparently been living and farming among them for years. The *real* message that Gareth needed to deliver was urgent. He didn't have years to build up trust.

Yes, his plan was risky, and probably full of holes. At best, there was a 40% probability that it would come off right. Still, it was worth the risk, given that he needed an opportunity to get Phillip and Jonathan together. He saw no other way to accomplish it. It was believed in El Paso and in New Rome that Phillip and Jonathan had not spoken in years—in fact, the Aztlanis wanted the two rebels to stay estranged more than they wanted just about anything else. Above all, then, Gareth wanted to rekindle the relationship between Phillip and Jonathan.

Even if he had failed, Phillip would have eventually learned of the Duke's plan, but weeks and maybe months of preparation time would have been lost.

Yes. It had been worth the risk. Jonathan was a good man with a spectacularly sharp and curious mind and he had pierced through the cloud of confusion and correctly interpreted Gareth's intentions. Phillip, though he was still cautious, had, at the very least, determined that—regardless of his intentions—an assassin was valuable for gathering new intelligence. Exposing Getz as the spy had been a painful bonus that had earned Gareth a reprieve in Phillip's eyes—at least for now.

"Quit staring out of the window you assassin dog," Phillip snarled, "I need answers from you!"

"What could you possibly still want to know?"

"For a good part of the last week, you've been rather delirious from your feigned infection. I've humored you because you are weak and obviously addle-brained. But now I want to go back over some things again."

He sighed deeply, rolling his eyes in exasperation. The game continued. Phillip mixed up his questions, changing directions randomly, asking about various facts of which he already had perfect knowledge, trying to trip him up, or catch him in a lie. The interview was peppered with well-planned diversionary questions, often followed by long stares and a nodding head designed to keep Gareth talking.

"We've had a rolling guerilla war with the Duke for many years. Why has he decided to engage in a full-scale attack now?" Phillip asked.

"He is being pressured by the King who has some intentions on moving his borders eastward but cannot do so as long as a huge chunk of Central and Eastern Texas remain either ungovernable because of militia activity, or in the hands of the Vallenses. The Vallensian people reject his authority along with that of the Church. There are even rumors that the Vallensian colonies in the Piney Woods have signed a treaty with the Duke of Jackson in the former Mississippi."

Phillip pulled up a wooden chair and sat next to Gareth's bed. "I guess I just don't see much here that is new or surprising. Why the change? What is the plan?"

"You have to understand that the King has both a dream and a nightmare. If you understand those two things, the rest of this is easy," Gareth said.

"Then talk to me; explain those royal dreams and nightmares."

He rose up in the bed, propping himself up against the headboard. The sounds of cicadas, katydids, and birds drifted in on a warm breeze. He reached down and took a long drink from his ever-present mug of beer.

"The dream is simple," he said, wiping foam from his mustache, "the Duke of Louisiana is a very religious man, and he has fully embraced the faith of New Rome. He is secretly allied with Aztlan, even though he is nominally under the authority of the King of the South States. He is also very ambitious.

"Aztlan and Louisiana have you in what could become a very effective vice, and they intend to squeeze at any moment.

The King dreams of uniting the entire South of what was once the United States into a single Southern Kingdom."

Phillip shook his head. "Considering that there are tens of thousands of us who will never submit to New Rome, it is a problematic dream at best. In addition, we could rely on the support of the King of the South States, who is friendly to, or at least tolerant of, our religion and overtly hostile to the beast that is Aztlan," Phillip said.

"Now, we get to the nightmare," Gareth continued, pointing towards his own head to emphasize the point. "The King's bed is drenched with night sweats when he envisions two very scary possibilities. The first is that the King of the South States, with all of his ample resources, might come to the aid of the Vallenses. The other... actually the more frightening of the two possibilities, is that Jonathan Wall will cast off his reckless and defeatist pacifism and join you in a rebellion against Aztlan."

With that, he drew closer to Phillip. There was excitement in his voice and a sparkle in his eyes as he spoke.

"Jonathan is the key. With one word, he could unite the whole world against Aztlan. He is admired or feared everywhere, even in New Rome. It is most probable that the King of the South States will not move, even on the Vallenses' behalf, unless Jonathan Wall agrees to fight."

He sank back against the headboard, clearly exhausted by the interrogation. "I cannot say that all is lost if you cannot convince Jonathan to join you, but...," he let the thought linger, as if to suggest that the danger is unspeakable.

"Jonathan will never fight. This I know," Phillip said softly. "We waste time speaking of it, because it isn't going to happen. If you don't know that, then you don't know Jonathan. We have to plan to make war with Aztlan without him."

Silence fell on the room, as the Ghost and the Assassin pondered on all the possibilities... if only Jonathan would fight. Before long, Phillip shook his head as if he was shaking off the remnants of doubt, or cleansing himself of his wishful thinking.

"Let's talk about Aztlan. How many soldiers is the Duke bringing and how long until they get here? Which way will they come, and what arms will they carry? Sit back up you assassin dog, and tell me what you know!" He was deliberately harsh in addressing Gareth, as if scared of becoming too friendly with him.

"They will most likely come up the remnants of the road that used to be called Interstate 10, at least as far as the trading post in Ozona. They'll stay south, and won't try any direct route across the badlands. They know that the militia is in control out there. From Ozona, or possibly Sonora, they will turn northeast and stage in San Angelo.

"Up until now, San Angelo has really been a border town between the desert badlands and the beginnings of the 'ungovernable' lands in Central Texas and eastward. I would say that the Duke plans to carry out a devastating attack, using as many as five-hundred to over a thousand soldiers, hoping to wipe out any militia units he encounters along the way. Then he'll try to march east, killing and burning as he goes, destroying villages and hamlets until he gets to Bethany, which is considered the capital of the rebellion."

Gareth stretched out his wounded arm and, wincing quite a bit, swung his legs over the side of the bed, before finishing his thought. "You know what he'll do if he gets to Bethany."

"Lay back down, fool!" Phillip interjected. "I don't need you falling out of bed, fainting, or passing out from the excess of beer."

Gareth laughed. "I need to stretch a bit, and I'll need to be more mobile if you are going to hang me any time soon."

Phillip gave in and helped him to his feet, probably figuring that he indeed needed to start moving about. At first, he wobbled a bit, but soon steadied himself against the bedpost.

"I'm still not sure about what you are telling me, Gareth," Phillip said, shaking his head. "You are talking about the Duke marching five-hundred to a thousand men *or more* across the desert, in the height of summer, with no supply lines and very little support along the way. They'll have to carry everything they need along treacherous terrain and unmaintained roads. I-10 hasn't been a highway in almost two decades. It's more like the surface of the moon since most of the pavement has been dug up or removed. The Duke is either very stupid, or very sure of himself."

"Well, Ghost, I don't think that he's stupid. But he is certainly arrogant, which will work to our advantage."

"So, you're sure that he's coming?" Phillip asked, head cocked to one side, eyes squinted at Gareth.

"I am."

"Then, we'll just have to make sure that he never gets to Bethany."

Chapter 3 - Ruth

Ruth Wall stood as still as the old ugly mannequin in Mrs. Palmer's sewing shop down in Bethany, her spear poised only inches above the dark mouth of the coon den. She was backed into a salt cedar bush, leaning on the lowest branches for her balance, moving nary a muscle as she waited for the huge she-coon to stick her head out.

Minutes passed, and she started to be concerned. The sweat was beading down her face and the drops were gathering on the tip of her nose. She blew upwards, hoping to disperse the gathering droplet before it dripped down into the opening of the hole—scaring off the she-coon.

She looked up for just a moment, feeling the slight breeze on her face as she turned her head very slowly towards the sun. It was almost four o'clock, nearly time to be heading back home.

Just as she had almost convinced herself to give up and head back to the ranch, the she-coon made her appearance. Warily, the creature poked her head out of the den. Like lightning, the spear came down with tremendous force and pinned the animal's head to the ground. Ruth drew her knife effortlessly from her homemade leather sheath. She bled out and gutted the coon in minutes.

Ruth tossed the coon into her hunting bag, picking up her walking stick, her bow and a quiver full of arrows. She gave a short whistle for Louise, her yellow blackmouth cur dog and, feeling quite satisfied with herself, glanced back at the sun. After re-checking the time, she started her short hike back home.

Louise came trotting back from the edge of the woods where she had been laying in the shade, trying to stay cool. She was a good pig dog, which was almost a necessity in these parts, but didn't care for coon hunting one bit. Louise lived and breathed for chasing and hunting pigs.

At fourteen years old, the redheaded Ruth was quite an accomplished hunter—not nearly as good as David, her older brother, but pretty good nonetheless. Her father told her that she was the best female hunter he had ever seen, and that was praise enough for Ruth.

Hunting was almost a full-time job, especially when there were guests to feed. In particular, now that the Aztlani assassin Gareth was staying with them and was eating them out of house and home. Not to mention all of the militiamen hanging around as guards and escorts. For a ranch owned by pacifists, home had come to resemble an armed camp.

Ruth loved to hunt, so she wasn't complaining. Still, it seemed like a thankless task, as she did notice that Gareth seemed never to be full. Even when he was sick and delirious with a fever from his infection, he still had a huge appetite. Ruth was just glad that she didn't have to do all of the brewing it would take to keep up with his penchant for Vallensian beer. Gareth still couldn't figure out how the Vallenses had icy cold beer in the summertime, which was a good source of humor, since no one would tell him about the icehouse.

The ghostmen usually provided for themselves, and prepared most of their own meals out in the woods away from the house. Her father, being the kind man that he was and a gracious host, would still impose on them to send a few men each day for a full-on supper at his table. Though they really didn't like any attention and were uncomfortable in the company of many people, they appeared to be tremendously honored to be asked to sit at the table with Jonathan Wall. Despite their discomfort, there were usually at least two of them at supper every night, most likely just to please and honor her father.

She was glad that there was nearly always fresh game for the table. Father told her that just about everyone had figured it all wrong before the crash. In almost all of the post-apocalyptic literature, he said, it was usually predicted that over-hunting would have wiped out all of the game after a collapse. He explained that, because most writers had a bias towards industrialism and the status-quo (he called it a *Normalcy Bias*, or the *Ceteris Parabus* fallacy), they automatically assumed that almost everyone was going to survive any collapse.

The books, many of which Ruth had read, usually did predict millions of deaths, but generally assumed some kind of eventual return to "normal," irrationally assuming a return to the system her father believed had caused the real crash when it happened. In reality, the true number of deaths had dwarfed the fictional estimates. Most people didn't even realize how at risk they were. Father called them 'unviable', and said that, throughout their entire lives, they had existed suspended on nothing and sustained by a system that could never last.

The fact that only a small percentage of the entire population actually survived through the first few years after the crash didn't surprise her father, and it had changed everything. There was *no* shortage of game, at least not in Texas. In fact, there was such an abundance of game that many of the predators that had once been abundant in Texas had returned and were fast multiplying. The wild pigs had actually become a nuisance. Like mesquite trees, they were fine and beneficial in reasonable numbers, but of late, they had become a real problem. They had no respect for fences, could devastate a wheat field in a single night, and were constantly destroying property.

Ruth could not even remember a time when there had not been wolves, mountain lions, and even some bears. According to her father, before the Industrial Revolution all of these predators had once been quite at home in Texas. However, prior to the collapse, only coyotes, some bobcats, and the occasional mountain lion lived in Central Texas, and the bears and wolves had been mostly eradicated.

Whenever her father talked about the times 'before the collapse', she was fascinated. To her it all seemed unreal. Just imagine the foolishness of those people! They didn't even know how to hunt or grow their own food! Ruth would hush and listen intently when the older folks talked about that time. She really couldn't get a good hold on what it had been like back then. It all seemed so bizarre. Father had said that there were over 25 million people living just in Texas before the collapse! Ruth shook her head as she tried to imagine it. Some things she would never really grasp. She could understand it, but it wasn't truly *real* to her.

But it *was* real. She had read many of the books in Father's library. She especially enjoyed reading the history books that portrayed life as it had been in the last fifty years before the crash. It sounded like another world. *It was another world.*

The fun part was when the older people would talk about technology. *What magic!* She had seen some of the devices, although they were all powerless now. 'Phones' no bigger than a stone, which were used to talk to people anywhere at any time without any delay. There were also computers, all linked together to share information across a huge 'web' called the 'Internet'. As a result, you could find out anything in the world just by typing questions on your computer. It all seemed very useful, but Father said that people soon became addicted to the technology, and risked their lives and the lives of their families by being dependent on it. The Vallenses were referred to as 'legalistic' or 'quaint' for rejecting most of the technology, or at least any dependence on it.

As Ruth walked along, deep in thought, she noticed the tell-tale silence of Louise locking into a ready and listening stance. Then, like a shot and without any command, Louise rocketed into the oak grove down by the creek. *Pig.*

She moved with practiced precision. Before Louise even reached the trees, Ruth had dropped her game bag and her stick, and had drawn an arrow from her quiver, smoothly feeding it onto the bowstring and drawing it back. She knew from where Louise went into the trees, and from the sound of her bark, just where the pig would most likely come out.

She took a deep calming breath, just as her brother David had taught her, willing her heart rate to steady, as she sighted down the arrow. Just before the feral hog broke through from the trees, with Louise snapping at her heals, Ruth had a strange and untimely thought. *I wonder if Tim is watching.*

The thought passed in an instant. Timothy was responsible if he was hit by an arrow, she reasoned. She calculated the lead, and let the arrow fly, watching as it found its mark, striking the hog just above and behind the left shoulder, traveling into the chest area, piercing organs along its path, and exiting low and on the right side of the pig's underbelly.

The stunned hog slowed down enough for Louise to catch up with it. The dog grabbed it by the back leg and spun it to the ground, evading the hog's head as it swung around gamely trying to gut the dog with a swipe of its 3-inch tusks. As Ruth approached, Louise finally pulled back, barking up a storm.

This was the most dangerous time, when the boar was wounded but not dead, so she advanced slowly in a crouch with her knife drawn and ready. She trusted that Louise would have intercepted the pig if it had tried to charge her, but she was cautious anyway.

After a few minutes, the pig had lost all of its energy, and—giving up—it lay its head down in the dust. Ruth moved in quickly and carefully, pinning the head down with her foot, as she jabbed her knife into the pig's neck, cutting the carotid artery. She made a clean slice across the pig's throat to give the blood a route out of the body, then dragged the rear-section of the pig uphill in order to use gravity to facilitate the bleeding.

She guessed that the hog weighed somewhere in the neighborhood of 90 to 100 lbs. Not a huge pig, but it would provide anywhere from 35 to 40 lbs of meat for the Wall's table tonight. She was glad that the pig hadn't run off with her arrow, as she and Louise would have had to track it in this heat for a quarter of a mile through the brush. That happened more often than not. This kill-shot had been nearly perfect, and had destroyed at least three major organs as it passed through the pig. According to David, piercing three organs was the ideal if you wanted to drop the pig where it stood.

As soon as she was sure the pig had bled out completely, she went to work almost mechanically, gutting it, using the hillside to provide gravity to make her work easier. She made certain to keep most of the organ meats, but threw a small handful to Louise as a treat and a reward.

"Nice kill, Ruth! Not bad at all... *for a girl.*"

Ruth turned around to see Tim watching her from the edge of the woods. She figured that he'd be around here somewhere. Tim was one of Phillip's ghostmen. He was 18 years old, and it had become obvious in the past week that it was his job to watch over her like some kind of bodyguard. She was unsure of how she felt about that.

Tim did a good job. She usually couldn't figure out where he was, though it had become a bit of a game between them, as she was always trying to locate him whenever she was hunting. She almost never could. He kept his distance, moved almost soundlessly, and was never upwind.

"That was an expert kill-shot, Timmy. Not one of you ghostmen, not even Phillip, could have done it better," Ruth boasted, working with her knife without pause on the pig carcass.

"I don't know; I've seen Phillip kill a pig without even loosing the arrow. He just thought about it and the pig surrendered."

"Whatever, Timothy," she retorted in a mocking tone. "Hey, be a pal and help me get this meat back to the house." They trussed the pig carcass onto the walking stick and carried it back to the house between themselves.

Ruth really didn't like hunting for pigs in the summertime. Pigs were usually winter food, but their numbers had multiplied so much over the last few years that it had become necessary. As a result, they were hunted in large numbers even in the summer. The Walls didn't mind the extra meat. When they didn't have visiting guests (which wasn't very often), they would grind the meat into sausage, lacto-ferment it, smoke it in the stone smokehouse, and dry it. Dried, smoked sausage was one of the primary foods for the Walls whenever they travelled, because it was perfectly preserved without any added processing. It was also very convenient because it could be carried in a backpack, a pocket, or a satchel, ready to eat at any given moment.

This pig, though, would be tonight's supper for the Walls and all of their guests. The old cook Wally (she called him 'Walleye') would roast it on a spit over an open flame. Ruth's mouth watered just thinking about it.

As they walked back to the house, Tim and Ruth talked about hunting and the hot summer, as Louise trotted back and forth, darting underneath the pig as if she wanted everyone to know that she had been the one to find it.

Technically, according to the *ordnung* of the community, she and Timothy were never allowed to be alone together. Tim was supposed to watch from afar and keep her safe. But no one would say anything to him for helping her carry a heavy pig back home. And she really did enjoy his company. Timothy was nice.

Back at the house, Wally half-heartedly scolded Ruth for bringing him another pig so late in the day. "This is the third pig in five days, girl! And here we are only hours from supper!"

Ruth knew that, in truth, Walleye was always pleased when he could cook up a nice pig for supper. She would tease back by telling him, "Ok, Walleye, sorry about that. I'll feed it to Louise and the rest of the dogs." Then he'd say, "No, no, no... it's alright. I'll cook it up anyway."

Everyone was always happy with roast pork on the plate. Ruth liked it slightly charred and glazed with honey, served with onions and basil from the garden, accompanied by pickled beans from the root cellar, and *nopal* cactus juice sweetened with honey. No one ever complained if supper was a little bit late when they knew that a pig was on the menu.

Ruth went into the stone springhouse to sit down for a moment, relishing the cool air inside. The springhouse actually wasn't built on a spring, as most springhouses were. It was built mostly below ground, about 20 feet from the large icehouse. The stone walls of the structure were nearly two feet thick. The ice-melt from the icehouse flowed down an underground pipe through the thick wall and into the springhouse. Stone gutters had been built around the inside walls of the icehouse, and the icy water filled the eight-inch deep troughs. When the dripping water had risen enough that it crested the dam on the trough in the south wall, it flowed down into a deep cistern where it could be pumped up via a hand-pump when it was needed. The icy cold water was the perfect place to store perishables, such as cheese, butter, leftover food etc., and the trough was nearly always full of jars and crocks of goodies, along with sealed jars of beer.

Ruth would hang meat from hooks in the ceiling rafters of the springhouse where it would stay cool until Wally could come, usually in the early morning, and cook it for breakfast, or process it for longer-term storage.

After she had cooled herself down a bit, Ruth hung the skinned and gutted coon carcass from a hook. She then walked down the stone pathway past the woodshop to the tannery where she gave the coonskin to Ana, who dropped it into a bucket of cool water she had recently pumped up from the springhouse cistern. From her bag, she took out the brains of the hog that she had wrapped in grass after gutting the beast, knowing that Ana would find them useful in her tanning process. Tanning was still somewhat of a mystery to Ruth.

Ana was a widow, about 45 years old, dark-haired and beautiful. She was the official tanner of the Wall ranch. Tanning was a full time job on the ranch and Ana was known throughout the Vallensian territories as one of the best tanners around. Ana's skins, at least all those that were not used right there on the ranch, were bundled and taken to Bethany where they would be traded for salt and any other necessities that could not be produced on the ranch. Ana, like all of the other workers on the ranch, was well taken care of. Ruth's father treated them all as if they were part of the family.

Ana had come to live and work on the Wall's ranch many years before Ruth was born, and she told fantastic and often frightening tales of life before the crash. Ruth sometimes got into trouble with her father for repeating Ana's tales. Father said that Ana would have been a great fiction writer, and sometimes even he would sit and listen, fascinated by the stories Ana could tell. But, on those rare occasions when he would fall under Ana's spell, like clockwork, after about 20 minutes of listening, he would shake his head and gruffly order everyone back to work. "Distractions!" he would say.

Ruth didn't have time for tales today. She thanked Ana and headed back to the house to clean up. Father would be home soon, and she wanted to talk to him about her day. She could not wait to tell him about her pig, and the perfect kill-shot that had even impressed Timothy the ghostman. She also

47

wanted to sit at her father's feet and hear him talk about whatever news he had from Bethany.

In the olden days, Father told her, people would sit around a glowing box and be entertained by strangers who hated them and wanted to brainwash them and do them harm. That didn't make any sense to Ruth. What nonsense! People must have been silly back then, or really stupid. How could watching devil's plays in a magic box be anywhere near as entertaining as hearing Ana's tales, or father's news, or playing tag in the yard with the other children, or hiding from work in the springhouse?

Ruth's father arrived home from Bethany just as everyone was sitting down to the table. Gareth, Phillip, and Timothy all sat at Father's table. It was the first time that Gareth had been to the great room to eat. Everyone was a little excited to see him, as it meant that he was getting better. He smiled a lot, joking that it was the beer that had healed him.

To Ruth, Philip and Gareth seemed to be like close friends, comfortable enough to argue incessantly and tease each other something awful.

Ruth bowed her head as her father made a speech and a prayer about the Walls being blessed to have such honored guests. He reminded them all that, in such trying times, it was good to have friends, even if they did not share the same views on everything. Then he told everyone, like he usually did, that Ruth had gotten the pig for the evening's supper. Ruth always liked that part, as everyone smiled at her, thanking her for the delicious meal. Then Tim told everyone the story about how she shot the pig. She protested that he had made it seem more dramatic and heroic than it really was, but she still blushed and was happy about the whole thing.

Then, suddenly, everything went horribly wrong.

It started when three of the militia men interrupted the supper to speak to Phillip privately. Ruth watched as Phillip put his hand to his mouth and silently shook his head. He spoke in hushed tones to the ghostmen, before returning to the table. He didn't sit down.

Phillip was ashen faced and his eyes had closed to mere slits when he began to speak. Ruth felt her stomach sink, and it seemed like all of the air in the room had been sucked out of the back window. She closed her eyes. Whatever it was, it was bad news.

Phillip said, "I apologize for interrupting your meal. I've just been alerted that two of my men are dead. My wife and two daughters are missing. They've been taken."

Chapter 4 - English

Whether he liked it or not, Sir Nigel Kerr was called 'English' or even 'Sir English' by everyone who knew him. He no longer disliked it. It had become who he now was. He reasoned that it could be worse—he could have been called *Sir Kerr*. After all of these years in America, and three years now in El Paso, he now preferred just this nickname. It was like being a dog named dog. His being an Englishman called "English" was, in fact, the only authentic thing about his place of work.

The ducal castle in El Paso, if one could even call it a castle, could have been considered eclectic if that word really meant 'a dissonant mix of ugly and disconnected styles'. Still, one thing could not be disputed—the ducal headquarters were appropriately named. The castle was called La Chimenea—*The Chimney*, and as the name would aptly suggest, it was always hot—brutally and relentlessly hot.

La Chimenea had not been designed or constructed to maximize or capitalize on any particular cooling principles. Though the main structure appeared to be covered in adobe, and slightly resembled what could only be called a Southwestern desert version of a medieval castle, for some reason the castle was bereft of any of the expected cooling benefits of either adobe or medieval castles.

Through some flaw in design, construction, or both, the castle more closely approximated a large earthen oven—gathering the extreme heat throughout the day, and exuding it throughout the night.

The obsession with castles, keeps, and siege walls, and basically all things medieval, was a natural result of necessity, combined with the mentality born of a return to monarchy. Post-modern survivor instincts, shaped by hardship in this new and often violent middle age, almost naturally resulted in monstrosities like the ducal castle in El Paso. But, La Chimenea reflected both the spirit of the city and the duchy it sheltered.

The 400-year-old city of El Paso, 'The Pass of the North', along with the Mexican sister city of Ciudad Juarez across the Rio Grande river, had once claimed a population of over two million souls. Though the metropolitan area itself was one of very few densely populated areas not completely destroyed by riots, bombs and fire, the population had diminished steadily from the nearly two million at the time of the collapse, to around 50,000 people only twenty years later. This number did not take into account the ducal army that was usually quartered outside of the city, which numbered around 8,000 men.

The urban area had been reduced in size to a few square miles, around which had been constructed a 30-foot high concrete and steel wall, mostly built out of abandoned materials and debris—remnants of what used to be a highly populated city. Unlike other areas, El Paso had not been reduced by bombs and fire, but rather by the inevitable deconstruction that usually accompanies the death of an empire.

Once the Duke had accomplished the task of enforcing some stability and peace on the city (along with the state religion of New Rome), he had cordoned off several blocks of the downtown area, including the old Camino Real Hotel. From the hodgepodge of late 19th and early 20th century buildings, he had proceeded to fashion what he thought was an acceptable version of a medieval castle. A late 20th century addition to the hotel, a 17-story tower, was what had earned the castle the *Chimenea* moniker.

Soon, workers had been summoned to remove most of the vestiges of the radically contrasting and contradictory architectural styles and facades. Battlements, bastions and parapets had been added, and in order to somehow homogenize the gruesome beast, most of the visible surfaces had been coated in some kind of adobe mixture. The outcome was rather dreadful.

A more practical result of the Duke's projects was a city and castle that were legitimately defensible against a moderately

51

sized army using mostly medieval style weaponry. Still, there was no denying that La Chimenea was an ugly stain on Texas, and on the Rio Grande valley. Moreover, English found it an almost impossible environment in which to work.

Every so often, he would make a mental note to ask the Duke to have the chief architect and builder of the castle drawn and quartered, or hanged for incompetence. Executing the perpetrator of this heinous abortion of a structure was not likely to ever happen, since the Duke himself had been the designer and chief contractor of the castle; but the joke always made English feel better and always irritated the Duke.

El Paso's heat usually made him think about the cool air of the northern mountains of Aztlan, which inevitably channeled his thoughts into a rut wherein he re-examined again all of the circumstances that had so radically changed the trajectory and reality of his life.

He had no time for that just now, as he had a stack of correspondence and intelligence to go over with the Duke. But, even as he willed himself to do his duty and give his report and get it over with, the warm air and the view from the castle window dragged his thoughts into that rut of reflection.

El Paso was still foreign to him. This place could not be any more different from either of the two other places he had once called home.

It seemed a hundred years ago that Nigel Kerr was a 25-year-old foreign visitor on holiday, skiing with friends in the high mountains of New Mexico. That was when the collapse happened and everything in his young life changed.

He never imagined that his fun-filled adventure to America was going to be permanent. He could still vividly remember his parents' home in the English countryside, even though he had not seen it in over 20 years. He could remember the day of his departure. He was saying goodbye to his parents, telling them that he would be home in a month or two. He made a promise that, when he returned rested and refreshed from his skiing trip, he would buckle down and take life more seriously.

English had been raised on his parents' farm where he had slopped pigs, shepherded sheep and milked cows. As a boy,

52

all he had wanted was to get away, see the world and have adventures. Now he knew that the ignorant dreams of children often determined the way of old fools.

At the age of 18, he had joined the military. As a soldier, in only a few years, he had indeed traveled the world and met exotic people. He had killed them because his government wanted him to, not because of any wrong they had done him. Various socio-political and economic reasons were routinely offered as an excuse for state-sponsored violence, but those reasons only salve the consciences of those who are already suffering from internal corruption and denial.

He had returned home spiritually depressed, morally confused, and with an intense desire for peace and simplicity, hoping to—in some magical way—purify his conscience.

At 25 years of age, he was back to being a student. Farm life was just not working out for his generation, what with the endless need for money and all the expensive rules, laws and hindrances. Farming, though now attractive to him, seemed an idyllic and unreasonable fantasy. Higher education promised a more realistic answer to his overwhelming angst.

For his twenty-fifth birthday his parents gave him an all-expenses paid trip to America. He had determined to spend the bulk of the trip skiing in the Southern Rockies. He hadn't determined to pass through what had always been referred to as 'The End of The World as We Know It.'

His passage to America had been uneventful, and without portent. The early stages of his trip were just as he had imagined. Then THE DAY arrived.

On the morning of the collapse, he and two American friends rode horses through the drifting snow to a remote cabin owned by an artist they had met while exploring around in Santa Fe. Why they had chosen that day to ride into the mountains, he could not say.

This particular artist lived on a mountainside just east of what was once known as Taos, New Mexico. Taos was then well known as a haven for artists, beatniks, leftists, environmentalists, and other assorted potheads and hippies.

The artist, Goffrey Byrd, was about stereotypical for the area, which made the day trip interesting, as one of English's American friends was a right-wing, special-forces, mercenary type genius that he had met while serving in the mountains of Afghanistan.

After a spectacularly insightful argument between the artist, who happened to be a communist, and the mercenary, who happened to hate communism, the group had decided to work out their political differences with copious amounts of alcohol and a good old-fashioned snowball fight.

The snowy battle was in full swing when Goffrey received a call on his cell phone. He barely had a signal, but he caught enough of the message to understand that things had gone very, very wrong in the world.

Goffrey's closest neighbor with a television was higher up the mountain, several miles up a twisty snow-covered road. The group rode silently and pensively, wondering what was going on, and how it would affect them. The mercenary was full of speculation and supposition, most of which turned out to be correct.

Staring out at El Paso shimmering in the summer heat, he shook his head. The rest of the memory blurred, like the waves of heat rising above the city—the endless reports of the economic crash, and then staring at the television while society just unraveled in real time; the panicked actions of an impotent government as the dominos cascaded outward from the crash; riots in stores, in neighborhoods, and then in whole cities. Within days (rather than weeks or months, as some had predicted) the world had changed forever.

Within a week of the crash, all communications and electrical power had been lost permanently.

The next few weeks the group spent learning how to survive a winter in the mountains without power. He recalled long, endless hours of guard duty; eating wild cats and hares trapped from the forest; bottomless cups of pine needle tea; shooting at looters and bandits, while simultaneously trying not to waste ammunition.

54

After a period of five weeks passed with no news at all from the outside world, the men had seen the mushroom cloud, or at least the uppermost part of it, rising into the clear blue sky to the south. They rightly guessed that the cloud had been a nuclear device going off in Albuquerque. To this day he still did not know who set off the nukes. In books, there were always answers. In the real world... not so much.

His present way of life was entirely different to what it used to be. The world was now monumentally different. What he called 'the world' had grown to immense proportions after the crash. England might as well be on the moon, and he could just as well have gotten on a spaceship when he left home twenty years ago.

He smiled as he watched the endless mule carts being pulled through the open portcullis at the main gate of the castle. He was on another planet now. He had gone back in time, even if he was in the future.

The terror he had felt back in those first few days, weeks, and months on that mountainside in New Mexico seemed overwhelming to a young man accustomed to life's luxuries. Still, English knew now that he would trade everything he had today, including his titles, his lands, and his prospects, to go back to those days. Things had been clearer back then... and cooler. Now, he was playing this deadly game, permanently soaking wet from the sweat. How could he escape this infernal heat?

In the three years since the King had sent him to El Paso as Secretary to Duke Carlos Emmanuel, English had complained about the heat incessantly. Even in the winter. He had hoped that his endless vocal protestations of discomfort would cause the Duke to send him back to New Rome, and to his home and lands there. Alternatively, he could eventually have enough of my moaning and decide to kill me, English thought, which would be almost as good. He took out a handkerchief and wiped down his face. Even the bloody breezes were hot here!

English had no love for the Aztlanis, no real love for his King, and even less love for his current master the Duke Carlos Emmanuel. In his own private correspondence, he referred to the former drug dealer and current Duke of El Paso with the acronym CEPIC which stood for *Cocaloco Everyman, Pretender-In-Chief.* He laughed to himself, thinking that, if the spies ever opened his mail, they would be forever trying to figure out what CEPIC meant. He also referred to the Duchy of El Paso as 'The Duchy of Wastelandia', but usually only under his breath or into his cup.

Being an Aztlani Knight on paper didn't erase the reality that he was, for all intents and purposes, an unwilling slave to the King, sent to the court of Carlos Emmanuel as a spy pretending to be his ducal secretary. And that was only the first play in the game.

English gathered the latest correspondence and intelligence from his own secretary, a young man named Pano, and exited his large office into the Great Hall that lead to the office of the Duke. In his mind, he called this walk the *paseo de la vergüenza* which meant 'the walk of shame'. It was funnier in his head and with his English accent.

The Duke was already waiting for him so he approached the desk in his usual formal manner, and greeted His Grace with a bow. "I have the latest communications and intelligence to share with Your Grace."

The Duke was a tiny joke of a man, a clown-royal, known before the collapse as an extremely violent middle-man who would do anything, betray any friend, violate any trust, and murder anyone necessary to maintain his position and to move up in the Juarez drug cartel.

Carlos was only a few inches taller than a grade school boy, and he wore silly elevated shoes that, rather than making him appear taller, only succeeded in making him look completely ridiculous. He further attempted to augment or amend his youthful looks with a cartoonish handlebar mustache that connected and outlined his face via a very thin beard-line that bordered his overly effeminate jaw. English always thought that Carlos was a caricature of a miniature Mexican bandit with self-image issues.

"No whining about the heat, then?" the Duke said, glancing at his secretary out of the corner of his eye.

"Were they to heat the furnace in this desert hell-hole seven times more than it was wont to be heated, Your Grace, you should not hear a peep from me."

"Don't tempt me, English. I'll hear your report, but zhooo should know that the King is going to want to hear news of the Crown Prince. I do hope zhooo are working on something to tell him?"

The Duke tried so very hard to mask his heavy Mexican accent, but he could not. No matter how hard he tried, whenever he said the word 'you', it usually came out sounding like 'jew'. When he was especially successful, like today, it came out more like 'zhooo'.

English had prepared a response for this very issue. He smiled reassuringly at the Duke. "I am writing to the King personally today, Your Grace. The Crown Prince was sent here to be trained and disciplined, so that he will be ready to rule Aztlan one day. That is what the King has commanded, and that is what we are doing—we are training the Crown Prince."

He walked towards the full-length window that looked down into the Duke's private courtyard. The heat and the topic made the sweat run profusely under his woolen officer's tunic. By rule, he only had to wear the official tunic when he was in the presence of the Duke, or in royal company, but he had chosen to wear it almost all of the time as a silent protest and to emphasize his own personal suffering to himself. It was his version of the 'hair-shirt' once worn by priests and others to cause private discomfort and irritation. Its purpose was supposedly to bring on humility and a disregard for the flesh, so that the individual would become more spiritually aware. He needed every victory he could get... and even private victories counted. His constant wearing of the tunic, along with his unwillingness to have it laundered in the castle laundry, had become a running joke among many of the workers of the castle.

"I think, perhaps, the King may want more detail than that. For example.... His Highness may want to know where the Crown Prince is *right now.*"

"I will prepare a wonderful answer for the King, detailing the glorious exploits of his eldest son, under the tutelage and training of those appointed personally by His Grace the Duke of El Paso," English replied, bowing curtly.

"That sounds great, Sir English, but sometime we gonna have to tell the King the actual location of his son, since he is not really training under me."

"Military training, Your Grace, requires discipline, practice and—above all—secrecy," English said, clasping his hands behind his back. "You are preparing for a military invasion of the badlands, with an incursion at least as far as San Angelo and maybe farther. This has not been done before, at least not with a force this size. I am certain the King would love to have his son and heir among the host, fighting against his enemies. However, Your Grace, we cannot risk letting the enemy know the whereabouts of the Crown Prince of Aztlan. The letters to the King could fall into the wrong hands. Surely both Your Grace and His Highness must understand that."

"So zhooo will craft this response to the King? In the way you have relayed it to me?"

"I will, Your Grace."

"If something happens to the Crown Prince, Sir English, I assure zhooo that 100% of the fault will be laid at your own door. I know nothing of the training or mission of the young Prince. I will deny everything."

"I understand, Your Grace."

"And, should the young Prince meet such misfortune, I will send the notice of the Prince's death in a note placed in the box with your head." The Duke nodded at English with satisfaction at his own creativity. "What else do zhooo have for me?"

English rifled through the papers, scanning them as if he were looking for something, though he had the contents memorized. "Let's see... as you know, the attempt to kill the post rider sent from Jonathan Wall to the King of the South States failed. We have no word from the assassin we sent, but we are assuming that he is dead."

"I see," the Duke noted, obviously unhappy with the news.

"There is more bad news, Your Grace, but the day's correspondence will end on a positive note, I assure you."

"Go ahead with it then," the Duke sighed.

"The failure of the assassin led to some of our other assets being compromised. The Ghost militia went on a spy hunt and uncovered several other agents we had strategically placed within communities in or near Bethany."

"What does this mean?" the Duke asked impatiently, "We have no spies among the Vallenses anymore? And we are so soon to launch our attack?"

"Yes, we do, but most of them have been exposed, or, having been exposed, have subsequently fled."

"But we still have men there? We still have means of finding out what they are planning?"

"We do, I can assure you, Your Grace. But there is no doubt that our intelligence gathering among the Vallenses has recently suffered a great setback, Your Grace," English said.

"I assume that the Ghost militia and the Vallenses know that we are going to attack?" asked the Duke, shaking his head.

"We have to assume that they are aware that we are coming, Your Grace. However, I fail to see what they can do about it. The Vallenses will not fight. Every piece of intelligence we have indicates that Jonathan Wall will not join forces with the rebels. The Ghost militia themselves can pester us, but we believe they cannot field more than 100 men at one time and place without risking everything. In any conflict, we will outnumber them ten to one."

"Ok. And zhooo say zhooo have good news?"

"News *you* might enjoy, Your Grace," English said, doing his best to hide his own disgust.

"Well... tell it to me, don't keep me waiting!"

"A little over a week ago, five of our spies, knowing that they had been compromised, took a wild shot in the dark. They had heard from a fisherman that some militiamen were guarding a shack down on the Colorado River. They did not know what they would find there, but they had hoped that, whatever it was, would be valuable to Aztlan. They disguised themselves as Vallensian farmers before approaching the militia guards, and were thus able to catch the men unawares. The freemen guards were under the command of the terrorist known as Phillip, and it turns out that they were guarding Phillip's own wife and daughters. Our spies were successful in overpowering the guards and taking Philip's family into custody."

The Duke's face lit up as he rose quickly to his feet. He tugged on his ridiculous mustache in his excitement. "Where are these prisoners? Please tell me that they are being brought here to me?"

"Your Grace, it would have been impossible to get them across the badlands without the militias catching up with them. Phillip has used most of his available resources, as you can imagine, trying to recover his family, and the Vallenses have helped too. Hundreds of the plain people have been working in teams with the militia, scouring the area. However, our spies took them to a safe house a hundred miles North of Bethany. When Bethany is burned by your army, Your Grace, we will gather all of the captives, including Phillip's family, and we will bring them back here safely with the soldiers."

The Duke, obviously excited at the turn of events, came around the desk. When he was excited, he looked even more like a cartoon villain—dark and swarthy, with the look of the weasel to him. *Cocaloco*, English thought, as he adopted his most subservient look for the Duke.

"We may not need to bring them here, then, English. We will send a letter under the white flag to Phillip himself. Zhooo will tell him that when our army arrives in San Angelo, that he is to surrender himself and all of his militia. If he does not do so, his wife and daughters will be tried as heretics and burned at the stake." The Duke paused for a moment, looking his secretary in the eye.

"I am not bluffing. We will do it."

"I assumed that much." English swallowed with difficulty. "Is that your wish, Your Grace?"

"It is my wish."

"I will send the letter, Your Grace."

"One more thing, English."

"Yes, Your Grace?"

"The assassin zhoo sent to kill the post rider," he paused, looking out the window, "he is dead, I assume?"

"We must assume so, Your Grace. Most likely killed by the terrorist Phillip himself," English lied.

"Have zhoo told this man's family?" the Duke asked.

"I was planning to draft a letter to his father today, Your Grace."

Chapter 5 - Phillip

The Ghost Militia didn't build fires at night. There were no cozy campfire scenes with the hypnotic, dancing, orange-yellow glow of diffused firelight emphasizing the faces of weather-hardened cowboys. Phillip's militiamen were both hunters and hunted, and most of them had lived their entire lives in this manner—outside, exposed to the elements, usually in close proximity to a horse. They knew that an open fire at night could get you killed.

At night, as in the day, Phillip's men disappeared into the surrounding hills and brush. They didn't have to be told what to do. Except for his current guests, each man had been in the unit for so long, that they moved as a single entity. When it was time to sleep, the men melted into the environment as creatures natural and indigenous to it. Each man would quietly eat his supper of sausage, jerky, or pemmican, with hardtack or maybe a dried tortilla. Tonight, perhaps a few of the men had spread a bit of sugared lard on their bread—those blessed enough to have any lard left from the trip to the ranch.

He chewed slowly and deliberately on a piece of dried sausage as his eyes, fully adjusted to the darkness, scanned the area and the horizon. What little moonlight there was gave a blue-black tinge to the juniper and low mesquite brushes that dotted the hills.

On nights like this one, you relied mostly on your ears. His guards knew the idiosyncrasies and peccadilloes of both horse and man. Each man standing guard had a baseline of expected sounds; they knew which man snored, and how loudly; which horses whinnied, how often, and why. From this cacophony of natural sounds and silence, the guard was able to determine if anything was amiss or deviating from the norm. Experience became a sixth sense.

Sometimes two or three men might break the routine, bunch up for a short while and talk in hushed whispers. But this, too, was part of the overall pattern. The need for interaction and camaraderie was understandable and even welcome. They were still human. Still, if they did congregate to talk, they were expected to operate as additional watchers. In their gatherings, they talked in low tones, with eyes and ears open, alternating between talking, listening, and scanning the area. During these powwows, no two men ever talked over one another, argued, or raised their voices. Within this warrior unit, even fellowship was military in its discipline and bearing.

He heard Gareth's heavy and untrained footsteps, as he approached. Phillip didn't bother to turn around, remaining crouched down low on the sandstone ledge.

"Greetings, assassin dog," he said. "If you intend to cut my throat, you'll have to do better than that. You sneak like a sasquatch."

"I know that you have eyes in the back of your head, Sir Ghost. I would never try such a thing. Most likely, if I was inclined to kill you, I'd shoot you from a great distance," Gareth replied, laughing.

"I'm no knight, friend," Phillip retorted, "so stop with that 'sir' talk. I'll take your insolence only so much. *Ghost* is one thing, 'sir' is another."

"Yes, sir!"

He shook his head, and then held up his hand for silence, focusing his ears on a sound from the brush. "Ah... young Raymond Stone went to water a bush. So, why are you still up Gareth? Can't sleep under the stars? I'll admit, it can be difficult to find rest with both God and your conscience looking down on you."

"God sees through barn roofs just as well as castles. There is no hiding from Him. But, in case you were wondering, I've been sleeping just fine during this fortnight with you, Phillip. I'm becoming more at home out here as the days pass."

"Good to hear. Good to hear." Phillip pulled out his battle knife and sliced off a piece of the sausage, handing it to Gareth, who accepted it gratefully.

63

"I know that you didn't want me to come with you," Gareth said, seriously. "I hope I haven't slowed you down."

"Not too much. We've been unable to track the Aztlanis this way anyway. We'll wait now for any word from the other militias, or from the Vallensian searchers to the north." His head moved slowly and deliberately like radar, as he "watched" with his ears. "Tomorrow, if the Lord wills, we will meet up with an old friend of mine. He's been at New Rome, and we're hopeful he'll have some news for us."

"You... have a friend who's been at New Rome? Wow. That's an interesting twist."

"Yeah, I figured that since you are an Aztlani spy and assassin, you'd enjoy a visit from New Rome."

Gareth dropped his head, and responded seriously, "Phillip, I came along to help you find your wife and daughters. I know we joke around a lot, but I want to find them just as much as any of your men do. I want them to be safe with you. I pray that we find them soon."

"I know, Gareth. I don't doubt you, though I know that many do."

"I am your friend, Ghost."

Phillip looked upward. The sky was clear, and the stars were uncountable in their number, and unfathomable in their beauty. "In our line of work, you'll understand that we don't trust words very much. These men began riding together for their own reasons—out of their hatred for Aztlan, or because they refused to worship according to the dictates of New Rome. Some of them are here because their families were killed, or because they merely wanted freedom and saw the militia as the best way of obtaining it. Some came because they were orphans and they had no family. Now, they ride together because they *are* a family—a clan.

"Like family, they are united in the fundamental opinions of life and living. Yet, unlike a traditional family, they have bled and died together. Out here, the word 'friend' means something. In fact, it is from the Hasinai Indian word for 'friend' or 'ally' that we have the name Texas, which is our home. You might recall that, in the Book of John, Jesus said to his disciples,

64

'Henceforth I call you not servants; for the servant knoweth not what his lord doeth: but I have called you *friends.*" With that, Phillip went silent for a moment, listening and watching, before he continued.

"You know, monarchs rule by right of blood—each son ruling in the place of his dead father—even if they despised one another in life and even if they had different beliefs. Thus, in a system of divine and royal right of heirs, the concept of 'blood' can be distorted and confusing. Out here, things are much simpler. We are kin by providence, and not by blood."

"I understand," Gareth said, pondering Phillip's words.

The militia commander turned to Gareth and whispered, "These men do not value words. They ride with you, but they watch you. They'll fight with you and die for you, or... they'll cut your throat. I can't tell which is more likely."

"Well, let's hope they *judge righteous judgment,*" Gareth said.

"It's strange and ironic, you know," Phillip added, "that one of the Indian words for 'friend' that some people believe became our word for Texas was the word *Taysha.* That conclusion is up for debate, of course, because others believe that our word Texas had to come from the Hasinai word for 'friend', the word *techas.* Anyway, one thing most everyone who discusses such things agrees on is that the word *Taysha* is also the Mayan word for *spy.*"

"You sir," Gareth said, smiling, "are a fount of etymological irony. Good night, Ghost."

"Good night, Assassin."

The night passed uneventfully, and Phillip managed to grab a few hours of sleep before he was wakened by the sound of approaching horses. He jumped to his feet, prepared for anything, when he saw his militia outriders returning from their reconnaissance mission.

Soon, the entire camp was up and moving organically, preparing for the day's ride. Very small fires—fires that did not smoke—were started, and each man would take coals from the fire to heat his own breakfast. A small hole, maybe four or five inches deep and five inches in diameter, would be dug into the hard ground. A small hand shovel-full of coals would be placed into the hole, over which a small pot would be placed.

Heating up the mesquite coffee always came first. Each man carried a ration of roasted mesquite pods, and each prepared their own cup of coffee each morning. It was more practical this way. It would take too long to heat large pots of coffee, but only a few minutes for a small cup of water. When the water boiled, small broken bits of mesquite pods, roasted black, would be tossed into the water and boiled for a few more minutes. The sweet, highly caffeinated concoction was then poured through a rough cloth into a drinking cup and the 'grounds' were set aside to be buried with whatever other evidence might be left over from the night's stay. It was said that if the Ghost militia was ever tracked and caught by an Aztlani army, it would be by the smell of mesquite coffee oozing from their pores.

Phillip credited the mesquite coffee with the great health and vitality of the militia—that, and the abundance of lacto-fermented foods in their diet. The militia had been riding for nearly 20 years, although most of the men were actually younger than that. Still, it was notable that disease was almost unknown among the freemen militias who lived primarily off the land.

After the coffee was prepared, the militiaman would refill the pot with a small amount of water to which he would add a handful of grains and maybe a pinch of salt. Sometimes, in the lean times, when there were no grains, another chunk of sausage or jerky would be added to the water and cooked into a broth. There was always plenty of meat. On good days, maybe an egg, or some other delicious local creature or plant would show up in the pot.

When there was fat, the men might cook a portion of it down with a sprinkle of dried agarito berry powder or fresh prickly-pear cactus fruit added to the mix. They had become experts at providing what their bodies needed, and very little more. As a result, they were lithe and fit, and with the exception of Rollo The Mountain, the huge and muscular man-child of the group, none of them would have been considered large.

The outriders rode directly to Phillip and, by way of salute, each of them gave an almost imperceptible nod to the commander before sliding off of their horses. The riders split into three groups. From this point on, the motions of each of the men was akin to a choreographed ballet. Phillip crouched down with one of the outriders, as men surrounded him wordlessly, facing outward. There was no way of telling when they might be being watched, or when a sniper might be observing the entire scene from a thousand yards away via a high-powered scope. Thus, in an over-abundance of caution, whenever Phillip talked to outriders, spies, or whenever he received reports, the militia made sure that even his lips could not be read from afar. This scene was repeated three times, as each of the outrider and militia segments mimicked the routine Phillip and his sub-group followed. Only the man who approached Phillip had the real report. The other two meetings were diversionary. In this way, a watcher might not even know which of the militiamen Phillip was. No man wore any insignia of rank or identifying regalia. In every way that was apparent, Phillip was just like the rest of the men. Still, even without an outward sign, to his men, he was not only the leader, but also their hero, and their father.

"What news do you bring?" Phillip asked.

The outrider looked down, with some sadness. "We have no good word yet of your wife and daughters. We've almost come to the conclusion that they did not ride for New Rome, or for El Paso. We're focusing our attention north now. The Vallenses believe that they have found some indication of a party traveling northward at approximately the correct window of time."

"I want our men up there and in charge," Phillip said, "I don't want the Vallenses stumbling upon the kidnapping party and mucking things up. They are superb trackers, but they are not killers, and they'll ruin any possible rescue attempt if they find them first."

"Yes, maestro. We had anticipated that this would be what you wanted, and we have sent a force of twenty men to take over the northward search."

"What else?"

"A little over a day ago, we captured an Aztlani messenger riding under the white flag towards San Angelo. He had a message for you." The outrider handed the message to Phillip. It was sealed with the ducal seal of The Duke of El Paso.

"What did you do with the messenger?"

"We told him that we did not recognize or honor the white flag at this time. We said that until the captive women and children were released, along with all captives held by Aztlan, the militia in Texas will be operating under the black flag and had every right to kill messengers. No surrender, no captives, and no hostages. We went on with the threats for a while before letting him go. We assume that the black flag message will make its way back to the Duke."

"I'm sure it will," Phillip agreed, as he opened the letter.

* * * *

Attention: To the Insurgent leader named Phillip, and to all of the leadership of the illegal Rebellion against the Rightful King of Aztlan.

HEED THESE WORDS!

In order to put an end to your cowardly acts of terrorism and your continued unlawful war against the rightful Liege Lord of the Kingdom, the wife and children of Phillip the Insurgent have been arrested and taken to New Rome, where they are to be tried on charges of Heresy and Treason!

Upon their conviction by the New Office of the Inquisition, they will be turned over to the secular authority to be burned at the stake.

Upwards of 20 times you have been warned to cease your activity, Phillip, but you remain in league with all of the enemies of Aztlan. For this, you are bound to see your wife and children perish—unless you are willing to give up your fruitless war, and surrender yourself (and all of your men) to the proper authorities. Your lives in exchange for those of your family, Phillip, those are your choices.

68

A day's hard ride could free your loved ones, if only you will surrender.

We look forward to your positive response, and to seeing this rebellion come to an end. Enough blood has been shed on both sides. Your own sacrifice could bring the peace for which all good men pray.

Sincerely,
Duke Carlos Emmanuel, Lord Provider of the Duchy of Texas, by the hand of His Royal Secretary.

Phillip read the letter through aloud so that the leaders among his men could hear it. Then he smiled faintly, almost imperceptibly.

"Why the smile, maestro?" Only Rollo, the huge, muscular man that most of the militiamen called *The Mountain,* had noticed it. "Your wife and children are in danger of being killed, and they've been taken to New Rome! Even we, as good as we are, can't invade New Rome to save them."

"They haven't been taken to New Rome, gentlemen." He looked at the outrider. "You and your men were right, they've been taken north—60 miles away. 20 leagues."

"How can you know?" asked Rollo. "How can you possibly be so certain?"

He looked up and the smile faded from his face. "It's a code. The Duke's secretary is an old, old friend of mine. We even survived the collapse together 20 years ago. He's ex-British SAS and he's been helping us from inside for a very long time. Now, he's told me where to find my wife and daughters and he's risked his life to do it."

Gareth whistled. "Oh, what a web we weave!"

Phillip looked at Gareth, "Deception goes both ways, Assassin. So maybe you thought yours was the only side with spies?"

"I thought no such thing, Ghost man. I know for certain that that is not the case," Gareth responded, "I know Sir Nigel Kerr very well too. English and I go back quite a long way; not so long as you, but I've known him for almost all of my life."

"You'll have to fill me in on that later. I'm interested to find out how else you and I might be connected." Phillip looked to the outrider, "Is there anything else?"

"The guests you are expecting have been spotted approaching from San Angelo way. They are alone. We've sent a guide to bring them to you. They should be here momentarily."

"Ahh," Phillip noted, "more friends from Aztlan." He turned to Gareth and pointed, "You should be starting to feel at home."

"I'm not sure that is exactly how I feel, Ghost, but I do have the feeling that things are just starting to get interesting in our friendship."

Gareth, Phillip, The Mountain, and a few other militiamen sipped mesquite coffee and discussed the plan to free Phillip's wife and daughters. It wasn't going to be easy, they all freely admitted. First, there would be the hard ride north in this heat. Phillip had assumed from the letter that they needed to move quickly... *A day's hard ride could free your loved ones.*

As the group made their plans, the guide returned with the two men riding in from Aztlan. Again, the ballet of men went into action to obscure events for those who might be watching from afar. As the choreographed scramble of men continued wordlessly, Phillip scanned the horizon in every direction. They were miles and miles away from anyone. He wondered if the protective machinations even mattered, and if anyone would even be watching. *No,* he thought, shaking his head. *Diligence and obedience are ours; results belong to God.* Our decisions do not depend on the enemy. We do our duty and do things right regardless of how safe we may or may not be.

Phillip ducked down into the small group that now surrounded him, and greeted the militia guide—Tyrell of Terrell the men called him—and the two men who had just ridden from Aztlan.

Like Gareth, the men had been given 'uniforms' that approximated the dress of the Ghost militia—black or brown cotton pants girded with heavy leather in the knees and backside.

70

The high leather boots were strapped up the leg, to guard the rider against mesquite thorns, cactus, and rattlesnake bites. A long leather coat was worn over a tan cotton shirt while riding, even in the summer. It was only partially as bad as it sounded. "Leather breathes; that's why cows wear it," Phillip liked to say. The coats had pockets throughout in which pounded steel or iron plates could be placed as makeshift armor, but these were kept in a secure location, and were only very rarely worn. Only when the militia intended to fight in traditional battle array—which was almost never—would they wear any armor.

Likewise, the militiamen very rarely carried guns, although they had access to them. Guns were heavy, ammunition was rare, and the Ghost militia survived and thrived by moving quickly and silently as an invisible recon force. Only a few times in the past ten years had the militia ever used guns in a battle.

Phillip embraced Rob Fosse, who was his best friend and often operated as a spy in New Rome, and greeted Sir Gerold Holcutt of Riverdell, Rob's traveling companion and a supporter of the insurrection against Aztlan.

Rob looked over the militia contingent and beamed. "Well, isn't this a strange court? And me so underdressed for such esteemed company!"

Phillip could not help but laugh at his old friend Rob Fosse. Rob was the funniest man he had ever met. *This ought to be interesting,* he thought.

"Greetings in the name of The Most High God," Phillip announced formally. "We humble servants of Jesus and lowly militiamen of Texas do kneel before Your Graces, newly arrived from Aztlan."

"Stand up, man!" Rob said, laughing. "We are the ones who ought to be bowing." He and Sir Gerold bowed down on one knee and dropped their heads.

Rob looked up with a grin on his face, "I didn't know that you kept company with royalty, Phillip, but you cannot have friends much higher than the Crown Prince and future King of Aztlan himself!" He turned his attention to Gareth. "Our surprised but heartfelt greetings to you O' great Prince Gareth and peace be unto you."

Phillip's eyes went from Rob Fosse and Sir Gerold to Gareth as they bowed to the Crown Prince, and his hand instinctively went to his sword.

For only a split second, confusion set in on the faces of Phillip's men; but instantly that confusion cleared and the men set into motion. The sound of swords being drawn all over the camp was both awesome and terrifying. Rob and Sir Gerold staggered backwards at the frightening sound, as blades appeared from everywhere, pointed at Gareth. "He's a traitor and a spy!" someone shouted.

Phillip's sword was drawn, but his was soon intersecting those of his men. "Easy boys!" he said with a smile on his face, "I know what you're thinking, but the Crown Prince is with us."

Chapter 6 - Jonathan

Ruth smiled as she struggled to lift the stringer of twelve largemouth bass to show her father. Jonathan estimated them all to be at least 14 to 16 inches long and meaty too. He smiled back at her, clapped her on her shoulder and helped her carry them to the concrete worktable behind the springhouse. Although Wally would cook them, both knew that he wouldn't clean them. Over the years, the old cook had made sure everyone understood that. Jonathan and Ruth got to work with their fillet knives while Ruth chatted excitedly about the day's events, minutely dissecting the finer points of her fishing success.

Fishing had recently become a very popular pastime at the ranch, but it seemed that now folks were fishing more for sport rather than mainly for food. Jonathan could remember back when Ruth was too young to go fishing alone. Back then, he had been forced to assign fishing duty. Almost no one wanted to fish, especially in the hot dog days of summer. Now, Ruth's excitement and energy about anything to do with fishing, hunting, or trapping had started to rub off on everyone else.

Sometimes, when he walked past the lower tank on his way to the woodlot, or to check on the cattle in the bottom acres, he would see four or five people fishing with Ruth. Very few days passed without there being fish on the menu in some form or fashion, or, at the very least, bass fillets hanging in the smokehouse for long-term preservation.

The tanks on the Wall ranch were man-made ponds that had been originally designed to provide water for the cattle. Tanks were usually built on the lowest parts of a piece of land, where there was evidence of regular run-off from rains.

Only a few years prior to the collapse, several of the small cattle tanks along or beside the creek had been expanded to increase the total amount of water catchment, and to enable fish farming as an additional source of protein. The lower tank had been steadily expanded until now it encompassed about four acres. It was a pond, even if everyone still called it the lower tank.

In order to maintain a good population of fish in the tanks on the ranch, Jonathan had finally been forced to adopt both a flexible fishing season, and a quota. Every time a fish was caught out of any tank on the property, it had to be logged into the ledger hanging by the cleaning table behind the springhouse. Jonathan kept a close eye on how many fish were being taken from the tanks on the ranch, and would put an end to fishing season if too many were being caught. In addition, any servants who took fish from the tanks had to return a specific amount of food for the fish in the tank. Fish feed could be anything from old eggs past their prime that were scrambled up for fish food, to small pieces of meat, bits of rattlesnake or possum, or, preferably, buckets of grasshoppers caught in grasshopper traps.

Jonathan had been so excited when he discovered plans for the grasshopper traps in an old, antique book that included plans for hundreds of old-timey farming devices.

The large grasshopper traps were screened boxes, some as wide as twelve feet across, with partial openings on their bottoms. The traps could be dragged through the fields and grass behind a horse or mule. The grasshoppers would jump and get trapped in the boxes. When the boxes were full, they were left out in the fields until the grasshoppers dried up; then they could be bagged and stored as chicken or fish food. Dried grasshoppers were one of the primary forms of chicken feed on the ranch, and provided most of the protein that would one day become eggs for the inhabitants of the ranch. Excess eggs (and there were a lot of those) were usually cooked up and fed to the pigs, but would sometimes also become fish food. The guts and heads of Ruth's fish, when cleaned, went into the bucket of stuff to be fed to the chickens; and any unproductive or culled chickens would be fed to the pigs. It was quite a system! Because of it, and with the regular hunting, the Walls and their ranch staff had quite a variety of meat regularly appearing on the menu.

74

After he finished helping Ruth clean all the fish, Jonathan washed his hands in cool water that was pumped up from the cistern. He used a bar of homemade lye soap to make sure he got rid of the stench and the stickiness from his hands.

Every time he washed his hands here, he thought of the 'grey-water' system they had installed on this sink. The used water swirled down the drain, into a pipe that ran eighteen inches below the ground. As the pipe ran past three large pecan trees that shaded the tannery and the root cellars, the water seeped out through tiny holes that had been drilled in the pipe several feet from the trees. The pipe with the holes drilled in it passed through a bed of coarse gravel so that the mud and dirt wouldn't compact around the holes and plug them up. Owing to this method, these productive trees regularly received some watering, even between rains and during droughts.

He and and his wife planted these three pecan trees 25 years ago, not long before she gave birth to David, their first child. Now, a quarter of a century later, the trees were fully-grown and in full production. The lifespan of these trees was not usually expected to be much longer than that, though some pecan trees in this area had been known to live and produce for many, many decades. There were pecan trees in the Wall's orchard and along the creek and down by the lower tank that were already 30 years old, planted there when the Vallenses first came to this land. Although they were still healthy and strong, the Vallenses planted more nut and fruit trees every year, planning for the future.

When he looked at the towering trees heavy with green pecans, he remembered the day they had planted them. He could recall Elizabeth—pregnant with David—watching and laughing at him. It was spring, and back then, Jonathan had thought it was the spring of their lives together. But God had seen fit to take her, and it was not up to him to question the wisdom, goodness, and severity of a Sovereign God.

He still had David, and his two daughters Elizabeth (who had been named after his wife), and Ruth. Betsy had been married to Paul Miller for five years now, and had given him his two grandchildren—Jon and Thomas.

David was his friend, his partner, and his constant worry. His son knew perfectly well the reasons and the apologetics for the pacifism of the Vallenses. Still, in the past few years, as the attacks on the peaceful communities of believers had increased and had become more heinous and violent, David had become more militant. He still obeyed the wishes of his father, and submitted to the commands of the Church, but he was constantly—albeit within the bounds of what would be allowed—agitating for war with Aztlan.

He was still too young by five years to be an Elder in the Vallensian Church, but a year ago, David had asked to speak in front of a meeting of all of the Elders, even those from distant communities, and he had made a heartfelt plea and argument for active Vallensian material assistance to the militias. His argument had been so good that it had split the community—a split that remained to this day. Though both sides had agreed to listen to and to tolerate one another, and though the Vallenses' official position on violence had not changed, Jonathan knew that a significant number of God's people in the Vallensian Church were now in support of active participation in the war.

He also suspected that many of the Vallenses, although maybe not in Bethany or in this region, were surreptitiously giving direct aid to the militia. If discovered by Aztlan, this behavior would be considered an act of war.

An act of war, Jonathan mused. *Aztlan commits acts of war against us on a regular basis.* But he still believed that pacifism was both the wise path, and the path of Christ. In this way of thinking, he had always been almost Tolstoyan. Leo Tolstoy—the famed author of War and Peace—had also been an extreme pacifist, and Jonathan had studied his arguments against violence for many years. In other ways, Tolstoy was unorthodox, and probably even a heretic, but his arguments against the use of violence were solid and well grounded.

Jonathan had heard all of the arguments in favor of violence, and he understood his opponents on the subject very well. But history had shown that the pacifistic plain people had been preserved for over 700 years, while any militaristic group formed during that same period, including the empires of

England, France, Japan, and the United States, had ceased to exist. Who knows, maybe the Swiss, up in their Alpine chalets, were still safe and sound with their guns and ammo; but if they were, they were the exception that proved the rule.

Defensive violence was a valid philosophy in the short term, but in terms of long-term survival, eventually all violent nations or groups ceased to be. The Amish and the Vallenses still existed in what used to be America. In contrast, The Hell's Angels and the U.S. Army no longer did—at least as far as he knew. Knowledge of the true nature of the outside world didn't extend very far.

Before he knew it, lost in his own thoughts, Jonathan found himself strolling in the orchard. The air was markedly cooler there—sometimes by as much as 20 degrees—than elsewhere on the ranch. Jonathan plucked a peach from one of the trees and examined it. Not quite fully ripe, but getting close. The Walls and all of their people would be swarming over the orchard soon, bringing in the harvest of peaches.

He sat down in the shade of the trees, to enjoy the sweet fruit, wiping the juice from his mouth on his sleeve. His wife Elizabeth would have scolded him for that, but Winnie, his laundry maid, never said anything. Elizabeth hated to have to scrub the juice out of his shirts in summer.

Jonathan's thoughts rolled back through the years and he saw Elizabeth as a young woman, before they were married, hefting spade and pick and post-hole digger as dutifully as any man as they dug the holes for some of these very trees. Phillip had been there too, but that was before they had quarreled over her, and over Phillip's mercenary activities, and over just about everything else that you can possibly imagine.

Now Elizabeth was dead, but Phillip was back, and war was looming on the horizon. Everything he and Elizabeth had built was now in jeopardy.

Phillip's own family was now kidnapped. Their lives were in peril, and the Ghost had ridden off with most of the militia to try to find them and rescue them.

God's ways are mysterious, mused Jonathan. *Still, we know that He is perfect and good, and that we can trust Him.*

In the distance, he could see Timothy riding towards the orchard at great speed. He stood up and walked out to meet him.

Timothy quickly dismounted. The young militia soldier was strong and handsome, as well as humble and intelligent, Jonathan observed. He wondered what had happened to the boy's parents and to the rest of his family. The pastor made a mental note to ask him sometime.

In the weeks Timothy had been at the ranch, Jonathan had not learned much about him, except that he was diligent in his duty, and committed to keeping the Wall family safe.

Under normal circumstances, Jonathan would not have allowed militia guards to watch over his family. However, Phillip had not only insisted on providing protection, but had made it known that the Walls were going to be guarded whether they liked it or not. At least, this way, Phillip reasoned, Jonathan and his family could have some communication and relationship with the men who guarded them. He had reluctantly agreed, so long as no Vallenses were to engage in violence. The young man had shown himself to be extraordinarily committed to the safety of the Wall family, Ruth in particular.

Timothy and David had also grown close, which greatly troubled him. David already had the propensity to be inclined towards violence as a means, and he was worried that his son would now grow even more 'militia minded' than was good for any Vallensian. The two young men, along with another young ghost militiaman named Robin, who they all called 'The Hood', had been spending an inordinate amount of time together.

He often wondered what it would be like to have been born and raised after the collapse, and to have never known hearth or kin. In many ways, even literally in most cases, the young men of the militia were orphans. They were a band of brothers, sworn to one another and to their cause. They were modern Cossacks or Spartans. They had no homes, no real property, and very little likelihood of ever finding love or marriage. He admired them, even as he pitied them. His son just simply admired them. Jonathan longed for a day when there

78

would be no need for the militia; yet, he knew that that day wouldn't come until the Lord returned.

Timothy interrupted this solemn train of thought, "The Elders of your people have requested that Your Honor gather with them for a meeting in Bethany. We've just heard news via post rider from there."

"Stop calling me Your Honor, Timothy"

"I'm sorry Your Honor, but we have to obey our code and rules, as created by Phillip. Hence, a request for you not be addressed formally would have to come directly from Phillip."

"What if I were to fight you over it?"

"Some folks might find that rather refreshing."

"I understand," Jonathan said, knowing he would get nowhere arguing with Ghost militia reasoning. "What news from the post rider? What is this all about?"

"Well, Your Honor, that was the complete substance of the message to you. However, in questioning the rider, I learned that the Duke's attack force is a day's ride from San Angelo, and will be here in less than three. Their numbers are estimated at about five-hundred men."

"Five hundred men!" These days, forces that large were almost unheard of. Once upon a time, armies of thousands and tens of thousands had marched through Texas and the South; post-collapse, a force of even a few hundred men was difficult to mobilize and command.

"Will you let them take and burn San Angelo? What is the militia going to do? We have to evacuate the frontier... but there isn't time. Five hundred men? For what?" He was exasperated and angry, "Five hundred men to kill pacifists, farmers, and traders?"

"The situation is not good. Phillip is out with a sizable force, attempting to rescue his wife and daughters. We were not expecting the Duke's army for another couple of weeks or so..." Tim rubbed his youthful beard and began to fiddle with the grip of his sword. To Jonathan, he seemed almost ashamed that the Ghost militia was caught unprepared.

"They must have marched by night or traveled on some course we did not expect them to take. Though even those options seem unlikely," he paused for a moment. "In fact, Your Honor, I cannot say how the Duke's army got here this fast without being noticed. But, that is all beside the point. I am confident that militia outriders and recon units will be sent along the path of the Aztlani army. They will harass them and thin their numbers some, but as things are now, no attempt will be made to defend San Angelo... it's always been considered indefensible. Every trader and merchant there knows it."

Jonathan stared southward, pondering on the implications of these words. When he finally spoke, his voice was distant and cold, despite the heat of the day. "It's the Winter Massacre all over again."

In his mind, he was back on the frozen rolling hills East of San Angelo, loading bodies of his own people—mostly women, children, and the elderly—onto a haycart, to take them to Bethany for burial.

At that moment, his son David and two other militia riders approached in haste.

"We have to ride, Father. The Elders are gathering and there is no time to waste," David urged.

Timothy interjected, "Perhaps we can bring the Elders of the Vallenses here to the ranch? We have two small units in and around Bethany, and a more sizeable unit here. It's likely that the Vallenses can pull back from the frontier in time, if we send word now. The Aztlani goal is to raze Bethany, and they will do it, without a doubt. This place, however, is defensible. It is built on high ground. Any way they try to approach this ranch, they must come uphill."

"This isn't the Alamo, Timothy. It's a farm."

As they spoke, Ruth rode up on Jonathan's horse Laredo. Louise trotted along behind her obediently. Ruth had a large leather satchel that riders called a 'wallet', and after dismounting, she stowed it in the saddlebag. "There's food and supplies here for several men for a few days."

Jonathan thanked Ruth, and kissed her on her forehead. "You take care of everyone here. I'll be back sometime tomorrow... if the Lord wills." Ruth just nodded in reply.

"Please listen, Your Honor," Tim spoke with a growing sense of urgency, "we can ride hard to Bethany and bring the Elders here. Our orders are to keep you and your family safe."

Jonathan shook his head. "According to Gareth, the Aztlanis have no desire or plans to harm me or my family."

"We still don't know if Gareth is an Aztlani spy or not, but that is all the more reason for you and the Elders to meet here and not in Bethany."

"It's out of the question," Jonathan replied softly, "our colonies between here and San Angelo would be cut off; and, if we do not ride now, we'll lose a whole day that might be used to get some of our people to safety."

"Father's right, Tim, we have to ride to Bethany now," David agreed.

"Besides, this isn't about me," Jonathan added.

"I'm sorry to disagree with you, Your Honor," Tim said with his eyes down. "This has always been about you."

Chapter 7 - David

The heat was oppressive again, but David could see that the white cumulonimbus clouds off to the South and West were beginning to conglomerate and build skyward, looking like a giant volcanic eruption towering to perhaps 40,000 feet—an ominous portent of possible severe weather. The clouds were forming a squall line, probably still several hours away off to the south and west towards San Angelo. *Maybe those Aztlani soldiers will get an appropriate welcome to the tornado belt,* he thought. David hoped some rain would cool things down, and maybe hinder the Aztlani advance. Weather in Texas is notoriously unpredictable, and quite often such storms just blow by without dropping any rain at all, or they simply disappear.

His father had sent messengers to gather at Bethany as many Elders and members of the council as could be reached on short notice. Jonathan Wall was trusted to act on behalf of the community in case of emergency, but he felt strongly that the situation required some unanimity in opinion among the leadership. That would be hard, considering the current differences of opinion on the defense issue.

As the Pastor's party rode south, the dust from the road was so heavy and thick that everyone had bandanas or balaclavas pulled over their mouths and noses.

They negotiated the county road at a pretty fast pace, considering the heat and season. Still, on occasion, they would have to detour, following wagon-rutted tracks behind cattle barns, around catchment tanks, or through fields of golden wheat. The locals knew where the county road had been blocked, cut, or otherwise made to be impassible. None of the old paved roads between the ranch and Bethany existed any longer.

Almost immediately after the collapse, the paved roads had been blocked by trees and boulders, mostly by locals seeking to stem, or at least slow, any bandit traffic. Later, the pavement itself had been ripped up and used in dams and other infrastructure projects. The plain people had no use for paved roads, and saw them as a tangible evil—both a symptom and cause of everything that had gone wrong with the old society.

"Paved roads allow you to move faster," Father had said. "Moving faster leads to the sins of covetousness, impatience, over-specialization, and inevitably produces the idolatry of efficiency and utilitarianism. Eventually, these sins lead to the death of faith, family, and just about everything else. Paved roads shrink the world, but increase the real distance between parents and children, friends, and brethren. Everything you should hate is brought near, but everything you should love and cherish moves far away from you." His father repeated this message many times, and the current state of the world after the collapse bore witness to his beliefs. "Everything man-made that shrinks the world," his father would say, "is, at some level, an assault on God who made the world."

Great minds must think alike, because he couldn't remember a paved road around here that was still intact. Many years ago, when he was still a boy, his father had taken him, and many of the men from the ranch, to the old city of Penateka, two long days by wagon eastward from Bethany. Penateka used to be the largest city in the area, and was a regular shopping destination for most of the Vallenses prior to the collapse.

There was no city of Penateka, Texas any more. David had seen pictures of the city in old newspapers that his father kept, but within ten years of the collapse, the city was gone. It hadn't been destroyed by bombs or fire. No one would have ever wasted an atomic bomb on the town. Nevertheless, in a decade, the city had been disassembled by hand. Penateka was destroyed as a result of covetousness and greed, but it had disappeared out of *necessity*. Piece by piece, the city, which had once been home to almost 30,000 souls, had been torn down and hauled off in wagons and carts by people who needed the materials for homes, barns, caskets, fires, or... whatever.

A decade ago, there were still some passable roads in Penateka. There were no street signs or telephone poles, or abandoned buildings. There were many abandoned cars, or rather, frames of abandoned cars, but there were no houses, fences or gates. In many places, even the sewer and water pipes had been ripped out of the ground.

David vividly remembered seeing a chunk of concrete jutting out of the ground, where someone had tried to drag it off by chaining horses or a team of oxen to it, but they obviously had given up. The chunk was probably too large or maybe the chain had broken. Father had said that it was a chunk of street curbing, but that it represented the old world. Around seven billion people had tried to drag it someplace God didn't want it to go... so the chain broke. *And the meek had inherited the earth.* Well, the meek, along with a whole lot of covetous, militaristic scumbags like the King of Aztlan—who wanted to destroy the meek and steal the earth. Despite his militant tendencies, David resolutely believed that God had a plan for everyone, including the King of Aztlan and those like him.

In every era of time, he thought, God had raised up a champion to defend His people and destroy His foes. Moses, Joshua, David. Now, the Vallenses had a champion in Phillip and the Ghost militia, even if Father couldn't see it.

On their way to Bethany the group stopped from time to time and he and his father would ride up to houses, barns or fields to inform the local Vallenses of what was happening. Father told them to pack up whatever food and supplies they could muster into wagons and head up to the Wall ranch. Many wouldn't leave immediately because they were concerned about their animals, but they dutifully promised their pastor that they would get prepared and would come quickly whenever they determined that trouble was near. Some of the more creative ones had already devised a system during the construction and arrangement of their farms whereby they could leave their animals unattended for days, even weeks, and the animals could feed and water themselves.

David knew that an exodus would soon begin and the road the men had just traveled would be jammed with horses, buggies and wagons heading northward. It was very likely that some of these people might never see their farms again. Father would say, "Fields can be replanted. Farms can be rebuilt. We have resources and man-power, but we cannot replace our lives."

David honored and respected his father, but he could not see how teaching his own people not to defend themselves, especially in such an extreme situation, could in any way be protecting their lives. The son had concluded that inordinate pacifism—pacifism in the face of inescapable aggression and annihilation—actually bred violence. All that he could think of was—*we need to fight!*

The road began to rise as they approached the Bethany pass. The town was now situated only on this side of the pass, but before the collapse, another, smaller town had existed on the south side of the 'mountains' (as the locals had called them). The mountains were actually twin mesas that rose up about 300 feet above Bethany. The pass between the mesas was 100 yards wide but was made narrower by thickly growing mesquite and brush, along with large piles of rubble and boulders on both sides of the road.

At one time, just after the Civil War, the southward path through the mesas had been a military road along which the Apache and Comanche tribes had been driven northward out of Texas. Before the collapse, the road had become a small and lightly traveled state highway. Now, the pass was a narrow wagon path between the twin mesas of Bethany.

After the collapse, wiser minds among the Vallenses had determined to build a new trading village north of the mesas. In this way, in case of an attack, the pass could be shut down or blocked in order to give the town folk time to evacuate the village.

The town could still, albeit with some difficulty, be approached from the west. However, crossing Jefford's Creek was no easy endeavor, making the western route far less appealing. Jefford's Creek had once, indeed, been a creek, rather than the river it was now. Father told him that it had been dammed up by the WPA back in what they called 'The Great Depression', and that Jefford's Creek Reservoir 30 miles to the west was once the water supply for most of the towns in the area.

Once the dam was completed in the early 1940s, the creek had become nothing more than a seasonal overflow from the reservoir. Back then, it was only fed by the draws, run-offs, and creeks from there to here. By the early 21st century, it was at best a wide creek, but sometimes it was just a trickling stream.

The reservoir had been gone now for almost twenty years, and there weren't many people diverting water for agriculture anymore. For all intents and purposes, Jefford's Creek had become a river again as it had been throughout most of history. From just west of Bethany, the river flowed serenely through the lowlands and valleys for awhile northward before making a giant bend only a few miles north and east of the Wall Ranch. From there, it flowed into Lake Penateka, a day's ride to the east-northeast of the ranch. Lake Penateka was one of the only man-made reservoirs in the area that still held water.

From the east, Bethany was virtually inapproachable north of the twin mesas. The mesquite brush, juniper bushes, and sharply undulating terrain made it almost impossible to traverse on horseback, or en masse, especially by anyone who didn't know the area. The militiamen knew of paths and switchbacks, and they could, and did, successfully send outriders and recon units through the brush they referred to as 'The Big Thicket'. Given that for any army, that approach was not practicable, the Aztlani troops—if they planned to destroy Bethany, which undoubtedly they did—would have to come through the narrow Bethany pass. Five hundred men was a formidable force, but David was of the opinion that Bethany could and should be defended.

If Phillip were here, he thought, there would certainly be a fight, and perhaps, with God's help, the resistance could even ruin the Duke's plans. However, with the heart and soul of the Ghost militia away—and likely ignorant of the pending attack—and only a handful of the militia present, it was very unlikely that any attempt would be made to defend and protect Bethany. It would all burn.

There was going to be a debate in the council. That much was sure. A relatively large number of the Vallenses

86

believed that the time to fight had arrived. If only he would be allowed to speak maybe he could convince his father and the Elders to let each man act according to their consciences.

If he would be allowed to speak.

That was in no wise a certain thing. He was not old enough to speak freely during a debate because you had to be 30 years old to serve as an Elder; besides, his feelings were well known among the Vallenses. The division and disagreement that had come from his last speech in front of the Elders and the council had still not been resolved. The issue was boiling just under the surface. Now, it seemed to be coming to a head.

As they approached Bethany, David looked up and saw his father's eyes intently peering at him over a green-dyed cotton bandana. The eyes were the softest brown, flecked with gold, platinum and bronze; they had always struck him as being almost uniquely alive.

As a boy, he had heard his father preach about the deadness of the world and of the carnal man, speaking of deadness in the eyes of 'worldlings'. He used to say, "Those who are fully given over to the world and to their love of it have the eyes of the shark. They have doll's eyes. There is a deep and pervading deadness in them like inky pools of hopelessness." His father was not talking about any particular eye color. He was talking about a lack of life behind those eyes. In contrast, David had always—from his earliest memories—noted a particular and sparkling glow of life in the eyes of his father; and it was this life that was looking at him now. He could not see if his father was smiling or frowning, but he knew that he was studying him. His father's lively eyes missed nothing.

The group rode into the town and agreed to meet at the Public House in half an hour. His father sent messengers throughout the village, alerting the inhabitants of the imminent danger, urging them to pack up and head northward as soon as possible. Two militia men were sent to find and alert the Ghost units that were supposed to be in the area.

David dismounted in front of the Cobbler Shop and unlashed a large Longhorn hide from behind his saddle. Ana the Tanner had asked him to deliver the hide to Mr. Byler the Cobbler in exchange for some boots for herself and the Wall family. If things were coming down for good in Bethany, the Walls would need those extra boots.

The first cool breeze flowing from the distant squall line pushed through town, as David removed his straw hat and entered the cobbler shop. The old cobbler stood up slowly from his work and approached the large oak counter to meet him.

Mr. Byler was probably only in his 70s, but as an *oldling* he was quite rare. To the 'younglings'—those who had been born just before or immediately after the crash—anyone who had been a full adult at the time of the collapse was called an 'oldling'.

Because of the nature of the crash, there were a few peculiar demographical anomalies in the world, or at least in the world that David knew. Human society was now stratified very clearly between oldlings and younglings, even if only the young folk used those terms. There was a noticeable lack of any substantial intermediate generation (the *middlings*), as well as an absence of many people who were very old. Basically, there was a *stratum* or age group which was mostly missing.

The missing generation consisted of those aged 18 to 35. Very few people in that age group had survived—David himself was one of them, and so was his sister Betsy—maybe only a few hundred of them existed among all of the Vallenses.

Many of those who were small children or babies at the time of the crash had died not too long after. It was a tough time, and high infant and youth mortality rates arrived with the perils of the times. Among the Vallenses, this loss was stayed within a few years, as relative stability returned to the Vallensian region, but the noticeable lack of many twenty-somethings was a reality of David's world.

Likewise, it was pretty rare to find oldlings who were much more than about 65 years of age, as so many of what were then known as 'senior citizens' had also died. Thus, Mr. Byler was quite a rarity. He was one of the oldest of the Vallenses living in the area. He had served his time as an elder, and though he still offered his council and advice freely, he no longer attended council meetings. He found them to be tiring affairs.

"I hear in the winds that we are to have some excitement, and I'm not talking about some little rainstorms," Mr. Byler said in a serious tone.

"Yes sir," David replied, "things are looking a bit scary at the moment. We really need you and everyone else to evacuate Bethany as soon as possible—as early as tonight, if the weather allows. You'll find camps being set up near our ranch, but we might have to keep moving north and east until we find out what is going to happen."

"I was just closing up. I've got your boots ready and I'll pack them up on your horse for you," He paused for a moment, looking down. "I hope there will be a Bethany here when we return."

"God will provide, Mr. Byler," David said, maybe a bit unconvincingly. "We've made it through hard times before."

"Some folks are saying that there'll be a fight," he lowered his voice to almost a whisper. "Are you going to fight, young David?"

"I don't know, sir. I just don't know."

The Public House was mostly quiet as everyone filed in. David was not on the council, and was not an Elder; still, as a part of Jonathan's party and as one of the most notable members of the group who wanted to fight, he was confident that no one would object to his attendance. The mood of the room was restrained and the hustle and bustle of evacuees, carts, and buggies out in the street—as people prepared to make their way north—further solemnized the atmosphere in the pub.

His father approached him as he entered and, leading him by the elbow, guided him over to the counter.

"Several members of the council have asked that you speak on their behalf." His father looked him in the eye. His manner was respectful, but David could tell that he was still concerned. There was an unspoken declaration in his father's look that told him that though they were to be opponents on this issue, it did not affect his father's affection for him.

"Thank you, Father. I will not speak without your permission."

"You have my permission, David. I am not surprised to see that so many in the council have respect for you and your opinions. It is gratifying to an old man to see his son so honored." His father smiled at him, "I have an important announcement to make, after which you may speak. Please, keep it short because we all have work to do."

"Yes sir," was all he could manage.

His father brought the meeting to order, and introduced the Elders who were present.

There was old Arness Barron, the man who had organized the Vallenses to help the Walls after his mother died. Standing almost at attention in the corner was Jeremy Saldano, whose family built nearly all of the Vallenses' carts, wagons, and buggies. Seated by the window was Maurice Stannis, accompanied by his older sons Lance and Walter.

Many of the men present had, years ago, taken the family name of their trade. There was Grayson Smith—usually called 'Smithy'. There was Davidson Cooper who ran the Cooper shop and made barrels. Standing by the door was Nicholas Brewer, who not only was a brewer, but he owned and operated the Public House; and standing next to him was Sheldon Wright, the wheelwright in Bethany.

There were about 30 men present at the council meeting, including the Elders, the four members of the Ghost Militia, and David himself.

After introductions all around, his father began.

"I want to thank everyone for being here. We have urgent news from San Angelo, but before we start, we need to pray, and then we'll sing the 2nd Psalm."

With eyes closed, the gathered Vallenses and the militiamen joined together in solemn and heartfelt prayer. Throughout the singing of the Psalm, David could sense the passion and sincerity in the voices of the men surrounding him. He was moved as never before. Trying times have a way of focusing the mind and the heart. How many times in history had the Psalms been sung by groups like this who were suffering tribulation?

As the last note of the Psalm faded, David's father raised his hand, as did the men of old when indicating that they would speak.

"When we arrived in Bethany not an hour ago, we received word from a militia outrider concerning the situation in San Angelo." Looking around, David could see the tension in men's solemn faces, as young and old alike awaited their pastor's words with anticipation.

"The people of San Angelo, and many Vallenses among them, took it upon themselves to burn the city as the Aztlani host approached. The city is in flames. Several smaller frontier towns were burned and pillaged by the heathen army as they marched towards San Angelo. Thus, the people there decided to leave nothing for the enemy, but scorched earth. A mass evacuation is taking place, and most of those folks are heading here, burning their own fields and any other structures or supplies on their way. They hope to make it through the pass in front of the army.

"However painful, it is a wise plan. The Aztlani army is, no doubt, forced to carry their material supplies with them. No supply lines or resupply bases are available to them as they move across the badlands and militia territory. They have undoubtedly counted on pillaging and stealing what they need as they travel. Resupply in a large frontier town like San Angelo would have been a critical element in their plans. Like the Russians before Napoleon, our brethren to the south are leaving the invader with nothing to scavenge."

David grinned for a moment before he fully grasped the implications of such plan. Thousands of refugees would be heading northward through the pass in the next twenty-four hours.

"Maybe we should burn Bethany before Aztlan does!" shouted Grayson the Smithy.

"We will be discussing our options in time," his father replied softly. The pastor of the Vallenses dropped his head and stroked his beard for a moment. "We certainly have to consider every option."

There was a stony silence as each man in the room considered what was coming. They pondered on the fact that life—as they had known it up until now—had fundamentally changed.

Whether they chose to fight or not, the peaceful Vallenses of Central Texas were now at war.

Chapter 8 - Timothy

Refugees had been arriving for over eight hours, some joining the pilgrim tent camps that were rising spontaneously throughout the area around the Wall ranch, others stopping for water and a short break before continuing on to the north and east. Those who continued on, generally the more pessimistic ones, hoped to cross Jefford's Creek at Blackmun's Crossing before either one or the other of the armies chose, for strategic purposes, to destroy the bridge.

From horseback, Timothy, Ruth, and Jack Johnson were supervising the arrival, giving instructions, and watching diligently for Aztlani spies, or any unknown or unusual people moving among the Vallenses.

The three were blessed that the moon was out and that the storm had only lightly clipped them as it made its way east. The ground was barely damp, and there was enough light to be able to see what had once seemed to be an almost endless flow of refugees coming up the road. Finally, in the last hour or so, the flow had started to abate.

Tim handed Jack a metal cup, then poured in some hot mesquite coffee from the insulated leather bag Ruth had brought over from one of the camps. Jack Johnson was a close neighbor to the Walls, and the two young men had become friends over the past few weeks.

Jack, who was about his own age of 18 years, had the given name of Andrei Nikolayevich Bolkonsky. Tim had learned Jack's real name and its spelling during all the hours spent with him and Ruth in the past several weeks. Andrei and his father Nikolai, like many immigrants, used more Americanized names, but strangely enough, neither had chosen the English language equivalent of their Russian names. For some reason, unknown to anyone but himself, the father had taken the name John. The son took the name Jack, which—to make the issue even more confusing—actually used to be a nickname for the name John. Since Jack was John's son, soon enough the Vallenses began to call the young Bolkonsky by the name Jack John's-son. From that, and somewhat illogically, the father had come to be known as John Johnson, even though Nikolai Bolkonsky's own father had been named Pyotr. To all of the Vallenses, the Russians were known as the Johnsons.

Tim was learning that naming conventions that had become so staid and stiff prior to the collapse, had, in many cases, reverted to the more flexible form of earlier centuries. Without computers, tracking IDs, microchips and passports, people could pretty much be called whatever they liked.

Identification was now solely based on who knew you and for how long. Trust was not easily won, but meant everything, and neither did a sordid past, long repented of, haunt those who now chose to live rightly. The Vallenses never did trust many words; thus, a person's character, honor, integrity, and faith was their only identification. Strangers realized that it was what you did, and how you lived over a long period of time that would make you accepted as part of the community, not paperwork, government papers, empty words, or mere intentions.

According to many of the *oldlings* and Elders that Tim had spoken to, it was actually harder to spy or get away with a con or cheat today than it had been before the collapse. People were more wary; strangers were watched more closely. People were also more reliant on their intuition and relied more on their natural senses. Nobody relied on inanimate objects, or data divorced from context, to make decisions. It had taken the spy Ronald Getz and others like him many, many years to infiltrate the Vallenses to the point that one of them had an opportunity to kill Gareth the assassin while in militia custody.

He was beginning to see the multiple threads of love, care, humanity, and community that bound the Vallenses together like a tapestry—threads that, in the old world, had been replaced by electronics, numbers, and a virtual life. In the times before the collapse, people's lives were governed by distant

94

strangers and tyrants no one knew—those with no accountability or loyalty to the family of faith.

Ruth had told him that the Johnson family (the wife had kept her Russian given name—Natasha), had been the Wall's neighbors to the south for almost 25 years. John Johnson and Jonathan Wall had been close friends for all of those years, and Jack and his father were the first ones to arrive to help organize and situate the refugees arriving from Bethany, as well as from the south and west.

Sipping his coffee, Tim watched as the refugees passed the Walls' main gate. Some turned in to join others at the camp, whilst others continued their perilous journey into the darkness.

Some families, Tim had heard, had already crossed Jefford's Creek and were heading for the intersection with the Old Comanche Road as it moved northeastward. By continuing to move northward and eastward, they hoped to find a place to wait out the attack. It was generally accepted by the Vallenses that Aztlan would be satisfied with burning and destroying Bethany. No one believed that they would continue to follow the Vallenses further north, because—by doing so—they would be moving farther away from their own homes, with no bases and no means of re-supply. History told them that even the greatest of armies had their limits—even Napoleon had stopped at Moscow.

The general opinion of those Vallenses who stopped near the Walls' ranch was that the Aztlani army would return home after burning Bethany. The destruction of San Angelo before they could pillage it had likely robbed the foreign army of their will-power and their desire to chase a rabbit they could not hope to catch.

Sometime around midnight, Tim and Jack rode over to a militia unit that was just arriving—it was one of the units that had been stationed in the Thicket, east of Bethany. Ruth, who had gone to get more coffee, caught up with them just as the Ghost militia rider began to give his report to Timothy.

The debate was over... the Vallenses were not going to fight. *I already knew that*, Tim thought. *Why did anyone think that they would?* Both militia units that had been stationed near Bethany, as well as the outriders that had been tasked with pestering the invaders all along their advance from San Angelo, were returning to the Wall ranch to protect the family. Their only hope now was to guard as many of the Vallenses as possible during their retreat, and to consider a possible defense of the Wall ranch if the invaders decided to keep moving northward.

There had been no way to plan a full-fledged defense of the village. Phillip and the bulk of the Ghost militia were still gone, and were probably unaware of what was going on in Bethany. If, vastly outmanned and outgunned, the remaining units had tried to mount a defense, and if they were defeated—which was very likely—there would be no hope for the fleeing Vallenses. The war would have been over before it started.

"So we are just going to give them Bethany?" he asked. "Why didn't the Vallenses just burn it down, like they did San Angelo?"

The spokesman for this militia unit was an impressive rider they all called Piggy. Tim had given him the name a few years ago for his excellent and unique ability to take down a wild boar by throwing a knife from horseback—a feat no one else would even attempt, much less accomplish.

"It's a very complicated situation," Piggy responded, leaning forward in his saddle. "I think everyone agreed that Bethany should be burned before the Aztlanis could loot it. But, no one wanted to burn it if there was still the slightest possibility that the Aztlani army might give up on it."

Tim pondered the likelihood of such an outcome for a moment. He couldn't imagine the enemy retreating without destroying the town. "What makes anyone think that they will leave Bethany intact? Why ride all this way and then quit?"

"Ok, I know that this sounds confusing, but it's actually not when you consider it carefully, and when you have all of the information. After the council meeting, a handful of militiamen, along with David Wall, decided to stay and fight when Aztlan tries to come through the Bethany Pass. They are hoping to slow them down long enough to allow for a defense to be planned and executed here on the high ground of the ranch," Piggy explained, almost sheepishly, shrugging to indicate that it had not been his idea.

"David Wall?" Tim almost hollered the name. "David Wall decided to fight? What the hell is going on? He's a Vallensian! Fight? How many is a handful?! I need to know the details of all that is going on Piggy, right now!"

"Ok, ok!" Piggy tried to placate him, putting up his hand to slow the conversation down. "Let me run through it quickly." He took a deep breath, "After the council meeting, Jonathan announced that any man who felt strongly compelled to fight had to make a decision if they were going to be Vallenses or Militia, given that the Vallenses are not permitted to fight. He said that he would understand it if anyone wanted to join the militia. However, if they chose that part, they would henceforth be considered militiamen and not Vallenses, and though they could continue to live and work among the Vallenses and attend some Vallensian functions, they would no longer be permitted to participate in the communion or close fellowship of the Church.

"Regardless, David Wall announced that he would fight with the militia. The only other Vallensian who crossed over was Grayson Smith, the blacksmith. No one else was willing to forego the communion in order to fight what they considered to be a losing battle."

"So what is this about fighting? I still don't get it. What is happening now?"

"Easy, Tim, give me a moment to lay it all out" Piggy said softly. "When David and Grayson crossed over, we had already decided that the fight could not be won there without risking everything. We were all pulling out. However, a few of our men decided to stay and help David in slowing down Aztlan. As far as I know, there are maybe five men, counting Wall and Smith, left to defend Bethany."

"*Maybe* five men?" he asked.

Piggy began counting on his fingers, "Ok, there is David Wall and the Smithy, and among the militia there is The Hood, Enos Flynn, and Pachuco Reyes. When we left, Hood was preparing the town so he could ride through and burn it in a moment's notice. The rest were rolling boulders down off the sides of the twin mesas and doing whatever else they could to block the pass."

"So five men are going to fight five-hundred trained Aztlani soldiers?" Tim asked, clearly bewildered at such a notion. "This is their plan? It's a suicide."

"Actually it's only four," Piggy added. "Hood can't be risked, because if they all die early in the battle, no one will be able to fire the town."

"Ridiculous!"

"It's a sacrifice, Tim."

"It's a useless slaughter!"

"They didn't see it that way."

"They should have just burned the town!"

"They needed to slow them down. Listen, you weren't there, Tim; you can't know how it went down."

Tim sighed deeply, rose up on his saddle before settling back down into it. After a moment of thought, he looked at Piggy. "I've been charged with protecting the Wall family by Phillip himself. I have my orders. There are enough of you here to start preparing the defense of this place. I'm riding south. What are the plans there?"

As he spoke these words, he heard a slight, almost imperceptible gasp escape from Ruth. When he looked at her, she had her hand over her mouth. When she saw him looking at her, she dropped her hand and averted her gaze.

"*All* of your family is my responsibility, Ruth," he said gently.

"I understand," she replied, "and I would ride with you, if I thought you'd let me get away with it. But you won't."

"No, I won't."

Piggy interrupted, "They are expecting the Aztlanis to arrive at sunrise. The storm and the burning of San Angelo slowed them down, but not for long."

"I've got to go then."

"I'll be going with you," shouted Jack, who had remained silent through the whole exchange.

"If you do...," Tim cautioned, leaning forward.

"I will be kicked out of the fellowship, I know. But my family is indebted to the Walls for their friendship and help when my parents first came to this country. David is my friend... I've known him all my life. I will go and fight."

"I can't stop you," Tim replied. "Jonathan said that each man had to decide for himself. Go quickly and say goodbye to your parents, and get what weapons you have. If we ride through as fast as we can, and barring any unexpected delays, we can be there an hour or so before sunrise. The road isn't as jammed with refugees as it was an hour ago, and the northbound traffic will grow lighter. I know a few shortcuts too. I'll meet you here and be ready to ride in thirty minutes."

Jack rode off into the shadows, and the rest of the militia began to ride into the camp. Piggy stopped his horse next to Tim's and the two shook hands.

"Thank you for your report, Piggy."

"I'm just doing my job. I know that you are too. May God keep you and protect you."

"Thanks, man. You keep all of these folks safe—especially my best friend Ruth here, ok?"

"Will do, Tim," Piggy replied, as he followed the last of his unit through the gate.

Tim turned to Ruth, who was sitting stoically on her horse, absentmindedly clutching the coffee bag. The two looked at one another for a few moments in silence that spoke volumes. Tim reached into the pocket on his leather coat, pulled out an old arrowhead and handed it to her.

"I found this by the creek the day you took down that pig with one shot. Why don't you hold it for me until I get back?"

Ruth rubbed the arrowhead in her hand, looking at him searchingly. "I'll do that, Timothy."

After another moment of silence, Tim pulled the reins, spurred the horse and headed for his tent.

As he passed by the pilgrim camp and the people moving about setting up tents and preparing fires, he wondered if the Vallenses knew what the militia was doing, and why they found it necessary to fight. He figured that they did know. They must know. Somehow, he knew that they were grateful. He also knew that most of the members of the Ghost militia were also grateful for the Vallenses, and for all they had done to stabilize their world after the collapse, providing some light to the world cloaked in deathly darkness. What would the world be without them? *What a weird sight we must all be to the world.*

His thoughts strayed to the issues that divided, and those that united these two unlikely allies. Maybe, deep down, he wanted—maybe even more than he was willing to admit—to be a Vallensian, and to have a family. Kin was something he had never had in his short life. Yet, he knew that for a soldier home life and family were not an option. Phillip himself had tried to keep a wife and now the Ghost's own family was held by Aztlan.

He had been raised in the militia. He didn't even remember having a family, nor could he know what that meant outside the family he had among his Ghost brethren. His duty and honor were the only two things of consequence that he owned.

He had only faint memories of being an orphan, running with a pack of what could only be called feral orphan boys out west and south of what had once been Wichita Falls. How old was he when the militia found him? Seven? Six? Probably seven—it was hard to tell, with no one to remember his birthday or locate any remaining records.

The militia outriders picked up the eight homeless orphans and offered them real food and a place to sleep. And then they had trained. For the next seven years, they had trained almost every day. They didn't just learn to fight and ride. They learned to read and spell. They learned history and philosophy. Phillip did not believe that a warrior could remain on the side of right if he was uneducated and if he was ignorant of history, philosophy, and religion. The Ghost militia was not made up of coarse and vulgar killers. They were killers, without a doubt, but they were educated and noble in their pursuit of justice.

Phillip had called them his Spartans, and had taught them what that moniker meant. He told them that many years ago, three hundred Spartans had faced off against between half a million and a million Persians at Thermopylae, and had fought there to their death. It was an honor to be called Spartans.

Phillip had also taught them the militia honor code, and they had all learned the art and business of guerilla war. At eighteen years of age, Timothy was one of the brightest and bravest of Phillip's own troops; and now, he was heading towards his Thermopylae.

Reaching his tent, he grabbed another quiver of arrows that had been fitted with a leather cover and a shoulder strap and threw it over his shoulder. Then he loaded his saddlebag with dried meat, extra containers of water, and a few extra flints. If they were to fight with guns, which they did on occasion, someone else would have had to have gotten them. Phillip did not usually allow them to keep guns with them. They were too heavy, and too easily relied upon. The militia stash of arms was hidden and only accessed when the whole militia would be engaged in an action. Most likely, the Ghost units would be using arrows, swords and knives against Aztlani guns and maybe even cannon.

After he was certain that he had everything that he needed, he sat down with a quill pen, dipped the tip in a small bottle of ink he had bought the last time he was in Bethany, and wrote a note to Ruth on a piece of cotton paper.

He wrote that the time he had spent guarding the Walls had been the best time of his life, and that he had really enjoyed knowing her. He told her that he admired her more than he did anyone else in the world—other than, maybe, her father and Phillip. She'd understand that. He reminded her to keep her faith, and be a good help to her father, and that he hoped that someday she'd marry and raise a good Vallensian family. He placed the note on his cot, knowing that Ruth would find it if something happened to him. Then he mounted his horse, looked back one more time over his humble home, and rode back towards the gate.

As he approached the main entrance, he met up with Jack who had evidently informed his family of his plans. The Russian just smiled a crooked smile, indicating that it had probably not gone too well. Tim didn't ask and Jack didn't volunteer.

As they rode in silence through the gate and turned towards the road to Bethany, Tim slowed down and pulled his horse up. He looked back, and in the moonlight, he could just make out the outline of Ruth, seated on her horse, silhouetted by Vallensian fires.

He didn't wave goodbye.

Chapter 9 - Ruth

It wasn't much different from hunting. Her horse Peloncio stood patiently and without fidgeting as they waited in the dark shadows of the copse. A warm breeze swirled lazily through the trees, and she kept her breath steady and regular as she sat motionless in the dark.

Traffic on the Bethany road had thinned to the point that only an occasional straggler passed by—either families to the north of the town who took a longer time to get ready to leave, or those who had made it through the pass just before it was closed down.

Every part of her had wanted to rush down to Bethany. She knew shortcuts that no one else even knew existed, and she could have probably arrived long before Tim and Jack got even close. She had waited a good thirty minutes before starting to follow them southward. Now, she waited patiently in the dark.

Her conscience would not allow her to do what she so much wanted to do, which was to disobey Timothy, her father, and the *ordnung* of the community, and go fight those who would attack and kill her people and destroy their property. Still, her inner voice urged her to, at the very least, make sure that Tim and David were safe, even if she had to die doing so. But the obedience she had learned all of her life, and her love and respect for her father, would not allow her to rush south to Bethany without his permission. So she waited.

Her father would have left Bethany only after the last of the stragglers had gotten out of the town, so she expected him to pass by here at any time.

She was not surprised that a few minutes later her father and a group of friends and Elders appeared, riding up the road in the moonlight. She rode out where she could be seen, and sat waiting for them as they approached.

"Ruth?" her father asked. "Is that you, dear?"

"Yes, Father."

"What are you doing here, Ruth?"

"I was waiting for you. I need to ask your permission to ride scout to Bethany. I know that you won't think that it's wise, but please let me do it, Father. Somebody needs to be able to warn the camp—someone who knows all of the shortcuts and the hiding places also needs to be able to ride back and warn everyone if the Aztlani soldiers keep coming north. I'll stay hidden, and away from the battle... I promise."

"Ruth..." her father sighed. "Ruth, you're still a young girl, and you know nothing of war. Scouting is a grown man's job. We'll send someone to do this."

"Father, hear me out." She paused and concentrated on not being emotional, and on not sounding scared or childish. "Father, no one knows the area like I do. No one can ride as fast, hide as well, or get in and out like I can. Even Tim says that only Phillip himself rides like me. I promise you, I will stay safe, Father."

She raised her eyes, sat up in the saddle, and looked her father in the eye.

"When I left home, I had every intention of riding all the way to Bethany, of disobeying you, and of joining in the battle... but I know that such an emotional and rushed decision was wrong. I did as you said, Father, and I listened to my conscience. You know I will do as you say, but you also know that I can do this. Please let me go, Father."

Her father shifted around in his saddle and looked back down the road as if he were waiting for some kind of sign. Then he turned back towards Ruth. "Stay off of the roads once the battle starts. Keep your eyes open, and your back to the sun when it comes up in the east. Don't allow yourself to be silhouetted against the sky. The Aztlani army has been hesitant to send out scouts because the militia kills them all, but that doesn't mean that they won't do it. Keep an eye on your surroundings, and don't let anyone get behind you. Pick a point far enough away from Bethany to watch without being seen, and stay out of shooting range. Do not get involved! If things go bad, head east into the Thicket; you know your way around there, and no Aztlani unit will be able to follow you."

"Yes, Father." She stifled her desire to shout with joy.

"Your job is to watch from afar, and get word to us if the army moves northward from the town. That is it, do you understand me?"

"Yes Father. Thank you."

He rode up to her and embraced her, patting her on the shoulder. "Be safe, little girl."

"Yes sir."

As her father rode away, he looked back over his shoulder and smiled at her. She knew that he did not want her to go, and that others would likely second-guess him for doing so. Still, he was responsible for thousands of people, and he knew that she was the best at what needed to be done.

She pulled Peloncio around, and rode off through the oaks heading south.

Ruth arrived outside of Bethany at almost the same time as Tim and Jack entered the town. She turned eastward and rode until she was into the Thicket, just east of the easternmost mesa. She tied Peloncio to a low mesquite branch and then hiked back a quarter of a mile to the west, where she scrambled silently up a low hill until she commanded a good view of Bethany and the twin mesas. It was still quite dark, but light was just starting to spread across the sky to the east. She stayed lower on the hill and beneath a salt cedar bush, so that she would not be silhouetted against the sky, as her father instructed.

As the early light of morning began to spread across the land, she could make out a few of the men as they made final preparations for the assault.

She didn't like this spot. While it gave her a good view of Bethany and of most of the pass, she was still too low to be able to see if the Aztlani army had arrived. From her vantage point, the view to the south was blocked by the twin mesas. She needed to get closer... and higher.

Everything her father had told her replayed repeatedly in her mind. She did intend to stay safe, and she wanted to obey her father, but she knew that she needed to get up on the east end of the easternmost mesa in order to be able to command a good view of the battle.

The militia would have at least two and maybe three men on each of the mesas looking down into the pass. However, the other end of the east mesa—the end she was near—was slightly more elevated and would allow her to see everything clearly.

She started moving before she could have time to talk herself out of it.

It's just like hunting, she told herself, as she moved stealthily through the brush and mesquite that dotted the foothills of the mesa. From where she was, only a few hundred yards to the east, was the Thicket where Peloncio waited patiently. The Thicket curved around from northeast to southwest and ended at the easternmost tip of the east mesa. If she was forced to run, she was confident that she could be back in the Thicket in minutes.

When she reached the base of the mesa, she concealed herself in another cedar bush and sat perfectly still for another ten minutes. If some Aztlani scout was trying to come around the mesas, or was intending to get up to the top of the mesa, she wanted to know about it before she began her climb.

When nothing moved, she began her ascent. It took her 20 minutes to scramble to the top, and when she did, the gray light of morning had chased away the darkness of the long night. She crouched low and moved forward, keeping her eyes trained to the surroundings, looking for danger. There were several large boulders on top of the mesa, and she used them for cover as she crawled forward quietly.

Near the south edge of the mesa, she found the perfect vantage point. Crouching behind some very large boulders, she could now command a view of the entire area. She could see Bethany, and most of the Bethany road that came down from the north. There were no militiamen on the top of the mesa, but she figured they were just below the peak, making sure that they could not be seen from the south. Stretched out below her to the south, she could see for miles and miles, and she caught her breath when she saw that the Aztlani army had arrived. With

106

banners flying, they were forming up, a half-mile south of the pass.

She could also see Aztlani scouts, two of them, sneaking up towards the south entrance of the pass, staying low, and creeping from cover to cover. She wanted to scream out a warning to the militia, but she knew that it would not help. She reached for an arrow from her quiver, but stopped herself when she remembered her father's command. *Do not get involved!* The men were too far away anyway. It would be a miracle if her arrow reached them.

She was just starting to notice the warmth of the new day, and the light changing from gray to more orange-yellow, when she saw one of the Aztlani scouts pitch backward, an arrow sticking out from his throat! *Yes!* The other barely had time to register the fact that his partner had been killed, when another arrow entered his chest and he too flopped into the dirt.

Ruth could not tell from whence the arrows came, but she was ecstatic and felt the adrenaline pump through her, knowing that the scouts had been spotted.

It seemed like forever, but it was probably only another 15 minutes, before the Aztlanis tried again. This time, there were ten men, all approaching from the West. They were close to the westernmost mesa, and hoped to use the mountain as a shield to get close to the pass. Again, she felt the scream rise up in her throat as she strived with every thread of her being not to do something to warn militiamen guarding the pass.

Death, in this instance, did not come by arrow, at least not at first. As the advance unit came close to the entrance to the pass, each man clinging as closely as possible to the face of the mountain, they did not see until it was too late as five or six huge boulders came crashing down the mesa on top of them. This time, she saw the militiamen moving quickly back away from the edge of the mesa, and she saw a single arrow strike the back of the only Aztlani soldier with the ability to crawl away from the pile of rocks. Then all became still again, except for the moans and cries of broken men, crushed from above by rocks not much smaller than horses.

As she wiped away a bead of sweat, and tried her best to calm herself, she heard her brother David's voice as he shouted to the men guarding the pass.

"They'll come heavy this time boys! Shoot and move. No more than two to three shots from one place then move! Keep under cover! Remember... Shoot for the officers! Shoot anyone giving orders first! Then anyone on a horse! If they are wearing armor, the throat and under the arm are the weakest spots! Shoot and move! Don't let yourself get trapped! Keep a way out behind you! Make them panic! Make them crawl over their own dead bodies to kill you!"

She had to steady herself from the effects of fear and excitement. Timothy had told her that the body goes into shock at the beginning of a battle, and that there can be an intense fog and confusion. It happened to everyone, but the men who could remain calm and let it pass were the ones who survived. She forced herself to concentrate on her breathing and used every method she knew from hunting to remain calm.

Off to the south, she could see that the army was preparing a full-out assault on the pass. A hundred men and twenty horses stepped out from the mass of men, and began to advance—slowly at first, and then faster as they got nearer the pass. When they were 50 yards from the south entrance of the pass, they were moving as fast as they could go.

Arrows rained down from both sides of the pass, and it wasn't long before all 20 of the cavalrymen were unhorsed and lying wounded on the ground. The infantry hesitated, as they realized that they were going to have to climb over the rubble to advance. For many of them, their hesitation was their last cogent thought, as arrows pierced their bodies. A young officer tried to rally the men by brandishing his sword and pulling out a pistol, but his cry was cut short by an arrow that passed cleanly through his head.

The Aztlani assault faltered as man after man went down. Within seconds, those who were not wounded or dead were retreating as fast as they could run.

Ruth was so focused on the assault, that she had neglected her duty to stay aware. Her error occurred to her in a

108

flash when something moving off to her left caught her eye. She swung around the boulder she was lying against just in time to see an assault force of 20 men moving in towards the east. *They are trying to flank the militia by coming around the mountain!*

She knew that she was not supposed to get involved, but before she could stop herself, she let go a flurry of arrows, five in all, in a long arc in front of the flanking force. Her intention was not to hit and kill anyone; she wanted it to seem like there were many men guarding the easternmost edge of the mesa.

Her ploy worked, as the men, who had just seen the slaughter of almost a hundred men trying to take the pass, thought better of their orders and fled back to the main body of the army.

There was obvious confusion among the ranks of the Aztlani army. Many of the highest-ranking officers had been killed already, and most of the 350 men remaining really wanted nothing to do with trying to force the pass. Someone finally took charge, assembled the rabble back into ranks and ordered a full out charge on the pass. This time, they were all coming.

Terror filled Ruth's heart as she saw the army approach. She had never seen, or even imagined, such a terrifying sight. One hundred men on horseback and twice that number on foot. Panic was evident on the soldier's faces, most of them screaming as they ran. These men were 600 miles away from home, away from any base of resupply.

No doubt, the officer that had rallied the troops told them that they were all going to be killed if they did not take the pass. Each man had rape and pillage before him if the pass could be taken, and almost certain death waiting for him, if he retreated and returned home beaten.

Many of the men pulled out pistols as they rushed forward and began firing wildly into the rocks and boulders, hoping to frighten the men waiting there. The men in front were slowed again as they had to traverse the last 50 yards over the bodies of their fallen countrymen. Several horsemen had their horses killed beneath them, and the panic-stricken animals often trampled living infantrymen who got in their way. All the while, the steady stream of arrows flowed forth from the defenders stationed in the gap.

As the Aztlani army surged forward, they were so intent on a last, desperate attempt on the pass, that they did not see the huge force of militiamen sweeping up behind them on horseback. Ruth saw them, and she did scream this time. It was Phillip and the main Ghost militia force!

Ruth cheered aloud as she saw Phillip, who rode standing up in his stirrups, his sword gripped tightly in his hand. Alongside him were Gareth and the man they called The Mountain, leading the charge.

It was too late when the Duke of El Paso's army discovered what was happening to them. Some of them may have heard hoofbeats coming from behind, but most of them did not. The front echelons fell from arrows fired by the men in the pass and, as the assault slowed upon crashing into the boulders, Phillip and the militia cut the army to shreds from the rear. The entire action lasted less than five minutes, but the five minutes of battle resulted in a bloody slaughter.

None of the enemy force was left alive, and no one was allowed to surrender.

Later, as they gathered themselves and tended the wounded militiamen that were brought into Bethany, Phillip explained that the men were free to surrender before the battle had begun. "Once the battle begins," he said, "the time for surrender is over. We do not have the time, the manpower, or the inclination to babysit Aztlani prisoners. The whole nation of Aztlan may surrender right now, if they like. But if they come here to take the spoils, we will water the ground with their blood."

She found Timothy and David tending to the wounded in the makeshift hospital that had been set up in the Public House. It seemed to her that not many had been wounded at all. When she walked in, both Tim and David greeted her with a scowl of contempt and confusion, but after she explained that she had received permission from her father to scout the battle, they relented. She gave them a quick report about where she had

110

been throughout the battle, and what she had seen. She carefully omitted the part about the five arrows she had shot.

Tim, seeing that she was still overwhelmed with what she had seen, came over to her and pulled her aside.

"I can't imagine how you must be feeling, Ruth."

"I'm doing fine. I was just so worried about you and David... and all the men. I was so scared." She looked at him, checking him up and down for any signs of harm. "Are you injured?"

"No. Just a few scrapes and bruises from scrambling up and down the mesa. Shockingly, of the six men who had held the pass, five of us are alive and unhurt."

"Five?"

Timothy looked down, and then took her by her shoulders. "Ruth... Jack Johnson was killed by a stray bullet... a ricochet."

"Oh, my," she let out a sigh, feeling a little weak in her knees. He guided her to a chair that was not occupied by the wounded. She looked out of the window, and could see that high in the air, the vultures had already begun to circle for the feast.

"I know that you've known Jack for your whole life, Ruth, and that he was very close with your family. I'm sorry. Maybe I could have talked him out of coming... I don't know."

"He came because he wanted to come, and because he wanted to protect David. You couldn't have stopped him. Besides, my father said that any man who wanted to fight, could fight." She looked at him again, "No... you couldn't have stopped him. This is God's will."

"I don't know about that, or if I even understand what you mean by that, Ruth. I do know that I've been in quite a few battles, and it is never easy to lose someone you care about. This will affect your family and the entire Vallensian community. I don't know what else to say."

"Then let's just do what we can to help these men," she said, standing up and smoothing her dark headcovering. She walked past Tim to see what she could do to help. As she started to move away, Tim stopped her.

"Don't think that I don't know what you did up there," he said, smiling.

"What do you mean?" she replied.

"We saw that flanking force move out to the east. David had already started moving with two other men to try to meet them on the backside. Then we saw the men stop, turn around, and flee. We couldn't figure out why they retreated. Now I know."

"How could you know?" Ruth said, acting as innocently as she could.

He pointed at the quiver on her back. "You're a little light there. I'd say, maybe five or six arrows light, but who's counting?"

She looked down, then back up at him, "I must have dropped them on the ride down."

"Sure you did," he said, smiling warmly.

Ruth blushed, and as she walked by him, she silently found his hand and placed into it the arrowhead he had given her when he left the ranch.

Part Two

Chapter 10 - Gareth

There is a personal terror that surpasses the carnal fear that every warrior feels when going into battle. That ultimate terror is not the fear of death, but the knowledge that he might live, while his loved ones die. Gareth did not know this terror first-hand, but he could see it on the face of Phillip as they inventoried the weapons and material gained in the battle at Bethany.

The urgent message that San Angelo had been burned by the retreating Vallenses, and that Bethany was soon to fall, had come just as the Ghost militia was planning their attempt to rescue Phillip's wife Juliet and the girls. The Ghost had to make a decision, and he had to make it fast. The militia leader sent Rob Fosse and Sir Gerold the rebel Aztlani knight, along with 20 militia soldiers northward to attempt the rescue of his wife and children.

Gareth, Phillip, The Mountain, and almost 200 Ghost militia warriors immediately rode south at full speed to try to flank and overwhelm the Aztlani army attacking Bethany.

It would be days and maybe even longer—depending on the outcome—before Phillip would find out whether his wife and daughters were safe, but the Ghost leader never said a word about his concerns. Gareth was impressed that Phillip always maintained a professional demeanor, and that he focused on keeping up the morale of his troops, especially after the lightning victory at Bethany.

Arriving at the twin mesas, the militia force almost instantly overwhelmed the struggling Aztlani attackers, but most of the credit for the stunning victory went to David and that handful of brave warriors standing in the gap at the twin mesas.

As a Prince, he had learned the art of war at the hands and feet of the greatest military minds of Aztlan; and his father, the King, made sure that he received the best military education that could be procured. Still, he had never seen acts of heroism and bravery such as the defenders at Bethany had displayed.

The hardest, and most important, work in a battle of this sort is the warfare that takes place in the minds of men. The Aztlani forces had been defeated in their minds long before they died on the field. A handful of men with arrows had made Bethany seem impregnable in the opinion of the average Aztlani soldier, and this mental reality made Bethany impregnable to him in real life. The invaders knew they were going to die... they just chose to die moving forward, rather than retreating.

He could only assume that the Aztlani force must have concluded that they were outmanned and outgunned. In their minds, they had already resigned to a mental state that means the death knell in any engagement... they had succumbed to panic and fear.

Fear, in and of itself, can be a great motivator in battle, but when that fear becomes irrational and is coupled with the type of panic that silences the better voices of wisdom and circumspection, the battle is all but over. There is nothing left for that army to do but die.

For Gareth, this had been his first engagement in war. He had practiced and drilled since he was a boy; but, until Bethany, his steel had never been forged in battle. How could he have ever known that his first real battle would be against Aztlan?

Silently flanking the Aztlani army, the militia force had double advantage—the elements of surprise and position. Entering the fray, he felt the thrill and terror of battle and, for the first time, had experienced a phenomenon about which his mentors had taught him. When in battle, fear and terror, as well as the resulting adrenaline surge, must be recognized, and then controlled and channeled productively. He felt the fog of war and the numbing dullness of uncertainty and confusion when he first drew his sword in battle, but as the killing progressed, the fear and panic had transformed into concentration and purpose.

A part of him knew that he was traitorously killing his own men—men who had sworn themselves to his father, the King, and to himself as Crown Prince and heir to the throne.

Still, he had to rest on the knowledge that in order for his vision for a greater and more peaceful Aztlan to prevail, for a time, Aztlan had to be the enemy. The lowly soldier could not know what private forces had driven him to abandon his father and side with his father's enemies.

Prince Gareth of Aztlan did not believe that he had rebelled against, or abandoned, his country. He might be a traitor to his father, but not to his country. All of the actions he was engaged in were *for* his country. Sometimes, in order to support and love your country, you must oppose and fight the government of your country.

As a young prince, he spent many years with Sir English at New Rome, and his father's adjutant had taught him that in order for there to be peace in any Kingdom, there must be freedom—typically purchased at a heavy price.

It was the King's job, English taught him, to punish evildoers, while rewarding and defending the righteous. Any Kingdom that has a tyrant as a sovereign will eventually fall; and any nation built on endless consumption, the drive for empire, and the oppression of its own people, would inevitably consume itself and perish in a storm of violence and death.

History is the long tale of empires rising to power founded on vision, hard work, and productive capability, only to be eventually morally poisoned by the insatiable drive for conquest and domination. If anything could be learned from the collapse of America, it was that consumption as a creed, and comfort as a maxim, would lead any nation to ruin.

Aztlan, under the reign of his father, had followed the beaten path that leads to destruction, and would certainly fall if something radical were not done to stop it.

Posing as an assassin and a spy, joining forces with the rebel army, and actively supporting his father's greatest enemy would be considered an act of treason—that much he knew. Yet, it would have been a greater treason to allow Aztlan to continue on its way to destruction.

As a prince, he proposed to follow the path of freedom and peace, but, if his father could not see his own folly, the kingdom would not survive long enough for him to be crowned.

116

There were good people in Aztlan—people who wanted peace; yet, for it to be restored, first the better angels of their nature would need to prevail by removing the foul and wicked rulers who oppressed them. Although Aztlan had been born an outlaw nation, there was no reason that she must remain so. Gareth firmly believed that, if his father could be overthrown, there would be hope for Aztlan and her people. If not, then he would rather die having stood against the evil empire—even if it was ruled over by his own father.

Here at Bethany, though the battle had lasted only minutes, there were moments that, for him, seemed to last an eternity. Plunging into the tumultuous and surging mass of men, some on horseback and some on foot, all fighting to the death, was one of those times.

The militia troops had long been at war with Aztlan, and were adept at such skirmishes. Most of the Duke's men, to the contrary, had merely been involved in destroying peaceful villages, riding down unarmed citizens, or fighting small groups of relatively untrained men trying to defend their towns or lands. Even with the numerical odds in favor of Aztlan, this was a slaughter, rather than a battle.

In the assault, as he had engaged his first enemy soldier on horseback, there was a moment when the man recognized him. In the heat of battle, with death dancing on every side, the man had looked up to see Gareth of Aztlan, the Crown Prince of the realm and heir to the throne, advancing on him with sword drawn. Their eyes met for what seemed like minutes, but could only have been seconds.

The man was instantly overcome by a wave of confusion, lowering his sword to his side he tried in vain to process the reality of what was happening.

When Gareth swung his sword, the shocked man was barely able to parry the strike. More instinctively than willingly, he had raised his weapon just in time to intercept the first blow, the reality of being attacked by his own Prince still not completely understandable to him.

117

Just as Gareth raised his sword to strike again, another militia fighter riding by plunged his sword into the hapless man's neck, instantly ending the Aztlani soldier's battle for clarity in his thoughts and worldview.

Looking down as the soldier bled out into the Vallensian soil, Gareth faltered for just a moment, as he realized that the man had died because he could not assimilate the sometimes incomprehensible and contradictory winds of life, politics, and battle.

Slowly, clarity returned. Some men had to die in order for the dream of peace and stability to reign in this world.

Spurring his horse, he returned to the business of bringing that dream to fruition. These Aztlani men, at the command of his father and the Duke of El Paso, had chosen to wage a war against a peaceful people. In his mind, death was the wages of that sin.

After the battle, he looked out over the field of dead and dying men, his own sword stained with the blood of his countrymen, and he shook his head at the irony of it all. In order for life to come, there needed to be death. For peace to reign between Aztlan and the Vallenses, the peaceful Vallenses would need to be brought into the war against Aztlan. This was his mission. Like war, irony is a fickle business.

He now stood with Phillip, David Wall, and several of Phillip's soldiers, and watched as the spoils of war were loaded onto wagons.

"Over 250 pistols, 100 rifles, somewhere north of 400 battle swords, not to mention ammunition, some armor, boots, a ton of other standard issue soldiering goodies and supplies," reported Rollo, the man they called *The Mountain*. "The men have also rounded up around 50 horses, all of which are now expertly trained and experienced in not getting killed in a battle."

"We have dead on the field, Mountain, so let's keep the humor and japes to a minimum, shall we?" replied Phillip.

"Of course, sir. My apologies. Apparently Jonathan Wall is on his way here to retrieve the body of the Vallensian man who was killed in the gap."

David looked up at Phillip and nodded. "My father will want to take Jack back to his parents as soon as possible, but I assume he will also want to meet with you so he can be apprised as to the situation here in Bethany. There are thousands of refugees encamped within a mile of our ranch, and thousands more who have fled north and east of Lake Penateka. Father will want to know if it is safe for the people to return here."

Gareth helped Phillip latch the back of the wagon, and then the men all stepped out of the road into the shade of a towering pecan tree that loomed over the south side of Main Street in front of Grayson's smith shop.

Looking eastward down the street he could see men with wagons and oxen moving up the Bethany road, as crews continued work pulling Aztlani dead from among the boulders near the base of the mesas in the gap.

When he looked back at Phillip, he said, "I can't imagine that it is safe for anyone to return. We don't even know if this was the main Aztlani force. We don't know how they got here as fast as they did, although I suspect your outriders will learn that they used trucks to get across the badlands, at least as far as San Angelo."

Phillip shook his head, "Since the crash, no army I know of has used trucks or burned precious fuel to get to the battlefield." He rubbed his beard and then scratched his head, "Our men are searching south and west of there. We suspect that you are probably right, though I don't understand why they wouldn't have come all the way to Bethany if that were the case. I know the roads are bad, but they are worse from El Paso to the frontier."

Gareth tried to put himself in the mind of the Duke of El Paso, who would have planned the assault himself. "I suppose," he said, scanning the street as the work there progressed, "that fuel was the final arbiter of how far they could go. It would determine how much they could carry, and how much they would need for the return trip. When your men find the trucks... *if* they find the trucks... we'll know more. There should be a fuel truck with them with enough fuel to get at least half of the trucks back to El Paso. If there is no fuel truck, and if there is clearly not enough fuel on board for the trucks to return home, then all bets are off."

David spoke up. "That would mean that it was a suicide mission?"

"Could be," he said, "or a test. Possibly even a diversion. Perhaps it could mean that the Duke felt that the initial force might be sufficient to take and burn the town, but if that attack failed, we'd think that the war is over, when it is not."

"So there could be another assault coming?" David asked.

"Oh, I can assure you that another assault is coming. The question is whether this first battle was a colossal failure on their part, or the first move in a broader campaign."

"I don't know," Phillip said, sighing demonstrably. "Aztlan has proven to be just arrogant enough to believe that this assault would accomplish their designs. I guess, I really don't know what to think yet. When the outriders get word to us from San Angelo, we'll know more. Until then, we'll need to prepare for another... another larger battle."

"We've work to do, then," Gareth said, looking from Phillip to David.

"We do," Phillip replied as he put his hand on David's shoulder, pausing for a moment before continuing. "You've done a phenomenal job David. Every man and woman in the area now owes you a debt of gratitude. I know that this action has cost you a lot personally, and might have a... negative impact... on your relationship with your father. But had you not acted when you did, and in the way that you did, Bethany would have been lost, and we would have been fighting uphill to try to stop Aztlan from destroying all of the Vallenses."

"I, like you, must obey my conscience," David said.

"Well, unhappily, you must now obey your conscience *and me*—since you are now a militia soldier. I'm going to ask you to handle the arrangements and the meeting with your father. You know everything I know. I'd be glad to meet with him if it is necessary, but there is nothing that I can tell him that you cannot convey yourself."

"Yes, sir," David replied.

Gareth and Phillip began strolling back down Main Street, walking slowly and silently for some time, as they each considered what the future might hold.

At the Livery, horses moved about and whinnied as men treated wounds on the battle-wearied mounts. Between the Livery and the General Store, there was a small park with wooden tables and some red mesquite chairs shaded by massive pecan and oak trees.

"I continue to pray that your wife and children are safe, Phillip," Gareth said as they sat down on two chairs, one on either side of a mesquite table.

"It won't help to send anyone northward for word of them," Phillip replied almost, but not quite, unemotionally. "We cannot make the messengers arrive any faster by wasting more men to ride out to meet them. We'll just have to wait."

"I'll wait with you until we hear."

"Thank you, Prince."

"No more 'Assassin'?"

"No more, Prince Gareth."

He pointed at Phillip. "I've been meaning to ask you. When did you figure out that I was the Prince? Thinking back, it seems you had known for awhile."

"I suspected it almost immediately from conversations and letters I have received from English over the years. Sir Nigel Kerr is very fond of you, and often spoke highly of you. I did not know for certain until the other night when we were talking in the darkness at camp up north, just before Rob Fosse and Sir Gerold showed up to confirm my suspicions. You said something that was curious to me. You said, *'God sees through barn roofs just as well as castles'*, and I think it was at that moment that I absolutely knew that I was speaking to the Crown Prince of Aztlan."

Gareth laughed. "Yes, I suspected as much. Not a minute later you said, *'Monarchs rule by right of blood—each son ruling in the place of his dead father'*. I think that was when I realized that you knew. I'm just grateful that you figured it out. Your men would have killed me right then."

"Yes," Phillip said, smiling, "they would have. In fact some of them still would like to go ahead and kill you just to be safe."

"Perhaps, in time, they will grow to like me."

"Fat chance! Still, I do think that they respect you for your integrity, and for your courage and bravery in the battle."

"I don't think I was very Princely."

"Probably not, but it was your first engagement. You did well enough."

They were silent for a moment as they reflected back on the battle.

"We've lost twelve men," he said, as he scanned Phillip's countenance for some clue as to what that meant to him.

Phillip nodded. "Twelve good men. Twelve friends. I have known, trained and fought with most of them since they were just boys."

"Do you ever grieve?"

"I never stop grieving," Phillip replied as he looked to the top of the mesa. His eyes were clear and blue. The afternoon had grown hot, and the mesas blocked the southerly wind, which was one negative in the placement of the town of Bethany.

"Will you stop riding... stop fighting, if there is peace with Aztlan?"

"There will never be peace with Aztlan until they are defeated."

"What then? When they are defeated; when Aztlan is humbled; what becomes of the Ghost?"

A wagon piled high with corpses to be buried rumbled by. "I suppose that I'll end my days like those men, but if I don't... If I don't... I'd like to stand on the top of that mesa with my wife and look out over a free and independent Texas. Maybe that vision is God's will, or perhaps it is just what my flesh wants. All I can do is fight until I know the difference."

"Do you fear God's wrath, Phillip?"

"I know that, if we let these people be slaughtered by Aztlan, I'd have every reason to fear it."

"Will the Vallenses fight now?"

122

Phillip shook his head. "No."

As they sat in silence pondering the wrath of God, an outrider came riding hard from the direction of the thicket. Phillip jumped up from his chair, and met the rider in the street.

"Is it my wife and children? Are they safe?"

The rider dismounted, nodding a salute to Phillip. "I come from the south, sir. We've found the trucks. There are ten of them, hidden in a caliche pit about ten miles northeast of San Angelo."

"Was there a fuel truck? Or any means of refueling for the trip home?"

"Not that we found, sir. The trucks were disabled and burned. A complete loss, sir. They were just blackened shells. It seems the Aztlani men were never intended to make it back home."

Chapter 11 - Ana

Her hands moved swiftly and expertly as she gathered the wheat into her left hand and cleanly cut the stalks off near the ground with her sickle. When the sheaf in her hand became difficult to carry easily, she tied it off with a few strands of wheat straw and then stacked it, grain heads up, with the other sheaves on the ground, creating a pile known as a 'shock' or a 'stook' of wheat.

In a few days, provided it did not rain and the wheat had dried sufficiently, other workers would come by with a large flatbed wagon pulled by two draft horses and they would grab the dried stooks with large hayforks and bring in the sheaves to the threshing barn to be threshed and winnowed.

War had come to Central Texas and to the Vallenses and now there were thousands of mouths to feed in and around the Wall family ranch. Every hand was needed to help bring in the harvest. Each family that needed help with sustenance would be getting a weekly ration of wheat, so long as they were unable to return to their homes. The harvest teams were also traveling to nearby farms to harvest those crops, knowing that every kernel would be precious if the war was to last very long.

Ana didn't mind helping with the harvest; in fact, even if the war had not come, she would have been out here. She always pitched in during the wheat harvest, even if her position at the ranch did not mandate it. She liked it, even on the hottest days. Harvesting reminded her of all the parables of the Bible regarding wheat, threshing, and winnowing. Seeing the grain processed from the beginning to the final product as bread or cereal grains impressed and amazed her.

Almost automatically, her hands worked the wheat and she continued rhythmically up the row. Her thoughts detoured from the parables of God, and retreated to the path of her old life and what it had been like once upon a time. She constantly told herself not to dwell on the past, but the flesh is weak—especially when you are alone with your thoughts.

Before he died, her husband wanted to avoid—at all costs—the agrarian life she now prized. Five years before the crash, she was compelled to start studying and looking into a simpler and more sustainable way of life. The world had become a frightening place to her, and the trite answers of the mainstream religious authorities, as well as the prophetical inferences that had once enamored her, had become wholly insufficient to offer her any comfort at all.

Her studies led her to Jonathan Wall's books on biblical worldviews, simple living, and Agrarianism. Her husband Hamish vehemently rejected everything she had started to believe was the truth. He told her that God had given men advanced and curious minds, and that using their minds to make their own lives easier and more comfortable was the fulfillment of God's wishes.

His utilitarian religion wholly embraced and encouraged his utilitarian thinking. Expediency was his only rule and law. In fact, Ana had learned that utilitarianism had become the religion of the entire world, no matter what name or title was put on it. There were many religions and denominations, but almost all had joined the one-world cult of *efficiency*, which did not allow for any doubting or questioning of technology, modernity, or the ways of the world. The cult of modern religion promoted the view that whatever coddled the flesh or made life easier and more comfortable, was a blessing from God and ought to be wholeheartedly received—no matter what the real effects were to the individual, the society, or the culture.

She tried gently and lovingly to help her husband understand that the Bible taught otherwise, and that the immoderate creature comforts of modern life were actually what had caused modern religion to apostatize, but he would have nothing of it.

Her husband had received the seed of his faith among the thorns. He heard the word, but the cares of this world and the deceitfulness of riches had choked it out. Consequently, he banned her from reading anything Jonathan Wall wrote and forced her to continue in, and increase her dependence on, a modern world rocketing towards collapse. The more the world stumbled and reeled from gluttony, greed, and consumption, the more Hamish insisted that everything was just fine, and the angrier he became with anyone who even hinted at abandoning the sinking ship.

The fact that she was still alive had nothing to do with preparedness, survival training, or anything of the sort. She had survived—she believed—by the grace of God alone.

When the crash came, Ana and Hamish were two of the very, very few people who made it out of Fort Worth. How many coincidences could there be? They just happened to have a half-tank of gas; and they just happened to choose a route out of town that hadn't already been closed off by the police, burning cars, rioters, or looters, or all of the above. They managed to make it two hours west of the city before the worst of the violence and mayhem consumed most of those who were left behind.

They ran out of gas outside of the small town of Albany, Texas. As they walked on the service road, terrified at everything that was happening around them, her silent prayers were answered when they were picked up and taken in by an older retired couple, the Haltoms.

Ana paused for a moment in her harvesting and took a whetstone out of the horn sheath that she kept tied around her waist with a section of rope. As she reflected on the aftermath of the collapse, she drew the whetstone along the edge of the blade. *It is amazing, sometimes, to consider what events are necessary to sharpen us and to hone us to make us of any use,* she thought.

The Haltoms were a very nice couple, and she really liked them a lot, but they were hopeless and helpless against the mind siege that accompanied the collapse. The day after they arrived at the Haltom's home, Hamish offered them money to take him to town, but Doc Haltom wouldn't take any money. He said that he was just being neighborly, adding that things were going to "get back to normal soon," and that he was only doing what he hoped someone would do for them under the same circumstances.

The four of them piled into the Haltom's car and drove into Albany to buy supplies and groceries and maybe fill some gas cans so they could retrieve the car from the highway. She had always been told that there was at least a three-day's supply of food at any grocery store, but that lie was exposed pretty quickly. Now, she knew that the supply would last for three days *so long as nothing was wrong.* If things got bad, the supply was only good for a couple of hours... maybe. The store had been cleaned out, as had the feed store and the hardware/sporting goods store. The commercial part of town had, for the most part, been abandoned.

Doc's wife May pronounced firmly that everything would be ok, and that things would come around soon enough, so they all went back to the house to wait for the return to normalcy that had been always been promised to them. At that time, they hadn't considered that the promise had been made by everyone with a vested interest in the status quo.

The promise of 'normalcy' was a mantra and maxim of that unholy trinity of bad ideas and ungodly living—the world, the government, and the church.

For a few days, things went as well as could be hoped under the extreme situation, as they all waited anxiously for things to "return to normal." They paced the house and talked a lot, making rather superficial preparedness and survival plans. Hamish and Doc Haltom inventoried what food and supplies were left in the house, and made lists of what might be needed if they could find someone with whom to barter, or if they could somehow get to Abilene.

The news on television waxed worse and worse; and eventually there was no news, because even the reporters, cameramen, producers and directors had families and needed to start fighting for their own lives.

When the reports of riots, fires and death in American cities and around the world stopped repeating incessantly on the flat-screen television and were replaced with an emergency broadcast scroll asking people to 'stay tuned', there was a moment when a palpable sense of panic crossed the faces of everyone in the room. Still, old Doc Haltom actually seemed cheerful when he announced that "nothing really bad can happen here. After all, we're Americans!"

They were all wrong. The Haltoms and Hamish were gunned down in the Haltom's living room as they stared at the TV vainly hoping that something, anything, would come on to replace the scrolling 'stay tuned' that had been their only message for two days.

Ana had walked down the alley behind the Haltoms' small house in order to see if she could get a sense of what was happening outside. She needed a walk and being cooped up in the house for days had done nothing to ease her anxiety and fear. *Jonathan Wall talked about this*, she had thought then. *He said that all of this was inevitable.*

She knew that the Vallensian community was only a few hours south of Albany, and she wondered if Hamish would now consider listening to what Jonathan had to say.

Maybe there was enough gas left in the Haltoms' car to make it south to the Vallenses. Maybe. Then she wondered how many thousands of people might be flooding into Central Texas hoping that the Vallenses—the same plain people who they had all once considered cute, quaint, or even crazy—would provide for them. Why would the Vallenses help any of these people? After all, they had willfully chosen not to heed the warnings that were all around them and had failed to provide for themselves. The least she could do was talk to Hamish and Doc Haltom about it, she concluded. She had just committed to that plan when she heard the gunshots.

Shocked and frightened, she ran back towards the house, but before she could even make it into the backyard, she saw what seemed to her like twenty gunmen ransacking the house. She crouched behind a dumpster until the men left.

She paused from sharpening the stone, and despite the heat of the summer day, a chill went down her spine. Even after 20 years, the image of the scene she encountered in the house was still vivid in her mind.

128

Hamish and the Haltoms had each been shot in the head, their blood mingling together and soaking into the upholstery. Almost everything in the house of any value had been stolen, and she could hear gunshots as the gang moved down the street.

In movies, things are explained and the viewer usually gets to grasp the 'why' behind the plot. The script usually answers your questions and the ending always makes sense. In real life, when the invisible and often imaginary threads that hold a society together are violently ripped apart, there are no pat answers. When the superficial veil of order gives way to the real chaos that reigns underneath it all, sometimes murderers just disappear down the street and you never know their back story or when or if they ever met with some kind of cosmic justice. Either way, Hamish was dead and she was alone.

Everything in her being told her to just run and try to get away, but panic, confusion and grief had washed over her to the point that she couldn't move at all. The only thought that made sense to her was that the gang who had killed her husband and the Haltoms wasn't likely to return. So she stayed in the house, hiding in the Haltoms' bedroom for two days. Finally, the stench of death got to be too much for her and she decided to walk southward under the cover of darkness. The entirety of her plan could be distilled down to one word—s*outh*. With that in mind, she had walked.

Ana looked up and she found that in her reverie she had walked to the threshing barn and the sun was starting to dip lower into the western sky.

In just a few days, if the Lord willed it, this barn would be a beehive of activity, as men and women carried in the sheaves and the business of threshing and winnowing would begin. Long flails—sticks with thin boards lashed to the end of them using leather straps —would be used to beat the sheaves placed on the threshing floor. When the sheaves were sufficiently beaten, the straw would be removed, and the doors on the opposite sides of the barn would be opened to allow a breeze to pass through the barn. The mass would be thrown into the air, the wind separating the wheat from the chaff.

She was convinced now that God knows just how much of a beating it takes to get rid of the chaff. She nodded her head at that thought. The world was God's field. First, the tares were ripped up from the field, and burned. Then the wheat was beaten to remove the chaff. From all of this, God brought forth the crop that he intended. Ana laughed. How different the reality was from the religious prophetic fantasies that had overflowed the world in the decades prior to the collapse!

Ruth walked up as Ana was in the doorway of the threshing barn, looking down at the six-inch board that had to be stepped over to get in or out of the door.

"That's a threshold, Ruth."

"I know that Mrs. McLennon! I've lived here all of my life!"

"Did you know that in the world the people call the entranceway to any door a 'threshold', even though they have no idea what that means?"

"No. I didn't know that."

"A threshold keeps the wheat in so when the wind blows the lighter chaff away, the heavier wheat falls to the floor and is kept in the barn by the threshold board." Ana looked at Ruth and smiled. "Both the wheat and the chaff are blown by the wind, but since the wheat kernel has the weight of God's goodness in it, it drops and is separated from the lighter and worthless chaff. It is kept safe by the threshold."

"I never thought of it that way, Mrs McLennon. I just always thought it kind of made sense not to let the wheat blow out through the door."

"Everything around us is there to teach us how God deals with us, Ruth. I never knew or cared for such matters back when I lived in the world—back before the crash. The modern religious world wasn't in the business of teaching us such things." Ana took a deep breath, then put her arm around Ruth.

"So, how are you doing... I mean, since the battle, and Jack's funeral and everything else going on. How are you holding up, young Miss Wall?"

130

"I'm doing fine, thanks. Father told us that it is very likely there will be another Aztlani attack soon. But I don't think we know much yet about when or where or what to expect."

"Although there is no doubt that your father is a good man, he doesn't tell you everything, Ruth. He protects us women from the very imminent and real danger of us knowing too much and thus worrying."

The brightness of the summer day had given way to the softer light and longer shadows of evening. Dozens of Vallenses were departing the fields and heading back to their camps, some talking quietly and others laughing at some quip or joke.

"We must head home now, dear Ruth," she said wiping dust from her apron. "Wally will have supper ready soon."

As the two walked, they talked about Ruth's day. Ruth told her that three large pigs had been caught in the traps, and that there had been a frightening event near the camps when some of the Vallensian women had seen a mountain lion cross the road only a half mile from the front gate.

"It seems that the predators are getting an upper hand for the time being," she told Ruth.

"Father says that the system of predator and prey eventually balances itself out, but I can tell you this... we have never seen so many wild pigs. We may get fat... *if* we aren't killed by them while walking to the outhouse at night!" Ruth exclaimed.

"A mountain lion brave enough to come so close to people frightens me more than some silly old pigs," Ana said, laughing.

"That's because you've never been face to face with a charging wild boar!"

"That is true, dear. That is true," she admitted.

As they drew near the gate, they heard the sound of horses behind them and turned to see a militia contingent approaching. Timothy was in the front, riding abreast of Piggy. Behind them was Tim's best friend The Hood, along with Enos Flynn, and Pachuco Reyes.

"It seems that your father has invited the heroes of the Battle of Bethany Pass to his table to share in some wild boar roast this evening."

Ruth smiled in response, "This ought to be interesting."

There was muted joviality and much conversation over a supper of tender roasted pork, browned sweet potatoes drenched in butter, sautéed onions, slow-cooked black beans, and a delicious desert of peaches and heavy cream. Ruth and Timothy caught up on the day's happenings and Ana told them funny stories of her earliest failed attempts at processing deer hides.

After supper, in the pale moonlight, Ruth and Ana were accompanied by Tim, Hood, and Piggy, as they walked out among the campfires and tents of the refugees and visited old and new friends. The party arrived at the tent of Ruth's sister Betsy and her husband Paul, and Ruth began to chase and play with her nephews Jon and Thomas while Ana helped Betsy with the supper dishes.

Elizabeth Miller, who Ana had always known as Betsy Wall, had grown into a strong and capable woman. She had her mother's strawberry blonde hair, as well as her strong hands and will. She had developed into every bit the hearty, intelligent, and industrious Vallensian wife that her father had trained her to be. She was not the deadly hunter that Ruth was, nor was she as avid a reader, philosopher, and thinker as her brother David. In truth, Ana thought, she had become what every Vallensian woman wanted to be. She was a good woman, a good wife, and a good mother.

"You know that you are all welcome to come and eat at the house with your father, Betsy."

"Oh, we know, Ana," Betsy replied, smiling. "We just don't want to be an added burden, and we really feel that we belong out here in the camps, with our neighbors and friends. Father would take every one of the Vallenses into his home if he could, and we all love him for that. But he raised me to love and care for our people as much as he does, and Paul and I really just want to do what we can out here to help those who need it."

A gentle breeze was dispersing the heat of the day, and an occasional firefly would twinkle by in the night, catching their attention. As the two women dried the last of the wooden dishes, they could hear Hood, Tim and Piggy laughing over some joke with Paul, so they joined the men around the campfire.

Before long, Jonathan and Wally the cook came up and joined the group. The moonlight had faded and in the darkness, the Milky Way came clearly into view. Ana never grew tired of Central Texas nights, and she stared up into the sky in awe and wonder at the beauty of it all.

Piggy and Tim were arguing about the name of some constellation or another, when Phillip suddenly, and silently, approached from the road.

The militiamen stood up, and everyone grew silent when they saw the serious look on the militia leader's face.

Phillip bowed slightly in greeting, and looked from his men to Jonathan with a pained seriousness etched on his features.

"I apologize for disturbing your evening. Trust me, I would have not done so without a good reason."

"Go ahead, Phillip," Jonathan said. "Please tell us whatever it is that troubles you so."

"We have received outriders with news, and I thought it would be prudent to share it with you. One rider arrived from the east, and one from north. Both, I am afraid, bear... difficult news."

"What is it, sir?" asked Tim, unable to bear the tension silently.

"From the north we have heard word concerning the attempt to rescue my wife and daughters." Involuntarily, Ana's hand came up to her mouth, and her heart pounded in her chest. "The attempt was apparently betrayed... somehow... and the men rode into an ambush. Rob Fosse and two other men escaped. Sir Gerold and the rest of my men were killed. We suspect that the Aztlanis have fled the area and there is no word concerning the whereabouts of my family."

Betsy gasped, and Ana clasped her hand in order to silence her.

Jonathan approached Phillip, who still sat on his horse, and reached for the hand of his old friend. Neither man could find words, so they stood there for some time before Jonathan finally spoke. "Phillip, we are all with you in your sadness and grief, and we will remain with you in prayer until your family is returned to you."

"Thank you," Phillip responded gravely, straightening himself in the saddle and clearing his throat.

"From the outrider who rode east, we have heard that some of your people... a large number..., the refugees who fled before the Bethany battle—those who did not stop at the banks of Lake Penateka—were overrun by an Aztlani force of unknown size."

"We don't have any details, and I'm sorry to be the one to bring this news. We fear that there has been a great slaughter. We've sent outriders to try to gain news of what happened. Apparently, some of the Vallenses had stopped on this side of Comanche, and others had continued as far as Chalk Mountain. I don't know when we'll know the full details. I... I just thought that you would want to know as soon as possible."

Ana watched Jonathan's face, as the information Phillip shared washed over him and slowly became a part of his new reality. His eyes looked glassy and damp as he looked up and nodded to Phillip again, this time patting him on his thigh as a sign of thanks, appreciation and unity in their mutual suffering.

She knew that Phillip, by all measures, had led a rough life; but he did have the mannish outlet of war and violence. She wondered if he could ever know of the sufferings of the Vallensian pastor. When she looked back at Phillip's face, and saw in it the stoic shield that guarded him from any outward display of his own grief, she knew that Phillip did know.

In the darkness, the fireflies carried on with their business, and the soft summer breeze continued to ruffle tent flaps and lift sparks from the fire high into the Vallensian night. Ana followed the sparks with her eyes, saddened by the news and impotent to do anything at all about it. The fireflies reminded her that as bad as things were, she was glad that her new world wasn't limited to a blackened screen with a scrolling message that said 'stay tuned'.

Chapter 12 - English

It was now fairly obvious that the Duke had double-crossed him. He had to face the unpalatable fact that, until now, he was being used, and this could mean only one thing—the Duke was aware that he was a spy; and if the Duke knew, then so did the King of Aztlan.

Based on the report that Pano, his long-time assistant, had just given him, it was obvious that Duke Carlos Emmanuel, that quintessential royal buffoon, had used him to plan the assault on Bethany as an elaborate diversion. Maybe the pretender-in-chief wasn't that buffoonish after all. He thought about that for a moment. Maybe the whole affair had been part of the setup.

He had always figured, at least in some deep recess of his consciousness, that he would be caught. Especially after he had sent Gareth to meet, and try to unite, the old friends Jonathan Wall and Phillip. Still, he had always somehow managed to file that knowledge away so that he didn't have to really consider it, not to mention the consequences that would necessarily follow once he was exposed. Oh, if he could just be back on his parents farm, slopping the pigs!

English sat pensively at his desk in the tower of the Chimenea Castle and went over all the facts. Could it be?

Ok, he thought, let's assume that the Duke has known for some time that he was a spy, and that he would be passing information to the Vallenses and the Ghost militia. The Duke then allowed him to plan the assault on Bethany knowing and expecting it to fail. Maybe he didn't care—he would still benefit from its success. The Duke's plan must have accommodated the likelihood that English would find some way to warn the Ghost that the attack was imminent. The Duke had, unknown to his own secretary, already sent a larger army to the south, bypassing Bethany and proceeding to the east to cut off any Vallensian escape. Skirting Bethany would also allow the army to eventually attack from the east where the Vallenses were more vulnerable.

Moreover, if the Duke already knew that his secretary would send the Crown Prince to warn Jonathan Wall and Phillip of the attack, *and* he allowed that plan to proceed, then that means the King was in on it too. The King must have expected or hoped that Gareth would fall in the battle, and it would have been a great way to get rid of a troublesome and rebellious son.

Unless Gareth was in on it too.

No. Now he was just being paranoid. He knew Gareth just as well as he knew Phillip. Gareth was an idealist and a true believer. In fact, if anyone had a just cause and the right motivation to see the King of Aztlan fall, it was Gareth, the King's own son. *Just stick to what you know.*

He had to assume that Gareth was supposed to die. If that was true, then somewhere out there, to the east among the Militia, was someone whose job it would be to kill Crown Prince Gareth of Aztlan; and he wouldn't be able to warn him.

The kidnapping of Phillip's family had not been just a chance happening, stumbled upon by escaping spies.. The militia leader's wife and daughters were clearly a part of the plan to lure Phillip away from Bethany.

English rubbed his head with both hands and took a deep breath. It was all too confusing. How had he let himself be outwitted by a half-pint drug dealer? There was no way that the Duke of El Paso had come up with, and actually accomplished, such a subtle and layered plan. Someone else; someone higher up—perhaps the King himself—had devised this plan. Or... there was a mole so close to Phillip that even The Ghost didn't know who he was.

So Phillip, far to the north of Bethany, had been forced to decide between his own family and saving the Vallenses—a win/win scenario, as far as the King was concerned. If Phillip had decided to save his family, the Aztlanis holding his wife would already be aware that a rescue attempt was coming, and would execute a carefully planned ambush. Most likely Phillip would have been killed along with all of his men. If Phillip decided, as he did, to rush back to Bethany, there was no guarantee that he would arrive on time. Maybe he would be killed in that engagement, or otherwise assume that the Bethany attack was the main attack and let his guard down. It would be very unlikely for him to realize that the attack at the Bethany Pass was just a diversion. He certainly wouldn't be expecting the real attack force to be way east of Bethany.

What a disaster! *And now I've been exposed as a spy. But given that I haven't been arrested yet,* English thought, *the Duke must assume that I have not yet figured that out. My arrest must be imminent.*

His assistant Pano sat patiently in the overstuffed chair, waiting for his boss to speak. English finally looked up at him and smiled.

"Perhaps you can go through that list again, Pano. Indulge me. I apologize if I am a bit... distracted."

"Yes sir, I understand. Finding out that you have been exposed as a spy—and a poor one at that—cannot be easy."

"Perhaps you could have done better?"

"Oh, I don't know boss. I'm not the one whose head is about to be cut off."

"Would you just read the report, please?"

"Around 2,000 Vallensian pilgrims were captured and killed outside of Comanche by the main force there, and any eastward escape route has been, for the most part, cut off. We don't know if there is another army heading towards Bethany from the west or the south, but I'd bet there is.

"The Duke has sent a formal letter to Jonathan of the Vallenses denying Aztlani culpability in both the Battle of Bethany, and in the slaughter at Comanche. He claims that rogue elements in his government—presumably by that he means YOU—working with rebels and agents of the King of Mexico were responsible for these atrocities against the peaceful Vallensian people."

"Those are all lies."

"I don't know. I wasn't with you the entire time. Maybe it's true," Pano said, trying to mute the grin on his face.

"They are lies, Pano."

"Yes sir, but very believable lies—at least to the Aztlani people in New Rome, and those in other Kingdoms that pay attention to such things. Certainly the King and the Duke expect to use these lies in their propaganda efforts."

"Ok," he said, rubbing his head again, "go on."

"The letter from the Duke to Jonathan Wall encourages Jonathan not to react rashly to the massacre, and also states that any assistance or aid given to the rebel militia would be considered an act of war by the Vallenses against the Sovereign King of Aztlan."

"A war that Aztlan has already declared, and is already waging on the Vallenses!" English shouted, slapping his hand on the desk.

"The Duke has called for a full meeting of his council this afternoon. You are expected to be there, and he specifically requested that you be in full dress uniform."

"I am always in full dress uniform. So, I take from this that I am to be arrested in front of the council this afternoon?"

"That would be my guess," Pano replied, nodding.

"And I don't suppose that I will be allowed to leave the castle, or the city?"

"Certainly not by any of the... normal routes."

English cocked his head and glared at Pano. "You have an abnormal route you can suggest?"

"I think I can arrange it, boss. In fact, I do have a plan. But you aren't going to leave me here to handle the Duke's wrath. I'm going with you."

English stood up, walked to the window and looked down into the outer bailey and the main gate. He assumed that the Duke had doubled the guard at all of the gates. An escape was a doubtful proposition.

"How might you arrange such a thing?" he asked.

Pano smiled. "I've brought a wig and some prostitute's clothes."

"Would you please be serious?"

Pano shrugged, "I know a way out that no one else is aware of, but I won't reveal it to you until you promise to take me."

"Ok!" he sighed, "I'll take you, but if we're going to go, we need to get moving. I seriously doubt that we can even get out of this office, much less leave the castle or the city."

"We'll get out," Pano reassured him, smiling. "Now take off your tunic. We've got to get it mended."

"I never take off my tunic!"

"Take it off, boss, if you want to get out of here."

Pano moved quickly as English reluctantly took off his coat. Bending over, the assistant pulled a boot knife and cut two of his collar buttons. English stared at Pano as if the man had just committed a sacrilege.

"Ok, boss, you have to pull this off. Acting shouldn't be hard for you since you've been a spy for so long. Here's the deal... you do not know that they know that you are a spy. Put that out of your mind. Everything is cool. You've just popped some buttons on your tunic, and we are taking it to the laundry mistress to have the buttons re-attached."

"Why would I go with you? Why wouldn't I just send you? After all, you are my assistant... although, if I weren't going to be beheaded, I'd fire you this instant."

"Listen, boss, everyone knows how you feel about this coat. You are a freak. Nobody understands your attachment to it, but everyone knows about it. You'd never let it out of your sight. You even launder it yourself. People would be more suspicious if they saw me walk by with it without you following me like a pit bull that just had his bone stolen."

"I like my tunic."

"No, boss, no," Pano said, wagging his finger, "something weird is going on between you and this coat. Still, that is what is going to get us out of here. You have to look as if you aren't expecting to be beheaded today, so there is no reason for us to be stopped. This is a castle, and they figure that you can't get out, so just act like yourself... you know, a bit angry, narcissistic, sarcastic, and irritable."

"Now you are just being mean. What do we do if we get caught?"

"What are they going to do, execute you?"

He gave Pano an exasperated look, "Will you please take this seriously?"

"I will... *if* you say that you're sorry for calling me 'Puddinhead' in front of the Duke last week."

"I'm sorry for calling you 'Puddinhead'."

"Ok. I forgive you."

"When we get out of here, I'm going to ditch you."

Pano laughed, "I doubt that you'll want to when you see where we're going."

"What is that supposed to mean?"

"Are you ready?"

"I suppose I have to be."

"Then let's go..."

The trip down to the basement of what was once the old Camino Real hotel was rather uneventful, as most of the staff had no idea that anything out of the ordinary was going on. They were stopped twice by curious guards, but when English acted irritated and obsessed with the missing buttons on his coat, the guards dismissed them with little fuss.

Medieval castles were built mainly for defense purposes, but that changed around the 14th and 15th centuries, when comfort became a priority.

The Chimenea Castle was designed along the latter lines, and since the main tower had been constructed out of a hotel, the Chimenea had hundreds of rooms that had been combined and converted into spacious and decadent suites for important visitors and guests.

The basement of the old hotel was not only home to the laundry facilities, but it had, at one time, been a part of the civil defense and emergency management system for downtown El Paso. A large portion of the basement was still unrenovated, and it had devolved into a large open storage area with unused offices off the main great room.

Upon reaching the basement, Pano stopped in the laundry area and stole some clothing from lockers that lined the wall; then they ducked into the abandoned civil defense shelter and Pano led English to one of the offices in the far southeast corner of the basement. Closing the door behind them, Pano tossed him some of the stolen clothes.

"Here, put these on. I'm sorry if they don't fit. I had to grab what was there."

"These aren't even Aztlani peasant clothes! They're worse! This shirt looks as if it was chewed by a dog," he said. This time he wasn't faking his irritation.

"If we were escaping into Aztlan, you'd want Aztlani peasant clothes, but we're not ... we're going to Mexico."

"What?" English stopped dressing with one leg partially into the hideous pants that seemed to have been loosely woven from cast-off hemp. "This city is in Aztlan, Pano. El Paso is Aztlan. Aztlan is all around us."

"Just keep dressing, boss; you'll understand when we're underway."

"If this is some attempt to turn me over to the Duke dressed like a mentally disturbed coffee picker from the mountains of South America so that I won't have the honor of being executed in my uniform, I shall be quite put out with you, Pano."

Pano started laughing. "No, but only because I hadn't thought of that; just please finish so we can go!"

When he pulled on the magnificently offensive green overshirt, Pano abandoned all attempts to control himself. He pointed and almost doubled over with laughter. English looked down at himself, and then just gave a low bow before squinting in an implied threat.

Pano started moving several pieces of rotted wood, an old Plexiglas display stand, and some clothing racks, uncovering a large shelving unit base that had once served as a makeshift filing cabinet. He understood from Pano's grunting that his assistant wanted him to help move the cabinet, so he grabbed the free end and shoved it away from the wall. Under the cabinet was an ancient carpet remnant, covering ten treated 2" x 10" boards, all laid flat as if they had been stored there some time during construction decades ago. As they began to move the boards, the entrance to the tunnel started to appear.

142

English looked down into the tunnel, which was as dark as the darkest night of the soul that could possibly be imagined; then he looked back up at Pano. "A tunnel?"

"Yes, a tunnel."

"To where?"

"I told you, to Mexico."

"How long is this tunnel?"

"Ten miles. Straight south. It's an old drug tunnel."

"Are you telling me that they used to mule drugs into the emergency law-enforcement headquarters of one of the largest cities in America?"

"Who did you think was selling the drugs?"

English shook his head. "I thought that you were going to get me out of here. I assumed that we were going to ride leisurely up to New Rome on horseback and have margaritas at some inn up in the mountains. You want me to go farther south? In the summer? I'll melt."

"You can't go back to New Rome, English. Ever. You are a fugitive and a traitor to your King... and you won't melt because I threw away your tunic."

He looked back down into the tunnel, trying to discern if it did, in fact, have a bottom. There was an old, rickety, wooden ladder that led down and disappeared into the darkness.

"Will there be margaritas in Mexico?"

"Well, I know a place in Monterrey that has the best Mezcal you've ever had, and the worm at the bottom of the bottle is delicious."

"Are you kidding me?"

"Yes. If you were to get down to the worm—which you wouldn't—you would find that it is actually tasteless. It tastes just like Mezcal."

"I think I'd rather be beheaded."

"That is the other option."

English sighed again then looked back the way they had come. "They better have margaritas." he said as he gingerly climbed down into the darkness.

Chapter 13 - David

"**A**gain!" Piggy yelled as David watched the last knife bounce harmlessly off the target. "You have to feel and watch the rotation in order to make minute adjustments according to the distance. The knife is a tool—an inanimate object, sure, but one with a will. It *wants* to fly right, straight and true. That is what it was made to do. A rock dropped from a height wants to fall, right? A thrown knife *wants* to stick into stuff!" Piggy smiled at David and pointed at him. "Just let the knife do what the knife wants to do. Now, try *again!*"

David wiped his brow with his sleeve and dismounted in order to retrieve the knives. Before today, he'd never thrown a knife at all, much less from the back of a horse.

The day was hot and brutally still and, given that the militia lived and breathed training, there were few breaks. Hydration was always necessary, but a rest break was all but non-existent. The men didn't see training as some chronological interference into their lives. Training *was* their life; and to them was as enjoyable as anything else they might have been doing. If you were too tired, you could sit down and catch your breath. If you were hungry, you would eat. The rest of the time, the militiaman trained.

David's short time in the militia had been quite educational. The Ghost militia was a strange concoction of professional army, guerilla unit, desert cavalry, and Special Forces recon fighting group.

Phillip had modeled the group loosely on the fighting concepts of the Moorish and Berber desert cavalries of the late medieval period in Africa and the Iberian Peninsula, combined with the tactics and lifestyle of many of the mounted insurgency groups he had fought in Asia in the early 21st century.

The group's motto, if David could discern one from what he was constantly being told, was "First train, then train. When you are done training, you train; and when you rest, you train. When you are not training, you are training your mind. Only when you die, do you cease to train."

The militia rarely wore armor, because it was heavy, hot, and cumbersome; and, given the way they fought, it was usually more trouble than it was worth. The men wore long, but loose fitting sleeves, usually weaved of cotton, which protected them from the sun and allowed for perspiration and evaporation, but were also heavy enough to give them light protection from spent arrows or projectiles. When riding or fighting, they usually wore long leather coats that also served as some protection from glancing blows, as well as from cactus and mesquite thorns.

Although the Ghost militia did have the equipment, ability, and skills to fight with guns, they preferred using arrows, javelins, knives, and swords. Every Ghost militiaman was an expert in *all* edged weapons. This had been drilled into David since the day he joined. In order to survive, he needed to know how to ride and how to fight. They lived with their horses, and they fought primarily with edged weapons. Hence, drilling and training in these two disciplines never ceased. As David was already considered to be even beyond an expert with a bow and arrow, his training focused on areas wherein he was deficient.

David wiped his forehead with the ample sleeve of his tan cotton blouse and remounted his horse. He looked at Piggy, who was tossing his razor sharp knife up and then catching it and spinning it on his hand, mindless of any danger.

"Nobody else throws knives from horseback, Piggy, so why are we doing this?"

"Because you are training with Piggy, David Wall! If you were training with someone else, you wouldn't be throwing knives from horseback. It's really quite simple."

"I mean, shouldn't I learn to throw knives from standing on the ground first?"

"Some might believe that. I don't. I believe that you should train for the way you would fight. When you learned to ride, did you sit on a saddle on the ground first, or did you climb up on a horse? Piggy's way is to *do*."

"I'm not sure that those things are the same," David said, frowning.

Piggy waved off David's objection. "Nothing is the same with anything it is not. Besides, it doesn't matter if they are the same. This is Piggy's Way!" Piggy laughed and spread his arms wide. "If I can train you to throw knives effectively from horseback—and there is no telling if I can, as I've failed with all these monkeys I live with—but if I can train *you* to do it, then you will have a skill that will help you and even feed you for the rest of your life. If I fail—which I am likely to do—then you can learn to throw a knife from the ground like any one of the monkeys."

"Ok, Piggy."

"Again!"

The training, both mental and physical, had been brutal and consistent. In a very short time, David had learned to sleep on his horse without falling off; how to stay up all night on watch; how to move almost soundlessly through just about any environment; and, most importantly, he had learned how to *blend in*. To blend in, you first had to move without being seen; and, if seen, you must move without being noticed; if noticed, you had to move without raising suspicion; however, if you raised suspicion, you had to move without any risk of being caught.

Phillip's teaching was simple in its philosophy, and difficult in its practical application. He wanted an army that was as natural to the environment as the mesquite tree or the diamondback rattlesnake. It needed to be able to stand perfectly still and be unnoticed; it needed to be able to move quickly and definitively without being tracked or monitored; and it needed to be able to strike anywhere, in any direction, at any time, from a position of strength and surprise.

Phillip taught David that the primary battlefield was that of the mind; thus, his military needed to be able to overwhelm the minds of the enemy. He firmly believed that, if you triumph in the mind, you would almost certainly triumph in battle.

146

Like Stonewall Jackson's brigade, Phillip wanted to be able to break every maxim of war. He wanted to be able to divide his forces and simultaneously attack two or more enemies, dozens of miles apart, each with superior numbers. He wanted to be able to attack one enemy in the evening and then move rapidly 80-100 miles over rough terrain overnight to attack another. In this way, his forces would seem to be 10 times larger than they were in reality. By traveling light, living off the land, and blending seamlessly into the environment, the Ghost militia would be everywhere and nowhere. He did not believe in 'campaigns' as they were traditionally fought. He believed in attrition—slowly and methodically destroying the enemy's will to fight, and thus their effectiveness.

Phillip always told David that the militia's greatest asset was Texas itself. He would say, "The land and the people of Texas are, by their nature, ungovernable, except by God." They had, for well over 150 years, allowed themselves to be ruled over by their lust, greed and covetousness; however, that period was an anomaly never to be repeated so long as he lived.

David threw the knife at the target again, this time forcing himself to keep his elbow high, his arm path short and under control. He had a mental image of the rotations as the knife left his hand, and, as it stuck in the board, he felt an elation run through him that he had never felt before.

"Excellent!" Piggy exclaimed. "Now, the trick is to do that repeatedly, so that you develop muscle memory *and* thought memory. It needs to be as natural as brushing your teeth."

David smiled broadly, "When do I learn to hit a moving target?"

"New Rome wasn't built in a day, Brother David. Training is our credo and our life. Now... do it again!"

Around midday, the men gathered in small groups spread around the perimeter that Phillip had outlined for them. Their meal was a large hunk of pemmican—ground up and powdered meat solidified into chunks with rendered fat and berry powder. It was to be eaten with hard, dried, flat biscuits that would be dipped in water to make them soft. At each mealtime, one small group out of the entire unit would elect a single member in rotation whose job it was to try to move around the perimeter without being seen by the other groups. It almost never happened, but it was a constant reminder to stay focused and alert even when relaxing. Still, this exercise was never attempted at night because, inevitably, the scout would have been killed by the hyper-alert militia watches. On occasion, different members of the militia would be invited to have a night off, when they were expected to dine at his father's table.

The only unit that was exempt from the usual training regimen was the small unit of personal guards assigned to the Wall family. Since he was now a member of the militia, David was excluded from this duty. Piggy was generally a regular member of the protection unit due to his expertise in close quarters combat, but he had requested training duty with David, and Phillip had conceded to the request.

After they had eaten, as the sun reached its apex in the sky, Piggy mounted his horse and called him over to resume training.

"Up you, Master Wall! The day is still young and we have only just begun."

"So, no *siesta* then?"

"Ghost militia men sleep only after death, sir."

"I've heard that before, but I thought I'd give it a try."

"We've more training to do, and you might like what I have planned for the afternoon."

"Throwing knives from the back of a flying bird?"

"That, sir, is a skill I keep to myself. Let's ride."

As they rode off eastward, Piggy made light-hearted banter and they discussed the history of the Ghost militia, and the events that lead to Phillip becoming the fly in the soup of the King of Aztlan.

"At some point, at least a decade before the collapse," Piggy said, "your father and Phillip split up... for reasons we can all imagine, but which no one ever really talks about. Phillip, just as your father did, saw what was coming and that the collapse was inevitable, but they disagreed on what to do about it. They both believed that the collapse would bring on a long period of chaos,

148

disorder, and lawlessness, which it did. However, Phillip believed that only through armed resistance and group defense could the free people remain free.

"Your father, obviously, believed that by building a new and separate infrastructure, and by focusing solely on obedience to God in life, living, and worldview—without any plans or designs for violence or defense—people would be defended by God supernaturally."

David scanned the horizon and pushed his hat further forward on his head. "It's hard to argue who was right. It seems contradictory, but I sometimes wonder if combining both approaches were necessary," he said.

"If you believe in the sovereignty of God," Piggy nodded, "then you have to submit to the fact that God has everything under control, and that, perhaps, we overreach ourselves when we try to intervene or figure it all out."

Pulling up on the reins, David brought his horse to a halt. "Prince Gareth is intent on finding a way to get my father and our people to fight. It consumes his thoughts. How can so many people, with so many agendas all be right?"

"I'm not sure that this is about 'right' in a moral sense, David. I mean, if one man says to skin a cat from the bottom up, and the other says from the top down, which one is morally right?" Piggy asked. "We're in this fight, and we're all trying to obey our consciences and do what we think God wants us to do without selling our souls. Some people can argue this morally, but I am not one of them—I'm too simple for that. The Prince believes that the only way that his father the King will be overthrown is with the moral authority and numerical might of the Vallenses, but... does he risk and harm that moral authority by encouraging them to fight? I don't know."

"So what do we do?"

"You chose to fight, and by doing so, you obeyed your conscience, which is the only safe thing to do. As for us, we are the Ghost militia. This is our life and our lot. We are King David's mighty men. 'Obedience is ours,' as they say, 'and results belong to God.'"

David began to be increasingly curious as the pair rode farther and farther away from the camp. After about five miles of conversation, he turned to Piggy and asked him where they were going.

"About five more miles to a small rise the boys have come to call 'Mayberry Mountain'. I'll tell you why we are going there when we get there," Piggy replied without breaking his own train of thought in the conversation.

"Your father and many like-minded families started their off-grid life and community about ten years before the crash, and about five years before you and I were born, David. Phillip left the community almost immediately after the schism and started to recruit only the men that fit his vision of what the militia should be.

"Phillip was well aware of most of the failures of militant 'anti-government' groups that came before the crash. One-hundred percent of those groups were fully infiltrated by government agents or paid informants, and almost all of them were founded on some really dodgy political and cultural philosophies and ideals. Phillip never received anyone into his group unless he himself had recruited them, initiated contact with them, and knew them in a way that precluded them being an agent or a paid informant. He recruited just like the intelligence agencies recruited. He focused on intelligent and resourceful men that were disenchanted and powerless. Surprisingly, he recruited heavily from the military and law-enforcement. So many of those men had an insider's view of what was wrong with the world.

"He trained his men very carefully, and avoided anything that looked or seemed openly militaristic. Moreover, he only recruited Christians that rejected politics as a solution. He did not want anyone who wanted power or leverage in the post-crash world."

David listened intently as they rode. Some of this he knew in a kind of superficial way, but most of the details that Piggy had just revealed were new to him. "How did they stay under the radar?"

"Well," Piggy continued, "as I said before, they avoided political involvement and almost never used the Internet, except for very innocuous reasons. They spent little of their time or money on guns, other than to purchase basic hunting and self-defense weapons. They never appeared in public or trained as a complete unit.

"The government had—by using government grants, think-tanks, social media, executive orders, secret legislation, and other such machinations—created the most immense and omnipresent data mining entity in history. Very complete and in-depth files were kept on any person or any group that even smelled faintly of being militant. Phillip diligently taught his men how not to 'smell'.

"When the crash happened, almost every so-called 'anti-government' group was taken out by the government or their private contractors in the first days and weeks—during the brief period when command and control was still quasi-available for them. This was easy for the government, since, as I said, almost 100% of these groups were already infiltrated and corrupted by imbedded agents and informants.

"In the thirty years prior to the crash, the government had, in fact, *become* the anti-government/militia/patriot movement. Most of the leadership, and most of the 'stars' of that movement were what were known as *agit-props*—agents of agitation and propaganda. These people stirred up dissent, while managing to keep people engaged without ever really motivating them to do anything productive or relevant. They put out videos and other materials exposing the wrongdoing of government agencies, but they did so in a way that allowed them to manage the fall-out and keep track of anyone who stepped too far over the line.

"Militia meetings, militant anti-government radio programs, and even survival and preparedness groups were started by, and remained under the control of, agents or *agit-props* of the federal government.

"This is where your father and Phillip were in perfect concord, for they are still seen as the only ones capable of recognizing someone that was a witting or unwitting agent of the

151

enemy. They both said, 'If anyone stirs you up but gives you no concrete solutions on how to live in and through the troubles that are coming; if anyone fails to encourage you to provide for yourself and your family, to obey God, and to separate yourself from the corrupt system that is bound to fail; then, whether they know it or not—and usually they do—those wicked counselors are nothing but puppets of the corrupt system they pretend to oppose'."

"Both Phillip and Jonathan Wall preached that in order to separate from the beast, you had to live separate from it, and you had to quit enabling and supporting it."

David looked at Piggy, surprised that the militia soldier was so educated on the history of the collapse. He encouraged Piggy to continue by making a rolling signal with his right hand.

Piggy shrugged and continued, "Phillip knew all of this before he got started, so he was way ahead of the game in the art of remaining invisible and off the target map. Phillip was probably already the foremost expert in the entire world on being invisible when the crash happened. The Central Intelligence Agency could have learned something from him!

"Having been a special forces operative and a highly paid mercenary, he was well aware of what governments looked for in the way of opposition, and what mistakes insurgencies made in opposing governments. Phillip's credo was 'Know what they are looking for, and don't be that. Know what they are not looking for, and try to emulate it.' It helped that Phillip had no plans or designs on actions against the government, and never planned on using violence towards that end."

"So when the crash came, Phillip was ready for it?" David asked.

"Surprisingly, no," Piggy answered, shaking his head. "He knew that the crash was coming, but there had been so many drops and mini-crashes and soft-landings as precursors to the big one, some of them preceding the crash by a decade and a half. After so many years of false alarms, even Phillip had let his guard down. When the crash finally occurred, he was up in the mountains of New Mexico, in the heart of what would become New Rome, recruiting a former British SAS soldier that he had

152

known some years before. He never expected to be so far from home when it happened, but, as it turned out, it ended up working out for the best."

David stopped his horse and took a big swig of water from his leather *bota*, turning to look at Piggy. "So, he had between 25 and 40 men when the crash went down, but there are very few *oldlings* left in the Ghost militia today. Where did they all go?"

Piggy took a drink from his own *bota*, before turning around in his saddle to scan the area they had just covered. "Well, there are some of the original militia men left, but many of them died shortly after the crash. While they were all well trained and earnest, they had lived most of their lives within the comfortable realms of the industrial/consumer pre-crash world. They weren't indigenous militia, raised in the bush. They were more susceptible to sickness and disease, their bodies accustomed to the world's diet. Their senses weren't as highly attuned to nature. There were many reasons, but it was a matter of attrition."

Piggy strapped his *bota* back on his horse and resumed the ride eastward. He gestured towards David, "Most of the militia men who fight today are even younger than you are, making you a *middling*. Being 25 years old in the militia today makes you an old man. But it also makes you a survivor, and worthy of honor and respect."

As they approached the low rise called Mayberry Mountain, Piggy reined up about a quarter of a mile to the west, in a small, low draw surrounded by brush and boulders. The draw had a small amount of water in it, so they dismounted and let the horses drink. Behind them and to the north stretched the almost impenetrable area known as The Big Thicket—an area that David grew up hunting in, and knew well. Ahead of them was the low Mayberry mesa.

"Ok," David said, "so what is the plan?"

"We often use this mesa as a tower to watch out to the east. From near the top, you can see for almost 20 miles out, past Lake Penateka and towards Comanche. If the enemy marches this way, you'll be able to see them from up there."

"So I'm to keep watch?"

"You are."

"This doesn't sound like training," he said, doubtfully.

"Remember what I told you, Piggy trains by having you *do.*"

"Sounds risky."

"Only if you fail in any of the duties I assign you... which you will not."

Piggy squared up and looked David in the eye. "You will not sleep. You will not go to the top of the mesa unless it is pitch black outside with no moon. Keep the sun to your back during the day, but do not go up to the top because you will be silhouetted in the sky. You will not start a fire, and if you urinate or defecate, you will do so on the west side of the mesa, and bury the evidence."

"Ok," David said, "and how long will I be here?"

Piggy made a high piercing sound mimicking a hawk and, within a minute, a Ghost militia soldier appeared next to them, having crawled around to the west side of the mesa.

"You will remain here until you are relieved of your duties, or spot the entire Aztlani army, in which case you should hurry back to inform us."

"And what are the odds that they are coming?"

"On a long enough timeline? One-hundred percent!" Piggy adopted a feigned serious look. "I'll leave you with this, Brother David," he said, raising one hand dramatically:

"To-morrow, and to-morrow, and to-morrow, Creeps in this petty pace from day to day, To the last syllable of recorded time; And all our yesterdays have lighted fools The way to dusty death. Out, out, brief candle! Life's but a walking shadow, a poor player, That struts and frets his hour upon the stage, And then is heard no more. It is a tale Told by an idiot, full of sound and fury, Signifying nothing." Breathing deeply and melodramatically, he winked at David, "that's Macbeth, in case you were curious."

154

David watched as Piggy and the militia soldier they called Longbow rode back towards camp. In what seemed like only moments, he was alone.

Chapter 14 - Jonathan

Jonathan had never seen Bethany as busy as it was this day, except maybe on the day before the battle, when the town was the single escape route northward in front of the Aztlani advance.

On this day, the general din from horses, wagons, cattle and people gave the small town the feeling of a mid-19th century boomtown. Oxen laden with bags filled with wheat jostled against mules pulling wagons full of watermelons and cantaloupes.

All of the stores and shops were busy, even Grayson the Smithy's blacksmith shop. Grayson had returned to work at the shop and the story of his removal from close fellowship in the Vallensian Church was as popular as were the tales of his heroics at the Pass. He was still their friend and their neighbor, and was treated as such; but tension was almost palpable in the whole community. Grayson and David Wall had been the first to step away from the Vallensians' long-held pacifistic views, but now there were others considering it. Jonathan hoped the trickle would not become a flood.

The endless clear, blue days—the signature of summer in Central Texas—paraded onward, and the squirrels still ran in and out of the park by the Livery. Vultures circled lazily in the distant sky, as if nothing of importance had ever happened there.

He was amazed at how quickly things had returned to some semblance of *normalcy*, even with the solemn news from the east that nearly 2,000 of the Vallenses had been killed by the Aztlani army they had hoped to escape. Driven by their fear, they kept moving eastward, hoping that they would be safe... and now they were dead.

And he hadn't stopped them. In fact, he hadn't even considered that Aztlan might attack from the east. No one really had.

For Jonathan, there was no *normal.* Not anymore. He felt the pain and personal responsibility for each one of those deaths, just as if they had happened right here in Bethany.

Some of those who died had been his friends, his neighbors, his countrymen, and his parishioners. Even though most of the dead had been those who lived out on the frontier to the west and south of Bethany, he still felt the weight of their deaths as one would feel the weight of stones in an avalanche. *The dead Vallenses won't even receive a proper Christian burial,* he thought, *the Aztlani commanders had seen to that.* He had heard that the peaceful and plain farmers had been stacked into huge funeral pyres and burned as heretics by the officers of the Inquisition of New Rome who were always present among large Aztlani armies.

In the Public House, there were the usual sights and sounds of Vallensian activity. Bartering and trading went on, and there was talk of harvest and of planting for the fall crop. Still, the discussion inevitably turned to war and with the implications of the Aztlani army remaining out to the east. Everyone who came in and out of the Pub greeted him, and a few stopped for a chat; still, most were busily trying to get their business done, not knowing when they might have to flee again.

Jonathan had come to Bethany to meet with David, but had just learned that his son was away on a training mission, and that Phillip himself was to meet him within the hour.

He sipped on a cold glass of *nopal* fruit juice sweetened with honey. The pinkish purple liquid was not only delicious, it was alive with beneficial compounds and enzymes.

The Wall family had stumbled onto the drink when they first moved to Central Texas, but soon thereafter, they learned that the juice derived from the ripe fruit of the *optunia* cactus had been harvested for jellies and jams for centuries. The Comanche had used the fruit as a medicine to reduce inflammation and as an ingredient in countless other natural remedies. It turned out that the ubiquitous cactus fruit was both healthy and delicious, and had thus become one of the most popular and readily available beverages among the Vallenses. Some of the *oldlings* called the drink Cactus Cola.

Almost everyone made wine from the *nopal* fruit, especially when grapes were not available. Some enterprising folks even made a pretty strong hard liquor, sold at the Public House and the General Store.

His wife Elizabeth had been a big proponent of the cactus juice as an overall health booster, and had prescribed the drink for everything—from headaches to sore ankles and knees to back aches. Between naturally bottle-fermented beer, and *nopal* juice, pretty much every infirmity was treated with some kind of beverage. The exception, of course, was garlic that, in the Wall household, was another cure-all for everything, especially any affliction or bacterial or viral infection.

Compared to how things were before the collapse, the Vallenses were extremely healthy and vibrant people, and most folks attributed this vibrancy to the Vallensian diet, rich with lacto-fermented foods, such as pickled vegetables and beans, sauerkraut, chutneys, sausages, and cheeses. Elizabeth had focused intently on learning historic long-term food preservation techniques that by-passed the old standards of pressure canning and other methods that killed all of the good living organisms and enzymes in the food.

Elizabeth had been dead now for thirteen years. She had died from blunt trauma suffered after being thrown from a horse only a year after Ruth was born. Before she died, in her weakness and pain, she had joked that falling from a horse was one of the few catastrophes in life that could not be fixed with garlic or cactus juice. Jonathan could not drink the juice now without thinking about her—which to him was not a bad thing.

It was not at all surprising to him to see Prince Gareth come into the Pub. He had figured that the Aztlani Prince would want to speak to him once it was known that he was in town for the day. Gareth approached him with a friendly smile, and asked if he could join him.

"I've come for some of the remedy," Gareth said rubbing the mostly healed knife wound he had suffered at the hand of the spy Ronald Getz.

"This is the place to get it," Jonathan answered, "though the beer here is nowhere near as good as the stuff we make at the ranch."

"I concur completely," the Prince replied as Nick Brewer brought over his mug of beer.

Gareth bowed his head and paused for a moment, "Please allow me to express my sincere and heartfelt condolences for the needless and senseless murder of so many of your people at the hands of my own."

"You had nothing to do with it. I know that, and so do all of the Vallenses; but I do appreciate your condolences."

"I know that you desperately desire to be free of any more discussion on the matter, but I would be doing myself—and all of the good Aztlani people that also live under tyranny—a disservice if I did not encourage you to revenge this dreadful wrong by helping the Ghost militia to destroy the Aztlani army."

Jonathan smiled at the Prince, but then closed his eyes and shook his head. "Revenge is a motive that is forbidden to my people, Gareth."

"You can call it justice if you prefer."

"Justice is also in the hands of God," he said softly, "rather than mine."

"I do not mean to add to your burdens, Jonathan, but please bear with me as I do my duty, even if you feel that my effort would be futile."

"I understand, Prince, and I sympathize. It is not as if I do not understand the carnal and temporal motivations that drive men to war. In fact... right now, I think that I am in touch with them like no one else could be."

"All carnal and temporal motivations are not, by default, sinful, as you surely know," Gareth interjected. "Fear motivates us to avoid danger, hunger motivates us to eat; and we drink to alleviate thirst."

"Still, a hunger for anger and a thirst for revenge ultimately drive men to steal and kill. Listen, Prince, I am not

159

judging you, Phillip, David or the militia. I understand that people need to obey their conscience. I just cannot fathom why I am constantly being pressured to disregard mine. Am I the only one who is to ignore his conscience?"

"Unhappily, Jonathan, your conscience is currently nothing but a stumbling stone to your people, many of whom would like to fight, but still follow and obey you without question."

"I would hope that they are following their convictions and the voice of wisdom embodied in our sincerely held position on non-violence."

"Ideally, yes—we would all hope that—but in reality, I do not believe that this is the case. If you gave the word, the Vallenses, and other similar groups throughout Texas, could field an army of 10,000 men—enough to put an end to Aztlani tyranny for good."

"True, but that would create fear, trepidation and jealousy in other Kingdoms across North America and maybe even around the world. Or worse yet, we would become the masters and civil magistrates and become tyrants ourselves."

"It doesn't have to be that way."

"Unless the hearts of men have changed, then it does."

The Prince sat back in his chair and gazed out of the window as horse-drawn buggies navigated around carts parked on the street in front of the Pub. "I have to believe that you are wrong, and that righteousness can rule as easily as malevolence and tyranny."

"History says otherwise, Prince."

The two men looked at one another for a moment, before Gareth drained his beer and set the mug down firmly on the table. "You do understand that I had to ask?" He stood up and shook Jonathan's hand with a firm and friendly grip.

"Let me leave you, Pastor Wall, with a bit of a prophecy." The Aztlani Prince stood up and reached into his pocket. He withdrew two hand-cut iron nails—payment for the beer (one of the many acceptable forms of 'money' used in Bethany)—which he dropped on the table. "The Vallenses will fight... eventually. Whether you or I are here to see the day, I
160

cannot say. Still, the Vallenses will fight, or... or they will cease to exist as a people."

"Perhaps," Jonathan replied, thoughtfully, "if God wills it; but if He does erase us from the earth as a people, He will lift up the torch of the apostolic faith in some other place... or He might just return and end all the speculation."

Gareth nodded briefly, thanked him for the conversation, and left to join another table of Vallensian farmers who were engrossed in an argument about which was the best method of storing wheat.

After sitting and pondering for a while, Jonathan paid for his own beverage with a small spool of hand-spun thread that Ana had made and headed out of the Public House towards the Cobbler's shop.

As he walked the short distance to Mr. Byler's shop, he watched the people loading and unloading supplies. He was grateful that Bethany had been spared the fate of San Angelo. He felt no real conflict within himself and that surprised him, but he knew that God had often, from unlikely sources, raised up a defense for His people. It troubled him that David and Grayson had been that source, but he could not question what he felt God had done in preserving Bethany. He supposed that surrounding the Vallenses with the militia couldn't be much different from his own hope that the King of the South States would send aid.

He thought about the letter he had sent via the post-rider. Maybe his message would be read and heeded by that distant King, or maybe help was already coming. Whatever its source, he hoped that help was on the way.

Outside of the Cobbler shop, he ran into Mr. Byler, who was securing a large load of pelts to the bench of a Vallensian wagon. When the cobbler was done, the two men retired into the shade provided by the overhang in front of the shop to exchange usual pleasantries and affectionate greetings.

"I was wondering if you might have a need for several large Longhorn hides that Ana is working on?" he asked the cobbler.

"Of course. Of course. There are so many people wanting to have new boots before..." Mr. Byler's voice trailed off.

"I understand," Jonathan replied. "Since you mention it—and without any desire to add to your burdens—I also need another pair of heavy boots for Ruth. She goes through them so fast, you know. But, whatever value you place on the hides—up and above the price of the boots—I'd like you to keep on account for the Johnsons. I've taken some sheep from them in trade."

He paused for a moment, the reality and weight of the issue impeding on his thoughts. "You know," he said, "with Jack gone, they can't keep as many sheep. Things will be tough for them for a time. We're helping out as much as we are able."

"This is a sad, sad business, Jonathan. I had hoped, at one time, that we were past all of this. But I don't suppose we'll ever be beyond persecution and suffering."

The two men stood in silence for a while, before Jonathan finally spoke. "We'd also like to have you up for supper soon. I know you are so busy, but Betsy and Ana would love to see you, and they don't get to town as often as they'd like."

"I'm afraid that, with current events being what they are, I might be living up there before long, but that all depends on what happens with the Aztlani army, doesn't it?"

"It does."

"Tell Ruthie that I'll have her boots for her in a week, and, Lord willing, I'll bring them to her myself."

Jonathan smiled, and shook Mr. Byler's hand. "I'll tell her, Mr. Byler. We'd all love to see you, and we look forward to it."

As the two men parted, Jonathan saw Phillip approaching, and went out to meet him. The two old friends shook hands before Jonathan pulled Phillip towards him and embraced him.

"I hope things are well Brother Phillip, and that your news is not too dire. It's been a rough week."

"That it has, Jonathan."

They walked eastward without any particular destination in mind, but before long, they found themselves at the end of the

162

main street where it met the Bethany road as it turned towards the Pass. The rocks and boulders blocking the pass were still there and, from the street, Jonathan could see at least a half dozen of the Ghost militia guards manning their posts up on the twin mesas.

Phillip stopped walking and looked him in the eye before looking away again towards the Pass. "Our troubles are likely to come from the east this time, and I would be surprised if they weren't focused more up north... up at your ranch, rather than at Bethany."

"I figured that that would be the case."

"We haven't seen any movement yet. Whatever the Aztlanis are doing, it hasn't involved any kind of lightning attack westward, which is what we originally expected."

"Do you have any guess as to the size of their force?"

"Our scouts have estimated it at around 1,000 men, but there could be more. We've sent scouts northward and southward too to make sure that we weren't being enveloped. My guess is that they will attempt an assault en force on the Vallenses encamped near your ranch, and I'd be surprised if we had another week to prepare."

Jonathan looked at Phillip, "We've got to evacuate the people again; only this time we need to know for certain that we aren't sending them directly into the path of the enemy."

Phillip nodded respectfully, "We anticipated that you would want to move your people north and westward toward Vallensia, and already have outriders patrolling that entire area. Based on our intelligence, we think that we have a good idea of which way they will come. We're going to plan an ambush between the old city of Penateka and the Lake Penateka dam. There is a throttle point there at the dam that we can use to our advantage. We already have men guarding that critical point."

"Will they make it through? I mean, you can't have enough men to take them on face to face, right?"

"We never fight that way. Traditional frontal assaults are not part of our repertoire. This time, we will use their own guns against them, and we'll have a few other tricks up our sleeve. They will make it through the choke point, but hopefully, we can thin them down enough so that only a few hundred are still around to make the assault on your ranch. If we can do that, we feel like we can win."

"So there will be a defense of the ranch?"

"Yes, sir, there will."

Jonathan exhaled deeply, rubbing his beard. "I will need to leave with the people going towards Vallensia. I won't send them off into the unknown alone again."

"I figured as much."

"Well... then you'll need to come up for a visit, Phillip. There are things I'll need to show you. A few years ago, we were having some serious problems with the wild pigs getting in and destroying our fields and crops. We tried everything to get rid of them, albeit with little success. So... in order to get ahead of the problem we installed some... structures... that might interest you near most of the corners of our property."

Phillip smiled, "Oh, really?"

"Basically, they are like what you call 'pill boxes'—reinforced defensive enclosures—from which we could shoot the invasive herds of pigs without being seen or attacked."

Phillip tried to hold it in, but finally gave up and began laughing uncontrollably, and it took a minute for him to stop. When he finally pulled himself together, his eyes were red, and he was still giggling a bit when he put his hand on Jonathan's shoulder.

"Brother Jonathan," he said, before breaking into more giggling. "We've known about your 'structures' for some time, and we've already made plans for their use."

Jonathan didn't know exactly what to say to that, so he just looked at Phillip with a sheepish grin. "Good... then... good."

At that, Phillip shook his hand and walked away in the direction of the guards manning the pass. After a few steps, he swung around and Jonathan could see that he was still laughing. "Here's to reinforced defensive enclosures!" he shouted, before shaking his head again and walking away.

Chapter 15 - Phillip

Having the guns, ammo and other supplies brought up from Harmony had been the easiest part of the preparations. Even though San Angelo had ceased to exist as a habitable frontier town, the militia's Harmony location was still intact. When the Ghost militia showed up to retrieve their munitions from one of their central hiding places, they found it undisturbed. Hauling the materials to Bethany had been a pretty straightforward task, but distributing everything to units spread out over hundreds of square miles turned out to be more challenging.

Once the Vallenses were almost fully evacuated from the vicinity of the Wall Ranch, Phillip saw to it that most of the reserve arms and ammo, along with the largest number of his troops, were in place there. With the exception of the two units he had sent to guard and protect the Vallenses in their retreat, almost all of the Ghost militia would be engaged in the oncoming battle with Aztlan.

After abandoning a plan to send wagons on a long, dangerous, and circuitous route to distribute weapons to the militia units that were already in place, it was finally decided that each unit or position would be responsible for sending a sufficient number of men back to the Wall Ranch to pick up the necessary arms and supplies. This meant that the transport troops needed to move extremely fast, and that the supply troops working at the ranch needed to be prepared and efficient. So far, the plan was moving along pretty well. Almost all of the troops stationed at the Penateka Dam had already received their weapons.

For more than 20 years, he had made sure that the militia did not rely or become dependent upon guns. Nonetheless, each man and each unit was trained to use them expertly knowing that there would be situations, as the one he now expected, where guns would be beneficial.

He was expecting a two-stage fight, starting with the ambush at the bottleneck, as the Aztlani army attempted to move past and around Lake Penateka at the Penateka Dam. In order for his men to have any chances of success in the battle, at least 2/3 of the enemy forces would need to be destroyed at the dam. The second stage would only be realized if the Aztlani forces were to keep moving westward, as they were expected to do, and engaged in an assault on the Wall ranch. An active and energetic defense of the Ranch was the next critical part of the plan.

A stiff, hot breeze blew almost constantly from the southwest, and as he helped his men load wooden boxes full of ammunition into Jonathan's *'reinforced defensive enclosures'* —the pillboxes originally intended to be used for sniping pigs—he really began to feel the effects of physical exertion and mental stress, something he rarely noticed in the past.

Phillip tried to keep his mind on the more immediate tasks, since those were the only aspects of the current situation over which he actually exercised any real influence and control; but his mind could not help drifting to thoughts of the well-being of his wife and daughters. The latest word from militia spies in New Rome was that his family had, indeed, been taken to the Aztlani capitol, where, they were being held hostage in a castle near what was called the Old Town.

It was generally accepted that, at present, no legitimate attempt at hostage rescue could be attempted in New Rome. Although, in theory, Phillip knew that hostage exchange could work, the only person of value he had to exchange would be Gareth, and there was no way his honor would allow him to be disloyal to the Crown Prince, even if the lives of his wife and daughters were on the line.

Prince Gareth had, in fact, offered himself up to Phillip as a pawn to be used in such an exchange, but he had immediately, and somewhat angrily, rejected the Prince's proposal. There was one thing that everyone on both sides needed to know about him. His wife and his daughters knew, as would everyone else, that Phillip did not and would not bend to moral or political pressure. *Strange*, he thought, *in that arena I am really just like Jonathan.*

Many years ago, Phillip had embraced the possibility that his loved ones might be used as weapons against him in the war. In fact, he had broken his own rule in order to get married in the first place. Although Ghost militiamen were not forbidden to marry, he strongly advised against it; and now, his own situations served as a perfect example of why marriage and the militia did not mix.

He could not convince himself that his marriage had been a mistake. That he could not do. He loved his wife and his daughters more than he could ever show. However, the amount of suffering and distraction a soldier was going to be subjected to was bound to be in direct proportion to how connected that soldier was to friends and family outside of the militia. His was to be a cautionary tale on why militia members ought to be recruited from among men who have no hope or desire to get married.

For years, he had discussed the realities and dangers of the situation with his wife. She and his daughters understood that it might be necessary that they die or suffer for the cause they all believed in. He would no longer risk the war with Aztlan, or the lives of his men, on risky schemes to save his family. Already almost twenty men had died during the rescue that was attempted up near the Red River. That loss was unacceptable to him, and he vowed not to allow it again. The men of the Ghost militia were his family too, and he felt their losses as acutely if his wife and daughters were killed.

The wind howled almost incessantly and made it difficult to work without having to constantly angle one's head and squint to keep out the dust. The wind, combined with the bright sunlight and the oppressive heat, made the work that much more difficult.

When Jonathan and David rode up, accompanied by several militia riders, the last preparations to the defensive measures at the southeast corner of the ranch were being made.

The men dismounted and joined him as he made his final examination of the area.

167

"I never intended these structures to be used in a war," Jonathan said reflectively, shrugging his head towards the pillbox.

"Yes you did," Phillip replied, "you built these because you were at war with voracious invaders who wanted to destroy your ability to survive here... You just fail to recognize that some predatory invaders are of the two-legged variety, but are of the same character and nature."

"Well, I would say that God differentiates between the two as well."

"Ok, ok, ok!" David interrupted. "We're not going to get anywhere with that conversation right now. Are we? I don't think so. We came to have a final briefing so that I can get Father, Ruth, Ana, and a few other stragglers out of here and out of harm's way."

"Well," Phillip answered, looking at Jonathan, "why are you still here, Brother? What is it that you need to know?"

Jonathan looked down and shuffled his boots a little before finally looking back at him. "I was wondering if you could give us some idea of... this is hard to say... what you think your probabilities of success are. I just need to know so I can make plans to keep our people moving if need be."

Phillip looked at his old friend and smiled. "Jonathan, I am never over-confident, and I always leave room for surprises... but this place you have here is highly defendable. It is built on high ground, and we control the angles to every approach from any direction. We are watching the Aztlani army on their way in, and we are going to deliver a serious blow to them at the Penateka Dam. From there they will have a half day's march through rough and hostile country, under fire almost all of the way. Those who make it this far will be marching uphill into hellacious fire and they have no way of knowing what awaits them once they finally make it. I wouldn't want to be in any Aztlani force trying to take this hill."

Jonathan rubbed his beard and looked around, absorbing the information. "I see. So we are hopeful enough that we might be able to return here before long, and we shouldn't have to go very far north to wait out the fighting."

"Actually, we'd prefer it if you'd stay here with your family Jonathan. We can protect you better here."

"I cannot," Jonathan said, shaking his head, "so many of our people were killed after I let them run off without me. I could not bear it if it happened again."

"Then leave Ruth, Jonathan. She'll be safe here with Tim and Piggy guarding her. You should leave Ana and Betsy as well."

"Betsy and Paul have already left. Wally is staying because he... well because he refuses to leave this place, and he says he wants to cook for you. He thinks you are famous. Winnie, the lady who does the laundry, is here too; she didn't want to leave. Ana and Ruth are still here. Are you sure they'll all be safe?"

Phillip looked at his old friend, and clasped his shoulder with his hand. "Jonathan, I assure you that if things do not go as well as anticipated we will use all of our resources, skill, and ability to get your family and friends out of here. I do think that they will be safer here than on the trail out there somewhere."

Jonathan remained silent for a long time before replying. "I know that it is in God's hands, Phillip. I will ask Ana and Ruth to stay."

"Excellent!" Phillip replied. "I'll let Timothy and Piggy know exactly what is expected of them. They will have very explicit instructions of what to do during the battle."

"Thank you, Phillip," Jonathan said, before turning to his son and embracing him. "David... Son... I pray that God keeps you safe. I know that you know it, but just in case you didn't, I would have you know that I am well pleased with you. I know you are doing what you believe God would have you to do, and I am satisfied and pleased with your desire to be obedient. You pray for me as well, Son."

David gave his father a huge bear hug and squeeze, before releasing him. "I always pray for you, Father. I pray that one day this will all be over, and that we will go back to farming this land in peace."

"Me too, Son. Me too."

Jonathan looked back to Phillip and, as he walked back towards his horse, he said, "Keep David safe for me, please."

"I will do my best," Phillip replied, humbly.

He watched, as Jonathan rode away, accompanied by two militia guards, to join the rest of the Vallenses that had fled to the north, and he wondered if he had done the right thing by acting so confidently with Jonathan. Although he sincerely believed everything he had told the Vallensian pastor, he also knew that Jonathan trusted him, and now even trusted him with the life of his youngest daughter. *Stick with what you know*, he thought. *She's safer here. You did the right thing.*

Upon entering the Wall house, Phillip walked directly to the dining room, which had been set up as the command center for the coming battle. Maps—hand-drawn on cotton paper, skins or even on flat pieces of wood—were spread out on the heavy wooden tables. The room was full of many of his most trusted men, and most of them were in the midst of a heated debate when their commander entered the room.

"What's all the hubbub, gentlemen?" he asked.

"We've just received a report from Longbow about the Penateka Dam. You'll want to hear it first," replied Hood.

"Well, let's hear it."

Pachuco Reyes stepped up and assumed a formal stance before delivering the report. "Longbow reports that advanced scouts of the Aztlani force were doing reconnaissance on the dam. Our men already positioned there knew that they were coming, stayed out of sight and did not engage. The Aztlani recon team set explosive charges on the dam and then retreated. We immediately disarmed the charges but left them intact."

"So what are we arguing about?"

"Rob Fosse and I think that they were planning to blow the dam *after* they cross—kind of like Julius Caesar at the Rubicon; but others," he jerked his head in the direction of The Mountain, "think that they are planning on blowing up the dam earlier, because they are going to be coming from another direction."

"Ok, so what does our intelligence tell us?"

170

"Every indication is that they are planning to cross at the dam. They've been there three or four times to scout the crossing, and we've given them no reason to believe that we suspect that they are coming that way. We have a diversion force to their north, digging fake entrenchments and basically just making them think that we expect them to go around the lake that way. That force also serves as a stop-gap in case they do actually come that way." Pachuco pointed at the map, and emphasized his words with a wide sweeping motion, "If they come across the dam, this northern unit of ours will sweep in behind them to make sure that they cross."

Phillip looked at Pachuco, then over to The Mountain who seemed to have been the chief of the opposition party. Then, after looking at the map closely, he noted... "They will blow the dam *after* they are across only if they suspect that our northern unit is going to follow them. That would serve two purposes—it would not only make their own men know that retreat is not an option, but would also keep our men from flanking them and hitting them from the rear—which, by the way, we will do anyway."

Pachuco and Rob Fosse smiled at The Mountain, happy that the boss had taken their side. Rollo, not as happy, stepped up to the map. "So what happens if we are wrong? What happens if the move towards the dam is just a diversion? They've already done this to us once. If they turn north, there is only one unit to try to stop them from rounding the lake?"

"Rollo," Phillip said gently, "It is good that you are thinking like this. Always expect a double-cross. Always expect that you will be lied to by your enemy. You have all done well in your analysis. Now... *if* you are correct, and you may well be, then Aztlan will engage our northern unit as they attempt to round the lake around the north side. That movement will take them two days. We will have moved our whole force to meet them in half the time. Either way, we're in good shape."

"Phillip," Rollo said, "why don't *we* blow the dam now and force them to the north. That will give us more time to prepare."

171

"Three reasons. First, we don't want the dam blown. A whole lot of people count on fishing in that lake, and we are not engineers. We have no idea what ramifications blowing the dam will have to farms and villages that might be downstream. Second, the dam is strategically the best place for us to attack. They will not cross directly over the dam road, as that would make their entire army fully exposed, out in the open on the narrow road. In that case, we could hold them up with just 25 men and they won't risk that. Instead, they will cross just to the south of there, below the dam. It is not quite as exposed, but the tradeoff for us is that they will be below us and will be forced through a narrower bottleneck. That's when we'll hit them. Third, the battle at the dam needs to convince them that they've met and defeated our whole force. We need to hit them hard, but we need them to think that the worst of it is over. If we blow the dam, they'll know that we have bigger things planned for them and will be prepared."

"I see," Rollo said in resignation, "I guess, I'm not so good at thinking two or three steps ahead. It seems to me that we would just wait until they are crossing, and blow the dam."

"There's nothing to be ashamed of, Rollo. Most military minds would think that too, and that does accomplish the task if you just want your enemy to run away. However, you would have to fight that same army again. No. I'd rather fight here and now. I'd rather kill every one of these invaders, and have others think twice before coming here to take a spoil."

"Hear, hear!" the militiamen all shouted.

As the meeting devolved into a general din made up of a dozen separate conversations, Phillip glanced out the window, and was distracted by what he saw near the stone smokehouse. As he walked to the window to have a better view, he could make out that an injured man was being helped from a horse, and that David was hollering commands to those around him. He bolted for the door.

Phillip could hear the dining room empty out behind him, as the militia leaders, though they did not know why their commander had suddenly run from the room, all snapped into action. Their training kicked in, and in seconds, a defensive perimeter was set up around the ranch's primary structures.

He ran to the smokehouse as fast as he could, and there found a wounded militia rider, young Raymond Stone, being attended to by Ana, Winnie, and David. He was trying to figure out how Raymond might have been injured, when suddenly it occurred to him... Raymond had been one of the two men he had sent to accompany and guard Jonathan Wall on his journey north!

Raymond was seriously wounded, and was bleeding profusely from his thigh. It looked like his leg had been almost completely severed, and Ana was working hard to try to stem the bleeding from the femoral artery.

Phillip crouched down next to the man and put his hand on the man's shoulder. "Where is Jonathan Wall?"

The man cringed, and then settled himself, trying his best to remain calm. Still, he knew that he had been seriously, possibly mortally, wounded. "He's gone..."

"What do you mean 'gone'?"

"We were riding... three farmers... Vallenses... Jonathan stopped to talk... they killed Morell."

"Where is Jonathan Wall?"

"...they got to me before I could get off my horse..."

"Listen! I need to know where Jonathan is!"

"They took him! I... I couldn't stand up... I couldn't help..."

"I know, Raymond. You did well, soldier. Now... which direction did they go? West?"

"... I don't know," was all that Raymond Stone could say before his head sunk into his chest, and he died.

Chapter 16 - Timothy

Timothy spurred his horse and pulled a bit wider to his right as the other militia riders—Hood, Piggy, and the 16-year-old scout named Marbus Claim—caught up to him on the road.

As soon as Phillip gave the word, the Ghost militia had, almost automatically, launched into well-coordinated action, with very few spoken commands being necessary. Within minutes, he was out of the front gate and galloping down the road westward. At the gate, he noticed that Morell's mare, still saddled, had made her way back through the gates of the ranch, and was grazing peacefully under some oak trees.

He headed west, hoping to quickly spot the location where the abduction had taken place. From there, he would try to discern the direction the fake Vallenses had taken Jonathan.

The party reigned up about a mile from the Wall's front gate when they came across the body of the dead Ghost militiaman known as Morell.

Morell, or, what was left of the man, was in an odd position, lying partially up an embankment that led to the thick woods on the north side of the road. The body was stretched cruelly up the hill, and there was blood on the head and throat area. *Oh well*, he figured, *I don't suppose it matters how they killed him, because he's dead in any case.*

He dismounted and began to examine the road, as Piggy and Hood each went in opposite directions, looking for more clues.

He could see where Raymond had been struck in the leg and that the pool of blood had become sticky, already swarming with flies. As he continued to examine the area, Piggy rode back up and dismounted.

"It's pretty obvious that they rode off westward," Piggy commented as he walked over to the bloody stain on the dirt road. "We can track them, especially if Phillip sends The Hood, but we'll need to move quickly if that is what we're going to do."

Timothy looked up at Marbus and indicated that he wanted the young man to dismount and help him with Morell's body. They dragged the body down the embankment and over to Marbus' horse. "Take him back to the ranch, and then catch up with us. We'll leave some sign to let you know if we change our direction or leave the road."

"Yes, sir," answered Marbus, as he helped Timothy hoist the dead man up on to the back of his horse.

"Take his horse back too. I saw her back by the main gate. Ask Ruth to unsaddle her and get her some water."

He thought about Ruth and wondered what she would be doing... and thinking about. She'd lost her mother years ago, but she was very close to her father. Being an orphan, he couldn't really imagine how she might be feeling. If he was going to be tracking Jonathan's kidnappers, he hoped that Phillip would understand the need to assign someone to keep an eye on Ruth.

Marbus struggled for a few moments as he secured Morell's dead body onto the horse, and Timothy watched him with what bordered on amusement, until a flash of movement caught his left eye.

Too late to yell, he saw the mountain lion fly down the embankment and leap towards Marbus, who still struggled with the rope, trying to get it under the body and back to the saddle.

In the split-second when the lion seemed to be in mid-air, he saw Piggy shift his weight, draw a throwing knife, releasing it with a single, smooth motion. The knife hit broadside, but did little to slow down the momentum of the big cat as it flew towards Marbus and the horse. The horse panicked and bolted just as the lion made contact with Marbus, who fell backwards onto the road. As the cat roared in pain, an arrow buried itself into its neck. The lion kept rolling over in its death throes, screaming as Timothy had never heard an animal scream.

Phillip had told them once that in the old 'movies' (a concept he really couldn't understand fully), animals died instantly and peacefully. When you kill something in real life, it takes a painfully long time to die. That was the case with this mountain lion, which writhed on the ground screaming for what seemed like minutes as Timothy and the prone Marbus stared at it, transfixed. The only militia member who noticed and reacted to the arrow and its source, was Piggy.

Piggy stood with a knife raised in his right hand, poised to launch it. As Timothy's eyes followed Piggy's stare, he saw Ruth sitting statue-like on her horse off to the south of the road, next to some heavy brush. The bow was still in her hand, 're-loaded' with another arrow, in case the first one hadn't accomplished the task.

Timothy watched as Piggy lowered his arm and then turned to look at him with a huge smile on his face. "It's your girlfriend, Timmy," Piggy whispered, laughing as he knelt down to help the stunned Marbus up off the ground.

"She's not my girlfriend, Piggy," he scowled as he walked by the two militiamen and approached Ruth.

"What are you doing here, Ruth?"

"Saving that guy's life," she said, pointing at Marbus.

"I mean, why are you out here by yourself? Why aren't you at the ranch?"

"They took my father, and I'm going to find them."

"Ruth, you have to go back to the ranch. We're going to track them. If they can be found or caught, we'll do it. We'll stay on them until we get your father back."

Ruth rode by him and up onto the road. "Somehow, I doubt it," she said, a bit brusquely.

"Ruth, your father's gone, but you still have to follow the rules! I need you to go back to the ranch."

"My father's gone, there is a battle going on, and my sister's gone north. Under the circumstances, the old rules no longer apply," she said, softly.

"We'll track them, Ruth, I promise."

"You'll track them with me," she said matter-of-factly.

176

Piggy was laughing uncontrollably by this time as he helped Marbus locate his horse and finish securing the body. "I thought you were a pacifist, girly!" he said, "Look what you did to that housecat!"

Ruth dismounted and located her arrow that, after passing through the lion, had embedded itself in the embankment. Then she bent down and pulled Piggy's knife out of the side of the beast, which, by this time, had finally stopped thrashing about. She wiped the blood off the knife on the cat's fur, handing the knife back to Piggy.

"Cats are not people, Piggy; and, by the way, the cat was going for the body, not for Marbus. Before you arrived, she was dragging the body up that embankment. She wasn't going to let you steal it."

Timothy rubbed his black beard in his hands. "That makes sense. I couldn't figure out why a mountain lion, which usually avoids people, would attack Marbus."

"I'm just saying that what I just saw was pretty violent!" Piggy said, his grin wide and jovial, "Aren't you supposed to just forgive the kitty and make nice with it?"

"You ridicule that about which you know nothing," she replied calmly. "Pacifism is not the easy and wide road that violence is. My father ought not to be made fun of."

"Oh," Piggy retorted as he walked back towards his own horse, "I have nothing but the highest respect for your father. I'm just pointing out the... dynamics... of his daughter wanting to join this posse after violently killing a lion in front of our faces." He looked at Ruth seriously, "If you ride with us, dearie, we will kill many Aztlanis, and they will writhe and wriggle as much as that cat when they are killed."

"I'm not the saint that my father is, and perhaps the road of pacifism is too narrow for me. I don't know yet. But *I am* going with you."

Piggy bowed his head, "The more the merrier, darlin'."

As Marbus, clearly still shaken and ashen-faced, rode off towards the Wall's ranch, he tipped his hat as he passed The Hood and Rob Fosse, who were riding to join the posse.

Timothy saw Rob Fosse smile as he noticed the dead lion on the road.

"I suppose you all made it a quarter of a mile before you got hungry, and I further suppose the lass here is going to cook this beast up for our supper? That is what I must discern from this ridiculous scene."

Timothy just shook his head as Piggy made a 'zip-your-lip' signal with his hand before rolling his eyes towards Ruth. Tim figured that if Ruth was going to be riding with them, she'd have to learn to handle herself with militia humor. However, it seemed that she was up for the challenge, given that she'd handled herself pretty well with Piggy.

He couldn't help but be impressed with Ruth's killing of the lion, but he also knew that—although he could not stop her from going with them—he would be made to answer to Phillip, and probably Jonathan, for why he had let her join the posse.

In the end, he supposed that she was safer riding with some of the best fighters in the Ghost militia, away from the ranch and the battle.

Hood had been sent because he was the best tracker in the bunch. He guessed that Rob Fosse was there because Phillip trusted him more than just about any other man in the militia.

Together the new posse rode west and stayed on that westerly trek when the road turned south and became the Bethany road. The kidnappers had wanted to avoid Bethany and any substantial road traffic. As they moved westward, the road—once a paved county road, but now more of a footpath—meandered slowly as it ascended towards Jefford's Creek.

The posse traveled with the usual Ghost militia efficiency and speed. Every once in awhile, Hood would dismount and examine the ground or the surrounding flora, and when he did, the militia members would—without any orders given—spread out and inspect the area. Tim and the other riders never rode too close together, and, every mile or so, each one in turn would fall back—without a word or a signal—and virtually disappear to the rear to discern if they were being followed. If there was high ground ahead, one of the men would usually break off and take a circuitous route behind it, in order to make sure they didn't ride into an ambush.

Some short while after they crossed Jefford's Creek, they pulled up near an abandoned Vallensian farm and went into the large hay barn. Hood immediately went up the ladder into the hayloft and stood watch while the posse rested and talked.

Tim looked at the faces of everyone in the posse, and he could tell that, under the surface of their experienced, professional faces, they were worried. The kidnappers were making remarkably good time. If they were to get past San Angelo, it would be difficult to catch them as they crossed the badlands of the frontier. The good news, Piggy informed them, was that, judging by the clues, Jonathan seemed unharmed. He doubted that the kidnappers could move as fast as they were moving if the Vallensian pastor was seriously injured.

Hood gave a whistle indicating that Marbus Claim had caught up with them, and before long, the young militia scout entered the barn.

As the young boy dismounted and joined the group, Tim greeted him. As he shook his hand, he thanked him for dealing with Morell so the rest of the team could begin the search.

"Ah, here is our young friend *Carne de Gato!*" Rob Fosse yelled from across the barn. He over-emphasized the guttural 'g' in *gato* for comedic effect. "That means 'Cat Meat', in case you don't speak any *español*." Rob smiled as he cut off a piece of sausage and handed it to Marbus. "How does it feel to be rejected by a feline in favor of a corpse, and then get saved by a lady?"

Piggy howled with laughter, and even Tim found himself laughing at Rob, but he looked on in satisfaction as Marbus—who didn't talk much—just smiled and ate the sausage. As a 16-year-old militiaman, Marbus had learned that remaining silent and smiling a lot was the best attitude to adopt. The older men discovered that it was exponentially less fun ribbing him if they never got any rise out of him. Timothy noted that Marbus Claim was wise for his young years.

Ruth looked at him, ignoring the good-natured ribbing that was going on around her. "How far ahead of us are they?" she asked.

He walked over and sat next to her. "At least four or five hours. We can't stay here for very long... but the rest is for the horses, not for the men. Usually, when we ride scout, we can change horses regularly, but on this trip, these are all we have. In this heat, not getting any rest could kill them and then we would never find out where they took your father."

"I understand," she said, "but I need you to be honest with me. What is the likelihood that we will catch them?"

"Honestly? I'm sorry to say, but our chances are not very good. We can follow them, and track them to wherever they go. That is as good as we can do; but, if it helps... I do not believe they will harm your father. At least, not for a long time. He is too valuable to them."

"Gareth said that he was safe, that they wouldn't harm him at all."

"Things have changed, Ruth. Your father has capitulated a bit in allowing the Vallenses to work with the militia. His own son is now fighting."

"My father will never fight, Tim... you know that."

"I know that, but Aztlan doesn't. This means that they are getting scared that your father will permit the Vallenses to field an army."

"But he won't!" She clasped her hands in frustration. "This can't possibly help them," she raised her voice. "If anything, this will give David more control, and he'll be the one to lead the Vallenses into the war."

"You can't expect tyrants to be rational," Piggy said. All the joking had ceased, as everyone listened to what was being said between Timothy and Ruth.

"There is something you need to know, Ruth," Rob Fosse said, becoming serious for the first time on the trip. "I know Aztlan, and I've spent time spying in New Rome. I have some insight that others may not have."

"People in Aztlan fear your father more than they fear Phillip. The Vallenses aren't anywhere near as frightening to

180

Aztlan with David or anyone else leading them. Your father carries a moral authority that scares the hell out of the King and the Duke. Listen, the Crown Prince is a good man, but he's a dreamer. Even he fails to see that the conflict between Aztlan and the Vallenses is not really about land or strategic considerations. It is about power. All power is religious, it is sacred, and—most of all—it is coercive. Your father has power that he refuses to accept or wield, and that scares the King more than ten-thousand Ghost militia warriors at his gates. Aztlan would fear your father if he were alone in the wilderness with no one to lead. That, you can believe."

"My father is a peaceful and loving man! Why can't they just leave us alone?" Ruth asked.

"Why can't the sun rise in the west and set in the east?" Piggy replied. "The King of Aztlan hates the Vallenses because they exist, and he fears Jonathan because he is the conscience of the Vallenses."

Tim looked at Ruth and nodded his head. "Ruth," he stood up and walked towards his horse, "we are soldiers here, and we don't trouble ourselves with 'why' very much. I understand your reasons for wanting to ride with us, but it's important that you stop trying to impute reason, logic, and right-thinking to the people we are fighting. It'll slow you down, and it might get you killed."

As they mounted their horses, Marbus finally spoke up and informed them all that the battle of the Penateka Dam was under way. He didn't have any details, but when he left the ranch, the word had come from the east that hostilities had commenced.

It was about an hour before sundown when they left the Vallensian barn, and about five hours later, sometime around two in the morning, they began to approach the burned out ruins of San Angelo.

The posse resisted their usual and instinctual practice of skirting the town. Tim knew that they needed information, which meant that they would need to question anyone they came across. Even at this time of the morning, there was still the occasional trophy hunter, hauling away anything that might still be salvageable from the wreckage left in the town.

Rob Fosse and Piggy questioned a few men with wagons they encountered on the road, but didn't learn anything useful.

Tim saw an old highway sign that announced that they were on 'Highway 67', but that didn't mean much to him. He just wondered why the sign hadn't been taken away sometime during the past 20 years. Being a militia rider, you saw strange things.

They turned south towards the Concho River, and approached what had been the old downtown area. There, he was surprised to see so many buildings that, although they were crumbling and collapsing, had not been fully pillaged for the very nicely squared stones that made up the edifices. Rob Fosse told him that some of the buildings were almost 200 years old.

In the moonlight, they could just make out a man rushing away from them into the shadows, and Piggy was off after him before an order could be given. Not ten minutes later, Piggy rode up alone and gave his report.

"It was an *oldling*. And I mean an *old oldling*. That guy was probably here when those buildings were still under construction. I suppose he lives here, but somehow escaped the fires. I gave him some sausage, and once he warmed up to me, he told me that he saw ten 'bad men' ride out to the southwest, towards the Twin Buttes reservoir. That's not a mile from Harmony. We're going that way anyway."

Tim turned to Marbus, "You want to ride scout on this one? Or would you rather Hood go?"

"I don't know the area as well as Hood does, and I've only been to Harmony once. Maybe he should go."

Without a word, Hood galloped off to the southwest, and the rest of the posse rode down to the Concho River to water and rest the horses.

After about an hour, Marbus signaled, and, a few moments later, Hood galloped back up to the group and dismounted.

"What does it look like?" Tim asked.

"The old man was right. They made camp near the reservoir. They look like trouble. Jonathan is not with them, and they don't look to be officially linked to Aztlan, but these guys are bad news. From the looks of it, they are a pack of looters and killers. They are there on purpose, but I don't know what they are up to."

"How smart are they?"

"On a scale of one to ten?"

"Yeah."

"Maybe a two."

"Nice. Armaments?"

"Swords, spears, and knives."

"Excellent."

After reconnoitering the area, and setting up their plan, Piggy rode into the looters' camp, as the other members of the posse watched from the shadows.

"Up you uncircumcised Philistines! Wake up, you swine!" A few of the men struggled to leap to their feet as the others slowly rolled out of their bedrolls. It took awhile, but soon enough, they realized that they had a stranger in their midst, and started drawing their weapons, surrounding Piggy.

"Easy there, you Philistine dogs!" Piggy said, dismounting. "We're going to do this Piggy's way! I am Piggy, and I have you right where I want you! Drop your weapons!"

Chapter 17 - Gareth

Despite Phillip's protestations, Gareth was on the front lines when the battle began at the Penateka Dam. He understood that he was both a friend and a valuable tool of militia propaganda; hence, it was understandable that Phillip wanted him out of harm's way. Still, from the moment he saw Phillip's plans, he knew that he wouldn't miss this fight for anything in the world. Frankly, during all the years of training and schooling at the feet of the greatest military minds of Aztlan, he had never seen a more brilliantly devised defensive strategy. In his view, Phillip was one of the greatest generals since Stonewall Jackson.

Gareth's unique position and experience allowed him to examine the military plans of both sides impartially and objectively, as much as was possible. Thus, he had to admit that, if he were on the side of Aztlan, he would be doing exactly what the Aztlani general was doing. From their limited point of view, their plans made sense.

From what he had learned from militia scouts and out-riders, the invaders' plans were now quite evident.

Aztlan had brilliantly skirted Bethany to the south in the opening days of the campaign, using the diversionary failure of the attack on Bethany as cover. The Ghost militia didn't even know that Aztlan had advanced that far eastbound until it was too late and the Vallensian refugees had already been slaughtered. Once they had reached the area of Lampasas, the army had turned and marched northward, eventually making a forward line west of Dublin, stretching from Deleon to Comanche. From there, quietly and with purpose and precision, they had marched the entire front westward, sweeping the Vallensian refugees in front of them, and eventually enveloping and destroying the "heretics". Only those Vallenses who had traveled as far as

Chalk Mountain had survived. However, given that their numbers were so small, Aztlan did not consider pursuing them to be worth the effort.

According to the Ghost militia outriders, Aztlan had conscripted hundreds of civilian looters, thieves, and gangs to do the actual killing of the Vallenses, and had promised them all the rape, plunder, and pillaging they could possibly want if they would do the dirty work. In this way, at least to Aztlan, their hands were clean of genocide and the slaughter of innocents.

Gareth paused for a moment and his thoughts rolled back to his childhood and the days spent in his father's expansive library. He had read hundreds of his father's books, both fiction and non-fiction, of the time before the collapse, and he had been absolutely fascinated by them. He had especially enjoyed his father's collection of post-apocalyptic books because those had attempted, with varying degrees of success, to look into the future and see what life might be like after a million different collapse scenarios. One common thread amongst them all was the omnipresence of the inevitable and ubiquitous traveling gangs of looters and ne'er-do-wells. In the books, the gangs of low-life misfits were always pictured as inbred mutant-zombie-biker trash; clownish representations of the lowest dregs of white-trash society; prison escapees and assorted trailer dwellers that enjoyed raping anything that moved and kicking puppies for fun.

Gareth had to smile at the irony of how things had really turned out. For the most part, in the last 20 years, the looter gangs of pillaging gypsies had been made up of former middle-class suburbanites. They were cubicle drones and middle-management wannabes who had given up any moral high ground in exchange for moral relativism long before there was even any sign of collapse. After almost 50 years of brainwashing by the self-esteem cult, where children—irrespective of their natural ability— were mind-numbed by years of video games and sport into believing that they 'deserved' a corner office, a regular paycheck and a paid vacation regardless of their failure to attain even the lower rungs of mediocrity, the die had been cast for the few of this class that actually survived the crash.

When 90% of the population dies—most within the first year, due to their unpreparedness and their inability to think for themselves, adapt, and overcome the new challenges—some interesting statistical realities emerge. Of those who survived, in general, most were intelligent and engaged individuals who possessed an ability to process information in real-time. Survivors almost universally had the ability to innovate while under pressure, without panicking or giving up. However, there were a small percentage of survivors who—having already succumbed to moral relativism and the wicked philosophies found in video games and movies—fell rather naturally into the survival ethics of crime and the utilitarian pack mentality.

Sure, there were inner-city gangs and thuggish looters in the first days after the collapse, but those people perished pretty quickly—especially in Texas, where everyone had guns. The new class of criminals came from the upper and middle-class of disaffected urban know-it-alls and even rural ranchers and cattlemen, who believed that whatever you did to survive was good and right, even if it wasn't moral or just. Murder is easy when you have lived your whole life as an entitled brat.

The looter gangs of the last two decades didn't come roaring up on motorcycles, blowing up bunnies with hand-grenades. They looked like the poor and disheveled homeless of the early 21st century, and they might approach your ranch or community with women and small children out front, aiming to appear as poor, helpless people, just looking for a handout. They knew that someone was bound to feel sorry for them and would let them in. The rape and the pillage happened later, but when it did, the victims never expected it or saw it coming.

Such was the reality of what Aztlan unleashed on the Vallenses. Groups of looters followed large armies like sea birds would follow a shrimp boat, and these groups had a particular hatred for the Vallenses, because the Vallensian countryside—some of the most productive areas of Texas—had been patrolled ruthlessly by the Ghost militia for the last 20 years. The sweet and delicious heart of the Vallensian lands was now ripe for the picking, and the looters wanted all of it.

186

Hence, Aztlan had turned the looters loose on several thousand helpless and unarmed Vallensian refugees. Satisfied that their deed would be done, they had continued their slow and deliberate march westward, burning and destroying farms and villages as they went—the looter gangs killing the Vallenses before them, and devouring the land like locusts in their wake. Sherman's March was being revisited as Aztlan moved westward towards Bethany.

As the enemy approached Lake Penateka, their options diminished. While the decision to move all the way to the east and attack from there in order to avoid the Bethany Pass, the Thicket and all of the other natural hindrances to the south and west was a brilliant move, the Aztlani forces now had some difficult choices to make. If they were to swing south again, far below Penateka, they would be back to square one—they'd still have to deal with The Thicket and the Bethany Pass. To move northward was an even worse choice. North of the lake was extremely difficult country. In most of that area, county roads did not exist even before the collapse. The region was thickly forested, and the roads that did exist were extremely narrow. The trees came right up to touch the sides of the roads. An army marching westward down those roads for days would be picked apart by an enemy they would never even see.

The militia had put a Ghost unit to the north to make it look as if the militia expected Aztlan to move that way, but for Aztlan to go north would have been a real suicide on their part.

In effect, Phillip's plan had made Aztlan's decision for them. They would squeeze through the insignificant opening just below the Penateka Dam. They would think that it was a masterstroke, and that the militia wouldn't be expecting them there. Phillip had reinforced this idea by keeping all of his movements in the Penateka area completely shielded and invisible to the enemy. Even now, the hundreds of militia soldiers in place at the south and west sides of the lake and the dam were completely hidden from Aztlan. Thus, to keep the northern militia units from sweeping in behind them, Aztlan intended to blow up the dam behind them.

The most brilliant part of the plan was that Phillip had no intention of winning the battle at the dam. He *intended* to lose. He had to put up just enough resistance to make it look as if an inferior militia force had been overwhelmed by a superior army. Phillip intended to win by losing, and Aztlan had to be drawn into the trap because they would think that they were winning. The militia needed to kill so many of the Aztlan soldiers that by any accounting it would have to be considered a resounding loss, while at the same time convincing the Aztlani generals and soldiers that they were engaged in a great victory. Gareth was staggered by the genius of it all. He was never gladder not to be Phillip's enemy.

Aztlan, indeed, just as Phillip had predicted, swept in quickly and intently towards the dam. Gareth held his breath when, for a moment, it looked as if the invader would actually cross on the top of the dam, across the dam road, instead of continuing towards the easier and wider crossing below the dam. This wouldn't have been a tragedy, but it would have made the militia's position exponentially more difficult. Gareth himself, and all of the warriors hidden to the south and west, would have had to fight uphill to plug the dam road in time to keep up with the plan.

The Aztlani vanguard paused at the entrance to the dam road, and for some time actually considered crossing that way, before some officers rode up and ordered them to keep moving down the hill to cross just south of there where the lake overflow waters trickled southward as a shallow creek.

He heard a noise and looked behind him as David Wall rode up and joined him in the woods overlooking the battlefield. Their orders were for the militia cavalry to launch a surprise attack downhill, just as Aztlan began the uphill climb on the west side of the creek. They were to engage only briefly, before fleeing back up the hill in full retreat, hopefully drawing the 'victorious' Aztlanis along behind them.

Because the Ghost militia, as a policy, never, ever engaged in frontal assaults, anyone who was fully learned in their tactics might well smell a trap at this point. Indeed, this was one

188

weakness in the plan, which could not have been avoided. Time would tell if the Aztlani leadership was adept enough to sense that they were being led into a slaughter.

At some invisible and silent signal, the militia cavalry appeared mystically from the tree line, and Gareth could see the surprise and shock on the faces of the Aztlani troops as the Ghost militia appeared out of nowhere and was suddenly upon them. Some of those troops were able to take up their weapons and fire a few shots. Consequently, several militia riders were killed within the first seconds of the attack.

Regardless of the plans and contrivances of men, riding into enemy fire is very disturbing. Prior to this, he had only ridden into battle at Bethany, and in that instance, they had attacked from the rear, relying on the element of surprise. During the first few moments—moments that seemed to last an eternity—Gareth found himself unsettled, for he could actually hear bullets flying by his head. He felt the 'thump' of one as it pierced his coat as he rode forward, swinging his sword.

David was still on his right and Gareth heard the pastor's son shouting encouragement as they rode onward. He wondered if David was actually yelling at himself.

Within seconds, they crashed into the Aztlani troops, slashing their way into the throng of surprised men. Their job was to kill as many enemy soldiers as possible within just a few minutes, while listening for the signal to retreat. The slaughter was great, and he lost count after he personally had killed twelve Aztlani soldiers.

Fully half of the militia—those who had volunteered to do so—then killed their own horses with shots from hidden pistols, and proceeded to scream 'Retreat!' and, 'All is lost! Run for your lives!" The mayhem and confusion truly made it look like the militia cavalry had been routed, even though only a handful of the Ghostmen had been lost.

The Crown Prince and David, upon hearing the call to retreat, turned and began to ride back up the hill when David's horse was shot out from under him, tossing him violently to the ground. Gareth reached down and hauled David onto the back of his horse and, albeit with some difficulty, continued the retreat up the hill.

Aztlan's leaders, having watched the engagement from the distance on the east side of the creek, and seeing all the horses and dead men writhing on the ground, sensed an immediate and overwhelming victory and ordered a full assault. Aztlani soldiers poured down the hill and across the creek, and the militia let them come without firing, except for some token resistance fired by snipers up on the dam, and back to the west in the trees.

What came next was choreographed to perfection, as the militia, using the method of Genghis Khan, pulled back rapidly in the center of their lines—creating an enveloping bubble, as the Aztlani army moved westward toward the Wall ranch. The enemy officers, sensing a great victory, and wanting to be part of it, did not lag behind the rear-guard. Instead, they bolted forward towards the middle of the host, and were thus unaware when the militia's northern unit swept in behind the enemy army, effectively slamming shut the back door. The attempts to blow up the dam had failed, but there were few people there to notice.

Heedless and ignorant, the Aztlani army—albeit still in ranks—rushed forward in pursuit of what they thought was the bulk of the defeated and retreating militia. Gareth could see their faces contorted in the rapturous throes of victorious glee, despite the fact that, unbeknownst to them, for every five miles they marched, one out of every two of them was killed by snipers and crossfire. It wasn't until, a few hours later, when the Aztlani force arrived within two miles of the Wall Ranch, that the officers began to notice that their army had considerably shrunk.

Part of the reason for their ignorance of what was happening to them was that they had so far outpaced their rear-guard that they didn't even realize that they no longer had one. The militia had effectively destroyed almost one-half of the enemy without their leadership even realizing it.

Eventually, though, the reality of the situation began to sink in, and the Aztlani officers started to recognize that their army was now enveloped with no way to move but forward. Unhappily for their men, the officers reasoned that—since the
190

way forward was open, it had to be the way out. So, they kept up the march, hoping that they would soon outreach the forces that harried them on both sides, and from the rear. The path of least resistance was forward, and forward they went.

David had procured another horse from a dead Aztlani cavalryman, and had rejoined Gareth on the south side of the advancing Aztlani army.

"We must ride forward, Prince, and get to the ranch, so that we can participate in the defense," David said, the excitement of battle making him slightly short of breath.

"The way gets exceedingly narrow here," Gareth replied, "we'll be seen."

"Follow me. We'll shortcut through the Thicket. No one knows the Thicket like me, except maybe Ruth."

They bolted to the left and, soon, they were immersed in the Thicket. "Stay right on my tail, Prince Gareth, and don't make a mistake or you'll likely kill your horse and then you'll have to walk out!"

David expertly negotiated the almost imperceptible game trails and switchbacks of the Thicket, and Gareth did his best to stay directly on the tail of the horse in front of him.

In less than an hour, they were near the southeast corner of the Wall Ranch, and Gareth gave ample vocal warning that they were not the enemy, so that they wouldn't be shot by the troops manning the pillboxes.

They found Phillip in the command center set up in the Wall's dining room. Flushed with excitement, David reported to Phillip all he had seen and all that had occurred during the militia's planned retreat.

Strangely enough, Phillip was neither surprised nor excited about the news that his plan was proceeding flawlessly. His blue eyes never gave even a twinkle or shine as he stared out the window to the east. After a moment, he gave orders to The Mountain and several other militia leaders, and then began pacing the room back and forth.

"This is the worst type of battle for me," he said, "and the absolute worst time in the battle. I can do no good for my men in any of the pillboxes—isolated from command—neither can I assault the enemy because our forces are already hidden and in place. I have to trust my men to do their duty, and wait for the results." He paused and closed his eyes, "I feel just as I did when my Juliet was pregnant again, and I was waiting for word..."

With that, his strength gave out, and he slumped into a heavy oaken chair. Tears came to his peerless blue eyes, until he closed them again in silence.

Gareth sensed that the militia commander needed a moment, so he indicated to David to meet him outside.

"We ought to do something productive," David said. "However, since we aren't in command, maybe we should join the men in one of the pillboxes where we can watch the defense unfold?"

With that, the two men walked back to the southeast, and climbed down into the underground structure, joining the three militia men who were armed with fully automatic machine guns.

There was no conversation for some time as they awaited the ambush on the Aztlani forces. After a few minutes of silence, David looked at Gareth and a strange look of distress passed over his face.

"You royal idiot! You've been wounded!"

Only then did Gareth notice the blood that had pooled around his collar. The shot, he had assumed, must have gone through his coat, and had actually hit him in the shoulder, almost precisely where he had been stabbed by the spy Ronald Getz.

He prodded the wound with his fingers, before rolling his eyes and dabbing at the blood with a cloth he kept in his pocket. "I guess it's more beer and garlic for me."

David pulled back his collar and examined the wound. "It's not too serious. Through and through; but as soon as this battle is over, a hospital will be set up in the barn, and you are to immediately report to Ana for treatment."

Gareth painfully worked the shoulder before replying. "Certainly, David, I will do as you say."

The assault on the Wall Ranch was over almost as soon as it started. The guns in the pillboxes poured down incessant and deadly fire on what was left of the Aztlani forces. David and Gareth fed ammo to the gunners and reminded them to let the barrels cool when they got too hot.

After a few minutes of mind-rending fire, the militia gunmen pointed down the hill and Gareth could see white flags flying all along the Aztlani lines.

The dead bodies were piled thick and high as David and Gareth rode out among the surrendered forces. They looked around, as the men had thrown down their weapons and were huddled together now at the place that had been the center of the assault.

He estimated the remnants of the once great Aztlani army to be at less than 300 men, all of whom were now wide-eyed and pensive.

Pacing back and forth on his horse before the enemy host, he glowered down on their officers with unmasked hatred, as blood dripped from his fingertips, flowing down from the wound in his shoulder.

"Who is in command of this force?" he bellowed.

An Aztlani Colonel stepped forward, and finally recognized his Prince. He stood there in stunned silence for a moment before dropping to his knee in reverence.

"Stand up, dog!" he shouted. "Stand up you cowardly murderer of women and children! So *you* are in command of this rabble?"

"Yes, Your Grace!"

He paced once again the full length of the Aztlani front, and then returned to the quivering Colonel. "Command your men to pick up their arms and continue fighting! There is no surrender for you here! We are under the black flag, and you knew that before you began this murderous spree amongst the free and peaceful people of Texas!"

"Under the rules of war, Your Grace, we surrender our army to you!" the Colonel replied.

"Your army?!?" The anger and hatred of what Aztlan was, and what it had become, flushed through him as he withdrew his pistol and shot the Colonel through the head.

"I'll ask again... who is *now* in command of this army?!"

Another officer sheepishly stepped forward and bowed before the Crown Prince of Aztlan. "I am, Your Grace."

"Command these men to take up their arms and continue the battle! We are under the black flag, and there is no surrender for you. You will all die today for your crimes" he said as he pointed across the aligned Aztlani soldiers with his pistol. "You may fight and die like men, or you will be shot down or hung like dogs! Now... take up your arms!"

"Great Prince," the soldier interrupted, "the day is lost. We are beaten. We must surrender. Please honorably observe the rules of war, Your Grace, and accept our unconditional surrender!"

"Where were your *'rules of war'* when you murdered 2000 innocent Vallenses at Comanche? Where was your honor then?"

"We did not participate in the death of the Vallenses, Your Grace! Looters and highwaymen killed those people!"

Gareth raised the pistol, and shot the soldier in the face. The man fell backwards and started to twitch uncontrollably on the ground.

"Again! Who is in command of this army?!"

"You are!" several of the Aztlani soldiers shouted.

"Excellent!" he exclaimed. "Finally, I have a correct answer! Now, as the Crown Prince of Aztlan and as commander of this army, I order you to take up your arms and fight. Alternatively, if you are a coward, you may try to flee... However, what you will *not* do is surrender! You have thirty seconds to comply, or you will be shot as criminals one by one!"

Gareth rode back up the hill towards the militia lines. Seeing no way out, and desirous of ending the painful and frightening process, the Aztlani soldiers rushed to their weapons. They were cut down like weeds by the relentless punishing fire from militia guns.

It was all over in minutes.

The whole day would have been a smashing success, had it not been for the last news the command center received less than an hour after the final shots were fired. Militia dead were being buried, and the wounded were being hauled to the hay barn when word came that a lone Aztlani deserter had found and blown the charges on the Penateka Dam. The one flaw in the plans for the day was that no one had remembered to remove and secure the charges on the dam.

As the wounded were being treated, and as the spoils of war were being collected into militia wagons, billions of gallons of precious water—the lifeblood of hundreds of Vallensian farmers and fishermen—washed downstream as a fifty-foot wall of water flooded farms and villages, unceremoniously removing the bodies of the dead from the battlefield at the base of what had been the Penateka Dam.

Chapter 18 - English

As Pano worked above him to re-seal the entrance and to obscure any easy recognition of the existence of the tunnel, English clung to the ladder—an old, partially rotted contraption that clung precariously to its title only by the strength of some rusted nails and wishes.

The time he spent in the British Special Air Service as a young man taught him to remain calm even when in peril. However, no amount of training will make you feel comfortable or safe while in pitch darkness, suspended over a hole of unknown depth, clinging to rotted boards nailed together by uneducated drug mules over two decades ago.

About 15 feet down, all light disappeared into inky darkness and the ladder swung freely, hanging by hope and tradition more than by any really tangible reason. When Pano finished hiding the entrance to the hole, even the faint light from the top disappeared and the absolute darkness overwhelmed them.

"How far down to the bottom of this hole?" he whispered.

"It reaches all the way to the bottom, boss," Pano said, sarcastically.

"Idiot!" he muttered. "I'm about to plummet down this shaft, and I'd like to know how long I'll fall before I'm crushed into a bloody heap at the bottom... if there is one."

Pano exhaled loudly. "If you hang from the bottom rung you should be able to touch the ground... unless..."

"Unless what?"

"Unless a portion of the ladder has fallen off, then you might, indeed, plummet to your death."

At about 25 feet down, he reached the bottom rung and lowered himself cautiously until he felt his feet scrape the ground at the bottom of the hole. He dropped down and blindly moved to one side, feeling for the tunnel wall with his hands.

When, at last, Pano joined him, English had a million questions rushing through his brain.

"Ok, I'm going to ask you a series of questions. If you smart off, I'm going to choke you out, do you understand?"

"Yes, boss. Of course."

"Good, we understand each other. First question... what do we do for light?"

"Well, we could go back up, because there is plenty of light up there; but instead I recommend we use a torch. I've got one right here."

"A flashlight?" he asked.

"I don't understand what you are saying," Pano said.

"You have a torch?"

"Yes, boss."

"Would you light it, or turn it on, or whatever you intend to do with it?"

He could hear some struggling and muted motion as Pano readied the torch, then he heard a flint strike and a flame quickly lit up the area.

"Excellent," he said, "so now we are burning up the oxygen down here, which leads to my second question. Is there any oxygen down here?"

"Yes, boss. There are large pipes every so often that reach to the surface, providing oxygen supply over the entire length of the tunnel. Most are hidden in dilapidated structures and rubble or under rock piles on the surface."

"Ok, great. Next question!" He knelt down to feel the ground and examined the tunnel as best as he could with the flickering light that was available. "We have a ten mile trek ahead of us, and all of it is underground. How safe is this tunnel? Are there any gas deposits that are going to blow us up? Have any bears or rattlesnakes taken up residence down here? What about looters or deserters? Would the structure hold, or cave in? Does anyone else know about this tunnel?"

"Easy, boss; that's more than one question." Pano looked at him with a grin on his face. "First, let me say—and I mean no sarcasm or disrespect—that going back that way," he pointed towards the surface, "will get you killed with 100% probability. Head rolling on the ground, neck-spewing blood everywhere—the whole nasty mess that goes along with beheadings. However... going this way," he said as he indicated down the tunnel, "who knows? Maybe death, maybe not. So, I'll tell you what. Let's get moving and I'll fill you in along the way."

"Ok, Pano... you have the torch. You lead the way."

Pano took the lead, but kept a manageable pace, considering that they had a good half a day's walk ahead of them.

"This tunnel was built during the last decade of the 20th century, before the unprecedented violence that led to the border becoming one of the most violent and deadly places on Earth. It was managed on both ends by federal forces working in conjunction to maintain the monetary benefits and the necessary edifice of the so-called 'War on Drugs'.

"Although governments and protected cartels brought drugs into the United States on aircraft, boats, and even submarines, this tunnel was still one of the primary routes for 'official', or, 'white' drugs in the world. 'White drugs' were those that were imported illegally by government agencies, shell organizations, and some crooked local officials to finance and support black operations and the secret agendas of the power elite.

"One of the largest 'white drug' operations in the world had been exposed in the late 1980s. Members of the CIA and other covert operations agencies were exposed by some suicidal media types to be flying drugs into what was then Arkansas and a few other centrally located states. The contract mules usually flew into small rural airports where they would hand the drugs off to selected criminals, who would sell those drugs in the inner cities in Los Angeles, New York, Chicago, etc. The operations brought in billions of dollars for black operations around the world, and kept up an increasing need for higher taxes and government spending on the War on Drugs.

"After that operation was blown, it was decided that replicating it would be too complicated, it had too many moving

198

parts, and was too easily exposed. So, not long after that, this tunnel was constructed to streamline and simplify the system.

"As cover, the US and Mexican governments would 'discover' hundreds of drug tunnels in the opening decades of the 21st century; and they would be reported on widely. That gave citizens the mistaken idea that these types of operations were temporary, ineffective, and subject to exposure.

"All of that aside... when the collapse came, with everything else going on in the world; the eradication of most borders; the end of the drug trade; the death of most of the interested parties; the tunnel was abandoned and, soon, it wasn't even a memory."

"So how did you know about it?"

"That, boss, is a meaty mystery, wrapped in an enigma tortilla, smothered in creamy top secret sauce. It will, however, become clear enough in time."

"You aren't going to tell me?"

"As I said, you'll find out soon enough."

"Something tells me that I might have jumped out of the frying pan and into the fire."

"The tunnel does run both ways, boss," Pano retorted, dragging his finger across his throat, simulating a cut by a knife.

In a movement so fast that Pano didn't even have time to react, English seized the diminutive assistant by the throat and lifted him clean off of the ground, slamming him into the wall of the tunnel.

"Give me one reason that I shouldn't just snap your neck and leave you here to rot!" he growled.

Pano's face turned red, and he struggled to speak, his feet dangling helplessly in the air. "Because...," he grunted, "the people waiting for us... at the end of the tunnel... will be very unhappy if I am not with you."

He slowly lowered Pano back to the ground, releasing his grip. "I suspect you need to start being more forthcoming with me, Pano, if you don't want me to go ahead and just risk their displeasure."

"Sheesh, boss! Lighten up! We need to get you another tunic."

"How about you just tell me what is going on?"

"There is only so much that I can tell you, boss," Pano said, rubbing his neck, trying to regain his composure. "I assure you, that the people who wanted me to get you out of La Chimenea Castle are very interested in you, and they might be able to help you get whatever it is you want. You are just going to have to be patient. If they wanted you dead, you'd be back there, and you'd already be a foot shorter."

"You are the one who is too short to be a spy."

"And you are too grumpy and neurotic to be a knight."

The tunnel was tall enough that they could stand upright, but the feeling of claustrophobia increased with every step they made. About 6 feet wide at the base, the tunnel was reinforced along most of its run with concrete, and about every 50 feet or so, there were heavy supports made of steel or thick, wooden beams. Conduit with electrical cable running through it was attached along the roof, and there were lights—long out of service—evenly spaced about 20 feet apart throughout the whole length of the tunnel.

Without access to electric lights, Pano and English relied on the burning torch, and, as insurance, several more torches had been pre-placed at regular intervals along the way.

English had some experience working underground from his early days with the Scots Guards before he had done his tour in SAS. The Guard unit he was assigned to primarily served as a ceremonial unit, but they were also in charge of security in and around many of the prominent royal and governmental facilities in London. Their function often required that they work in 'Underground London', securing the tunnels, tubes, and underground railway facilities—some hundreds of years old—throughout the city, during state functions.

The Guards had taught him patience, respect, and the importance of form and tradition. However, his time in SAS had taught him to survive, to improvise, and to adapt. Unhappily, no one had taught him how to maintain hope and faith in a world that seemed to be collectively flying by the seat of its pants. In his current world, the things he despised the most—disorder and

200

chaos, interspersed heavily with tyranny and despotism—seemed to rule.

In the service, when he had worked in the tunnels under London, he may not have appreciated the mission, but he trusted in the system of order and honor he and his fellow soldiers lived by. In battle with the SAS, he may not have thought much about the politics and agenda behind his country's mission, but he absolutely relied on discipline and duty in order to stay both alive, and sane.

Over two decades ago, if he had been killed in the line of duty in Afghanistan, Libya, Syria, or Iran, his name would have been inscribed on the SAS regimental clock tower at Sterling Lines. Because of that, surviving a mission was referred to as "beating the clock." Oh, how ironic were those words today! He had indeed beaten the clock... and now here he was, centuries in the past, trying to find some way to get back home... whatever that meant now. He figured that the old regimental clock was probably gone now. *The mind reels*, he thought.

Inscribed on the base of that regimental clock at Sterling Lines was a verse from the *The Golden Road to Samarkand* by James Elroy Flecker:

> *We are the Pilgrims, master; we shall go*
> *Always a little further: it may be*
> *Beyond the last blue mountain barred with snow,*
> *Across that angry or that glimmering sea.*

He was beginning to realize that his hope was not in a return to some old and archaic sense of militaristic order, rooted in the inordinate reliance on enforced and inorganic systems designed to replace a more basic and natural life. That life now seemed so artificial. He thought of the Vallenses and all of their predecessors—*the meek of the earth*. For thousands of years, Kingdoms, princes and predacious religious authorities have tried to stomp out any peaceful people that—enabled and emboldened by their simple faith, their simple nature, and their work ethic—refused to become dependent on those same authorities.

He thought about those peaceful farmers and ranchers in the Vallensian lands. He knew that anger and hatred—the foul product of the dark and bitter hearts of men—would be relentless in their attempts to root them out of the land and erase them from the world.

The Vallenses were the real pilgrims... maybe they were even the last pilgrims. It was they who were always moving across the mountains and even the angry and glimmering sea if needs be, in order to find a place where they could live peaceably by the dictates of their God and their consciences. To English, they seemed to be the only truly free men—even amidst their bondage, struggles, and persecution.

Perhaps the order and peace that he sought could be found in helping those who so often would refuse to help themselves. Maybe he should just go start a farm and, in this way, return to that time of his life that held the best and most fruitful of all of his memories.

From his earliest days as a military man, he had always considered his uniform to be the last and best representation of the order and symmetry of life he had learned on his parents' farm. Whatever difficulties or hardships there were in farm life, they were made understandable and even enjoyable by the knowledge that the order of nature, and the right management of that nature, provided for and satisfied the fundamental human need for structure, order and a connection with the creation. Somehow, maybe sub-consciously, his mind had latched onto his tunic as a thread or connection with all that he had lost.

He signed on as an adjutant to the King of Aztlan, not because he admired the King, or because he saw goodness and right in the Aztlani cause, but because of a modicum of stability he perceived in the system and the opportunity for a return to order amidst the insanity and chaos that reigned after the collapse. He shook his head. *So foolish.* Order out of chaos... isn't that what governments and tyrants always offer men in place of their freedom? Safety and security have always been the legal tender used to purchase willing slaves.

Before long, he had learned that Aztlan was just another type of insanity. His friend Phillip had, providentially, been with
202

him on the day of the collapse, specifically in order to recruit him into the militia. It had been Phillip who had encouraged him to serve Aztlan. The militia leader wanted him to see from the inside what type of beast Aztlan might turn out to be. Now he knew.

As he and Pano trudged their way through miles of Mexican tunnels, he didn't know what future awaited him, but he did know that he was no longer going to be satisfied with a well-kept and immaculately tailored tunic. He wanted real freedom. Whatever that meant for him (and how could he know?), he did know it had something to do with the Vallenses. He was now a pilgrim, rather than a knight. It made it easier for him to see his journey as a pilgrimage, even if he didn't know his ultimate destination.

"I know, you've been so talkative, boss—a regular chatterbox—and I'd hate to encourage you," Pano smiled at him, "but we're getting close to the end here and I wanted you to know that... at the end of every tunnel, there is a silver lining."

"That's not even good enough to be a mixed metaphor."

"Maybe, but it's true. But I wanted you to know that I had your best interests in mind when I set about to get you out of the castle, and you need to keep that in mind so you don't overreact when... you see what the reason was."

"Oh, you are just a fountain of information and encouragement."

"I'm just saying that you should keep an open mind."

He stopped and stared at Pano with a look of resignation. "Listen, Pano, I am thankful that you got me out and saved my life. And I'm tremendously sorry that I almost choked the life out of you. I'm just ready to get on with this, and it doesn't help me for you to continue to act mysteriously."

Pano shrugged, and started to walk on before stopping to look back at him again, "I forgive you for choking me."

As they reached the terminus of the tunnel, he noticed that, on this end, the decrepit old ladder had been unceremoniously tossed to the side of the hole, and a newer version stood in its place. *Someone is expecting us*, he thought.

Pano threw the torch back into the tunnel and then ascended the ladder towards the light that streamed in from the circle above. He followed and, in almost no time, they were standing in a ramshackle shed surrounded by four men in light uniforms, each with their hands at the ready on the hilt of a sheathed sword. Pano greeted the men in Spanish and answered their few questions, before indicating to English with a nod. The soldiers seemed satisfied with his answers, as they relaxed a bit and nodded a greeting to him before turning to leave the shed.

The bright light and burning heat of the day reminded him that he was still in the desert, and that, despite the nice respite in the cool and damp of the tunnel, they had only traveled about ten miles from those who sought to kill him.

Cresting a small hill, English saw spread out before him in battle array an army consisting of perhaps 2,000 predominantly Mexican soldiers. Several officers, upon seeing the party coming over the hill, began to ride out to meet them.

When the mounted officers intercepted them, several of them dismounted and proceeded to greet Pano in Spanish. They then nodded their heads toward English in greeting, removing their hats.

"We are pleased to meet you Sir Kerr of Aztlan. We hope that your subterranean journey was not unpleasant," one of the officers, who seemed to be the highest in rank, addressed him. "I am General Rodrigo Loya, Commander of the armed forces of the Kingdom of Mexico. I am told that you prefer to be called 'English'; thus, I do hope you will not find it disrespectful for me to refer to you in this way."

English shook his head, indicating that he was not offended, but remained silent, waiting for the General to continue.

"English... We intended, all along, to remove you from your... situation... at the castle, but we were forced to move faster than we had originally planned. Apparently, the Duke desired to terminate the charade of your employment with him sooner than we expected. That, and another providential series of events has necessitated that our attack on La Chimenea be moved forward significantly."

English was taken aback. "Your *attack* on La Chimenea?"

Pano leaned over to him and whispered, pointing over his shoulder with his thumb. "Perhaps, boss, you didn't see the huge Mexican army hiding over there behind the General?"

English scowled at Pano, before turning back to the General. "I apologize, Your Grace, but would you mind filling me in on the details of the 'providential series of events' you mentioned?"

"I would not mind at all. We have learned that your friend, the man they call *The Ghost*, recently delivered a stunning defeat to an army of several thousand men near the Vallensian village of Bethany."

The General paused, looking intently at English, and seemed to be examining his face as he watched the information sink in.

"That victory, as unexpected as it was to almost everyone, has caused that ridiculous man who calls himself 'The Duke of El Paso' to make a horrible strategic error."

The General paused again and moved a step closer to English before continuing. "In his rage, and in order to save face with the King of Aztlan, he has sent the remainder of his forces—except for a few hundred men left behind to guard his castle—an army of almost 6,000 men, to attack and annihilate the Ghost militia and all of the Vallensian people.

"We intend to, as you English say, 'seize the day.' By order of our King, we are going to capture La Chimenea Castle and kill the Duke of El Paso... and you are going to help us do it."

Chapter 19 - Ana

Nothing in her life had ever been more devastating to her than the news that Jonathan had been captured, not even the violent death of her husband Hamish. She knew that this was true, but she really didn't know what that knowledge meant to her, or how she should interpret those feelings. She only knew that, no matter what the outcome of the war might be, she could not imagine her life without Jonathan in it.

She was barely hanging on emotionally, and her work around the ranch, though hectic, kept her from breaking down in grief and despair.

The aftermath of the battle of the Penateka Dam was traumatic and difficult to handle. Since the battle had culminated at the Wall Ranch, there were many wounded to attend to, and some of the militiamen had died within the first few days from their wounds, or from subsequent infections.

The hay barn had served as the original triage area, and in the blazing summer heat, it soon stunk of death and decay—a scent she knew she would never get used to and never forget. Those who were treatable, and who had a high probability of recovery, were moved into the house or to other suitable lodgings in other buildings on the ranch.

Those who were still dying in the hay barn were given whatever care and comfort could be offered them. Most of those who were left in the barn soon realized that they were still there because they were not expected to live. She was strengthened and heartened by how well the men accepted their destiny, and their strength made it easier for her to cope with the grim situation. She may not have been able to handle it if there had been hysterics and constant wailing in the barn. Perhaps that was her own selfishness, but she did have a grasp on the precariousness of her own emotional condition.

She had seen to it that Prince Gareth was returned to his former room in the Wall's home. So far, he had been spared the ravages of infection, and it seemed that he would recover fully with treatment and a sufficient amount of rest. He made constant jokes about his need for beer and garlic, and his levity and wit did help make things easier for her.

Ruth being gone had been one of the more difficult realities for her, especially since she was now worried sick over the absence of the rest of the Walls from the ranch. David was busy with Phillip and was away most of the time, so she was left in charge of both the hospital duties and the regular running of the place. Betsy and her family were still up north, and until she returned, there was no Wall presence at the ranch.

Daily she made her regular rounds, and Wally was very helpful in keeping everyone well fed and as happy as he could. The cook was one of the bright spots in Ana's rather depressing days. Wally kept the food coming, and the Wall's ample storage of grains, vegetables, and meats made serving so many people much easier than it might have been otherwise.

On the third day after the battle, Phillip and David arrived and reported that most of the Vallenses that had fled northward would be returning to the area around the ranch and should begin arriving soon. To her, the presence of the refugees would be a welcome sign, and with Betsy and Paul around, she knew that life on the ranch might soon return to some semblance of 'normal'.

The Vallenses, by their nature, were a very resourceful and helpful people. Most of them knew how to forage and hunt, and how to provide for themselves, as well as for any of their people who were weak or needy, in an ample way.

The peach crop from the orchard was a few days past being ready to harvest, so she intended on recruiting some of the returning Vallenses to bring in that harvest, which would add to the available food on the ranch.

With all of these thoughts running through her head, and as she busied herself with her duties, she was reminded of how thankful she was for God's providence in bringing her to the Walls' homestead in the first place. She had no just cause to be depressed. Not after what God had done for her thus far in her life.

Her mind wondered back once more to the time she lost her husband and barely escaped with her life. She remembered walking south—away, she hoped, from the devastating reality of death and mayhem she had left behind in Albany, almost exactly a week after the collapse. All she carried with her was a plastic grocery bag with three bottles of water and three tins of tuna. She had found a survival pocketknife with a can opener on it in the Haltoms' silverware drawer, and she was pretty sure she could make it work.

After the first day of walking, she had only made it about six miles from the Haltoms' house. She was slowed on that first day because she spent most of the time hiding—afraid of every shadow, every sound, and every movement.

She decided to avoid both of the highways that went south out of Albany. Highway 6 went to the southeast, but that would take her closer to Fort Worth and she wanted nothing to do with any big cities. She realized that she didn't want to go near any small towns either. The other highway, Highway 283, would take her straight south to the Interstate, avoiding any large metropolitan areas. However, she was just too afraid that she would run into the gang that had murdered her husband and the Haltoms. *Best to stay off any paved roads.*

She headed cross-country, which made progress slow and difficult. Most of rural America was then crisscrossed with barbed wire, and this part of Texas was also pretty thick with brush, cactus, and mesquite trees, sometimes growing so thickly that she would have to walk a half mile to the east or west just to find a clear route back in order to keep heading south.

Every so often, she would come upon a ranch road that continued for several miles almost straight south. Still, if she heard a sound or anything that might be construed as an engine, she would flee into the brush and hide—sometimes for over an hour—too afraid to move or to show herself.

She only drank half of the first bottle of water on the first day, and she abstained from eating any of the tuna.

208

The first night, she found an empty cattle shed, and she slept—or tried to sleep—in an old 1940s era bathtub that was evidently used as a seasonal cattle feeder. She didn't sleep much. Every animal sound frightened her, and every gust of wind made her sit straight up in the tub; her heart would pound in her chest and her imagination would create scenarios of horror that she could not ignore or forget.

At last, not long before dawn, she drifted off for an hour. She awoke more exhausted than she had ever been in her life. The sun, streaming through a crack in the corrugated steel of the shed roof, announced to her the coming of the new day.

The second day of her walk went much better as the ranches were large in this area, and she encountered fewer fences. She found a ranch road running mostly southward, and at some point, she estimated that she was about a half-mile from the highway because she could hear an occasional car or truck pass by.

She figured she had walked around 10 miles when she suddenly heard loud gunfire from the direction of the highway. She bolted into a copse of trees and stayed there until the sounds faded away once again. She could not help herself from wondering what had happened, and who—if anyone—had been killed by the gunfire.

By midday on that second day, she noted that she had never been so hungry or thirsty in all her life. She knew that her water and food would not last long and that she had to ration carefully. Eventually, she lost the self-control and drank the second half of the opened bottle of water, as well as another full one. Famished, she opened and ate one tin of tuna.

Towards the end of that day, she came upon an abandoned hunting camp. Whoever had leased the land had placed two campers and a picnic table there. She watched the area for a long time, making certain that no one was around—or, at least, no one *appeared* to be.

She didn't want to steal any food or break into the campers, but she found a well with a long garden hose running from it to one of the campers. The well obviously wasn't working—probably from the lack of electricity—but there was still water in the hose, so she used it to fill her empty bottles and she took a long drink to satisfy her thirst.

She didn't want to hang around too long for fear that someone might be using the campers, perhaps as their survival retreat. Maybe they were away hunting, or maybe they might be arriving at any time, so she quickly decided to continue on her way south, greatly refreshed in her mind and spirit by the acquisition of more water. She was no *Survivorman*, but neither was this the Serengeti. A spark of hope was enough to keep her moving.

She spent the second night in a low hollow in a copse of oak trees. Maybe it was because she was so tired, but she slept for a good part of the night and awoke rather rested. She ate her second tin of tuna, hoping that it would offer her enough energy for the day. Starting her trek south, she noticed that the early morning sun was still barely breaking above the horizon to the east, and the sun glistened off the little bit of dew that had collected on the tall grass.

After walking for only a few hours, she came upon a shallow draw that ran to the south. It was lined with tall oaks and pecan trees, so she walked along the side of the draw until she came to State Highway 576, which ran east and west. She took her time, just waiting and watching from the trees—making sure that there were no people around—before sprinting across the highway. After another quarter of a mile, she found another ranch road heading southward.

It was on the third day that she arrived at Interstate 20 and had to come up with a plan to cross it. It would turn out to be the most frightening endeavor of her life. In such a short time, she had already developed a survival instinct, and she knew that being out in the open where people were likely to be moving or traveling, was a very bad idea. She hadn't heard any news for almost a week, but everything that she had seen indicated to her that, globally, the situation was not getting any better.

In just a single week, her most basic instinct—her desire to avoid predators, especially the human kind—had developed to the point that she automatically knew that she needed to avoid any paths or patterns where "game animals" (people like herself)

210

would normally travel. Thus, crossing the Interstate was, to her, a very dangerous prospect, but one that could not be helped or avoided.

She found a place where she could remain hidden, but where she could still command a good view of the Interstate and, for the rest of the day, she just watched. What she saw both sickened and saddened her.

That day, watching over the Interstate, she learned what a thin and really imaginary veil of civility had separated the bulk of "polite" society from the more deadly and dangerous types of humanity. She was almost unable to tell the predators from the prey, as groups of relatively normally dressed people walking along the freeway would suddenly and violently assault any individuals or smaller groups approaching them, in order to rob from them whatever meager belongings they carried. Sometimes these attacks would lead to gunfights, and only rarely were those being attacked able to fight off and escape their assailants.

Sometimes cars and trucks would drive by at extremely high speeds and, in a few cases, the robbers would run out into the roadway and try to shoot out the windshields or the tires. Occasionally they succeeded.

She could not believe how quickly the world had descended into sheer barbarism, murder, and treachery. She supposed that if she had really been paying attention, she would not have been surprised.

One large group decided to make the hunting easier by making a roadblock. Whenever a vehicle approached, the bandits would shoot at the car and its occupants, then rob them of whatever they could find that was valuable. Some type of predator instinct prevented them from stealing the vehicles that still worked. They knew that they would become prey once they decided to get behind the wheel and drive.

As darkness approached, in the twilight, the bandits built large fires near the access roads of the Interstate, and they cooked up whatever food and delicacies they had stolen from their prey. She determined that the fires would benefit her and help her to cross the highway, because they would destroy the night vision of those who were feasting around them.

211

She waited until the entire group was seated around the fires, and, checking to make sure that there were no other people around, she started her sprint across the highway, a distance that she later learned was longer than a football field. Her mind raced as fast as she ran and, at one point, she thought that maybe she wasn't going to make it. She feared that she'd have to stop to lie down and rest in the median, but the urge to live and to get to Jonathan and the Vallenses overrode her fears. Huffing and gasping for breath, she made it to the south side of the Interstate, and, slipping over the barbed wire fence, she disappeared into the trees—glad to be invisible again in the darkness. *Maybe I am like a gazelle on the Serengeti*, she thought.

Back in the hayloft, she recruited the huge militiaman the Ghost soldiers called The Mountain, but whom she just called by his name—Rollo—to help her carry two recently deceased men to the newly inaugurated militia graveyard. She struggled with the weight, but Rollo was able to carry most of the load as they hauled the bodies to their final resting place. In the graveyard, eight militia warriors dug holes in the hard ground with picks and shovels, carving out graves in which to bury men who had been their friends and brethren.

Rollo seemed to be emotionally unaffected, but he was particularly quiet as they went about their dark task.

"The floodwaters carried away another 25 or so who died at the base of the dam... so at least we don't have to dig holes for them," he said.

"It would be nice if we could find them and give them a decent burial," she replied softly.

"Dead is dead, Miss Ana. When you're dead, it doesn't really matter if you were one of the 300 down that hill over there who we shoved into a mass grave, or one of our friends here who we bury respectfully and individually."

"I think there is a difference, Rollo. Those men were here to kill innocent people that only wanted to live in peace. These men died trying to defend them. There is a difference."

"I'm not sure the mother or father back in Aztlan who won't be seeing their son again will appreciate that difference," he replied, looking down at one of the graves.

She turned to go back to the barn, then stopped and looked back at Rollo. "All of these men chose to fight—which is against our way as Vallenses—but I do believe that there is a difference, Rollo. There is a great divide between good and bad, and wrong and right." She turned again and walked back up the hill.

An hour later, walking into Prince Gareth's room to change his dressings, she noticed that he was at the end of his bed, doubled over. He barely registered her presence and his face was completely disfigured with pain. He ground his teeth into the heavy woolen blanket he had put into his mouth to keep himself from screaming.

She was able to push him backwards onto the bed, and he let out an almost animal groan as he pulled his legs up to his chest and writhed on the bed.

"What's wrong?" she shouted to him, holding him by his shoulders and trying to get him to look at her.

"He... brought me a drink... medicine... told... me... to... drink." As he struggled with words, the pain must have become too intense because he passed out.

Poison. Someone had poisoned Prince Gareth. It seemed inconceivable. Who could have done this? *What to do?*

She had a good amount of activated charcoal in the tannery, which also served as a pharmacy and dispensary, so she ran out of the house and down the stone walk towards her workplace.

Coming around the corner near the icehouse, she could see David and Phillip, who were both mounted, near the drive by the front of the house. She shouted to them, and they both turned toward her. However, before she could say anything, she heard two sharp reports—akin to gunshots—and she saw both David and Phillip—one at a time—fall backwards off their horses. Men were shouting and running towards them, and she could see the shape of a man as he leapt onto a horse by the hay barn.

She froze for a moment, not knowing exactly what to do. It seemed that several of the militiamen had already gotten to David and Phillip, so she finally made up her mind and ducked into the tannery, grabbing a small crock, which she knew contained the activated charcoal.

Running back to the springhouse, she could see that the militiamen had placed David and Phillip on stretchers, and they were rushing them into the house. Wally was running out to meet them. She'd have to help them once she was finished trying to save Gareth.

She reached into the ice-cold water of the springhouse and fished out a quart jar of milk. With the milk and charcoal in hand, she rushed back into the house and into Gareth's room.

Her mind struggled to process the information, and she almost dropped both of her jars when she discovered that Prince Gareth of Aztlan wasn't in his bed. He was gone.

Part Three

Chapter 20 - Ruth

She was not at all surprised that she didn't feel that tired. Her adrenaline had been pumping regularly for the last several hours, and though she was highly on edge for the moment, she knew that when and if she finally did get to sleep, she was going to crash hard.

From the shadows, hidden in the darkness, Ruth watched intently as Piggy confronted the looter gang, and as the group of thieves—groggy from sleep—began to slowly surround the lone militia warrior. Piggy had dismounted, and his horse had retreated at his command.

Piggy, contrary to his name, was not fat at all, but like almost all of the Ghost militiamen he was wiry and very muscular. He was of medium height and build; his hair was black and curly, and a bit long beneath his hat; and he had a striking personal presence, even when he was silent. His beard was dark and full and complemented his impressive face. He was confident, maybe even brash or arrogant, and he never seemed to doubt himself even in the slightest.

Piggy raised his empty hands in a peaceful way, showing to the looters that they really needed to remain calm. His attempt made the looters more confused and suspicious, but seemed to keep them from being able to immediately decide to attack him.

"Everyone just take it easy and throw down your weapons," Piggy said with a playful look in his eyes. "It's possible that you all might make it out of here alive if you don't do anything colossally stupid... well... all except that guy," he said, pointing his finger at the biggest man of the looter gang, "because that guy has no hope. He's already dead, but the rest of you can still make it if you play it smart."

216

She sensed a very slight movement to her right and she looked and saw The Hood slowly and silently draw back his bow and take aim.

"I'm being very serious here," Piggy continued, as the group of looters circled carefully around him like a pack of hyenas surrounding a lone lion. "That guy right there is already dead, but the rest of you can save your own lives by just calmly putting down all of your weapons. Believe me, you want to do this Piggy's way!"

The large looter that Piggy had identified as a dead man straightened up a bit, and Ruth could see a mask of confusion on his face. "Why do you keep saying I'm dead? What's going on here? Who are you?"

"Shut up corpse! I'm talking to these other folks who can still save themselves. Quit being so selfish and shut your filthy trap because there's no hope for you."

"What... what are you talking about?" the looter asked, with a tremor in his voice that genuinely sounded like worry.

"Ok," Piggy replied, keeping his hands out and facing down, each slowly moving up and down in a calming motion, "the rest of you forget about the dead guy. Don't listen to him and just don't do anything stupid. I'm going to show you something you'll really want to see. In fact, it is amazing and I promise you have never seen it before."

Ruth watched as Piggy slowly raised his left hand in a fist, as if he were holding an imaginary bow. He then pantomimed pulling an imaginary arrow from his quiver, and he went through the motions of loading the invisible arrow onto the invisible string. He then drew back the arrow and pointed it at the large looter, who raised his hands as if, for some reason, he thought that the imaginary weapon was real.

"Calm... calm... calm," Piggy said softly, as he reassured the rest of the looters, and after a few seconds pause, he smiled and released the non-existent arrow. A slight sound of air splitting and a real arrow hit the looter right in the heart, and he fell over backwards.

The rest of the looters froze in place, and could not at all get their minds around what had just happened. After what seemed to Ruth like an eternity, a clumsy and stupid looking looter went for his sword, and this ignited a frenetic burst of motion as each of the remaining looters went for their own weapons. Just as they began to move, Piggy, lightning fast, drew out throwing knives and as he spun in effortless and artistic motion around the circle, the knives just seemed to find their targets—usually the heart or the throat. Simultaneously, arrows pierced the air, and looters were falling in every direction.

In only seconds, the ballet was finished, and all of the looters were either dead or dying. Piggy stood in the middle of the circle of dead men, still slightly crouched down, and holding a knife back and close to his right ear.

"I told you idiots to remain calm," he said with mock dismay and disappointment, "this was totally unnecessary!"

Ruth and the rest of the posse approached slowly from out of the shadows, each with their weapons at the ready. When it became obvious that there were no more immediate threats, they each lowered their weapons and walked closer to Piggy.

"I don't know," she said, confused, "why... why did you kill that big man first? Why kill him at all?"

Piggy looked at her sadly and took a deep breath, before pointing at a heap of what had looked to her like clothing and blankets on the ground, lying just outside of the looters sleeping circle. From where she stood, she could now see what looked like two Vallensian woman's headcoverings exposed beneath the blanket.

She let out a gasp as she ran over to the heap and pulled back the blanket. What she saw caused her to fall backwards in shock and horror. Timothy caught her as she plunged backwards, and she turned into his waiting arms, sobbing. The two Vallensian women were dead, and obviously had been tortured and probably raped as well. The most appalling thing about the condition of the women was that their assailants had left on their prayer coverings—perhaps as a joke or as a statement of disdain against the faith of the plain women.

After taking a few minutes to get over the traumatic sight of the dead women, she stood up shakily and with Timothy's help she walked slowly back towards the group.

218

"They haven't been dead long," Piggy said, looking at her. "If we had gotten here maybe a few hours ago, we might have saved them." He paused again. "That guy," he said, pointing at the first and largest looter, "still had blood stains on his knuckles. That's why I picked him out to die first. I knew that Hood would know what to do. It wasn't just for drama, Ruth. I wanted them to feel terror, just like those women did. I guess you could call it revenge, but I call it justice." He looked back at Ruth, "I told you if you came on this adventure, there'd be plenty of killing."

"These other people weren't innocent," Timothy told her, "they were just as guilty as the guy with blood on his hands. Piggy played it so that they would draw their weapons first. He knew we'd all have his back. But still I'd have to say that that was a phenomenal feat of knife throwing, Piggy."

Piggy was walking around the circle, pulling knives from dead looters. "This is why we never stop training, gentlemen... and lady."

The posse did a thorough inspection of the area to see if there were any other surviving hostages. There weren't, so they gathered together what looted food and materials they could carry, along with most of the weapons, and bound them into blankets that they strapped to their horses.

They wordlessly began preparing a site to bury the Vallensian women, and took turns digging in the graves with their fold-up camp shovels while Ruth wrapped up the women's bodies and cleaned up their faces. She didn't know them, but she felt like they were a part of her family. After the burial, they gathered together and Ruth quoted a psalm to them from memory, as they all bowed their heads.

"We're only about a mile from Harmony, so we won't have to carry this stuff very far," Timothy told her as they headed to the west. "We should be there not long before sunrise and we'll be able to get some rest."

The ride to Harmony was quiet and uneventful and each member of the posse seemed to be both pensive and reflective as they considered the death of the Vallensian women. Ruth figured that the women had been captured during the attack up near Comanche, and that the looters had been part of a group that had participated in the slaughter of the 2,000 Valensians there. She wondered how many more captive women or children might be out there in the soulless and cruel hands of looters, thieves, and rapists; and then she was forced to face the reality that her father was in the hands of the same kind of people.

Times like this truly tested her faith. She wanted to ask God how He could let things like this happen to such a peaceful people; but her father was always telling her that faith does not protect us *from* danger or trials or suffering... faith strengthens us and gives us peace *in* dangers, and trials, and suffering. "Nobody promised us a rose garden." he would always say.

Before she had time to get too deeply into her own thoughts on the matter, they were drawing close to the secretive place the Ghost militia called by its one-word title — 'Harmony'.

When they were still several hundred yards away, the posse reined up on the eastern edge of what looked like a large but shallow canyon. She steadied Peloncio as Timothy came up beside her.

"We have to signal from here. We'd likely be dead if we tried descending into the caliche pit without signaling."

"Caliche pit?" she asked as she examined the canyon.

"Caliche is a material that they used to use as a road base for country roads back before the collapse. 'Caliche' means 'clay', and there are pits like this all over Texas where they dug out the white, rocky clay to spread on the roads.

"Phillip bought this pit and several hundred acres around it almost a decade before the collapse. He set up a small company that sold caliche to farmers and ranchers. All the while he was building the Harmony facility in the wall of the pit. It was the perfect cover for an excavating operation."

"What is the Harmony facility?"

Timothy straightened up in his saddle, stretching out his back after the long ride. As he stretched, Piggy began making a very peculiar animal-like sound that Ruth could not readily identify; but he did it loudly enough that they were all certain that

220

whatever militia guards were out there would know that they had company coming.

"Harmony, in addition to being an armory and storage facility, is an orphanage, school, and training center for children and young men. I was raised and trained in a similar school up north of here that Phillip started after the crash. He had to open a few others because there were so many orphans around then. As the militia patrolled this whole area of Central and North Texas, orphans would be saved and gathered up and sent to the orphanages.

"Once the orphans arrived at a place like Harmony, they would be evaluated over several weeks as they were fed and treated for malnourishment or whatever afflictions they might have. If they were considered militia material, they were enrolled in the militia schools and they would begin their training. If it were to be determined that they were not militia material—perhaps they were too docile or what Phillip might consider to be inordinately sensitive—they would be placed in a regular school, where they would remain until they could be adopted out."

"How would that work?" she asked. "I mean, how did you adopt out orphans after the crash?"

Timothy laughed and gave her a sly look. "Well, your father may not know it, but there were Vallenses in and around San Angelo who knew Phillip and who quietly and privately supported what he was doing. They would never let any of the Vallensian elders know that they were materially supporting the militia, but I guess it was one of the worst kept secrets around before this war started.

"Out of 20,000 or so Vallenses, there were many, many people who believed that they were obeying their consciences by supporting the militias, even if they were not being completely open with their own eldership about it. Anyway, these Vallenses would take in the orphans whenever they could place them in good homes. Many of the Vallensian families wanted more children after the collapse, and some of them had lost some or most of their own. Your people love large families and highly prize children (she noticed a slight wetness in his eyes as he said this)—something that was another stark difference between you and those in the pre-crash world.

"I was one of those set aside for militia training."

"Did you enjoy it? What was it like?"

"It was all I knew. I never knew any other life, and I still don't. The time I have spent with you and your family at your ranch was the first time I've ever seen a glimpse that there might be another life available out there." He paused for a moment, looking down, "We need to go... the others are heading down."

Harmony was a huge underground facility built into the walls of the caliche pit. It was completely obscured from the outside by the boulders, rocks, and bushes that were carefully arranged outside of its entrance. Ruth didn't see any of the facility guards, but she was told that there were always 20 or more of the Ghost militia on guard at any time, protecting the facility.

Inside she was amazed at the complexity and size of the Harmony facility. There were teaching facilities, barracks, an armory, a kitchen, and a large common area the boys there called 'The Plaza'. During the day, when the children were not in school or in training, they were permitted to explore around the caliche pit while militia and training guards watched out for any individuals or groups that might be approaching. A simple signal from a guard would send everyone, with military precision, scrambling back into the facility. The students and the instructors had been very carefully and expertly trained in the defense of the complex.

At any given time, Timothy informed her, there were up to 100 students at Harmony, which was the largest of the militia training facilities. Regular supplies and materials, usually donated by participating Vallenses, or purchased, bartered, or traded with other traveling traders, were brought in militia caravans to the complex.

All of the students at Harmony, both militia and those who were assigned for adoption, received an education while they were there. She knew now why all of the militia men seemed to be so well-spoken and intelligent. Timothy told her that they were expected to read and write well and to be familiar with the

222

basics of different areas of philosophy and economics. They were also well versed in many of the classics of literature, which is why so many of the militia men were able to quote from those classics, and why they argued and debated esoteric points of Shakespeare and Tolstoy, often even while they were actively training.

Ruth was assigned to a room, and Peloncio was led off by an eager eleven year old boy who promised to feed, water, and comb the horse out for her.

There were no beds in the rooms at Harmony. Everyone slept on the floor. She was told that her room was actually extraordinary, in that it included a blanket and a homemade pillow. This room was only for guests and children slated for adoption, she was told. Militia trainees were expected to sleep on the ground, with only their coats and clothing for any added comfort. Most often they slept outside, and sometimes they trained by sleeping on the sides of the cliffs, or even on horses. She was glad to have a blanket and a pillow, and upon lying down, she was deeply asleep in minutes.

When she awoke, she wandered around the complex until she found Timothy and the rest of the posse in the kitchen, gathered around a long wooden table and drinking some kind of herbal tea. She didn't ask what it was when it was offered to her, but upon tasting it she decided that it was quite nice. She figured she'd probably rather not know what was in it.

"Glad to see you got some rest," Timothy said, greeting her with a smile.

"Look," Piggy said, good-naturedly, "it's the old ball and chain."

Ruth saw Tim scowl at Piggy and then punch him very hard in his upper arm.

"Ouch!" Piggy yelled, feigning great pain and emotional distress. "I will not be mauled and abused by the likes of you!"

"Quit being a jerk, then," Tim replied, shaking his head.

"That's it! I'm going to see if we can find a cook to scare us up some vittles... unless," he looked at Ruth with sudden mock seriousness, "unless you are planning on non-violently dragging in a panther or a T-Rex or something?"

"I could see to it that there is Piggy on the menu, if you'd like to keep it up?"

"Oh, no ma'am! I'll be good. Oink! Oink!" He pirouetted, before turning back to her and laughing, "Two legs good, four legs bad!"

The rest of the posse got up with Piggy, laughing at his antics. They all waved at Tim as they started out of the kitchen to see if they could locate the cook. As they were walking out, Ruth shouted to Marbus Claim to remain. He looked around, not understanding why, but obediently came back to the table.

"Marbus," she said, "the Vallensian *ordnung*—these are the unwritten but inviolable rules we live by—does not allow for a woman... or a girl... and man to be alone with someone of the opposite sex who is not their spouse. I'd appreciate it if you would stay here and join us."

"Sure," Marbus answered. "I don't get most of their jokes anyway. So I just maintain my right to remain silent."

"Probably a good policy," Timothy nodded, before turning to Ruth. "We've decided that it is most probable that your father has been taken to El Paso and not to New Rome. I'm sad to tell you that it is not likely that we'll catch the men who took him before they make it to the city. We could ride hard and fast and try to catch them, but from here on in we are going to be increasingly out in the open in the badlands, and it wouldn't be wise for us to try it. We might harm the horses, or ride into an ambush.

"So," he said, sighing, "we've decided to keep on moving methodically towards El Paso, and when we get there we'll try to figure out what to do."

"I see," she said.

"The militia has at least one spy in the castle at El Paso. We're hoping that when we get there, we'll be able to locate him and plan a rescue."

"Ok," she said resignedly. "I know that you men know more about this than I do. I'm in it for the long haul, and I know that you all want my father back safely as well. So, count me in.

Just... please make sure to keep me informed on what is going on. If something changes, or... if you receive bad news... I do want to know about it."

"It's a deal."

Later that afternoon, after a delicious meal of heavy acorn bread, lentil soup, and boiled potatoes, the posse gathered together in front of the entrance as their horses were led out to them by the boys of Harmony. As they prepared and checked their saddles and equipment, they heard the distinctive call of a militiaman approaching. They were all a bit shocked to see The Mountain ride up and dismount.

Rollo nodded at the group as he gave instructions to the boys to swap out horses for him. After he had arranged for a fresh horse, he approached the group.

"Phillip sent me to join up with you," he said, with a sideways look at Ruth. "I have an urgent message to deliver to her father when we find him."

Chapter 21 - Jonathan

Traveling across the badlands in the summer on horseback is a rough and difficult journey even if you are practiced, prepared, and intelligent. Trying to do so while stupid is a recipe for disaster. Jonathan was trying not to be uncharitable—even in his thoughts—but after his captors had killed their second horse, he was forced to conclude that stupidity may not be a sin *per se*, but it sure can be costly.

After covering almost 100 miles on the first full day after his capture, with temperatures nearing the century mark, his kidnappers had tried to duplicate the feat on the second day but had been forced to slow way down after the sudden death of the second horse. His captors had to be thinking that the militia would be hot on their trail, and they needed to get to El Paso as soon as possible in order to avoid being captured.

What they did not know, and probably could not even fathom, was that the militia posse—which was undoubtedly following them—wouldn't be willing to kill their own horses and strand themselves in the Chihuahuan Desert just to make haste. Instead, they would be tracking their quarry slowly and steadily—waiting for the Aztlanis to make a mistake. His trio of captors had made nothing but mistakes, and it was inevitable that there would be more errors in their future. His job would be to exacerbate those errors.

The initial operation of kidnapping him had been fairly well thought out, and it had gone off without a hitch. The three Aztlani spies, dressed as straggling Vallensian refugees recently arrived from the south, had called to him from the side of the road. When he approached them, one of the men grabbed his horse by the reins. The militia guards—Morell, and the young man they called Raymond—obviously believing that the three men speaking to Jonathan were Vallenses who knew him, rode over to see what was going on. That was when the Aztlani soldier named Leo suddenly ran Morell through with a sword that he had hidden under his cloak. Raymond had barely enough time to register what was happening, and to begin to react, when Leo spun around and caught him across the hip and thigh with a massive swing of the heavy sword. Raymond had escaped, but Jonathan knew that the boy was hurt badly. He hoped that God had spared the young man's life, but the wound looked very, very bad to him.

The kidnappers, he had learned, were Aztlani soldiers dressed in Vallensian garb that they had stolen during raids against Vallensian farms on the frontier. Leo, the leader of the group, was a rough and rude young man who evidently lacked both religion and normal human affections—including any respect for human life.

Leo had informed him that they had many spies among the Vallenses who were heading north, and if he didn't come with them peaceably, the spies were instructed to kill Vallensian refugees each day until he did so. Jonathan was certain that the spies would kill the Vallenses if they had the opportunity to do so anyway, but he had agreed to go peaceably for two reasons: first, because he had no alternative, and he had no intention of using force to try to free himself; second, because by keeping at least these three men busy guarding him, he hoped that at least a few of his people might be spared.

His main objectives over the last two days since the kidnapping were a bit contradictory, as he had been trying to slow the party down, while simultaneously encouraging them in whatever bad ideas their leader would concoct. Eventually he had decided that the second object—encouraging stupid decisions—would accomplish the first; and that had been exactly what had transpired. Leo's drive to escape capture and get to El Paso in some kind of record time had resulted in the death of two of the horses. Now, with the other two mounts nearly lame and suffering dehydration, with hundreds of miles still to go, their escape had slowed to a crawl. In the last 24 hours, it had become questionable whether they were even going to make it to El Paso at all.

Somewhere around his son David's age of 25 years, Leo was an uneducated and ill-bred know-it-all, whose ignorance was in direct proportion to his ego. He was quite tall, sallow skinned, with the look of a viper in his thin features and sharp cheekbones. His demeanor and carriage were offensive, even when he said nothing, and he treated his cohorts as something significantly less than subordinates. Any suggestion they made was immediately rejected regardless of merit, unless he later decided to introduce the same idea as his own in order to adopt it.

Troy was the silent one of the bunch, a young man in his late teens, tall, broad, and muscular. He obviously did not like Leo, and seemed to take umbrage at the constant barrage of insults coming forth from the mouth of the leader. The young man had offered some solid counsel to Leo at the outset—that they didn't need to rush, and that they would make better time overall if they spared the horses and took a more circuitous route. For some reason this wise advice had offended Leo to no end, and from that point on he had not spared Troy a tongue lashing if the boy dared speak above a whisper. Jonathan had curried favor with the young man, primarily by offering looks of understanding and commiseration whenever Leo would unleash an un-prompted attack against him. When they stopped for lunch on the second day, Leo had denied Troy any food in order to better feed his captive. Back on the trail, Jonathan had secretly given half of his bread to the young man, who seemed very thankful.

Atticus was the other Aztlani soldier, and he seemed to be the kind of guy who avoided conflict as much as possible by sucking up to Leo whenever he could, while simultaneously trying to be friends with Troy. He even pretended to be friendly to Jonathan when Leo wasn't watching. The only one of the three who seemed to be intelligent and thoughtful was Troy, so Jonathan had decided to focus his attentions and efforts on the youngest man of the bunch.

He had his hands full with a long 'to-do' list as they traveled. His first coup had been to side with Leo when the leader had commanded that they take the straightest route possible, rather than the longer route down south to what used to be I-10, or the northern route that passed through Midland and Odessa, where the trail met up with the old I-20 corridor. The area between the two old Interstate corridors was known as 'the badlands', and was purely militia territory. Jonathan figured his odds of being rescued were better if he tried to keep the group in the badlands.

The straight route through the badlands was extremely rugged and difficult, and Jonathan knew the area very well. It was also a trail almost solely used by the militia, and because of that, Aztlani traders and scouts would have never even considered going that way. The hot summer sun, the lack of water, and rough riding had made things much harder on the group, and especially on the horses.

By the middle of the second day, they were all on foot in order to save the remaining horses, so Jonathan diligently applied himself to leaving 'signs' in order to make tracking the group easier on the posse. He would absent-mindedly kick over rocks and stumble into yucca plants, breaking the thin spines over onto the ground. As they passed low-hanging limbs—when there were trees around, which wasn't often—he would break off twigs with green leaves on them and leave them on the trail behind them. Leo was too stupid to notice, and if Atticus ever noticed he didn't register it. Once, after flipping over a partially rotted branch with his foot, exposing the darker and bug eaten underside, Jonathan thought he saw the faintest of smiles touch the corner of Troy's mouth, but he couldn't be sure.

In addition to trying to leave behind easily noticeable markers, he also tried to keep firing a constant litany of questions, comments, and advice to Leo in order to keep him talking, arguing, and ranting, instead of thinking and planning. Leo seemed to like the attention, and he took every question or comment as an opportunity to speak about himself and his abilities.

As the shadows grew long towards the end of the second day, they were somewhere near where the town of Big Lake, Texas used to be. Jonathan had convinced Leo that there would be water in the 'Big Lake', and had used an old *Big Lake, Texas* road sign to assure Leo that it had to be so. What Leo did not know, is what Big Lake had always been famous for. The name 'Big Lake' was a joke, because the lake there was famous for being dry most of the time, especially in the summer. Since this had not been a very wet year, and there had also not been any recent heavy rains, there was nearly a zero probability that there would be water there. Leo didn't find that out until they came upon the lake and found wild cattle grazing on buffalo grass in the middle of the dry 'lake'.

Leo had gone on a tear after that one, and Jonathan was convinced for a few moments that he might take a beating for it, but Leo just vented his anger at him verbally, also cursing at the sky and any handy rocks that were around, before turning his wrath on his compatriots for not knowing a better route. Jonathan was both shocked and amused at the things that came out of the Aztlani's mouth, most of which he would never be able to repeat.

"I assure you," Jonathan said with a calming voice, "the last time I was here there *was* water in this lake." That, of course, was not a lie. Jonathan had grown up in West Texas, and knew that the lake rarely held water, except during the rainy season, and only then if the year had been particularly wet. The last time he had seen the lake there were about four inches of water in it, and the grass could still be seen above the water line.

After that, frustrated and angry, Leo had suggested that they make camp in some crumbling structures near the old town, and Jonathan had encouraged that idea too, hoping to have some down-time to rest and think and plan. It seemed to be Leo's plan to travel while it was hottest, and rest when it was cool, the opposite of what the militia posse would be doing. Jonathan just had to shake his head at that kind of reasoning.

They found a dilapidated old roadside motel just outside of town, probably built in the 1940s, and Leo chose it as their campsite. There was scarcely any roof left on most of the buildings, and no doors or windows, but many of the walls at the Travel-On Motel were constructed with cinderblocks, and were still standing.

After unloading their gear, and unsaddling the horses, Leo announced that he was going to hike around and look for water. He assured the two other men confidently that *if* there was water around, he would find it.

Jonathan knew several locations in the area where there was a very high likelihood that water could be found, but, even though he was thirsty and starting to suffer headaches himself, he didn't say a word. After an hour, Leo returned, smiling arrogantly and holding the crumbling remains of an old, orange Home Depot bucket, in which were a couple of inches of stagnant and rusty rainwater, along with what had once been about 20 or 30 nails and screws. Leo bragged about his find, but didn't dare drink any of the putrid water himself. Instead, he poured it into an old aluminum pan found in one of the buildings, and let the horses drink what they could.

As Leo went on to regale his partners with the story of his heroism in diligently searching out and finding water—as well as saving the horses—Jonathan announced that he needed to relieve himself, and stepped backwards out of the abandoned shell of a building. Looking around, he almost laughed out loud when he saw what used to be the motel swimming pool. There were several hundred gallons of nasty water in the pool—but it was wet, and even stagnant water can be purified with fire and/or filtration, *if* one had the know-how and intelligence to do it.

His captors didn't seem to care to watch him, since there was really no place to run or hide, so he was not surprised that none of the three amigos followed him as he stepped behind a wall that ran along and beside the old swimming pool.

As he walked he examined the area, mentally noting the abundance of survival materials and supplies that could be used in an emergency situation. There were numerous edible plants in the area, some growing up through cracks in the old concrete walks. He paused to pick and eat some succulent purslane leaves—which would provide him with both water and nutrients.

He was always amazed at how much "stuff" was really usable, but instead was quite invisible to people who didn't know *how* to think.

As he approached the rear of the building that once housed the motel office, he stepped onto a thin paving stone—about two feet square—that was almost completely covered over with weeds and debris. The stone made an interesting hollow sound, so he reached down carefully and flipped it over, nearly laughing aloud again as he found himself peering down into an underground cistern that was nearly 2/3 full of good water. He looked towards the office, which was one of the few buildings that still had a roof, and saw where steel roof gutters—still intact—ran into the ground, and obviously terminated into this cistern. He smiled to himself inwardly in his amusement.

They were in the borderlands of the Chihuahuan Desert at this time, and the people who originally built these structures were quite industrious, and would have taken advantage of even the sparse amount of rainfall received in the area. He figured that, conservatively, there were probably 40 to 50 similar cisterns in the immediate vicinity of the town.

He stepped out behind the office to urinate, and, when he had finished, he walked back by the cistern, stopping to replace the paving stone over the hole. Once he had the stone back in place, he kicked the dirt and debris back over it, and, satisfied that he had obscured the cistern, he looked back up to find Troy leaning against the cinderblock wall about 30 feet away, watching him with a "now we've got a secret" smile on his face. After a few seconds of eye-contact, and without a word, Troy turned around, walked along the poolside without giving it a second look, and strolled back into the building they had chosen as their home for the night.

The third day of his captivity dawned cold and fair, and despite the emptiness of his belly, and the burning thirst in his throat and mouth, he felt strong and alive. It had gotten quite cold overnight in the desert, and, although he knew it was going to be very hot throughout the day, he was glad when the first rays of warm sunlight arrived to take the chill off of the morning.

Troy's suggestion that they leave early in order to take advantage of the cool of the morning was gruffly vetoed by Leo, and Jonathan was not at all surprised when it was already after 9 a.m. and growing hot when they finally got underway.

The horses had not recovered much, and before long the heat of the morning began bearing down on man and beast, amplifying the effects of dehydration and hunger.

By noon they had reached the ghost town of Texon, Texas, an old oil-boom town that had already been abandoned—other than by a handful of souls—even before the collapse. Remarkably, though Texon was a ghost town, many of the buildings in the old town were still standing and in moderately good repair. *It's as if someone has been maintaining the place*, Jonathan thought.

His suspicions were realized when they saw an old man, walking with the help of an ironwood cane, come out of the old service station to meet them.

He noticed that the old man was particularly lively despite his age and the fact that he was obviously quite blind. Jonathan felt his heart go out in immediate concern for the man, especially when Leo approached him with a smile on his face.

"Well, howdy, Old-Timer!" Leo shouted, as he dismounted.

"Howdy to y'all," the old man replied. "You don't sound like militia... and if ya be traders, I've nothing to trade for right now, so ya might just be on your way."

"Easy, old man," Leo responded sharply. "We need water for these men and for our horses, and *we'll* decide if you have anything worth taking."

The old man leaned on his stick, his face pointed down, and he sighed deeply before he responded. "Ahh. I see... more looters. When will y'all realize I got nothin' left to steal?"

"Where's the water, old man?" Leo demanded.

"There's some water in the box over yonder," he indicated with the stick, "where the downspout runs off the roof. Take what 'ya need, but please don't mess with the box on account of it's my only source of water."

Leo walked up and poked the man heavily in the chest, sending him hobbling backwards a few steps. "You don't tell us what to do! We tell *you* what to do!"

"Take it easy, Leo." Troy said, with obvious disgust in his voice.

"YOU don't tell me what to do either, punk!"

"We're not all looters, sir," Jonathan offered. "I've been kidnapped and am currently being held captive by these men."

The old man looked up, blindly trying to gauge where Jonathan was, his head moving from right to left. In a moment it seemed that he had figured it out because he stared directly at him, smiling an almost toothless smile. "Well, then!" he said, his smile growing even wider, "you must be Jonathan Wall! I say it is great to meet ya, sir. I've heard great things about ya and I've been expectin' ya!"

Leo stopped in his tracks upon hearing this and shook his head before turning around. "What?"

The old man turned back to Leo. "What, what?"

"What did you say? How did you know that this man is Jonathan Wall?"

"Oh, I'm sorry. I should have said something earlier when ya first arrived. My apologies, then."

"What the heck are you talking about, old man?" Leo exclaimed.

The old man gestured with his thumb over his shoulder towards the service station office. "Them folks has been waitin' for *him.*"

As the last words escaped the old man's mouth, and as Leo turned to look towards the office, a knife plunged into the kidnapper's chest, throwing him backwards and onto his back.

Sensing what was happening, Jonathan—just as he had done with the post-rider bearing the letter to the King of the South States—reached over and with one lightning quick movement, threw an unsuspecting Troy to the ground, immediately covering the young man with his own body.

Arrows thudded into Atticus, knocking him over, as the old man leaned on his staff, listening and nodding his head in approval. The Aztlani soldier died still completely unaware of what was going on around him.

Jonathan was yelling by this time, and it took a few seconds for the attackers to realize that the leader of the

Vallenses was trying to save the young kidnapper's life. When The Hood ran up with his bow at the ready, peering down the length of an arrow set to fly, Jonathan saw a quizzical look cross the militia freeman's face.

"Everyone calm down," Jonathan yelled. "Nobody kills this one... I think he might be one of us."

Chapter 22 - Rollo

They all thought that they were so smart. *That is the trouble with them,* he thought, *they think they are the smartest people in the world.* All he had to do is run down a list of all the mistakes they'd made to prove that they weren't as good as they seemed to be.

Phillip had allowed a spy to attack a prisoner who was in his custody. Rollo smiled at that thought. Getz the spy was the man who had recruited him in the first place. He never had liked Getz and was glad that the man was dead. Silly old fool had accomplished nothing with his sacrifice except to make Phillip look weak.

Phillip had also let his wife and daughters get taken by Aztlan; then, with all of his resources he had let an entire Aztlani army sneak around him and butcher the Vallenses who were camped up by Comanche. Then he let Jonathan get taken from right under his nose. *Fools.*

Worst of all was the fact that Phillip had never sniffed out the spy in his own leadership! Arrogant leaders are always susceptible to one glaring weakness... they always believe and trust in the loyalty of their inner circle. That's why they always fail. *When I'm a baron... I'll trust no one.*

Rollo had risen up fast in the ranks of the militia due to his wit, his ruthlessness, and his ability to be in the right place at the right time. At first, he was just a mostly loyal mercenary, a hireling who fought with the militia just as he would have fought with anyone else who paid him well. Before long, though, the adulation and adoration that Phillip constantly received from the men started to grate on him. He silently sneered at the thought of it. The "Ghost" was just a fallible old man. Sure, Phillip was skilled, and he fought with some sense of purpose and honor; but all of that was just emotional nonsense. Phillip's infatuation with the Vallenses had turned him into a puppet to his own emotions and affections. Emotional attachment had no place in the bosom of a warrior.

Just when his resentment against Phillip had reached its peak... that was when Getz had approached him— recruiting him as a spy for Aztlan. Getz promised to pay handsomely—Aztlani gold now, lands and servants and titles once the Vallenses could be wiped out and erased from Central Texas. Getz had, by the authority of the King of Aztlan, promised him a barony, if, when the time was right, he would cut off the head of the rebellion.

In the meantime, he had served Aztlan well. It was he who had told the escaping spies where to find Phillip's wife. He had been the one who had suggested the plan of drawing Phillip away from Bethany, and of the diversionary attack on that village in order to get the main Aztlani force out to the east without it being noticed. He had been somewhat disappointed in the loss of that army, and he had hoped to be able to warn Aztlan of Phillip's plan of defense; but the attackers had served their purpose well by killing off over 2,000 of the Vallenses before they all died. Every bit of cancer that could be excised from *his* lands was a step forward in his opinion.

Cutting off the head. That meant engaging in a bold stroke by taking out the four major impediments to an overwhelming Aztlani victory. Three of those impediments—Phillip, David, and the rebellious Crown Prince Gareth—were now dead. *They have to be.* Two shots from a pistol, and some hemlock slipped into a cup of tea, and the brains of the resistance were now gone. *I wish I could have watched Phillip die.*

The plan hadn't gone off perfectly. He had hoped to use his first bullet on Phillip from point-blank range. But Gareth, who had always been a bit suspicious, had figured out the plot at the last moment. Too late for Gareth, though, because he had already taken a drink of the hemlock tea before he had realized what was happening; but, as Rollo had run out to meet David and Phillip, Gareth had shouted to them from his window. That meant that he had needed to shoot before he was really ready to do so. He could not let Phillip have even a second or two of

237

warning. The man was way too dangerous if he knew what was coming. So, rather than shoot Phillip first—which he had hoped to do—and because of their positions and his shooting angle, his first shot had hit David square in the middle of the chest. Center mass. The second shot had hit Phillip lower and towards his right side. Both shots had been significant enough to knock the rider off of his horse. *Three down... one to go.*

He fled to the horse he had packed and waiting for him by the barn. The confusion going on near the front of the house had been a perfect diversion for his getaway. With one posse off searching for Jonathan, and the whole leadership of the militia now in question, Rollo doubted if another posse could be raised and on his trail very quickly. He would finish his job and be on the way to New Rome before they could possibly catch up to him.

He found the posse at Harmony, where he had expected them to be. He had laughed. Anyone trained by Phillip was completely predictable if you knew what to expect. Militia thinking was so regimented and regular that their biggest weakness was a result of their biggest strength. They all thought like Phillip, and therefore he knew exactly where they would be by the time he arrived.

Now his challenge was to keep the group from being suspicious of him, and to find a way to accomplish his fourth task without getting killed. He'd hate to lose out on the barony and all of the benefits of being a noble, just because he'd let his guard down or did something stupid.

The posse was heading out to track Jonathan and his captors when he arrived at Harmony. With a new, fresh horse, he was ready to ride with them in minutes.

The party was an interesting one. Jonathan Wall's own daughter Ruth was part of the party. *Too bad for her that she's a part of this. She should have stayed home with Ana and the rest of the Vallenses,* he thought. Not that that would save her for very long. With the head of the resistance serpent cut off, the rest of the creature would die soon enough. Surely another, larger, Aztlani army was headed this way. The militia and the Vallenses would be sitting ducks without Phillip, David, or Gareth to lead them.

Hood was here. He was a good man and a good warrior, but was just too blinded by his own loyalty to know that he was fighting for the losing side. Rob Fosse was here too. Rob was Phillip's best friend, and probably was the man most likely to take over the reins of the militia now that Phillip was dead... so he'd have to go too. Call him the fifth casualty of the decapitation of the resistance. And then there was this Marbus Claim boy and the young man named Timothy. Harmless orphans, for the most part. The Mountain didn't know the Claim boy very well, and Timothy seemed to be a dreamer and not much of a threat. The two militia boys might live through this if they knew when to cut and run. *If not, they'll die for militia honor too.*

The one guy he had to watch out for, and that he did not want to mess with, was Piggy. Piggy was Phillip times two. Phillip had been raised by the world, and had become a militiaman as a grown man. By contrast, over 20 years younger, Piggy had been raised in the militia and it was his natural home and environment. Most militiamen were good fighters with strong minds and strong wills. Piggy was an *apex predator.* He had a mind that would dwarf some geniuses, yet he was completely at home and happy in the somewhat simple and structured militia world. As opposed to Piggy, Phillip was *just* a genius. Piggy was a phenomenon. Phillip was a deadly and efficient fighter. Piggy was a demon. Rollo himself had been forced to fight with Piggy during a training session. It had not gone well for The Mountain, he remembered all too well. No man - not any militia man—not even Phillip—had remained standing for more than 10 seconds when going into training combat with Piggy. Then, he had seen Piggy in battle. He was a force, an efficient and effective killing machine, an entire front of his own.

Piggy was a renaissance man, an artist and a poet, and probably the deadliest man Rollo had ever even heard of. He was a military Michaelangelo who could kill his enemies while painting the Sistine Chapel ceiling and not even sense any disconnect between the relative moral values of the two acts. He did not seem to struggle with philosophical concepts like death and life and meaning. He just *knew*. He existed in this complicated and dangerous world as confidently as a giant oak or a rainbow. Piggy just *was*. And any man who would come against Piggy did so at his own peril. *Someone might try to sneak up on him or get the drop on him, like I did with Phillip, but I wouldn't... not if I want to live.* Piggy was going to be a big bone to be chewed. The biggest.

As they tracked westward during the late afternoon on the 2nd day after Jonathan's abduction, it became very clear that the posse's task was going to be much, much easier than they had originally thought. Timothy told him that on the first day, the captors had made really good time. Because of this, they had basically given up hope of actually catching them in the desert. The posse had left Harmony resigned and expecting to have to try to rescue Jonathan from some cell in the castle at El Paso.

After finding a couple of dead horses, and the obvious trail being left behind by the pastor of the Vallenses, the posse had figured out that they were dealing with complete ignoramuses, and that they would probably catch up with the Aztlani party overnight.

Rollo shook his head as he checked off the list of grave errors made by the kidnappers. First, they had decided to take the direct route to El Paso. While that might sound like a good idea, it was a horrible one. The straight route was terribly hazardous, and for that reason it was the route the militia always used. The posse would know every inch of the trail and the route, while the kidnappers were completely ignorant of hazards, as well as where to find water, shade, or a place to rest.

Second, the kidnappers were trying too hard to make good time and in doing so they were slowing themselves way down. They had killed a couple of their horses, and now they were evidently on foot. A slower, circuitous route would have made tracking them infinitely more difficult.

Third, no one was watching the captive. Jonathan Wall was marking his trail so well that he might as well have left signs
240

with giant arrows on them. The kidnappers were making no effort at all to obscure their trail.

Fourth, the captors had been traveling hard by day—obviously leaving late in the morning as the day got the hottest—and quitting just as the cool desert night temperatures set in. They were doing the opposite of what they ought to be doing. By contrast, the posse had travelled by night, slept underground most of the second day, and had only left Harmony around 4 hours before sundown. Now, as the sun was beginning to set, they would plan on travelling all night, but by the look of things, they would be upon their prey sometime after midnight.

He had to admit, Aztlani soldiers were stupid compared to the well-trained and well-ordered militia forces. Aztlan won engagements only when they could present superior numbers and could stumble into some element of surprise, which almost never happened. Rollo attributed the epidemic of stupidity and sloth among the Aztlani army to their comfortable and consumptive upbringing, and their education in Aztlani schools. They were relics of the time before the crash. Aztlan had learned few lessons from the old world.

Now that he was knowledgeable of the means, methods, and training regimen of the militia, he planned on raising his own army once he received his barony in Central Texas. Who knows? Maybe he would get strong enough and declare his own kingdom in Texas! Defeating Aztlan would be easy enough, if only he had the manpower to do it.

For now, he was stuck working for the King of Aztlan, and he needed to figure out a way to do his duty without being killed by the likes of Piggy.

They came upon the small town of Big Lake, Texas at around two in the morning on the third day. Riding a ways past Big Lake, they had abruptly lost the trail; so they had doubled back. It was obvious that the kidnappers had chosen to sleep the night away in Big Lake, and the posse had easily tracked them to an abandoned motel outside of town.

After a long discussion, they had decided against trying to take Jonathan as his captors slept. It was too risky, and they much preferred to set up an ambush where they could take out the kidnappers with less of a probability of hurting or killing Jonathan Wall.

Riding westward, they identified the perfect location for their ambush in the small ghost town of Texon, Texas. It just so happened that, unbeknownst to probably just about everyone who was not in the militia, Texon was a militia way station, and the old man who lived there was the last resident of the old town, and a long-time friend of Phillip himself.

Approaching Texon, after giving a strong militia approach signal, they had been met there by the blind old man named Oswald. Oswald maintained the town as a militia post for outriders, and in exchange the militia regularly brought him food and supplies. The old man was generally left alone by looters, because they found him to be harmless and there was nothing *obvious* to steal from the ghost town.

In reality, Texon served a purpose not completely unlike that of the Harmony facility, only Texon was not an orphanage or a school. There were several hidden underground storage units and root cellars in the town that were still used by the militia outriders on a regular basis. In the early 20th century, when Texon was a booming oil town, the people were still smart enough to build root cellars under their homes. The homes were collapsed or gone now, but many of the root cellars remained.

Phillip and others had tried to convince Oswald to move out of the town—they really didn't need him there, and hated to expose him to looter violence—but the old man steadfastly rejected their offers. Texon was *his* town, and he only planned to leave it upon his death.

Oswald fed them an early breakfast and gave fodder and water to their horses. The old man had been fascinated to meet Ruth, and had talked to her and asked her questions throughout the short morning meal. The militia posse then posted guards while, two at a time, they were permitted a few hours of sleep. Hood had stayed behind at Big Lake to track the Aztlanis, just in case, for some unknown reason, they did something unexpected and avoided Texon completely.

They were not surprised, though, when the kidnappers did not arrive until nearly noon. As they waited, Rollo shook his head in disgust. The bums had probably slept until mid-morning, wasting the cool traveling time altogether.

Ruth, Timothy, and the Claim boy had taken up positions on the opposite side of the main street that ran into the ghost town. Rollo, Piggy, and Rob Fosse had taken the main attack position behind the old service station.

"How come you never took a wife, Rob Fosse?" Piggy asked, smiling.

"Oh, no woman with any sense would have me, Piggy! I'm way too beautiful, and they wouldn't want to compete," Rob answered, smiling back.

"And what about you, Mountain?" Piggy asked, looking at him. "Are you too beautiful to take a wife?"

"I'm married to my job; besides, I don't have time right now; maybe someday, after I retire from the militia."

"I never heard of anyone retiring from the militia. Even this old man Oswald is militia down to his bones," Piggy said.

"You'd be surprised," was all Rollo said in response.

Piggy turned back to him and replied with almost a frightening calm on his face and in his voice, "Oh, I'm never surprised, Mountain."

A cold chill went down his spine as, just for the briefest moment, he wondered if Piggy had figured out what was happening. But he let it pass. There was no way even Piggy could know what had happened back at the Wall ranch. The cold calm disappeared from Piggy's face as he looked back up the road. "Maybe after you retire, you'll become rich and famous, and you'll have a job for ol' Piggy!"

Rollo squinted his eyes at Piggy. What the devil is he up to? Probably nothing. Probably just an overactive imagination on my part.

Rob Fosse was laughing by this time, as he glanced up at the sun in order to gauge the time. "They should be along at any time now. Even Aztlani soldiers can't be this stupid."

Piggy chuckled. "It's not always stupidity. You'd be surprised at what mental mistakes even intelligent men make when they're out of tune with the reality that surrounds them... right, Mountain?"

"As per usual, I have no idea what you are even talking about, Piggy," he answered, the sweat starting to roll down his face in waves.

"Yeah, Piggy," Rob Fosse said. "What are you talking about? What is it to be in tune with the reality that surrounds us?"

"It's Piggy's Way," he said matter-of-factly. "Piggy doesn't do things artificially, or against the invisible but palpable flow of nature, honor, and good sense. Piggy's Way is kind of like my militia version of Occam's Razor." Piggy spun a knife heedlessly on the palm of his hand. "Occam's Razor suggests that, when faced with competing hypotheses that are equal in other respects, you are usually safer to choose the one that makes the fewest new assumptions. Piggy's Way suggest that there is an ebb and flow that is reality, and that it generally does not pay to be in constant struggle with the primal nature of things. Piggy's Way also often involves speaking of oneself in the third person."

"How, then, can Piggy be in conflict and war against Aztlan?" Rollo asked, smirking. "Isn't Aztlan the 'nature of things' right now?"

"You misunderstand Piggy's Way, Mountain. Piggy's Way does not assume that there is no struggle against evil, or sin, or greed. That is actually our most primal struggle, and we ought to engage in it heartily. If you go back far enough, there was no such conflict; and so the Garden of Eden establishes good and right *before* such things as treason, sin, or death entered in." Piggy stopped spinning the knife and used it to point off to the northwest, before continuing. "Aztlan... at least as it stands today, is in conflict with good and right, and therefore Piggy's Way is to be in conflict with Aztlan. It's really quite elementary."

Rob Fosse stared at Piggy, shaking his head. "Staggering. Truly staggering, Piggy. I have no idea what you just said, but... but... I think I love you!"

Both Piggy and Rob broke down laughing at that, as Rollo just stared at them, trying to mask his disgust at their levity.

Just as their laughter began to die down, they saw in the distance the outline of the kidnapper's party as they approached the outskirts of Texon.

The three men, through years of training and practice, instantly snapped into readiness mode. Rollo crept stealthily along a low wall that ran from the service station to an old partially collapsed building that he could not identify. He continued to move slowly and quietly as Jonathan Wall and his captors approached the old man Oswald, who had walked out to meet them. Still worried about Piggy, he glanced warily over his shoulder and saw the militiaman at the corner of the service station, focused on what was going on out front.

Feeling better, Rollo began to crawl again. He was hoping to be able to reach a spot where he could take a shot with his bow at Jonathan, and hopefully he could hit Rob Fosse too. If he could pull it off, it could still be explained away as "friendly fire." After all, things like that happen in battle all of the time. If he could not take out Rob Fosse without it looking too suspicious, he would bide his time in killing Phillip's best friend. Perhaps he could get Rob in his sleep, before high-tailing it to New Rome to claim his prize.

He finally reached an upright portion of the wall that stood about 48 inches high, and he steadied himself against it, waiting on a signal from Piggy or Rob Fosse that they were to open fire. He turned around again to look at Piggy. *Man, that guy has me freaked out!* But Piggy was still in the ready mode as Oswald spoke loudly to the leader of the kidnappers about water.

Rollo pulled an arrow out of his quiver and placed it onto the bow string. He peaked around the edge of the wall to see if he could get a good shot at Jonathan, and just as he pulled back he felt a heavy thump on the back of his head... and before he could register surprise, the lights went out.

Chapter 23 - Phillip

Being shot by someone you have cared for and fought with can be more traumatic than the carnal damage caused by a bullet tearing through flesh and muscle. Spies are an integral part of warfare, and he, of all people, was fully aware of that fact, having engaged and utilized spies both in New Rome and in El Paso. Still, one never gets used to treachery and disloyalty, especially when it happens within one's closest circle. He looked down at the dressings on his wound. *Getting shot is bad too.*

It had all happened so fast. He saw Rollo—the man he thought was his friend—raise the pistol and fire, and it seemed to him in that moment that time slowed down to a snail's pace. Although it happened in milliseconds, he seemed to be frozen in place. There was the crack of the first shot and David falling backwards off of his horse; then, The Mountain pointing the pistol at him. He was unable to react quickly enough and the second shot tore through his right side, unhorsing him as well. He hit the ground next to David.

He lay there stunned for a few seconds. Then he reached over to try to check on David, pulling himself up in order to try to help. The first shot had struck Jonathan's son directly in the center of the chest, probably taking out a good portion of his heart. David Wall was dead.

He lay down on David, and then he felt himself being lifted up onto a stretcher and hurried into the house. He was trying to give commands as his clothes were being cut off of him, but all he could remember saying at the time was... "Rollo... It was Rollo... Rollo did it."

Gareth was there, shouting orders and probing the wound, calling for alcohol for disinfectant and for some tools. The last thing he remembered before he passed out was seeing

Ana enter. She scanned the room, noting that Phillip was being worked on, and that David Wall was completely covered with a blanket. The recognition that he was dead seemed to wash over her like a tidal wave of dread and sorrow. Next, her eyes fixed on the Crown Prince, and she screamed "Gareth!" at the top of her lungs, before dropping some jars and crocks that she had been holding and slumping in a dead faint to the floor. He was trying to get up to help her when the edges of his vision went to gray... and then everything went to black.

He must have been out for quite some time because when he came to, he was lying on a cot with a pillow under his head and a cool, wet towel on his forehead. He could hear voices, and after some concentration and effort, he was able to make out what they were saying through the fog. Everything didn't make sense to him at the time, but Gareth was telling Ana why he wasn't dead.

"When Rollo came in with the tea, he said that you had ordered him to bring it to me," Gareth explained.

"I did no such thing!" Ana replied, obviously very frustrated and upset.

"I didn't know what to think, but I was suspicious. You had never done that before. I looked at the tea, and it seemed as if Rollo was very tense, and his jaw was clinched in a way that made me sense that something was wrong. And here is the clincher... you may not have a good grasp of such things, but, as royalty, I was raised with the ever-present threat of poisoning. From a small child I was taught to always be careful and suspicious of food and drink brought by someone when the situation is strange or unnatural. Also, we were taught how many of the most popular and notorious poisons smell. The tell-tale smell of dead mouse coming from that tea made it both unpalatable, and a candidate for poison—particularly hemlock."

Ana was still highly agitated. "So if you didn't drink the tea, then why were you squirming around on the bed, doubled over as if you had been poisoned?" she asked.

"Well, in one sense I was poisoned... I did take a drink of the tea, and was feeling some effects, but when Rollo left I immediately spit it out. I was experiencing some mild stomach cramps and numbness in my feet, which I expected, but the dosage that I consumed was minimal." He looked at her apologetically. "I'm ashamed to say that, in the heat of the moment, Ana... I... had a passing thought that maybe you might have been in on it. So when you walked in I feigned sickness in order to measure your reaction. As soon as you ran out like you did, I knew that you weren't involved, and I apologize for ever having entertained that thought. I am truly sorry to have hurt you."

"Oh, please don't be sorry!" Ana said excitedly. "I understand completely. Your suspicions saved your life."

"When you ran out the way you did, and I realized that you were not involved, I immediately tried to run after you. When I got into the front room here, I saw Rollo walk past the far window with a pistol in his hand. Rushing to the window over there, I saw David and Phillip ride up. I yelled to them, but it was too late. When I heard the shots, I tried to run after Rollo, but I was still suffering from symptoms of the hemlock, and my feet would not respond as I would have wished... I stumbled. When I did get outside, he was gone."

"Oh, my, my, my!" Ana cried, beginning to rock back and forth, "and now my beautiful David is dead!" She began sobbing uncontrollably, and Gareth did what he could to console her.

Phillip's head was throbbing, and his side was really starting to hurt. He sat up stiffly, and when Gareth and Ana saw him, they ran to him shouting that he should lie back down.

He refused them, and, sitting up in the cot, he shook his head to try to clear it. The throbbing pain in his side was familiar, and he knew he could handle the pain; the big threat now would come from infection. He looked at Gareth and clinched his jaw. "Give me a report, please, Prince."

"David is dead," Gareth replied, sadly.

"I saw that before I passed out." He looked to Ana and his face softened. "I am so, so sorry for your loss Ana. If I could have done anything...," he paused. "Please let us do whatever we can do to help you with this."

248

Ana looked up with tears streaming down her face. "There is nothing anyone can do to bring David back." She looked down and twisted a handkerchief in her hand. "His father needs to know."

Phillip just nodded his head. *What can I say?* No doubt Rollo was now on his way to meet up with the posse so he could kill Jonathan. *What can I do?* There is no way to catch a single, intelligent, trained militiaman alone on the run. The Ghost militia were trained much too well for that. *Our only hope is Piggy... or Rob Fosse. One of them will need to sniff out Rollo before he can kill Jonathan.* As much as he liked Rob, the only one he knew... absolutely knew... was better and smarter than The Mountain was Piggy. *Lord, I pray to you right now to give our brother Piggy wisdom and understanding. Let him know what to do!*

Phillip called for his inner circle, and then struggled to his feet. He was dizzy for a moment, but after a minute the dizziness passed.

Gareth looked at him and shook his head. "I guess you were right when you said that you'd received 'a dozen such nicks' and that you had never let them slow you down," Gareth said.

"No. I was wrong. What I said was, 'they never even made me sleepy,' and as you can see, I just woke up."

"Maybe you should take it easy for a few days."

"I will, Prince. I need to give some orders, and then I promise I'll take it easy."

"Something tells me that that promise is nothing but an empty shell."

"Let's just say that it is an honest reflection of my deepest intentions. Perhaps 'promise' was too firm a word."

"That's what I thought."

Within minutes, Pachuco Reyes, Longbow, Enos Flynn, Tyrell of Terrell, and Gareth were all standing around him as he stood by the table. Everyone was appropriately awed and saddened by the death of David Wall, but as militiamen they were all serious and ready for action. Death was an ever-present reality in war.

"I pray that that was the end of us having spies at the round table?" Phillip asked rhetorically, with just a hint of a smile. "We need to get back to work, because Aztlan is not sleeping. In fact, the beast is stirring. We have a slight advantage for now, because they will think that Gareth and I are both dead. That will embolden them. We'll be a surprise to them when they see us again in battle. Hopefully it will be like when the dead Cid, strapped to his warhorse *Babieca*, led his men against the Almoravids in Spain. Who knows, maybe Aztlan might even drop their weapons and run."

"Maybe," replied Tyrell, "after all, you are the Ghost. And I always wondered why you named your horse Babieca. It seemed to be such a strange name."

"I need you men to carefully and respectfully prepare David's body for burial. We will go ahead and seal his body in a coffin, but place it in the springhouse for now. It will do for a few days. We will all pray that his father returns in time to see him buried. If he doesn't, we will have the burial in three days' time."

"Yes, sir," Pachuco Reyes replied, "we will see that it is all done properly and that everything is ready." The militiaman paused for a moment in reflection, before continuing. "Most of the Vallenses who had fled north have now returned." Pachuco hesitated for a moment. "I must say, Maestro, that it is... necessary... that David's sister Elizabeth be informed of what has happened. She and her husband are camped in the main Vallensian camp at the front of the ranch."

Phillip pondered for a moment, looking down at the table. "Prince Gareth, I would like you to take Ana... when she is ready... and go do this thing."

"I will, Phillip," Gareth replied.

Phillip stood up straight, unconsciously stretching the muscle in his side that had been pierced by the bullet. "There is no doubt in my mind, that this attack was a precursor to a larger campaign. I expect that the remainder of the Duke's army is heading this way even now. I doubt they will use trucks as they did before—but they certainly could. We have some time to prepare, but it may not be much." He rapped his knuckles hard against the table, and frowned. "They think we're finished. They think that Prince Gareth and I are dead, and we'll let them keep thinking that. They think that they have 'cut off the head' and that the body will wither up and die. They will find out that they have been horribly wrong!"

"Where will we fight, sir?" Longbow asked.

"Aztlan cannot come from the east as they did in the battle of the Penateka Dam. They will have to come at us directly, from the west and south. They will expect us to do what we have done, which is to try to force them through the Bethany Pass," he looked down at the table, tracking his finger across the worn oak as if a map were there. "Not this time," he said, looking up into the faces of his men. "Not this time."

Phillip walked stiffly over to the window and looked out onto the drive where his own blood had mingled with that of David Wall. The stain was still evident on the ground. Then he turned back to his men, and raised his hand, pointing to the west. "This time we will hit them when and where they will least expect it... as they move across the badlands. We will hit them with everything we have."

"But, sir!" Enos Flynn said, with a shocked and confused look on his face. "They will likely have more than 5,000 men! Maybe *many* more! We've never engaged in traditional attacks against larger armies in the open field... never!"

"First, that is why they won't expect it. Second," he said, looking from man to man, "it won't exactly be in the 'open field'. Third... the term 'traditional' has become difficult to define in this age—especially after the collapse. Let's just say that, as far as the Ghost militia is concerned, this engagement will be far from traditional."

After several hours rest, and some more treatment for his wounds, he was back at work at the table in the Great Room, sending messengers to outlying units, and writing notes on cotton paper with a quill pen.

His wound was feeling much better now, and the throbbing had died down after the latest round of treatment. A poultice of antibacterial herbs, spices, and garlic had been applied tightly to both the entry and the exit wound. The bullet had traveled through the fleshy muscle and had missed perforating his abdomen and therefore hadn't hit any organs. The whole poultice had been drenched in what he was told was a tincture made of grain alcohol and the tiny fruit of an indigenous plant the Vallenses called "tickle tongue" or "the toothache tree." The whole mess smelled of limes and garlic, but he had to admit that the pain had been reduced quite a bit. He was experienced with these types of wounds—if not with the Vallensian treatment for them.

Every hour and a half he was made to drink a glass of Vallensian beer. Wally the cook told him that the body can process and eliminate the alcohol from one glass of beer an hour, and at his weight and height he should be able to handle the beer without losing any sharpness in his mind. He liked the beer, but he would be glad when this treatment was over. He was anxious to be back in the field, making preparations.

Wally was going around the room lighting the fat lamps when Gareth and the rest of his inner circle returned.

"We have informed Betsy Miller of the death of her brother," Gareth reported. "She took it quite well, considering. Something tells me that she wasn't that surprised. She said that David had chosen life in the militia, and that, although she was glad that he had obeyed his conscience, her father had taught all of the Wall children that 'those who live by the sword, are likely to die by the sword'."

"Ok," Phillip replied, sadly. "I don't pretend to understand these Vallenses, but I'm glad she handled it well. I hope her father and Ruth are able to handle it just as well."

"We have more bad news, Phillip," Pachuco Reyes said, looking intently at the militia leader.

"You might as well let me have it while I'm loaded up with this beer, Pachuco."

"Refugees are arriving from East Texas—from the Piney Woods. They say a large army is moving this way from Louisiana."

His head dropped to his chest. *I should have expected this.* He had almost stopped counting all of his failures in this war. "That has to be the Duke of Louisiana's army. Prince

Gareth told me I should be expecting this. I just had no idea... I had no idea this would all happen so soon."

Gareth looked at him and smiled a quirky smile. "Look on the bright side, Phillip. This way the blows will stop falling like sprinkles. Now it looks as if we'll get the brunt of the storm."

"I'm not sure if that is the bright side, Prince, but it does look like we are to be squeezed in that vice you mentioned to me."

"Perhaps," Gareth replied as he walked up to the table and pulled out a chair, "this would be the time to... impolitely and maybe callously... mention that with David Wall dead, and Jonathan gone, we might be able to encourage the Vallensian elders to let their people fight."

As Gareth sat down, Phillip stood up. "I cannot believe that, even under these circumstances, the Vallenses will fight." He stood for a moment but began to feel a little light-headed, so he sat down again.

"I will speak to them, Phillip. And, I hope you will accept my apologies for already doing so without your permission. I took the liberty of sending messengers to gather the Elders together tomorrow."

Phillip looked at the Prince, and after a few moments, he nodded his head. "So, do we have any word from the new refugees how large the Louisianan army might be?"

"All they said was 'thousands'."

"Thousands?"

"Yes, sir."

He sat back in his seat and put both hands up behind his head. "Longbow!" he shouted.

The militia soldier snapped to attention. "Yes, sir!"

"Let the Vallenses know that they are all going to be moving again."

"Moving, sir?"

"Yes. We're all going to Harmony. You and Tyrell are going to stay here and make sure all of the Vallenses pack up and start moving westward."

Prince Gareth looked at him quizzically. "Harmony? What's a Harmony?"

"You'll see soon enough, Crown Prince," he said as he started to gather up his papers and stuff them into a satchel. "We'll all see soon enough, because Harmony might just be where the Vallenses and the Ghost militia make their last stand."

"Maybe we should have called it Masada," Pachuco said, sighing deeply.

"Well, there won't be any suicides, but one way or another a whole lot of people are going to die."

Chapter 24 - English

Going back through the tunnel followed by 500 Mexican troops wasn't exactly what he had envisioned when he first escaped with Pano. *Good thing we brought better ladders*, he thought as they approached the north end of the tunnel, and the inevitable climb back up into La Chimenea castle.

The attack on the castle by the forces of the King of Mexico was a carefully timed affair. Above ground, 1,500 men had launched their siege on the castle the night before. The seige was designed to get the small force within the castle into defensive battle array for the protection of the castle and the Duke. Today, at precisely noon, the siege forces advancing on La Chimenea were to attempt to breach the castle walls, and at exactly that moment the tunnel force would emerge within the castle and fight their way to the Duke's private office and quarters. General Loya's hope was to take the castle with a minimum of actual fighting or loss of life. As a natural pessimist, English was not as optimistic. *No battle plan survives contact with the enemy*, they say. English didn't know exactly what to expect, but he figured it would go down somewhat differently than how it had been planned by General Loya.

English had not been in actual combat in almost 20 years. The last two decades for him had been spent in administration. He didn't know how he'd react to being back in battle, and frankly, he didn't look forward to it. *That part of my life is over.* The overwhelming desire for peace and order in his life smothered any residual attraction to the smells and sights of battle. He felt no need to prove his manhood. He had no loyalty to either side in this particular battle—though his disdain for Aztlan grew by the day. He had not quite codified the idea in his thinking, but deep down in the recesses of his heart, he desired to be a better help to Phillip, the Ghost militia, and to the Vallensian cause. The true longing of his heart was for peace.

Still, if the Aztlani army was marching towards Central Texas, then he wanted to be a part of stopping that army. He wasn't sure if taking La Chimenea would accomplish that task, but stranding Aztlan in the badlands with no means of support, no resupply, and no home base to which they might return, sounded like a good enough place to start. If he survived, and if the seizure of La Chimenea was successful, then he'd have to talk to General Rodrigo Loya about what the King of Mexico's next step might be.

As they approached the mouth of the tunnel and the entrance into the castle, there was some whispering and trepidation, mainly because it was still unclear if the Duke actually knew of the existence of the tunnel; and, if he did know about the tunnel, it was not known whether he might be expecting an attack from there. If he was expecting an attack, the tunnel force would be in a very precarious position, having to ascend through the bottleneck of the tunnel entrance and into tight quarters once they arrived in the old emergency center within the bowels of the castle.

By the command of General Loya, he was to lead the force, with his sidekick Pano beside him. One of the causes for his trepidation was that the attacking Mexican forces did not have guns, while everyone knew that the Aztlani guards absolutely would be armed with rifles and pistols.

English watched from below as Pano ascended the newly replaced ladder, trying to work as quietly as possible as he removed the boards that covered the hole.

What English absolutely did not expect was what the invasion team actually found—an almost empty castle, and the Duke Carlos Emmanuel with the entire leadership of the Duchy of El Paso kneeling in surrender on the hardwood floors of the Duke's lavish office.

The sounds of occasional gunshots could be heard outside of the castle, but resistance was light and didn't last very long. Many of the domestic workers in the castle had fled with
256

some of the guards when the Mexican army first appeared outside the city walls. The gates to the city were left open—obviously by the people fleeing the city—and the foreign army had marched in virtually unopposed. There were skirmishes and some light resistance from a few loyal Aztlani guards when Loya's army first reached the walls of La Chimenea, but eventually, as cowards and domestics fled from the castle, the citadel was breached as well. What he had thought would be a tough nut to crack was opened to the invading army with very few casualties.

The Duke of El Paso had indeed overplayed his hand when he chose to send almost his entire army in an attack on Central Texas; and, on a personal note, the Charles Emmanuel's stupidity had made it more than obvious that the his success in sniffing English out and manipulating him over the last few years was not the work of the Duke, but of some other offender. Someone, either in the castle or maybe among the Ghost militia, had betrayed him to the Duke, and it was likely that that someone was still in play. Perhaps the Duke could be... *convinced...* to give up that information.

Nobody in El Paso seemed to have expected the surprising attack by the new King of Mexico. After the dissolution of the first Kingdom and the rise of the King of Aztlan in California, Mexico had once again become an afterthought in North American affairs. It had been the official position of the King of Aztlan—based on information and 'intelligence' received from the Duke of El Paso—that Mexico was no longer a threat. English himself had not considered that there might be an element of Mexican nationalists still operating south of the old border, and though the Mexican force was tiny and poorly armed, they had very effectively concealed their intentions and masked their movements. When the inhabitants of the Duchy of El Paso woke up that morning, not one of them would have conceived of the idea that on that very day the city and the castle would be in the hands of the King of Mexico.

The clean-up operations were still continuing when General Loya and a few of his officers arrived in the Duke's office. The Duke and his closest henchmen were exercising their right to remain silent, as Mexican officers rifled through the desks and cabinets gathering intelligence and whatever else might be of value.

"Sir English," Loya said, with a slight bow of his head, "we are thankful for your assistance today. We will require your attendance—if you do not object—in our meetings for the rest of the day. There is a lot to do to prepare this place to be defended, and our intelligence officers will want you to be here to help us in our planning."

"Whatever I can do to serve you, sir." English looked over towards Charles Emmanuel, who was scowling at him with unmasked derision. "What do you intend to do with the Duke, here?" he asked, with an equal amount of derision. "There is some information I would like to extract from him, if it pleases you, sir."

"The Duke and his men will be removed to the basement where we are preparing a bank of cells for their pleasure. We'll be... debriefing... them there. What is it you would like to know from the Duke?"

"I'd like to know the name and current location of the traitor who blew my cover. I'd like to know the name and the current location of every spy the Duke has among the Vallenses and the Ghost militia, and I'd like to get an estimate from the Duke as to how many innocent pacifists he has had murdered so that he could curry favor with the King of Aztlan. Then... I'd like to see him lined up against a wall in the courtyard and shot."

"Well," Loya said, removing his gloves, "then it seems that for the time being we have the same agenda. Charles will be questioned... intently... before his trial. Then," the General glared at the Duke with a slight smile on his face, "provided he is found guilty by a court-martial made up of my officers, he will be shot by a firing squad."

Charles Emmanuel gasped noticeably. "Zhooo... Zhooo... Zhooo will not shoot me! I am a prisoner of war!"

"You," the General exclaimed, "are a murderous tyrant, and an enemy to your own people!" Loya slammed his gloves to the ground to emphasize his point, and his eyes flared in flames of fire. "You will now shut your miserable mouth, or I will make sure your *interrogation* is more intensive than you can possibly imagine! I will extract from you the name of every family member, every distant relative, every friend, and even every bastard child that you have ever fathered, and then I will systematically root the memory of your execrable name from the history of this world!"

The Duke's chin dropped to his chest, and he remained silent. Loya turned to English and closed his eyes for a moment, calming himself. "I apologize for my outburst, Sir English. I have a particular distaste for the likes of Charles Emmanuel and anyone of his ilk. Forgive me for losing my composure."

"I understand completely, sir."

Loya nodded to his men, and they quickly led the Duke and his entourage out of the office. After he had watched them depart, the General turned back to English.

"We will need to formulate a workable strategy for the defense of this castle and the city. Pano informs me that, despite the fact that you were treacherously exposed to the Duke as a spy, you have long been an able strategist and that you have a very capable mind. We have long desired that you might join us in our quest to protect ourselves from the carnivorous expansion plans of the King of Aztlan."

English nodded in thanks. "I appreciate your kind words, and your confidence General. I must tell you, though, that my allegiance has, for these 20 years, been with Phillip and the Ghost Militia." He walked over to the window, and looked down into the courtyard. Mexican soldiers were moving Aztlani soldiers, what few of them were left, into the yard of the Keep. "I suspect that your goals and those of the militia here in Texas are aligned, but you should know that I serve at the behest of Phillip, and Phillip alone."

"I understand," Loya nodded.

"From what I've gathered," English continued, "the Aztlani army of El Paso, ignorant of what has transpired here, is marching eastward with the intention of wiping out the militia... and all of the innocent and peaceful Vallensian people. What, may I ask, are your intentions in this regard?"

Loya sighed deeply. "I understand your concerns, and I share them. But we are a tiny army—only 2,000 men. These men were all that our king could spare, considering the concerns he has over his own southern border. We have no real cavalry, few guns, and very little experience. It seems that our best plan would be to stay here and defend this castle. We can recruit from among the locals—particularly among the Mexicans who have always disliked the King of Aztlan. We can seize any weapons left here in the castle, and we can train for the defense of El Paso. I do not see how we would be able to assist the militia at all." The General walked around to the back of the desk, as if he would sit, but he did not. He placed his hands on the desk and looked again at English. "Our mission... the order of our king... is to prevent the incursion and expansion of the King of Aztlan into Mexico. It seems to me that the best way to do that is to keep and defend this city."

English grimaced, and his eyes met those of the General. "If your honor will allow me... perhaps I can just offer a few more things to consider." Seeing Loya nod again, English put his arm behind his back and began to pace back and forth in front of the Duke's large desk. "An army of 6,000 Aztlani soldiers left here days ago to engage in an operation in Central Texas against a handful of freemen militia fighters and thousands of unarmed pacifists. If that operation is successful, and it seems certain that it will be, that army will be coming back here."

"Our army would be nothing against such a force in the open field, English," Loya said, "but here in this castle—in the midst of a walled city—2,000 men ought to be plenty. Defending a walled city is far easier than trying to assault a superior army in the open field."

"That is true sir, *if* your 2,000 men are defending against an attacking army of 6,000. But let me say that it is very unlikely that the attacking army will be only 6,000 men. You see, sir, most of the castle defenders escaped; and you can bet that many of them are, at this moment, galloping on horseback towards

New Rome. It is very likely, General, in fact, I would say it is absolutely certain, that the King of Aztlan is not going to sit idly on his hands while his entire southern army is left homeless and while his largest southern city—which also happens to be his only defense against Mexico and any other armies attacking from the south—is taken from him without a fight. Surrendering El Paso would leave the whole of Aztlan, including New Rome herself, open to attack from the south! That isn't going to happen, General. No, sir. I can assure you that you will not be facing an attacking force of 6,000 returning veterans who consider El Paso their home. No. You will probably be facing another army—one coming directly south from New Rome—and that army will be upwards of 20,000 strong if I were to hazard a guess.

"If, however, we were to go on the offensive," English said, lifting his hand into a fist, "if we were to rush eastward right now and strike the Aztlani force from the rear while they are engaged with the militia," English raised his fist and eyes towards the ceiling, "if we would strike a stunning and unexpected blow on Aztlan while they believe that they are strong and virtually unopposed, then... then, I believe that we can destroy that army before New Rome can respond to what has happened here."

The General looked down, leaning over the desk for a while before standing back up and breathing deeply. "So it is your considered opinion that New Rome will gamble everything to attack us here?"

"I don't perceive it as much of a risk for them, General. The King of Aztlan is safe and cozy up in his mountains. Twenty-thousand men is only a small portion of his available forces. He risks little to gain back his southern borders by destroying you here."

"It seems, Sir English, with all due respect, that you have been purposely kept out of the loop for some time. There is a hole in your logic—not in your intellect, which, I grant, is remarkable—but a hole in your logic caused by the lack of some very important facts."

English looked at the General quizzically and raised his eyebrows. "Perhaps, sir, you can enlighten me? I would definitely benefit by having any logic holes closed as soon as possible."

"I take it that you are wholly ignorant of what is happening in the north?" Loya asked.

"In New Rome, sir? I am probably ill-informed, but I wouldn't call it 'wholly ignorant'. I spent a lot of years in New Rome, and with the King of Aztlan."

"No, Sir Knight. Not in New Rome—farther *north*, in the former northern United States!"

"I'd have to admit sir, we have had little or no information from the north in the last 20 years. We've had rumors from travelers and captured looters, fairy tales and myths spread by storytellers and minstrels. At one point we were informed that most of the industrial centers were destroyed by nuclear missiles and bombs, and that the large cities had been completely wiped out. Our Aztlani theorists and intelligence groups produced a white paper, maybe ten years ago, that concluded that the population of the northern states had been reduced by more than 95% from its pre-crash levels due to extreme weather, riots, race war, criminal gangs, and of course the nuclear destruction in the cities."

"That was ten years ago, Sir English. We received those reports as well, but a lot has changed in ten years. Let us just say that the monster to the north of Aztlan may be worse than the monster in New Rome. I think you have a lot of catching up to do." General Loya sighed again before walking back around the desk and up to English.

"Sir English, you have given me much to think about. It is hard to say what the King of Aztlan may do. My men will fill you in on all of the intelligence we have on Aztlan and on the situation farther north. After you have had some time to consider it, I will receive your report and your recommendations as to how we ought to proceed from here."

English shook Loya's outstretched hand and held on to it for a moment. "Worse than Aztlan?"

"Perhaps, English. But how can we know?"

How, indeed, he thought. He released the General's hand and nodded. "Let me just say, General, before I retreat to
262

my office to study and pray..." He backed toward the door as he considered his words. "The Vallenses must be saved, sir. Without them, all of this is just senseless violence, with power, greed, and covetousness as the operative forces in the world. If we... those of us who put on uniforms and fight one another... if we are not fighting so that free people can live in peace and raise their families and do good, then... maybe it would have been better if God had wiped us all off of the earth."

"I see what you are saying, English, and in principle I agree. Maybe God will wipe us all off the earth anyway. He's made a good start of it. And, I can't say that I blame Him."

"Then save the Vallenses, General. Because as far as I can see, that may be the only reason God still has us here."

General Loya of Mexico walked over to the window and looked down into the courtyard. "Who knows, English. Maybe you're right."

Chapter 25 - Timothy

When the dust cleared, the Aztlani spies named Atticus and Leo lay dead in the street. Jonathan Wall was on top of the third spy, the boy named Troy; The Hood, Rob Fosse, and Marbus Claim still had their bows drawn and aimed at the fallen spies; and the blind old man named Oswald stood nodding his head with a smile touching his weathered face.

Ruth, seeing her father prone on the ground, launched herself past Timothy and sprinted to where he lay in the street. Timothy rushed after her, intent on doing his duty to keep her safe no matter the cost. He caught up with her and grabbed her by her shoulders, not sure that the exchange was completely over.

"Daddy!" she screamed, wrenching herself from Timothy's protective grasp.

"I'm ok, dear," Jonathan said, steadily climbing to his feet. "You stay back a bit until we get this sorted out."

"Where's Piggy?" Hood questioned, looking back towards the service station. "I expected he'd be the first one here to make sure they were all dead." He looked askance at the young man named Troy, then continued, "Clearly they are not... all dead, that is."

Timothy looked around and began walking over to the station. "I'll go check on him."

As he approached the low wall, and the opening between it and the service station, Piggy suddenly appeared before him, dusting off his pants and coat with his leather gloves.

A bit startled, "I... uh... hey, Piggy," was all he could think of to say.

"Oh," Piggy said, looking up and noticing Timothy, "Hello Tim. What's up?"

"Well, everyone was wondering where you were, so I said I'd come check on you."

"Well... isn't that nice of them."

"Where's Rollo?"

Piggy grimaced, half smile and half scowl, before putting his arm around Timothy and guiding him around the low wall. Once they were clear and could see behind the wall, he indicated with his glove towards a bound and gagged Rollo, who seemed to be unconscious. "Rollo is tied up for the moment."

He looked at Piggy in confusion, but was unable to frame a cogent question in his mind.

"This is going to be quite... delicate, and maybe perplexing for a moment, Timothy. Perhaps we ought to join the others and we'll try to clear this all up."

As they walked back towards the group in the middle of the dusty street, Timothy noticed that Rob Fosse and The Hood had bound the hands of the third Aztlani spy behind his back. Jonathan seemed to be attempting to intercede on the young spy's behalf, and Ruth still had a stunned and bewildered look on her face.

Rejoining the group, he could hear Jonathan pleading a case for mercy and leniency for the spy he called Troy. Rob Fosse and The Hood nodded their heads and remained silent out of respect while Jonathan asked for the militia to spare the boy's life, but did not look to be moved by it, nor did they loose the boy's bonds.

During a pause in the proceedings, a loud groan, followed by a very muffled scream could be heard emanating from behind the low wall. Everyone stopped and listened for a moment, and The Hood, Marbus Claim, and Ruth all quickly and quietly readied their bows. Piggy held up his hands to calm them, and was about to say something when The Hood spoke out... "What is that? Where is Rollo?" As he asked the question, Hood's eyes met Piggy's and you could see a look of exasperation pass over the militia tracker's face.

"Piggy! Piggy, what did you do?"

"I eliminated... or at least I incapacitated a threat."

Hood bowed his head, shaking it slowly. "Rollo?"

"That very Mountain."

A long, low growl, much like that of a bobcat caught in a trap, could be heard from behind the wall. Rob Fosse looked at Piggy. "Did you kill Rollo?" he asked.

"Not yet."

They all stood in awkward silence for a moment, waiting for Piggy to explain. He didn't.

"At some point are you going to tell us what you did to Rollo and why?" Rob asked.

"I would love to do that very thing, but people keep asking me pointless questions."

"So?"

"Like that one," Piggy said. He looked around, and saw that the confusion and irritation he was causing was not as amusing to everyone else as it was to him, so he relented. "Ok, we'll go inside and get our guests some water. Then I'll tell you why I have arrested Rollo The Mountain."

Marbus Claim was posted as a guard over the prisoners. Troy was bound and seated, and a now fully awake and obviously perturbed Rollo was hogtied on the ground. Timothy wasn't sure he could take much more of the suspense. He was curious to talk to Jonathan about his ordeal. He was also interested in the plight of Troy the young Aztlani spy. But he was most curious about why Piggy had arrested, bound, and gagged one of the most famous militia warriors then living. Rollo was a legend, and he had fought on the side of Phillip and the Ghost militia for many, many years. No one had anything but respect for Piggy and for his often preternatural physical and mental abilities and talents, so they could not even imagine that he had breached protocol and arrested Rollo without ample cause.

As they sat around in a circle, drinking cool water dipped from Oswald's water catchment box, the tension seemed to be a weight pressing down on them that only time and answers could lessen. Piggy took a long drink from his cup, wiped his mustache and beard with the back of his hand, and began to explain.

"Rollo is a traitor and a criminal, and I suspect that he is guilty of murdering the leadership of the militia back at His Honor Mr. Wall's ranch."

The shocking statement was short and to the point and hit everyone in the room like a cold, bracing wind from out of the north. Timothy just shook his head because there were too many loose ends, too much unknown, for him to grasp what was going on. He felt like his whole foundation was perilously close to collapsing.

After a long, painful period of muted gasping and muttering around the room, Jonathan Wall was the first to speak. "I don't know you all that well, Piggy, but I do expect that you have some reason... or some information... or some evidence that supports this suspicion?"

"Piggy!" Timothy sputtered, finally finding words and interrupting. "Are you saying that Phillip is dead? How can you know that?"

Piggy paused for a moment, then stood up, pulling one of his throwing knives from a sheath attached to the inside of his vest. He tapped the knife against his hand for awhile, then began to spin it casually as he spoke.

"I do believe that I have sufficient suspicion to have acted, Your Honor. And Timothy... I do not *know* that Phillip is dead. I *suspect* that he is dead, or at least very seriously injured. I suspect that Rollo has attempted to kill Phillip and Prince Gareth, and anyone else that might have gotten in his way."

Jonathan sighed. "So... you are saying that David might be dead as well?"

"He very well might be sir, but again, I don't know that. I just have a very solid suspicion that Rollo has been working for Aztlan for some time and that he has taken this opportunity to betray Phillip and the militia. I believe he is here now to kill you, Your Honor, and would have killed you just now if I had not intervened."

Rob Fosse stood up. "Piggy, these are very serious charges, and they are against a brother. Everyone here, along with all of the Vallenses and the militia, have the highest regard for your mind and your abilities. Personally, as Phillip's best friend and an officer in the militia, I have the utmost faith in your judgment and your intellect. I'm willing to go along with you here for a while, but... I'm hoping you are going to tell us why you suspect Rollo of treason."

"Thank you for your support, Rob," Piggy continued, the knife spinning lazily on his hand as he spoke, "it means a lot to me, and I do hope that I have not disappointed any of you." He walked over towards the doorway and leaned against it as if he were very, very tired. "I have suspected Rollo of being a traitor for a long time. In fact, I have been expecting him to make an attempt on Phillip's life for a long while. For letting down my guard, I hold myself responsible for any harm that has come to anyone. I am a soldier and must go where I am sent, so I could not offer any added protection for Phillip when absent. Frankly, I was surprised that Rollo didn't attempt to kill Phillip during the battle of Bethany, when I was at the Wall Ranch. When he didn't, I began to question myself and my discernment. I thought that perhaps I was wrong about the guy. For the first time in my life I began to have second thoughts about my own intuition. You see, Rollo has always been a mercenary. I've always believed that his allegiance to Phillip and the militia was feigned and that his loyalty was for sale. He always resented Phillip, and I could read that on his face as easily as any of you can read a book. I've studied the man. I've watched him. He always was trouble, and I never once trusted him. I've trained with him, and I've intently examined his movements while in battle. He exhibits every trait of the treasonous agent, and I could never show you that in a way that would convict him in any court. So I just had my private suspicions, and I waited and watched.

"When the farmer Ronald Getz attacked Gareth, my suspicions grew. Rollo was a friend of Getz, and I saw them meeting together on several occasions. Those impressions didn't mean anything to me until after Getz was exposed as a spy.

"As I said, I began to doubt myself after the Battle of Bethany, when Rollo didn't make a move on Phillip and Gareth, but that self-doubt began to drop away when I saw that Rollo was never surprised by the fact that the Battle of Bethany was just a

268

diversion for the larger attack to the East. I watched his face when we learned that the Vallenses had been slaughtered out by Comanche... a faint smile was on his lips, and I'm probably the only one who was watching him intently and saw it. Again, what could I charge him with? Smiling? Who would listen to me? Phillip would have taken it under advisement and sent me with the posse anyway. Frankly, I was just praying I was wrong.

"Then, he showed up at Harmony, traveling by himself and obviously under stress. When he said that he had a message for Jonathan, that was when I became quite certain that the deed was done." Piggy stood up and began to pace, putting the throwing knife back into its sheath. "There is no way Phillip would operate like that. All of you took his word for it, and I appreciate that, but I did not. Rob, you are the second in command of this militia. Do you now believe that Phillip would send a message to Jonathan, bypassing you? Do you think that, considering all that has happened, and that we were operating away from home in hostile territory, searching for the leader of the Vallenses, that Phillip would not give this message to *you* to deliver?"

Rob Fosse looked down, thinking on the questions intently. "I suppose you are right. It was odd. I didn't have the suspicions of The Mountain that you have. I suppose I should have asked. Thinking on it now, it definitely violated protocol and was very un-Phillip like."

"Exactly. Then, after the first night of travel, I went through Rollo's bag and found this." He pulled a pistol out of his coat and laid it on the table. "It has been fired twice, recently."

"What is Rollo doing with a pistol?" Timothy asked.

"That is the point, Tim," Piggy replied. "What is he doing with a pistol? Whom did he shoot? Why all the secrecy? If we were to have guns on this mission, we could all have been issued weapons from the armory at Harmony. None of this tracks! It only adds up if you consider my hypothesis... what I already suspected but could not prove, that Rollo is an agent of Aztlan and that he is actively beheading the opposition." Piggy looked around the room. They knew he had more to say, so everyone remained silent.

"That leads us to this afternoon. I was watching him. I had already taken the gun, and he never knew it was missing. I was waiting for him to make his move on Jonathan when he appeared. His behavior even further proved my suspicions. He moved down that wall away from the conflict, supposedly to increase the triangulation, but I could tell that he was angling for a shot at Mr. Wall. His angle put him in a cross-fire position and it put you, Rob, at risk. He could have taken you both out with one or two arrows properly placed. This is completely against our training. And, he couldn't stop watching me. He knew that I knew something. He was afraid. He was taking a lot of time lining up his shot, so I threw a knife at the spies and then, without pausing I threw my hunting knife and hit him with the blunt end, knocking him unconscious. I bound him up, and now... here we are."

There was silence in the room as everyone considered the evidence against Rollo. No one moved, and it seemed that there was scarcely any breathing for a full minute. Piggy looked up, and then back around the room. "Based on all of my suspicions, on his blatant violations of militia protocol, and the importance of the issue, I acted. And here is the deal... if he is innocent, we will know when we get him back to the Ranch and find out if Phillip is alive and unharmed. We have no need to hear his case until we get back to the Ranch. Either Phillip has been attacked, or I am wrong. I am willing to stake my reputation and future that I am right."

Rob Fosse nodded his head in agreement. "It obviously is a critically important issue. I pray to God that you are wrong, Piggy."

"As do I."

Timothy stood up and began to pace a little around the room. "I trust you Piggy. I can't say that I ever trusted Rollo. I respected his position and his experience, but he always did seem a bit shady to me. I'm with Rob. I hope you are wrong, but I think you have done the right thing."

As the others around the room, including Jonathan began to nod their heads, an ear-splitting crash shook the room as the door splintered inward and the bound and gagged Troy

270

tumbled to the ground at Piggy's feet. Piggy already had a knife drawn, and Ruth had instinctively drawn her bow, only to be stopped by her father, who gave her a silent look of disapproval. Piggy reached down and lifted up the obviously distraught young man, who was grunting and yelling into his gag. Piggy pulled down the gag and Troy sputtered for breath before yelling, "He's escaped! He's escaped!" Blood trickled down from a scratch on his head where it had made contact with the heavy wooden door. "He knocked the boy unconscious, and he took off on one of the horses. I tried to stop him, but I couldn't yell. He rode off to the northwest!"

The militia members began to ready themselves for pursuit, when Rob called them all to a halt.

"He's gone. He's no good to us now. We have our answer. If he were innocent, he'd have been pleased to go back and prove that Phillip was unharmed. He knew what awaited him back there. This is absolute proof that what Piggy said was true. Let him go and live with his conscience. We have a lot to do. I pray that Phillip and everyone else is alive and well back at the ranch, but we need to prepare ourselves for the worst."

Piggy looked at Rob and nodded. "You are the ranking militia leader here. We are at your command." Ruth grabbed Timothy's hand and rushed out shouting "Marbus!" and the others followed them into the courtyard.

Young Marbus Claim was just then beginning to stir. He had been knocked unconscious with a blow from a rock behind his left ear. Blood trickled down onto his tunic and the boy was extremely groggy and disoriented. Piggy tended to him and Ruth got him some water to drink as the other militia men huddled with Jonathan Wall, discussing their options. In time, Piggy rejoined the council and pronounced that Marbus had a slight concussion, but should be alright in time.

Jonathan prevailed on Rob Fosse to loose Troy from his bonds and the young man was grateful, while still understanding that once he was back at the ranch he would be put on trial for the death of the militia man Morell, and for the attack on Raymond Stone.

The party headed back towards Bethany slowly, taking into account their injured and the heat of the day. At Big Lake they rested again, not heading out on that second day until late in the evening, as the cooler air invaded the desert. Timothy spent a good portion of the trip talking at length with Ruth. She was very worried that her brother might be dead, and she did not know what would become of all of them if Phillip had been killed. The worst part, she said, was not knowing. Timothy agreed, and he found himself entertaining thoughts of being a Vallenses. He wondered how he would act, and what he might do if he had been raised among the Vallenses. Both Ruth and Jonathan seemed to believe that David's fate, if indeed he had suffered violence, was a natural and expected result of his adoption of violence as a means, and of his uniting with the militia. This was a puzzle that Timothy was far from solving. The puzzle of the Vallenses, their relationship with the militia, and the use of violence towards good and noble ends, was perhaps too much for a young orphan to try to figure out. The two men he admired most—Jonathan of the Vallenses and Phillip of the militia—were on complete opposite ends of the spectrum on the issue of violence. *Maybe,* he thought, *it is something that each man must figure out for himself.*

As they traveled eastward the ground began to ascend slowly upwards towards a low mesa formation that overlooked several miles of lowland plain about 40 miles due west of Harmony, and the party moved very slowly upwards—not willing to push themselves, their tired horses, or their injured men too hard. As they crested the top of the rise, Timothy was the first to see the sight across the plain, and the impact of it took his breath away so that he could only gasp at the vision.

Spread across the valley, shimmering in the late summer Texas sun, arrayed as a single beast with banners, was the 6,000 man Aztlani army newly arrived from El Paso. Timothy blinked, hoping that what he saw was a mirage, while the heat rising from the valley in the distance and the many enemy flags unfurled and whipping in the wind gave the scene a frighteningly surreal quality. One thousand horses stomped impatiently in the dried

272

and rocky dirt creating small billows of dust that made the army look as if it floated ethereally on an evil earthen cloud.

Timothy and Ruth looked at one another and their wordless communication resounded outward to everyone in the party. *What hath evil wrought?*

Piggy alone was able to summon the words that no one else was willing to voice...

"Looks like we're not too late for the party."

Chapter 26 - Ana

The Wall Ranch was churning with activity. More and more refugees from the Piney Woods and parts east were arriving at the ranch daily, pushed as they were from behind by the threatening advance of the army of the Duke of Louisiana. Everything seemed to be a continuous swirl of motion with some refugees arriving even as others were loaded up and headed further westward towards Harmony.

A few days earlier the wheels of constant movement had slowed down just long enough to allow for the burial of David Wall over in the peach orchard next to his mother Elizabeth. Most everyone took the day off—it being the Sabbath—to attend an impromptu wake, and so many people came by to visit Betsy Miller and her husband Paul that the line of those hoping to extend condolences stretched well over a mile down the Bethany road. Eventually, Ana, Wally, and Mr. Byler the cobbler had been forced to ride down the line of well-wishers to bid them all go home. They explained that Betsy and all of the Walls understood and accepted their love and appreciated their condolences, but that the day long wake was much too tiring, and the pain of loss was still too fresh for it all to go on much longer. Still, although the flow of guests through the Miller's tent was staunched, very few people actually went home.

Long hours after Ana and John Johnson closed off all access to the tent where the Miller family was living, the line of Vallensian friends continued to pass slowly by on the road, continuing until well after midnight and into the early morning. The grieving friends stopped to look and pray before traveling back to their homes, or returning by lantern light to their own tents pitched among the throng of refugees.

Ana felt like she had been forced to bury more than her beloved David. Maybe she had to bury the insular feeling of safety and security she had come to expect since the day she had arrived at the ranch. The Walls were the only *real* family she had known in her life, and she had lived with them almost three times longer than she had been married to Hamish.

When she first met David he was just a little boy, five-years-old, bursting with energy, and in possession of an infinitely curious mind—one almost impossible to satisfy. Now he was dead... *and maybe his father is too.* She banished the thought from her mind. She could not even begin to think that Jonathan might be dead. And Ruth was gone with the posse. She smoothed her apron and dress with her hands, nervously. *God, keep the rest of the Wall family safe!*

Down in the wheat field—now cleared of all of the wheat shocks—the militia leaders were forming up units of new recruits formed primarily out of the ranks of the newly arrived East Texas Vallenses. Seeing the Vallensian units lined up in ranks was a strange and discordant vision to Ana. The Vallensian elders had ruled unanimously to re-establish Jonathan's recent decree that any Vallensian adult male who wanted to join the militia could do so, provided he understood that he would be unceremoniously removed from the close fellowship of the Vallenses' Church. Of the Vallenses from Central Texas, only a few hundred decided that the time had come to fight; but of the newly arrived East Texas Vallenses, most of whom had never known Jonathan personally, almost 5,000 men had immediately signed up to join Phillip and the Ghost militia as they marched west towards the onrushing battle. These Vallenses, though they were strong, smart, and shot well, were decidedly not battle hardened militia troops. These were pacifist farmers and tradesmen who had finally concluded, to the satisfaction of their own consciences, that they had no more cheeks left to turn. So, a strange reality had settled in among the free people of Central Texas; thousands of formally peaceful farmers were now drilling day and night for war, while tens of thousands more—those who would not fight—were again packing their belongings and heading into the unknown future that they believed God had ordained for them. All of them were now headed towards Harmony.

Ana knew that both categories of Vallenses were doing what they believed they must do, and that both were praying for God to help them and support their endeavors. But she could not help but think that everything might be different if Jonathan were here to lead them.

As she watched the newly formed Vallensian units learn to march in the wheat field, she saw old friends and acquaintances drilling among them, while others were watching from along the sides of the field. The *oldling* Lew Tibault the papermaker was watching from the high weeds along the side of the road. Lew was too old to fight, but his seventeen year old apprentice (and adopted son) Doug was there in the ranks, marching in place and trying to keep time in his head. Lew often said that Doug was a better papermaker than he had ever hoped, and that the boy seemed to have been born with the talent and wit to make paper. Now, young Doug was going to war with the sword and probably a gun as well. Over there, marching silently, was Maurice Stannis and his boys Lance and Walter. Few people had doubted that the Stannis men would eventually go to war. Grayson Smith, one of the heroes of the Battle of Bethany, and his friend Davidson Cooper were both there among the Vallensian militia contingent.

Ana hoped and prayed, with all of her heart and mind, that the trouble could be averted, and that something would happen to make it all stop. But the refugees from East Texas kept pouring in, pushed ahead of an incessant and insatiable enemy army from the East; and, on top of this, everyone knew that the Aztlani army was closing in on the ruins of San Angelo. There was no stopping the battle. This, she knew.

When she had finally made it across the violent clearing that was Interstate 20, Ana disappeared into the darkness again, continuing her long walk southward. As she walked she soon found herself in some very rugged terrain. The trees grew thickly and mesquite thorns grabbed at her clothing and she only made progress with great difficulty.

After another full day of walking, she made her camp in a heavily wooded copse of trees on what must have been a very large ranch. She found an elevated deer feeder made of an old 50 gallon metal barrel that still had some corn in it, so she filled her pockets and her plastic sack with handfuls of the dried kernels. About a hundred feet away from the deer feeder she found a windmill that fed clear water into a small concrete tank for cattle, so she finished off the water she still had, then refilled the water bottles from the tank.

Taking one of the empty bottles, she first filled it about halfway with corn so that, in time, the water could soften and rehydrate it. She sat down behind the water tank and ate her last tin of tuna, then returned to her copse of trees where she made a rudimentary bed and shelter of cedar branches before lying down and falling into a deep sleep that carried her through the night. Her last thought before drifting off was a very clear vision of what was still going on back at the Interstate. She shivered at the thought, though the night was quite warm. She was so glad to be across that border knowing that there were no other major Interstates between her current position and the lands of the Vallenses.

She didn't know if the Vallenses would take her in, and she could not blame them if they would not. She knew that she had nowhere else to go, so she rested satisfied in the thought that perhaps God had brought her this far, against impossible odds, because he had desired to bless the Vallenses somehow... through her. Maybe she was called to serve them in some fashion, or perhaps she could do something to help them. That thought pleased her, and having had food and water, before long she drifted into a deep and restful sleep.

She woke up to the sound of her plastic bag rustling loudly, and in the scant light of dawn she could see that a squirrel had worked his way into her grocery sack where he was happily stealing some of her corn. Instinctively more than anything, she rolled over and snatched up the bag, closing it before the thief could flee out of the opening. Without even considering what she was doing, she grabbed hold of the squirrel through the bag and, finding its head, she twisted solidly until she knew that the neck was broken. She had never killed anything before, if you didn't count a dog she hit with her car on the way to work when she was 19, but killing the animal didn't freak her out or alarm her. She had seen it done on hunting shows and in videos she had bought about processing chickens.

She didn't really know what she was doing, but before long she had taken out the pocket knife and, fairly effectively, had cut out whatever meat could be found on the squirrel. She wanted to cook the meat, but cooking without fire was a mystery she had yet to solve, so she ended up talking herself into eating the small bits of meat raw. She knew she needed the protein, and she knew that life as she had known it was now over. Her grieving period for Hamish and for the old world she had always known was over as well. That life, and the love of it, had passed from her during that interminable period spent watching the murder and mayhem happening on I-20, and she no longer doubted that she had to do what it would take to survive. So chewing the raw meat wasn't exactly how she wanted to start her day, but absent a nice cup of coffee it would just have to do.

Just for a brief moment, she wondered what she looked like—sitting there in the filthy clothes she had been wearing on the day of the collapse—with squirrel blood on her hands and chewing on the raw flesh of a rodent.

She had always been considered attractive—remarkably so, according to some accounts. Many of the problems and heartaches of her life, she had learned, were a result of her good looks—or at least the pride she had always had about her good looks. She had made bad decisions when it came to men, and even her marriage—she now knew—had been a mistake, largely enabled by the fact that Hamish had heavily fed her ego.

From Jonathan she had learned that a woman's beauty, in order for it to be real and not a tool of manipulation, must come from inside. She must have a beautiful mind, a beautiful heart, and be beautiful in her love of God and others. Her entire life she had used her looks to manipulate men, and she had grown miserable and sad from it. Humility and meekness were traits she needed desperately, and she wondered if her current adventure was how she was to learn these things.

She had hardly finished the meal, when she heard footsteps coming towards her through the trees. Panicked, she

278

ducked down and tried to hide, but it was too late, and she had been too slow. Looking up, she could feel her heart pound in her chest, as two men and two women came towards her pointing guns at her.

"Get down!" the largest man yelled at her, and she ducked her head while thrusting her hands up into the air. "Stay down." The four strangers came directly into her camp and began rifling through her meager belongings, while the large man—a clean shaven, dark haired man who looked like a salesman—kept the gun trained on her chest.

"I'm trying to go south to meet some friends," she sputtered, her voice betraying her fear and desperation. "My husband has been murdered. Our car died up near Albany. I'm all alone... I'm... all... alone," she said as she began to cry.

"Stop crying, lady," the salesman said pitilessly, "everyone has a sob story. We're just making sure you aren't a looter or some killer trying to harm innocent people."

"I swear to you I am not. I don't even own a weapon. I've been walking for days. I'm trying to meet up with some friends of mine down south of here. I promise."

"Did you just eat that squirrel raw?" Salesman asked. He looked at her askance, like she was some kind of beast.

"I was hungry," she replied, sheepishly, trying to wipe the blood onto her jeans.

"Well," the salesman continued, "you'll have to come back to the house with us. We'll get it all sorted out there."

"Ok... Ok... Good. Back to the house." She looked over her four captors. They did not look like your stereotypical 'bad men'. *Maybe they work in an office somewhere near here. Maybe a car dealership,* she thought. Their clothes were dirty, but of good quality, and they weren't tattooed or scary in any way. *Middle-class office workers.* Maybe she would be alright. Maybe they were just some people who were as scared as she was.

The long walk back to the ranch house was tense. Nobody said anything to her, and twice she noticed as the women looked at her in a strange way—looking away quickly when she caught them staring. *Almost as if they pity me.* She wasn't used to that. Why would they pity her? Maybe they were affected by the fact that her husband had been murdered. Wow. She hadn't thought of that. To her, the catastrophe up near Albany all seemed so long ago. Now, these women looked at her as if to say, "I am so glad I am not her!" *So strange, to not feel that pity for myself.*

When they made it back to the house, she noticed that the area looked as if a long gun battle had taken place there.

"We've had some trouble," the salesman said, almost too cavalierly. A black pickup truck was parked across the driveway, and it had been 'T-boned' by a silver sedan that had evidently been trying to back up speedily from the house. The sedan was riddled with bullets and there was dried blood and broken glass all over the place.

Upon entering the house, she began to be frightened again. The house was a mess, as if burglars or spies had gone through it looking for something. When she turned to ask what had happened, she felt the gun poke her in the back, and then the salesman grunted at her while pointing towards a closed door. "Down there, squirrel lady," he ordered, "down to the basement."

Now she was frightened. In the basement she saw more dried blood, and the whole picture began to congeal for her in her mind. *These are the bad guys! Why are they dressed so nicely?* She thought about running... about fighting, but there was no way she would make it. There was nowhere to go.

Salesman began to tie her up to a support post in the basement, while saying nothing to her at all.

"Why are you doing this?"

"Shut up, lady. Don't you know what is going on in the world? We all have to do whatever we have to do."

"No. No. In fact I do not know what is going on in the world! Tell me."

"The stuff hit the fan...just like everyone was saying it would. The whole world has melted down. There are riots everywhere. No place is safe. That's why we came here. Now shut up, because I don't need you whining or talking or making trouble."

"Making trouble? I'm an innocent person! My husband has been killed. I need your help!"

Salesman started to laugh. "You need *my* help? Really? No, lady, because you are screwed. Everyone's on their own. No rules. That's just the way it has to be. You belong to us now, and we'll keep you here as long as we might be able to use you or trade you. If you stop being of value, we'll kill you and bury you in the yard with the family that lived here."

"You... killed them? Why?"

"Because they killed my friends, that's why!" Salesman was growing emotional and was emphasizing his points by pointing a finger into her face. "Because they had stuff we needed, and they weren't about to give it to us! Didn't you see all that mess up there in the driveway? They killed two of our friends when we tried to take their car. Our truck was out of gas. We just needed their car, and they shot us! So yeah... we killed them. They got what was coming to them. They should have just let us take the car. But they wrecked it, and wrecked the truck and now we're stuck here too, and so are you."

He finished tying her up and then smiled at her.

"Someone will come along and want to trade, and we'll trade you for a car or a horse or something. Or perhaps we'll kill them and take a car... who knows? Anyway, I told you to shut up, so shut up. You better not make a sound. You see, I don't care if you live or die and I'm not in the mood for trouble. Just keep it quiet or you'll be sorry."

"I don't get it. You all don't look like murderers. Why are you doing this?"

"Listen lady, I have a family too. You're not the only one whose life sucks right now, ok?" He paused for a moment, staring upwards as if he were trying to remember something that might have happened ages ago. "We were working at one of our insurance branches in Abilene when it happened. Six of us were here from the Dallas office. After the stuff started happening, we hung around thinking things were going to get straightened out, but they just got worse. A couple of days ago we gave up waiting and tried to drive back home, but the Interstate was impossible. There were ambushes everywhere, and a couple of times we barely escaped being killed. So, we turned south and drove around looking for help until we came upon this place.

"We were on fumes, man. We decided that we needed a car with gas in it, and we saw these folks sitting in their driveway. Apparently they were planning on going somewhere... probably too stupid to know that the Apocalypse had happened."

Salesman was now rationalizing, trying to convince himself more than anything. "We had talked about it a lot while we were driving around trying not to get killed. The gloves were off, man. Everyone is, like, just doing whatever they need to do, so that's what we decided we would do. You try to play nice in this world and people will cut your throat. I'm not dyin' out here, lady! I've got a family to get back to. Screw you and screw everybody!"

She noticed that Salesman was no longer really talking to her. He was talking to himself. He was rationalizing his crimes, and he expected her to listen and agree with him. She decided that it was best just to stay quiet.

"We decided we were going to take the car," he continued, "and if they had just let us, no one would have gotten hurt. But, when we, like, rushed up on the car, the old man just started shooting! Do you believe that? Shooting at us! He killed two of our co-workers, Tyler and Reggie. They got it in the chest... up close and personal. So we rushed the guy and I knocked him out with a tire iron. You shoulda heard the sound! It sounded like a melon popping. He had it coming, the bastard. Anyway, so we killed 'em. Who cares. They killed my friends, so I killed them. Self-defense. That's the way it goes."

"You were trying to steal from them, that's not self-defense."

"It ain't stealing if you need it lady. And, everyone is doing it."

"Oh my."

"Listen, I don't need you judging me! Just shut up, I tell you!"

"You are animals!"

282

Salesman smacked her suddenly and forcefully across the face. He stood looking down on her with rage in his face, and then he spit on her before wiping his mouth with his sleeve.

"You don't mean anything to me lady. I'll kill you too. I've got a family to get home to."

"Would you like someone to do this to your wife?"

"Shut up, lady! Everyone's got a sob story. Maybe yours will end well. But I doubt it."

Salesman stuffed a small rag into her mouth then gagged her violently before disappearing back up the stairs. She was left alone. *I'm going to die here*, she thought. Then she prayed.

After a few hours, she heard a ruckus upstairs. There were some thuds and a few screams, but before long it got silent. After a painfully long time she heard the door at the top of the stairs open slowly, and she heard the sounds of footsteps carefully descending the stairs. She looked up and saw a rough looking man with a full black beard staring at her. Her heart began thudding again. *Oh God! Oh God!* The man was dressed in rough "field hand" clothing, and he had a very large knife. If her captors were dressed like "good guys", this guy looked like bad news. She thought that she might faint.

The bearded man looked around the basement carefully, then came over to her and crouched down near her.

"My name is Rob Fosse. I work with Phillip of the Central Texas militia. My men are upstairs. We're not here to harm you."

She closed her eyes and continued to pray, as the man named Rob cut her bonds and removed the gag from her mouth. Her jaw was sore, and she found it difficult to speak.

"Help," was all she could manage.

"Ma'am," Rob Fosse said, gently. "I'm sorry for whatever you've been through, but we are here to help you. Please come with me."

"I'm not going anywhere with you!" she screamed, "I just want to be left alone!"

Rob Fosse had looked at her and just nodded his head. On his belt he had a holster, and in the holster he had a military looking pistol. He drew the weapon, and locked his eyes on

Ana. "Ma'am, this is a Beretta nine millimeter pistol. Do you know how to operate one of these?"

"Yes," she lied.

Rob flipped the pistol around and handed it to her. She didn't know what to think. Slowly, she raised her hand and took the pistol, keeping it pointed at the strange man with the beard.

"The safety is on," he said, pointing at the gun, "there is one in the chamber." He turned and began to walk back towards the stairs.

"Halt!" she hollered, weakly.

"Halt?" he said, turning back to her and smiling.

"Just... stop for a minute, okay?"

"Okay."

"What's going on? Why are you leaving? Why did you give me this gun?"

"Because you obviously need it, and because you want to be left alone, and because you have no reason to trust me or anybody else."

"What happened to the people who... were here... the four people who killed the people who owned this ranch, and then took me hostage."

"They're being handled. Don't worry about them."

"More killing?"

"Ma'am, I couldn't begin to explain to you what all is going on out there... but then again, maybe you know already. There are no police. There is no law. The militia is the law for right now, and we're trying our best to stabilize the area. We have placed a cordon around the Vallenses, who are a peaceful, Christian group living just south of here. We're just operating in this area to try to keep Jonathan Wall and the Vallensian people safe."

"Jonathan Wall?"

"Yes. He is a good friend of Phillip, our leader."

"Jonathan Wall!" she shouted. "That is where I'm going! I'm going to meet Jonathan Wall! I mean... I'm heading south. I don't know Jonathan... but... my husband was killed. I..." she stumbled over her words, pausing before starting again. "...I am a

284

student of Jonathan's. He doesn't know me, but I've been trying to get to him since the crash happened."

"Well, then perhaps we can do this over again," Rob said smiling. "I'm sorry, Ma'am, for whatever you've been through, but we are here to help you. Please come with me." He held out his hand for the gun.

Slowly, she lowered the weapon and let him take it from her hand.

The Vallenses, both the newly recruited Vallensian militia, and the thousands of Vallensian refugees, were now all packed up and heading westward towards Harmony. The long, lonely train stretched for miles down the Bethany road. Ana was in the wagon with Betsy and Paul Miller and their children, but her mind was on Jonathan Wall. She hoped he was alive, and that she would see him again. She had fought so hard to get here. *If I ever see him again, I will tell him what I have failed to say for all of these twenty years... I will tell him that I love him... even if he doesn't feel the same way about me.* The slow swaying of the wagon emphasized the emotion and angst that seemed to wash over her mind and soul. Her head dropped. Once again, she was heading out into the unknown, and once again she felt like she was all alone in the world.

As Rob Fosse led her out of the house, she saw the four murdering looters lined up with their backs to the wall of an old red barn. The Salesman wouldn't look at her. Their hands were tied behind their backs, and they weren't blindfolded. They stood there with unmixed and undiluted terror expressed freely on their faces, staring at a firing squad of seven militia men with rifles. She didn't know what to think about that, but she caught the looter women looking at her guiltily as she rode by. She pitied them, and her eyes communicated that she was glad it wasn't her staring at readied rifles with her back to a barn.

Chapter 27 - Gareth

He was impressed with the setup at Harmony. How Phillip had been prescient and skilled enough to design and build such a facility—and actually, he was told, several of them—before the collapse, only deepened his respect for the Ghost.

He could see that years of silent and steady planning and work, along with thousands and thousands of dollars had gone into the design and construction of Harmony. Yet, however useful and well planned it was, the location was not an ideal defensible position. The facility was built into the walls of a caliche pit that covered many acres, meaning that the defenders—if indeed the plan was to defend the facility—would be on low ground, with their attackers above them... far from ideal.

Harmony was designed to store enough food and supplies for a very long period of time, but for hundreds and not tens of thousands. The facility was large enough to hold the throngs of Vallenses, but not comfortably, and not for any real length of time. An enemy could surround Harmony and just wait. Starvation, disease, and other miseries would finish off the plain people in short order.

Phillip had hinted that he had a plan, and no one doubted that he had, but thus far the plan was still hidden in the breast of the militia leader. If anyone knew the plan, Gareth was ignorant of it. Preparations to house the guests were proceeding furiously. Everyone knew (even the enemy, it was assumed) that the Vallenses were on their way. As of yet, only the newly recruited Vallensian milita units had begun to arrive.

Gareth watched the frenzy of activity from the back of his horse atop one of the cliffs that looked down over the Harmony "hole." He wondered if, as Phillip had said, this might be the last stand of the freemen of Central Texas. He knew from scouts that the army of the Duke of El Paso, maybe over 5,000 men, was on the way from the southwest. He knew that the army of the Duke of Louisiana, numbered in the thousands as well, was coming hard from the east. Gareth assumed, as all of the leaders of the Ghost Militia did, that his father, the king, was sending a large force from New Rome.

He shook his head. Even if the defenders of Harmony could fight off the maybe thousands of attackers from the west and from the east, which was not at all probable... even if they could defeat a force twice their size in the open field and from low ground—a precarious and difficult to defend position... even if they could outlast or outfight such a huge force... they would almost immediately be facing another army two to three times that size coming in from New Rome. *Bleak* was the only faithful and honest word to describe the outlook of the next couple of days.

He knew that Phillip was a phenomenal fighter, and a brilliant tactician. The comparisons between Phillip and Stonewall Jackson were legitimate and well deserved. Still, at some point, the odds became too great, the conditions became too difficult to overcome, and the likelihood of success dwindled to almost zero. Gareth knew that his own survival, logically, required him to flee and seek the forgiveness of his father, the king. But he also knew that he would never do that. His position was a principled one and not one of expediency or a desire for power. Aztlan must be resisted at all costs, and he was willing to die to make that point. If he did die, he would be portrayed as a rebel and an opportunist. He would be trumpeted as a traitor to his own people. The truth, he knew, was otherwise, and he was satisfied to let the God of Heaven rule on how Crown Prince Gareth of Aztlan was to be remembered.

As thoughts of martyrdom or ignominy washed over him, he did not hear as Phillip rode up next to him and sat quietly looking out over the massive hole in the ground that was Harmony.

Gareth looked up, and at last noticed that Phillip was sitting there quietly on his warhorse Babieca, examining the multitude of men who went about minutely following his commands in and around Harmony.

"Ah, Ghost... you never seem to tire of appearing magically without being seen or noticed."

"I cannot make others see or hear what they cannot see or hear. This stallion weighs upwards of a ton, and makes much more noise than he should. It's not like he's wearing slippers, Prince Gareth."

He smiled. Phillip really could not imagine why people were not more aware of their surroundings and ordered in their thinking. The Ghost did not see himself as gifted or special. He saw everyone else as plodding, dull, and particularly unconcerned about the limitations of their five senses.

Gareth looked at Phillip and nodded his head. "So we are to have Phillip's last stand in a hole with no possibility of escape? Am I reading this correctly?"

"Based on what you know, I don't blame you for thinking that this looks like a hopeless defense. I should tell you though, that our prognosis is far from hopeless. The addition of the Vallensian troops will help us tremendously. More than they can possibly imagine."

"But, how are we going to fight them? I've been to the best military schools available in the post-collapse world. I've never seen anyone as good as you, but I cannot fathom how you plan on holding out in this location against such a force coming from two different directions. Phillip... you know this is not the way we fight. The Ghost militia has never chosen to fight in this manner."

"As I said," Phillip answered, calmly, "based on the information that you have, I cannot blame you for your confusion."

"At any point do you plan on sharing your plans with me?"

Phillip sat still for a moment, looking out over the work going on at Harmony. After a long pause, he spoke again, "You said, 'we'."

"Excuse me?"

"You said, 'we'. You said, 'this is not the way *we* fight.'"

"I did say that," Gareth answered.

"Can I believe that? Can I believe that now that the prognosis looks bleak that I can trust the Crown Prince of Aztlan with my most critical plans? Can I conclude that Rollo, my trusted Lieutenant and friend has abandoned and betrayed me, while you—the rich and entitled son of my enemy—will remain by my side?"

"You know," was all that Gareth said.

The militia leader looked down and brushed the mane of his horse with his hand, before looking back at him. "Yes. I suppose I do. I suppose I must trust you and place all of this... our future, and our freedom... in your hands."

"If you do not trust me, Phillip, I ask you to kill me now. I am not here for fame, or fortune, or heroism, or adventure. I am not even here for a kingdom, which would be the most plausible reason for me to be at war with my father."

"Then why are you here, Prince Gareth?"

Gareth looked back over his shoulder to the northwest, squinting as if he could see all the way to Aztlan. Then, he looked into Phillip's eyes. "I am here because, as every man born into royalty ought to do, I love my people, and I desire to serve their best interests. I want them to be free of the tyranny and imperialism of my father. I want them to be free to live as you live, and as the Vallenses live."

"A lesser man could rationalize sacrificing us at this point, to save his own skin... all to 'help' his people, of course," Phillip said.

"It will be no help to me or my people for freedom to perish anywhere."

"You have no selfish motives?" Phillip asked.

"All of my motives are selfish," he replied, exhaling deeply. "I selfishly want you, the Ghost militia, and the Vallenses to rise up and snatch my father from the throne. I selfishly pray that the King of the South States will see our valiant and heroic efforts and come to our aid. I selfishly look for help in our cause from every quarter. I selfishly do not care how many men are lost in overcoming the evil my father represents on this earth.

"I must admit, Phillip, that I dream of sitting on the throne of Aztlan, ruling benevolently, as our friend and my teacher Sir English taught me. I admit that there is some ego involved with believing that I am born to this greatness, and deserving of this power. I am just egotistical enough to believe that I am able and worthy to rule Aztlan."

Phillip nodded. "I have to say, Prince, that such questions of government and rule are now beyond me. My life is very provincial, and I cannot see afar off. I am no Napoleon."

"This is why you are compared to Stonewall."

"Those comparisons miss the mark entirely, but I am powerless to stop them."

The two friends sat silently for some time, before Phillip began to speak again. "I hope you won't be offended if some small details of my plans remain private. The success of my plan requires that there be a 'need-to-know' application here."

"I understand."

Phillip looked out over Harmony, and began to point with his hand. "Our plan is to arrange our forces in rings, spreading outward from Harmony, which will be at the center. The outermost forces will confront the enemy from dugouts, trenches, and reinforced emplacements. The duty of these forces will be to cause Aztlan, from whatever side he approaches, to expend himself on an enemy he cannot see, and cannot quantify.

"These forces will not be able to hold out for long, maybe only minutes, but they will confuse and delay the enemy. When Aztlan breaks through, the first ring of defenders will scatter and form up behind the enemy. From there, the second 'ring' of forces will engage in what will look like a frontal defense, facing the oncoming armies; but the center of each line will collapse in the middle, much like what we did at the Penateka Dam, but with a substantive difference. We will draw the enemy in at the center of each line, while our flanks hold out and maintain their positions."

"Won't Aztlan suspect this move? Will they have intelligence from Penateka that you have done this before?"

"It won't matter. Perhaps they suspect it, perhaps they do not. If they do, then they will hesitate, and we will gain advantage. If they do not suspect that they are being drawn in, then they will come hard, and our flanks will surround them."

"This sounds very familiar to Hindenburg's brilliant defensive victory at Tannenburg in 1914."

"In some ways it is, though we will not likely have the benefit of Russian incompetence and arrogance," Phillip laughed.

"Don't underestimate Aztlani incompetence and arrogance, Phillip!"

"The advantage we have," Phillip continued, "is that the Aztlanis—despite your wonderful speech—are not a monolithic 'people' in the ethnic sense. The warriors of Aztlan are mostly mercenaries and slaves. They don't fight for your father, they fight for food, money, booty, or just because they are forced to fight. They lose heart easily, as we saw in your battle in the woods near the Wall ranch."

He nodded his head. "There will be many of them, Phillip."

"I know."

"And, don't forget that a larger army will be coming from New Rome. Maybe it is already here," he added.

"We will deal with the army from New Rome when they get here. First, we will fight the enemy we see."

Phillip looked down and saw that a militia signalman was messaging him from near the hidden entrance to Harmony. He pulled on the reins of his horse. "Shall we?"

As the two men rode slowly back down into the artificial canyon, Phillip continued to explain his plan. "As the enemy breaches through each concentric circle, the far ends of the line will flank them, while the inner portions give way and draw them in. Then those forces will disappear as they join the flanking forces. In this way, we draw Aztlan and the Louisianans into the center of the centermost circle."

"Harmony?"

"Harmony."

"Your plan is to make Aztlan defend this hole in the ground?" Gareth asked.

"That is my plan."

"My goodness!" Gareth exclaimed. "Who ever thought of such a thing? That is like opening the door of your indefensible castle to your enemy while you escape out of the windows... all so you can be the attacking force, while your enemy is forced to defend!"

"Precisely."

"Wow."

"It may not work, Gareth."

"Well," he said, "no one will ever accuse you of being overly cautious. It may not work, but it is brilliant nonetheless."

"It all comes down to execution, Gareth. If we can execute—and there is no promise that we can—it can work. Most of our force is made up of newbie Vallenses who have never fought a day in their lives. But if they can follow orders, then we can prevail against a much larger force."

"But what of the Vallenses? What of the refugees... the non-combatants? I see you are making plans to house them inside the Harmony complex. How are you to defend them when you let the enemy in the front door with them?"

"That, my friend Prince, is one of the secrets that is on a need-to-know basis. And, unhappily, you do not need to know."

Gareth shook his head heartily. "It boggles the mind, Phillip. How long did it take you to come up with this plan?"

Phillip looked at Gareth and smiled, "Thirty years."

"You aren't joking, are you?"

"Nope."

"Stunning," Gareth said, smiling. "Simply stunning."

As they approached the entrance to Harmony, Phillip began to shout orders to his officers.

"I want everything that is not mission-critical removed from the facility! We may have to get more than 10,000 people into this stinking cave!" Phillip turned to Pachuco Reyes, who was unloading boxes from a wagon drawn out from the armory. "You there! Pachuco! You make sure our guests are well received and comfortable! I want everyone to be comfortable, and we may have to pack them in like sardines!"

292

"Yes, sir!" Pachuco shouted back, saluting with a very slight nod of his head.

"Enos Flynn! You take Longbow and you make sure the trenches and emplacements are ready in two hours! Then make sure that the Vallensian units know *exactly* what is expected of them, *exactly* what the signals are, and *exactly* how to NOT mess this up!"

Gareth was impressed with the activity, and the high spirits of the militia. It would be hard to find a numerically inferior defensive force more cheerful than were the Ghost militia men when they knew that battle was near. He turned to Phillip and reached over to tap him on the shoulder in order to gain his attention. "Ghost... if you please. When will the Vallenses arrive? I am growing concerned that they are delayed."

"They are in good hands, and making good time. They will stay ahead of the Louisianan army. I have scouts who will keep an eye on the enemy and keep the Vallensian refugees on a tight schedule. Remember, Gareth, that our Vallensian brethren are quite experienced and adept at fleeing from conflict. And I don't mean that disrespectfully."

The militia continued diligently in their preparations, and Phillip and Gareth rode a circuit around the Harmony canyon supervising the building and digging of defensive fortifications as well as the distribution of weapons. Scouts arrived now and again with messages for Phillip, and before long Gareth watched as militia wagons began distributing and stowing caches of ammunition.

As the heat of the day began to sit upon them like a heavy woolen blanket, the work trailed off, and militia soldiers erected a tent city to the south of Harmony, where Phillip's command and control center was to be headquartered. He wondered why Phillip was not bunkering up in some hidden quarter of the underground Harmony facility, but then he remembered that Phillip had suggested that they may have more than 10,000 Vallenses to stuff into the subterranean complex. By contrast, the command headquarters were placed on the far side of a low mesa, so that they were obscured from armies to the east

293

and west, while the officers could still scale the mesa to watch the battle and send messages and commands at will.

At about 3 p.m. messages began arriving at a rapid pace. The Louisianans had been spotted approaching rapidly from the east, with banners flying. Not long after that, scouts arrived with tidings from the west. In the distance, Gareth and Phillip could see the large army of El Paso approaching purposefully in full battle array. Phillip sent outriders to circumnavigate the enemy armies and to determine their size and strength. He sent more messengers to each of the leaders in the concentric circles with last minute commands and instructions.

At around 5 p.m., hostilities commenced. The first attack was from the east, as the army of the Duke of Louisiana led his forces in a direct frontal attack towards Harmony. When this news reached the command center, Gareth's eyes grew wide and he stood up straight, looking around.

"The Vallensian refugees have not arrived!" he shouted.

Phillip looked at him seriously, but just shrugged his shoulders. "It seems that we must proceed without them."

"Proceed without them? They are the reason for this battle, Phillip!" he found himself shouting. "Without them, there is no moral victory! They are the reason we are here!"

"Calm down, Gareth. If they are not here, then they are somewhere else. We have no word of a slaughter of the Vallenses, and we have had scouts following the Louisianans all the way from the Piney Woods. The Vallenses are one more thing we will not have to worry about. Besides, our enemy is here on the field. We will fight him here. God protects the Vallenses."

"I don't understand your attitude, Phillip."

"It is not necessary that you do, Prince. As I said earlier, we are on a need-to-know basis. What you need to know has been made known to you."

Gareth was incredulous, and he found himself shouting even louder at Phillip. "I am the Crown Prince of Aztlan, Phillip! I have placed the Vallenses under my own personal care! Yes, I wanted them all to fight, but I will not allow them to be

294

slaughtered by forces subject to my father while I am still alive! Do you hear me? You mark my words, Ghost, if something untoward happens to them and you knew about it or you let it happen, I will hold you personally responsible!"

Phillip smiled calmly, and raised his eyes at Gareth. Throughout Gareth's tirade, he had merely looked at the ground, but now, he stared defiantly at the Aztlani Prince. "Do not ever, good Prince," he said quite coolly, "question my loyalty to Jonathan and the Vallenses. I've given my life to their defense; whereas you, with all due respect, are a johnny-come-lately with a chip on your shoulder trying to get out from under the shadow of your father. If something happens to the Vallenses, you can be certain that I will take responsibility."

Gareth looked at the ground as Phillip continued to stare at him. Then he raised his eyes and nodded at the militia leader. "I apologize, Ghost, for doubting you. I know that you have always been a friend to Jonathan and a faithful defender of the Vallenses. I am truly sorry. I guess maybe my feelings were hurt that you have evidently not trusted me enough to share with me all of your plans."

"It is not a matter of trust, Prince, and I appreciate your apology—it is accepted. This is a matter of mission security. You are a target of high value for the enemy, and parts of the plan needed to be kept from even you."

As the conversation ended, the command area began to take heavy fire. Phillip and Gareth ran to their horses, and in moments they were climbing the mesa in order to get a better view of the field. From the top, as bullets whizzed by them and shells exploded 'round about, they could see through the dust that the Aztlani army from the east was, according to plan, heading thoughtlessly towards the pit while the militia forces were forming up behind them and forcing them into the canyon.

Things to the west were not going as well. Part of the Aztlani army had broken off and had placed themselves between the command center and Harmony, and were beginning to entrench themselves there. Almost 1,500 men now formed up below the command mesa, and Gareth slowly realized that the command area was now cut off from the battle. The flanking move by the El Paso army had surprised many of the militia defenders to the south of Harmony, and the plan on that quarter of the field was now in total disarray.

"We have trouble," Phillip said, matter-of-factly.

"Yes, it seems we are cut off," Gareth replied as he peered through his binoculars. "If we had cannon, we could clean them out. We don't have cannon do we?"

"No, I think our troubles are worse than that."

Gareth looked up, and then followed Phillips finger as it pointed off to the south. From the mesa, they could see an army of over 2,000 men approaching Harmony from directly behind them. "Who is that?" he asked.

Phillip looked at him and shrugged, "I have no idea." The militia commander then shouted at an outrider who had just arrived and pointed at the army marching in from the south. "Who is that?"

"I don't know, sir!"

"Go find out!"

"Yes sir, I will."

Phillip motioned towards the approaching army. "Perhaps we should abandon this position, seeing that we're now sandwiched between two armies, and our plan seems to be coming apart."

Gareth looked off to the south, almost as if he hadn't heard Phillip. "Who the hell is that?"

As Phillip gave orders to strike the camp, and secure any sensitive materials or maps, two riders approached from the south with a white flag flying on a staff, and were intercepted by militia outriders. Gareth watched as the two men were brought to the foot of the mesa where he and Phillip were ready to ride.

Phillip nodded towards the white flag and shouted to Gareth, "Perhaps this army is surrendering to us?"

Gareth shook his head, "I doubt it."

When the two riders were within shouting distance, Gareth hollered down towards them, "Who are you, and what army is this?"

"Ah, Mate!" the reply came back. "It is I, your old friend English! Have I changed so much that you don't recognize me?"

Sir Nigel Kerr, spy and traitor to the King of Aztlan, good friend to Phillip of the Ghost militia, and mentor to Crown Prince Gareth of Aztlan, had arrived at the Battle of Harmony with his 2,000 man army, sent by the good graces of the King of Mexico.

"Perhaps we are too late to do any good?" he said good-naturedly, after greeting his two old friends, and introducing his adjutant Pano to both of them.

"Actually, English, your timing could not have been better," Phillip replied. "On the other side of this mesa, an Aztlani force of 1,500 men has just begun to entrench themselves, after they preemptively flanked our flankers. I need you to take your men and push them into that huge hole in the ground."

English smiled, "That sounds like fun!"

Gareth looked at English and shook his head. "How did you get put in charge of a Mexican army?"

"It's a long story, young Gareth, and it involves tunics, and torches, and tunnels, and ghastly castles, and a perfect gentleman soldier named General Rodrigo Loya."

"Not to mention a trusty sidekick who is both loyal, and clever," Pano added, brusquely.

"Oh, yeah," English added, jerking his thumb in the direction of Pano, "there was him, too."

"You'll have to tell us the story after this is over," Gareth said, smiling.

"It will be my pleasure, my esteemed Prince."

In short order, the battle was joined, and the tide again turned in favor of the militia. The attacking enemy armies, from every side, thought that they were gaining the upper hand, and they all had orders to breach and enter the Harmony compound to destroy all of those who were harbored there. The militia forces allowed them to proceed, while circling back to form up again behind them. Before long, the bulk of both enemy armies had gained access to the canyon, while facing only token resistance. The only enemy forces that were not willfully and gladly entering the pit, were those that English and the Mexican army forced into it.

The militia troops who were defending the Harmony entrance gave light battle, then fled out of the canyon before they too were boxed in. The enemy, delighted by the evident rout, and finally seeing plunder and rape on their horizon after days and weeks of endless marching across Texas, forced access into the entrance of Harmony, and wave after wave of the soldiers allied to New Rome fought one another to make their way into the underground complex.

When fully half of the invading armies had made entrance into the facility and the other half were now down into the canyon, the leaders of the enemy forces gathered to determine what to do with the material that they fully planned to seize.

From the mesa to the south, Phillip and Gareth watched as the militia army—now on the rim of the canyon, and in a superior fighting position—began to pour fire into the caliche pit. The noise and the results were awesome.

As the confusion and death mounted in the pit, a rumble began to grow from the bowels of the earth, growing and rolling forth over all of the soldiers from both sides who were engaged in the fight. The battle seemed to halt when what felt like an earthquake began to shake the ground so severely that even Phillip and Gareth, mounted and on the mesa, could feel the shaking. The implosion as the ground above the Harmony facility collapsed on the Aztlani invaders was so impressive, that a tower of dust and dirt was caught up into the sky and created a pillar that could be seen from miles in any direction.

As they steadied themselves, and as the realization of what had happened slowly occurred to him, he turned to Phillip with his eyes opened as wide as he could manage.

"You blew it up!"

"I did."

"You had it planned all along!"

"I did."

"The Vallensian refugees were never coming here!"

"They were not."

Just then, gunfire, as hellacious as any he had ever heard, erupted from the direction of the canyon as militia forces firing through the dust and debris began to finish the work that was before them. The forces of the Duke of Louisiana, and those of the Duke of El Paso—all those that were not killed when Harmony was collapsed with them in it—were wiped out in short order by militia gunfire. No surrender was accepted.

Phillip lowered his binoculars and looked at Gareth. "Brother... We sent the Vallenses north, with a defensive unit to protect them. I don't know rightly where they will go, or what will become of them. But they could not be here. I believe that they do go with God. I truly believe that. But they could not be here. In order to save them, I had to send them north."

A remarkable silence fell upon the multitude of militia soldiers and officers when the fighting was over. It almost sounded like rain as debris from the implosion of Harmony began to fall down over the whole area.

Heads were bowed throughout the militia ranks as Vallensian and Ghost militia veterans stopped for a moment to consider that they had survived. The pause did not last long.

Through the prayerful silence, the sound of hoofbeats could be heard approaching from the northwest. Before long, a lone militia outrider rode up to Phillip and nodded by way of salute.

"Sir," he said to Phillip. "Your Honor," he said, nodding to Gareth.

"What is it?" Phillip asked.

"It's Aztlan. *All* of Aztlan. At least 25,000 men!"

"Where are they?" Phillip queried as he rushed to his horse.

"They're almost *here*, sir!"

Chapter 28 - Rollo

Escaping from the militia posse had been easy enough. *Piggy must have been a fool to think that he could hold me with such whimpy knots! But... then again, Piggy is no fool.* What then? He wondered if maybe Piggy had played him. By breaking out and escaping he had proven his guilt. He had shed the posse of their need to watch him. Maybe he should have delayed them a few more days... protested his innocence to make them question Piggy. He probably should have sown confusion among them. Maybe then the whole lot would have been captured by the army coming from New Rome while they delayed and pondered his innocence or guilt.

So, did Piggy let me escape? If he did, maybe he is a fool, Rollo thought to himself. He knew he could do more harm to the cause of the Vallenses and the militia as a free man. And was he to conclude that Piggy had sacrificed that Marbus Claim boy? How would Piggy have known that he wouldn't kill the boy? *Or maybe Piggy did know.* It was all so frustrating. While he should be celebrating his freedom and his future barony, instead he was still trying to figure out what Piggy knew and when he knew it. *How did he know?*

He was still pondering the mysteries of Piggy, when he rode headlong into the advancing Aztlani army. Twenty-five thousand men strong, the army was being led by Sir Jarius Whiteside, the King's own Chancellor. Whiteside was the Chief Minister of State to the Kingdom of Aztlan. Sir Chancellor Whiteside was known by everyone—except to his face—as The Falcon. His nickname was influenced by both his predatory character, and his hawkish face and long hooked nose. The Falcon was no mercenary, like Rollo. In fact he was different than almost every other high official or confidant to the king. The Falcon was a true-believer, both in the deity and perfections of his Monarch, the King of Aztlan, but also in the religion of New Rome. He was the favorite of the Bishops and Archbishops and Cardinals, because he would spare no effort, show no mercy, and shed whatever blood was necessary to spread the monolithic and monarchial religion of New Rome. It was said that he even had himself in mind for Pope someday. Just the thought of it made his eyes glaze over and made his face flush full red.

Rollo was well acquainted with the Knight Chancellor, and, like most people, he feared the man. He came upon the army on his second day riding as they rested just south of Big Spring, Texas. The army was spread out in camp just southwest of Scenic Mountain (which was actually just a high mesa) on the remnants of the highway that used to be called Highway 87. He immediately rode to the command camp and asked the adjutant for the pleasure of meeting with, and reporting to, the Knight Chancellor himself.

The Falcon kept him waiting for several hours, which was to be expected, but eventually, towards the end of the day as the sun began its descent beyond Scenic Mountain, he was escorted into the lavish command tent of Sir Jarius Whiteside.

"Our friend and fellow warrior, Rollo Billings—the man called The Mountain—greetings and welcome to the army of your King. What word have you on your mission?"

"Your Honor," Rollo said with a bow, "it is my utmost pleasure to report to the King's Chancellor the success of my mission on behalf of the King."

"So the leaders of the rebellion are dead?"

"Your Honor," Rollo replied assertively, "while there is no way for me to know definitively the final dispensation of all of the leadership, I can report that the rebels have been struck hard. I personally shot David Wall, the son of Jonathan Wall. David had joined the militia and was acting in a leadership role. That was my first shot, and I can assure the King's Chancellor that David Wall cannot have survived his wound. I also personally shot Phillip of the Ghost militia. I cannot say whether Phillip died of his wound, but I can say that it is most likely that he did. I also personally poisoned Crown Prince Gareth of Aztlan. I watched him drink hemlock, Your Honor. I feel confident that the King's bastard is dead."

"And what of Jonathan of the Vallenses? Does he live?"

"He does sir," Rollo replied, with his head bowed a bit. He looked back up and continued, "Jonathan was saved from my blow at the last moment by one of his bodyguards. But he is separated from his people, and on the run somewhere between here and San Angelo. He will be dead soon enough, Your Honor."

"It is hardly true," Sir Jarius replied, "that you have been wholly successful in your mission, would you agree?"

"No, Your Honor, with all due respect, I do not agree. I know that with Your Honor's deep understanding of warfare, and his personal experience in such things, that he understands the difficulty in operating alone, as a spy, behind enemy lines and without backup or support. I believe that striking all of the militia leadership right before a decisive battle can only be deemed a success by Your Honor. I am certain that the rebellion is crippled and leaderless. I am certain that the threat to the throne posed by the Crown Prince has been removed. I am also certain that no man—save Your Honor, of course—could have done better in the situation... as it presented itself."

"I am confident, Rollo, that you have done all that you could, and that the King will be pleased with your service. I thank you as well."

Rollo bowed down respectfully. "If I may, Your Honor," he continued, "may I ask the King's Chancellor when I might receive the Barony promised to me by the King for my service? I know that the King has given all such powers into the hand of his royal Chancellor. Will I be honored to receive my Barony immediately, as promised?"

The Chancellor smiled beneath his long crooked nose, and his eyes squinted in amusement. "My honorable friend. You can be assured that you will receive all that has been promised to you by the King. I will personally bestow the Barony upon you when the time is right, and when the results of the coming engagement are known."

"Surely you don't expect defeat, Your Honor? You now face a decapitated force, likely of only a few hundred men. The Vallenses will not fight, and the leader of the Vallenses is absent and on the run. Phillip the Ghost is dead or disabled. Frankly, I don't even see the need for this great army, lead as it is by such an able and revered General, to be here at all."

The Chancellor's eyes, only moments ago shining forth in mirth, turned dark and cloudy. "Rollo, let me speak bluntly. The armies of Aztlan are weak and cowardly. We prevail and rule by means of numbers and not ability, bravery, or superior training. We all honor the King and respect him as is his due. To me, he is a god. But... his advisors are buffoons, and his generals fight for money and not loyalty. If this army were half its size, I would not dare fight even a hundred loyal militia troops. That, sir, is the sad but honest truth. We need brave and loyal men, and we breed cowards and cutthroats. What this Kingdom needs is more religion and more severity. That is what I expect from you, and what I expect you to impose when you become Baron of Texas."

"We are of the same mind, Your Honor."

"Good, then I will have you ride with me." The Chancellor pulled off his white gloves and stepped from around his desk. "Tomorrow we will ride hard, and we will reach this 'Harmony' fortress you have told us so much about. Our riders have said that some militia forces are preparing defenses around the place. Perhaps we will have our battle tomorrow evening."

"Please excuse my forwardness, Your Honor... but... Phillip would never do battle with an army of this size in the open field! He knows he is outmanned, outgunned, and over-matched! If there are defensive battlements being placed, it must be a ruse!"

"Well, sir, according to *you*, Phillip is dead or incapacitated. Others are now in charge. And even if Phillip is leading his forces, I am certain that he has no intention of fighting *our* 25,000 men in the open field. In fact, it is our opinion that whoever is in charge of the militia has no idea that we are even coming." The Falcon squared himself and faced Rollo, looking into his eyes. "Their preparations are being made to meet the

303

6,000 men approaching their positions from the direction of El Paso. Also, the Duke of Louisiana, at our request, has sent a sizable army of several thousand men that is approaching from the east. Those forces will converge on this 'Harmony' fortress. It is our plan to wait until that battle is over and then attack."

"But, sir...," Rollo sputtered, "if two large armies are surrounding the militia as we speak, what need have you of attacking at all? Don't you believe that the militia will be destroyed? A handful of militia men will be standing against between eight and ten thousand trained soldiers."

"I don't personally believe that at all. We have never successfully defeated any Texas militia of any real size. Aztlan's history in Texas is one of defeat after defeat. Only a fool would believe that the forces now arrayed against the militia are sufficient to do the job. But they don't know we're here, and I intend to surprise the Ghost militia *after* the battle is over, when, if they still exist, they are weakest and when they will believe that they have won." The Chancellor walked over to the door of the tent and peered outside. "You of all people, Rollo, should know that we should never underestimate an enemy that fights for honor and for freedom. However wicked they are in their religion, and foolish they are in their worldview, they are not mercenaries like that rabble we have here in our army."

"Is the King aware of your feelings, Your Honor?"

"No, he is not, and neither *will* he be made aware of them, Rollo. What this Kingdom needs is a strong and effective Pope. The King should rule at the behest and pleasure of God's representative on earth. Only then will Aztlan meet and surpass its potential. I am certain that an honorable and religious man such as yourself can see the benefits of such an arrangement?"

"I do, Your Honor."

"Our task, Rollo... our *mutual* obligation... is to defeat and destroy these rebels, and to erase the execrable race of Vallenses from *our* soil. When we do so, I believe that God will reward us, and the King will see that *you* ought to be allowed to manage Texas, and I ought to be given the authority over the visible Church of God at New Rome. Do you agree?"

"I do, Your Honor."

"Good. We will have Mass this evening, then we will ride in the morning and put an end to this rebellion."

"Yes, Your Honor."

By late afternoon on the following day, the army of New Rome pulled up about fifteen miles northwest of San Angelo in order to await intelligence on what was happening at Harmony. The late summer sun was blistering hot, and shade was a rare blessing in the scrub and low juniper. Rollo was sitting impatiently among the sycophants in the Chancellor's general staff when the Knight Chancellor himself rode up and reined his horse.

"Rollo Billings!" he shouted brusquely. "Here, good sir!" The Chancellor turned his horse to the southeast and rode about twenty yards away from the rest of his staff.

"Coming, Sir!" Rollo responded obediently, as he spurred his horse and rode to meet the Chancellor. "Your Honor!" he said as he approached the Knight.

"Rollo... good... ok. We are not far from the battle. I require you and your expertise for a mission if, of course, you are pleased to do it."

"Very pleased to help in any way that I am able, Your Honor."

"I want you to take 25 men and ride scout ahead. I want to make sure that we have not arrived too early and that we are not riding into any sort of militia ambush."

"Is there any specific information that Your Honor requires, sir?"

"We are virtually blind here. I need any information that you can provide."

"Yes, sir!" Rollo shouted as he again spurred his horse and rode back to the staff. He was appointed 25 men by Lieutenant General Weld of the cavalry, and after quickly outfitting themselves with arms and gear the scout squad rode off to the southeast at a gallop.

He was excited to be of use to the Knight Chancellor, but he was curious as to why he had been chosen to complete this mission. The cavalry was always tasked with gathering information and riding scout, so he was a bit suspicious as to why the Chancellor might have selected him to lead the party. *Perhaps he wants me killed so he can deny me the Barony?* No. That made no sense. The Chancellor had all power while serving as Commanding General of the Army. He could easily have had Rollo killed for failing to completely fulfill his mission to kill Jonathan Wall in the first place. If the Knight Chancellor wanted him dead, he'd be dead. *Why then?* Perhaps Sir Jarius didn't trust his own commanders? This was most likely the case. He had said as much the night before. Regardless, Rollo intended to do his duty and do it well enough that The Falcon would know without doubt that he could be trusted.

They rode hard for ten miles without incident, and they were not five miles out of San Angelo when they came upon what looked to be a militia scout unit moving slowly and furtively towards the recently destroyed city.

Rollo spurred his horse and shouted, "Ride hard, boys! Capture them all!" His spirits rose as he rode, and he knew that if he could capture a militia scout party, he would be able to extract information from them one way or another. Things were looking bright for him, and he could see himself being named the *Baron Rollo Billings* in no time at all. Maybe there would even be a knighthood in it for him. *That wouldn't be bad*, he told himself.

In no time the Aztlani unit had surrounded the party of eight, and as Rollo rode up he could see through the dust that the militia men had circled up—facing outward—with their weapons drawn... and that he knew all of them. The first one he recognized was Piggy, who had a knife near his ear and a smile on his face. Young Ruth Wall was next to him and she had her bow drawn and bent. The others—Timothy, The Hood, the turncoat Troy, young Marbus Claim, and Rob Fosse were all likewise ready for battle, and they had surrounded Jonathan Wall who had a look of concern on his face.

"Hold your fire!" Rollo shouted to no one in particular. "Put down your weapons Piggy... and you there Rob, drop them... all of you!"

"That will never happen, Rollo," Piggy snorted.

"This is hardly a fair fight, Piggy," Rollo replied.

"Yes! You are correct. You better go get more guys!" Piggy parried.

"If you don't drop your weapons, you will all die right now, Piggy, including the girl... of course, after we are done with her. Jonathan will die too. You are sworn to protect him, Piggy. Drop your weapons and give yourselves up and the Walls' will not be harmed."

"You were in Texon to kill him, Rollo, you traitorous buffoon. No way he lives if we surrender, so let's stop the chit-chat and get on with this."

"As you wish!" Rollo shouted and his horse reared up as he spurred him forward. The battle commenced with such ferocity and with such speed that it soon became hard for him to determine just what happened, and in what order. Piggy's first knife struck him in the upper chest and knocked him clean off his horse. He felt no pain, and as he extracted the knife, out of the corner of his eye he saw Aztlani soldiers falling to the ground, pierced by arrows. He identified the boy Marbus Claim standing amidst the fury of battle and from his knees he threw the knife at him, watching it strike home. *Thanks for the lessons... and the knife, Piggy!* At some point, he struggled to his feet and, regaining his wits, he charged into the melee as arrows whizzed by his head and the deafening sounds of swords colliding assaulted his ears.

Rob Fosse fell at his feet and was stabbed through with a sword by one of the Aztlani cavalrymen. Rollo fought his way into the center of the mass of struggling men, and through what could only be called a crack in the edifice of defenders he was able to strike such a blow to the head of Jonathan Wall that the Vallensian leader fell to the ground unconscious. He looked up and saw Wall's daughter standing calmly in the eye of the storm. She was smoothly feeding arrows into her bow like a machine, and Aztlani soldiers were falling from her arrows so fast that he was certain that she never missed a shot. It was almost like her arrows were trained to strike Aztlani hearts.

From his right he saw motion as one of his men pulled a pistol and carefully aimed at the young red-headed girl. Everything seemed to slow down, and he saw Timothy jump and grab her at the last second, so that the bullet that was meant for her hit him instead. He grinned at the meaningless, but heroic act. He started to laugh, but just as he did, he was suddenly knocked violently to the ground by a horse which clipped him as it rode by.

He looked back and now Ruth was clutching Timothy, and screaming his name as he slumped to the ground. He saw Piggy—whose horse had been the one that smashed him to the ground—snatch Ruth up with one hand and simply throw her like a rag doll behind him on the horse before riding hard to the north. Ruth held on, but she was looking back in terror and sadness knowing that she was helpless to save her father or the wounded Timothy. The Hood rode after Piggy, with the Aztlani traitor Troy hard at his heels. Ruth's horse Peloncio, riderless, galloped after them under his own command.

Rollo heard himself shouting orders, but his thoughts were muddled and the dust was such that it was hard to know if there were even any Aztlani scouts alive to whom he might direct those orders. Almost instinctively he lifted up the unconscious Jonathan Wall, and as he did so he saw a few of his men twirling around on their frightened horses, and he commanded one of them to take the Vallensian leader and ride hard back towards the army. The Aztlani cavalryman seemed to be relieved to be ordered to flee, so he hastily pulled the stricken Vallensian over his lap and galloped away as fast as he could. Rollo located his own mount, then he half carried and half dragged the militia boy Timothy onto the horse. It seemed that the boy might have received a mortal blow, but he was still breathing. *Best to take any living hostages.* He lashed the boy to the horse, mounted quickly, and rode off at a gallop to catch up with the few Aztlani scouts who were still left alive.

As he rode, he was surprised by his own intense feeling of elation. His hearing returned, and his vision widened. Adrenaline pumped through him like he had never felt before—and he was the veteran of many battles. In the brief skirmish, he saw that he had lost twenty men. *Twenty men!* Still, he had captured Jonathan Wall, and, perhaps the boy Timothy might live and be able to give them information as well. He felt the warm blood—his own—as it began to drench his tunic, and he could feel it pooling at his beltline. He laughed and reveled in the euphoria. The dampness of his own blood made him feel alive! *Two hostages in exchange for twenty men... When one of those men is Jonathan Wall, it is well worth it.*

Riding hard towards the army of New Rome, his thoughts began to again grow confused; the adrenaline that was keeping him going waned rapidly and he felt himself growing light-headed. He knew that he was suffering from blood loss, but he also knew that he would still be alright. *I'm a baron now! There is no way they can keep the barony from me!*

He awoke on a cot being attended to by the Chancellor's own surgeon. The dust of the day hung in the room like a curtain and the late afternoon sun illuminated the floating particles in the air. Squinting, he could just make out the face of the Knight Chancellor, and of Lieutenant General Weld. Several more officers of the Chancellor's general staff were in attendance... he heard their hushed whispers. They all stared at him in wonder.

"Baron Rollo Billings, it is good to see that you are awake, and to hear that you should recover completely from your wounds. Can you hear me and understand me, Baron?"

"Baron?" Rollo grunted.

"Yes, Baron Rollo. You are now a Baron and you are officially awarded the Barony of Texas on behalf of the King of Aztlan. Congratulations."

The Falcon stood over him, his hooked nose giving him the look of a deadly raptor about to feed on a fresh kill. "We have heard of your bravery and heroism in the capture of the heretic Jonathan Wall. He has already been sent back to New Rome to stand trial for treason and heresy." The Falcon leaned low and dropped his voice to a faint whisper, so that only Rollo could hear. "He will, of course, be examined before the Commission on the Purity of the Faith, and I am certain...

absolutely certain... that he will be declared unorthodox." The Chancellor stood upright again and raised his voice. "We are all in your debt, Baron Rollo, and we hope you recuperate soon. God is smiling down on us, Baron. We will need you in the coming days."

"Yes, Your Honor," he managed to say. "Thank you." Then his head again began to swim. A Baron! The Baron of Texas! *Why is it so dark?*

Chapter 29 - Ruth

Ruth felt nothing but despair. She had never killed men before... but, strangely, that part didn't really bother her as much as it should have. Perhaps that would come later. She had also never been in the heat of battle before... but, she felt distant from any excitement or trauma arising from the fight. Riding from the scene of the battle had been the most heart-wrenching experience she had ever known in her young life. Both her beloved father, and her good friend Timothy, lay stricken on the field, and there was nothing... nothing... that she could do to help them. *I don't even know if they are alive.*

She felt a choking sensation in her throat, and she suddenly struggled for air. She sobbed. Her heart pounded in her chest and she desired more than anything in the world to be able to go back in time... to kill them all... to save her father and Tim. She might have done it, if she hadn't run out of arrows. *I failed them!*

Piggy and The Hood tried desperately to help her handle her grief. After a few hours of hiding out in the brush north of San Angelo, they had crept back to the scene of the battle to try to figure out what had happened. They found the body of Rob Fosse, who was their captain and their friend, and that of Marbus Claim, their silent and faithful companion, dead on the field. Marbus had one of Piggy's knives stuck in his chest. Upon finding the knife, Piggy had cursed the soul of Rollo The Mountain, and swore vengeance upon him.

Jonathan and Timothy were not there. The area was searched and their bodies could not be found anywhere in the vicinity. Troy explained that this was good news. "They wouldn't have wasted time on their bodies if they were dead, Ruth." *Perhaps.* Maybe that was true of Timothy—that thought gave her hope for him—but they would certainly have taken her father's body, dead or alive. Parading a dead Jonathan Wall through the streets of New Rome would have a sobering effect on anyone harboring thoughts of insurrection. She steeled herself. *Timothy is alive...* at least he was when the battle was over. Maybe her father was still alive too.

She knew that she should grieve over them and let it be done, and that keeping hope alive was probably not in her best interests. It would be painful to hold on to hope, and then have to grieve all over again if it turned out that both of the men were dead. She could not help herself, though. Timothy was alive, and she had to hope that her father was worth more to Aztlan alive than dead. Nobody wanted a martyr.

Piggy grasped her firmly by the shoulders. "No one can tell you how to feel, Ruth. Death is a reality in war. I can't tell you to grieve, or to wait, or to forget. I need to tell you though, that both your father and Timothy had *purpose*. They both wanted to live in peace, and to be good and honest men. They both made choices that brought them to this place. Your father taught that God was sovereign, and that all things come to be according to the divine decree of God. I respect that, and I agree with it. Whatever you feel, you must bow to the knowledge that this is God's will. Since we know that God is good and right, we must acquiesce to His decision. However you feel, that is what you must do."

They all stood in silence, and they began to notice the buzzing of flies called forth to the bounty of so many bodies. Ruth lifted her head and nodded at Piggy. "We should bury Marbus and Rob."

"We will, Ruth. Why don't you go find some shade and maybe pray for the safety of Timothy and your father?"

"I want to help bury them."

"As you wish. Then let's do that," Piggy said, and for the second time in just a few days, they found themselves digging graves in the desert.

Several hours later they approached the vicinity of Harmony. A great battle had evidently been fought there—this they could see—and a cloud of dust still hung heavily in the air.

312

The bodies that littered the ground were coated with fallen debris, and, just as in the earlier battle, the flies here had been summoned to the corpses that lay strewn around the area. As they rode silently, Piggy signaled loudly to the militia, and the party entered the battlefield unmolested. Miltiamen, both Vallensian and otherwise, busily dug out and reinforced an extensive trench system on the northwest side of the battlefield. Ruth saw a group on horseback and recognized Enos Flynn, Pachuco Reyes, and Tyrell of Terrell. Piggy signaled to them and the three rode over and joined them.

"Hello Piggy," Pachuco said with a slight bow of his head. "As you can see, part *one* of the great battle is over. The armies from El Paso and Louisiana have been utterly destroyed, but Phillip believes a larger force is headed this way from New Rome. We're digging in. There are too many of us to move fast, so we're going to have to fight here."

Piggy smiled, "So Phillip lives! This is excellent news!" The smile didn't last long, and his features quickly regained their reflection of the seriousness of the moment. "Our greetings, brothers," he said. "Yes, we believe that Phillip is correct. Aztlan is on the way. We had a skirmish with a scout team from that army not three hours ago," he stopped and removed his hat. "I hate to be the one to report that Rob Fosse and Marbus Claim were killed. Young Timothy and Jonathan Wall were captured."

"Jonathan Wall? Captured? I thought they already had Mr. Wall," Enos said, then, noticing Ruth, he took off his cap as well. "My apologies about your father, Ruth." Ruth nodded almost imperceptibly.

"We have a pretty long report for Phillip, Pachuco, and I'd really rather not tell the whole story a dozen times. Where can we find him?"

"The command tent is behind that low mesa," Pachuco replied, pointing to the southeast. "Our enemy doesn't know that Phillip and Prince Gareth are alive. We would like to keep it that way."

"Gareth lives too? That is excellent news," Piggy replied. Looking around, Ruth perceived the emotion and tightness that had instantaneously passed over the faces of the three militia men. "And David Wall?" Piggy asked.

Pachuco looked at Ruth and remained silent, and for a moment it seemed that all of the air was sucked out of the area, before Longbow interrupted with a reply. "Miss Wall... we're so sorry... your brother David..."

"...was killed," Ruth said, finishing the sentence.

"Yes, ma'am," Longbow replied while lowering his eyes.

"Was it Rollo?"

"Yes, ma'am."

"Did my brother suffer?"

"No ma'am. He died instantly."

"Has he been buried?"

"Yes, ma'am. There was a full Vallensian funeral just days ago. Your sister saw to it that everything was handled."

Ruth paused and looked out over the preparations that were being made for another, larger battle. "We won't keep you if you need to prepare. I thank you for the news and for your prayers and assistance to my family. We need to go report to Phillip. You are welcome to accompany us if you wish."

"We will," said Pachuco, and after another heavy and quiet moment, the party rode silently out towards the command center of the militia.

She didn't talk while Phillip and Piggy briefed one another on all of the recent happenings. Phillip was obviously saddened by the news of the deaths of Rob Fosse—his best friend and second in command—and the young militia fighter Marbus Claim. In like manner, Phillip seemed particularly distraught when he had to tell Ruth about the death of her brother. The heaviness of the moment was only interrupted when Piggy reported to Phillip that Jonathan Wall had been seized by Rollo and the Aztlani army.

"Oh no, Piggy," was all Phillip could say.

"I know, sir," Piggy replied.

"No... Piggy... I don't think that you do know. Jonathan in the hands of New Rome is a disaster for us." Phillip looked at Ruth, apologetically. "Perhaps you ought not to be here, Ruth."

314

"I will stay," she replied forcefully, "speak freely."

Piggy raised his hands in order to indicate that he wanted Phillip to listen. "Phillip, I had a split second to decide to try to save Jonathan... which was my duty... or Ruth. Jonathan was down on the field, either dead or seriously injured, and I could not tell if he was dead or alive. So I chose to try to save Ruth. It was a split-second decision, and I did what I thought was right."

Phillip walked a few paces away, then took a deep breath and turned back to Piggy. "No. Piggy. You did the right thing. If you had tried to save Jonathan, we might have lost both of them... and you as well. You did the right thing. I apologize for second guessing you. I wasn't there. You were, and you did the right thing."

"Thank you, Phillip."

The group stood in silence for a long moment before Phillip finally spoke. "New Rome is coming. Probably close to 25,000 men are only miles away. We can't run. We've always been able to flee, but we have almost 7,000 men now, and we're not as spry as we once were. We're digging in."

"This isn't good, Phillip," Piggy said, looking at his leader with his head cocked to one side.

"No, it isn't."

"Do you have any tricks in your bag?"

"I have some cheap parlor tricks, but nothing that will sufficiently help us here. They think that Gareth and I are dead. We've got that. That might surprise them for a moment, but it won't last. We're going to have to fight them the old-fashioned way."

"We don't like that way," Piggy said. "That is *not* Piggy's Way!"

"Well if you come up with something, you let me know, Piggy," Phillip replied.

"Each of us will just have to kill four of them," Ruth interrupted seriously.

Phillip eyed Ruth, and then nodded his head. "Yes, young lady, you are right. Each of us will have to kill four of them."

"I don't see where that is a problem," she said, looking out towards the field of battle.

Phillip stood looking at her for a moment. "Well, Ruth, then that is what we will try to do."

She was heartened a bit at the thought of the coming battle. She didn't feel any fear at all. Piggy had taken charge of their unit, and she trusted him completely. He found them a spot in the trenches towards the center of the defensive line. Weapons were brought in, and Piggy saw to it that she had several quivers of arrows.

"Listen, this isn't going to be much of an arrow kind of battle, Ruth. The Aztlanis will have guns, and a lot of them. You need to stay down, and don't even think about getting involved unless there is a clear shot that you can take."

"I will do as you say, Piggy."

"This is going to get frightening. You will be more scared than you have ever been. Aztlan will have guns, cannon, and all kinds of things," he paused while he looked out over the battlefield. "You have to listen to me... all of you." Troy and the Hood both nodded in agreement. "If I give a command, you have to do what I say instantly. You can't hesitate. We're all counting on one another. If we have to retreat, the horses are tied to a post over east of the command tents. Make your way there, and we'll ride around to the east of San Angelo and then head north. If we get separated, leave plenty of sign and I'll find you." They all nodded in agreement as they checked their weapons.

"Ruth," Piggy continued, "I cannot tell you how important it is that you keep your senses. If we are bombarded with shells, it can become very disconcerting and confusing. If you feel you are starting to lose it, just look at me... ok?"

"Ok, Piggy," was all she could think of to say.

They didn't have long to wait. Soon they heard the rumble of the approaching enemy. Then it grew quiet. After about 30 minutes of near silence, shells began to fall in every direction. Ruth was at first stunned by the ferocity of the

316

bombardment, but then her senses became dull and a stark fear gripped her. Some shells landed so close that the gravel and dirt shooting through the air stung her face and hands. She pressed herself into the western wall of the trench and pulled her legs close to her chest. The sound was deafening, and for a while she actually thought that she had lost her hearing. The sounds faded away, but the shells continued to drop and she could feel the force of the concussions as they battered her. She began to feel a sense of panic and she looked up and saw Piggy watching from just above the ridge of the trench. He looked down and saw her, and then slipped down beside her. Saying nothing, he reached into his pocket and pulled out some cotton, which he tore into two pieces and balled up into his hand. He indicated to her that she should put them in her ears, and as he did so a shell exploded inside the trench somewhere to the north of their position. Piggy was tossed over her, and debris rained down heavily for several moments. When he got off of her, she quickly checked to see that he was not wounded, and she was grateful that he was not.

Then, just as quickly as the firing had begun, it stopped. Several minutes passed by in silence before Piggy poked his head up to see what was happening. He slid back into the trench, motioning The Hood and Troy to gather around.

"They're coming. This is it. Pick your targets. Shoot slowly and deliberately, and no indiscriminate firing. One shot, one kill. Aim for center mass. If they break through the lines, don't panic and keep firing. Ruth, you stay down. Hand us ammo if you see we need it, and if anyone gets behind us, or into the trench, you do your thing with the arrows... and don't miss."

"I won't miss, Piggy."

"I know you won't, Ruth. Just take your time and stay calm like you did before."

The three or four minutes that elapsed between Piggy's instructions and the arrival of the enemy seemed like an eternity. Ruth crunched herself back up against the wall and waited for the firing to start, but it seemed like it never would. *Why aren't they firing?* Then, she realized that the militiamen were holding their fire so that they would have better and more effective shots. The enemy was out in the open, and they needed every bullet to find a home.

She looked up to Piggy and he smiled at her as if he was just going to be target shooting. *Piggy is in his element,* she thought. Then she wished that Timothy was here with her; but, before that thought could fully coalesce, she put it out of her mind. *Can't think about Tim right now.*

Then the firing started, and she had never heard anything quite like it in her life... even through the cotton in her ears. The distinctive *whizz* of each bullet could be heard independently, and she could feel the thud of bullets slamming into the earth at the top of the trench. She dared to look up again, and she saw The Hood, Troy, and Piggy firing slowly and calmly, picking out their shots.

A few moments later, she heard Piggy shout, "They've broken through!" and she looked down the line and saw Aztlani soldiers pouring into the trench. She pulled out her bow and kneeled down, facing northwards. She let each arrow fly deliberately, and watched as man after man tumbled into a pile in the trench. As more men began to climb over their dead comrades, she picked them off with kill shots every time. *When will they all just die!*

She felt Piggy tugging at her arm, and looked over to him as he mouthed, "WE HAVE TO GO!" She nodded, and joined the other three as they jumped out of the eastern side of the trench and began to dodge their way towards the command area on the distant mesa. She felt numb and detached, and somehow separated from her body as she tripped and stumbled over rocks and bodies, and occasionally tumbled downwards into a shell crater. At one point, she fell headlong down into a deep crater only to find The Hood, Piggy, and Troy waiting there for her.

"Just wait here, Ruth. The firing has stopped. I think they may be pulling back!" They waited for a minute, then almost as one being they all crept up to look out of the crater and see what was happening. The enemy had indeed retreated, and for just a moment they all felt the elation of victory. But, then they noticed that only a portion of the Aztlani army had been

318

involved in the first attack. They seemed to be forming up for another assault.

"Oh my," Ruth exclaimed, "they're coming back."

"Just wait," Piggy said, and he pointed to an embassy coming forth from the Aztlani host, flying a white flag. They watched in silence as a militia contingent made up of Pachuco Reyes, Longbow, and Tyrell of Terrell rode out under the white flag to meet them.

"If we could only hear what they are saying," Ruth said, watching with intense interest. There was some wild gesticulating by Tyrell, and they could see the Aztlani officers shaking their heads. "It doesn't look like it is going well," she added.

The short congress broke up, apparently with nothing solved, and they watched as the militia contingent rode back towards their own lines.

The Aztlani army continued to form up for the next attack, when suddenly the whole battlefield grew silent. At first they noticed the lone rider appear to their northwest, in the no-man's land between the armies. It was Crown Prince Gareth of Aztlan. He sat stoically upon his horse, with no white flag, before standing up in his saddle so that he could be seen clearly by the whole Aztlani host.

She could hear a murmur pass through both armies, and then she noticed everyone looking back to the south. To their southwest, also stationed between the two armies, was Phillip of the Ghost Militia. He also allowed himself to be seen clearly by the army from New Rome. Following some sort of silent signal, the two men began to ride around the army of Aztlan in opposite directions. Some enterprising Aztlani soldiers took wild shots at them, but nothing seemed to come close to hitting them.

"It seems to be a demonstration devised to disconcert the enemy," Piggy said, laughing. "They all think that Phillip and Gareth are dead."

"I don't think it's working," The Hood said, calmly.

"A nice piece of theatre," Troy said, "but I think all it bought us was time."

The spectacle seemed to go on for minutes before the two leaders met back in the middle and turned towards the enemy army.

As the two men stood facing Aztlan, a thumping sound could be heard coming from... it seemed... *everywhere.* Ruth had never heard anything like it. *What can that be?*

The thumping grew louder, and everyone was turning around and around, attempting to locate the origination of the strange sound.

Phillip and Gareth had turned again and were riding directly back towards their own lines. Both men dismounted and ran towards the trench, sliding in between Ruth and Piggy.

The sound grew louder and the ground itself began to shake.

"What is it?" Ruth shouted.

"I think I know what that is," Phillip answered, slowly standing up in the trench. "Could it be?"

From the east, rising above the horizon, glowing eerily in the late evening sunlight, Ruth saw four black beasts flying towards them in formation. She hadn't a clue what they could be, but her heart was pounding in her chest, and her brain struggled to understand what in the world could be coming at them. "What is it?" she shouted again.

"Blackhawk helicopters," Phillip shouted back, as the aircraft slowly buzzed directly over their heads. "American military aircraft... from before the crash!"

"I've never seen anything like it in my life," The Hood yelled, holding his hood down firmly on his head.

"None of us has," Piggy replied.

"I have," Phillip said. "In fact I've been in one."

"Whose are they?" Ruth yelled.

"I have no idea," Phillip responded, as the helicopters suddenly and simultaneously opened fire on the stunned and frightened Aztlani army.

The battle was over in minutes. The carnage was unbelievable. What was left of the Aztlani army—and there wasn't much left at all—rode hard into the desert to escape the

320

unexplainable sky beasts that rained missiles and bullets down on them like fire from the gods.

As the battle ended, the four black helicopters landed softly in the clearing that had been the no-man's land between the two armies. Men disembarked from the aircraft and jogged towards the militia lines. Several of them were dressed in very ornate military uniforms, and one of the men was dressed sharply in a white coat and trousers. As they approached the lines, an officer shouted, "We are looking for Phillip, the leader of the Ghost militia!"

Phillip stood up and waved towards the approaching party. "I am Phillip, commander of this army."

"Well hello, Phillip, and greetings from the people of the South States!" said the man wearing white. "I am Richard the First, King of the South States. Your friend Jonathan Wall wrote me a letter asking me if I might be able to help."

A shout of joy and victory went out up and down the militia lines. There was much hugging and celebration as the knowledge that help had arrived began to sink in.

Ruth was still stunned at the appearance of the black flying machines, and found it hard to grasp everything that was happening. As the celebratory spirit began to surround her, she found herself smiling as Piggy, The Hood, and Troy all embraced around her, laughing and shouting for joy.

Meeting together with the King of the South States became a very formal affair. Tents were erected hastily and furniture and rugs that had been removed from the Harmony complex were brought in to make the tents comfortable. Ruth stood trembling as introductions were made, and she shook hands with the officers from the South States as they each made their rounds and happily embraced the militia leaders.

Soon, a conversation started between King Richard and Phillip, and the topic turned to the Vallenses.

"I desire to meet with and converse with Jonathan Wall of the Vallenses," the King said. "Without his letter... and his reputation... we certainly would not have come."

"I am sad to report that Jonathan Wall was captured by Aztlan earlier today," Phillip replied.

"I am very sorry to hear that, Phillip. Where has he been taken?"

"We understand that he has been taken to New Rome. He will probably be tried there as a heretic."

"I am so sorry, for you all."

"Ruth here," Piggy said, "is Jonathan Wall's daughter, and can speak on behalf of the Vallenses, Your Honor."

The King looked at Ruth with a kindly expression, and motioned for her to come forward. "Young Ruth, I am so sorry to hear about your father. Please let me know if there is anything I can do to help you... anything at all."

"Well, Your Honor, I thank you and I appreciate your offer. I'd like to take you up on it. Perhaps you can get back into your flying machines and go rescue my father from New Rome."

King Richard grimaced, and tried to manage a smile as he looked Ruth in the eye. "If only we could, young Ruth. If only we could. You see..." the King paused, trying to find the right words, "...we only barely made it here to help you. These craft were cobbled together with spare parts and pieces that we had to manufacture to get them to fly. We had some old mechanics that used to work on these things decades ago, but the machines sat unused and exposed to the elements for 20 years. I started the process of trying to get them flying again as soon as I received your father's letter. We did all we could to get here in time. We even concocted and cooked up the fuel we had to use to make them fly. But I've been told that what you just saw... that magnificent intervention in your war... was all that those old birds had in them. These helicopters were already old when the collapse happened. They were run, almost completely, by computers and we just don't have the technology, the expertise, or the infrastructure to operate them as they were intended to operate. You'd laugh if you knew how our mechanics made them fly for that one mission. Our enemy could have shot them down with slingshots if they hadn't been so afraid and stunned. Suffice it to say that it is only by God's own grace that we ever

322

made it here, and that we were able to intervene successfully. I feel comfortable telling you that those craft will never fly again. In fact, my military officers have advised me to scuttle the craft so that the weapons on them cannot be seized by the enemy and copied." The King looked over the assembled fellowship and smiled his best smile. "I fear that we have all seen the end—at least in our days—of aerial warfare."

Phillip shook his head. "How was it done, Your Highness?"

"With bubblegum and toothpicks is the technical answer, Phillip. The computers were all dumped and everything was made 'fly-by-wire'. Every bit of excess weight was removed, and we just had to pray that the birds wouldn't fall out of the sky. We made it here using very short jumps, never flying more than ten to twenty miles at a time before we would have to land and completely go through the fuel system and double check everything again. The only extra weight we carried was for fuel and spare parts. We left with six helicopters, and we made it here with four. If we had been forced to go 100 more miles, we would have been on foot. Frankly, I think God helped us and guided us—and that is the spiritual answer."

"So you cannot help my father?" Ruth asked.

"I am not saying we cannot help, dear Ruth. But our help will have to be more... traditional. I have an army coming here to join us. They are sweeping up behind that treacherous and treasonous *former* Duke of Louisiana as we speak. The ex-Duke has been captured, tried, and hung as a traitor." The King turned to Phillip and continued, "When they finish mopping up the resistance in Louisiana, they will come here to help you as much as they can. There are currently 8,000 men who will be at your disposal. More than that, I cannot offer. I hope you will be pleased to accept them.

"As for us in the South States, we are preparing for trouble from that tyrant to the north. We *all* need to be preparing to deal with him."

Phillip and Gareth looked at one another, then turned back to the King. "A tyrant to the north, Your Highness?" Gareth asked. "Are there problems to the north?"

"Problems to the north?   Oh, absolutely yes there are problems to the north!"

"Your Highness," Phillip said, "the Vallenses have just fled to the north. All of them! They headed that way just days ago to escape the clutches of Aztlan and to avoid being squeezed between him and the Duke of Louisiana."

"Oh, dear!" King Richard whispered, looking up towards heaven.   His gray eyes closed and he seemed to be praying silently for a moment, before his eyes opened again and he looked intently at Ruth.

"May the God of Heaven protect and keep the Vallenses!"

THE END of Book One

Epilogue

Before the collapse, it was easy for scoffers to deny that things could ever get so bad. There were three fundamental errors that were pervasive at the time of the crash, and that resulted in the failed worldview that predominated when the world as we knew it came to an end. These three errors were:

1. The *Ceteris Parabus* Fallacy (also called the "Normalcy Bias")
2. Denying Catastrophism
3. The "Strongest Will Survive" Fallacy

The human mind is naturally, but irrationally married to the idea of *Ceteris Parabus. Ceteris Parabus* literally means, *"all other things being equal or held constant."* The *Ceteris Parabus* fallacy holds that although there may be disruptions or slight changes, for the most part things will eventually return to some semblance of "normal." The problem is, that "normal" was usually defined by the early 21st century mind as "the relatively recent and historically aberrant ways of the modern world developed predominantly in the the 19th and 20th centuries." So, it was rarely ever assumed that "normal" might mean: *"the way in which men has lived for almost all of history, up until the very recent advent of the Industrial Revolution."* To modern man, the last couple of centuries of industrial and consumer living *were* the normal to which the world would always return. Although electricity and the ubiquity of machines and electronics-based production were a historically new phenomenon, man naturally believed that the new ways were the *normal* ways.

The second error made by the scoffers was that they always based their estimations on the idea that world population would always increase, and that even through interruptions, however grave, *most* of the people would survive. This is to say that, although most people accepted catastrophism in their religion or in their understanding of how the world was formed, they denied catastrophism could possibly continue on into the future. Catastrophism was always just a historical phenomenon. So, man assumed that catastrophe had formed and framed the world, had affected and influenced all of history, and had on many occasions wiped out entire civilizations, but now that we had computers and machines, all of those things were now in the past. They could never happen again. In effect, the more dependent mankind became on very tenuous and untrustworthy technologies; the more man grew soft from the lack of physical labor; the more man (in general) lost the skills and knowledge to survive, the more he assumed irrationally that his culture was not subject to failure.

The third error that led to the collapse was the historically disproven theory that the stronger a culture or an empire becomes militarily, the more likely it is to survive. However much history has proven that the meek of the land survive, and that empires fall and disappear into the dustbin of history, man insists that militarism and strength are the one thing needful to survival. What was the result of this irrationality? Mankind, as a whole, was completely unprepared for what was, historically speaking, clearly inevitable. Looking back, even Preparedness people, Survivalists, and Apocalypticists were grossly unprepared. Most of the world denied it could ever happen, but, of those who knew that it would happen, only a rare few were actually already living a simple, sustainable, and survivable life. Those who depended inordinately on gear and gadgets, or fieldcraft and short term survival skills—whilst still remaining dependent in the long run on a consumerist world that rejected production—perished with most of the willfully ignorant world.

One of the reasons so many people fell into these errors is because the prophets of modernity, both in and out of religion, were selling peace and safety at all costs. Comfort and ease are always easier to sell than hard work, responsibility, sustainability, and simplicity. Ways to satiate the conscience were provided;

326

there were endless charities and missions and causes, so long as no one actually decided to unplug and everyone stayed on the rails that delivered the world into the inevitability of collapse.

There were no guarantees of safety or survival for anyone when the world as we knew it came to an end, but history—that unmerciful and inflexible reality—tends to always re-impose itself (at least statistically) despite the erroneous and arrogant opinions of men who generally reject facts in favor of wishes. History is a stubbornly persistent spectre. Men, insisting that the survival of the fittest had shaped their present reality, were surprised to find out that their own worldview of dependence and consumption had resulted in them being phenomenally unfit to survive. How embarrassing.

Our Vallenses were far from perfect. They made mistakes and paid for them as we all must, but they had their own advantages, not the least of which was their insistence that they produce more than they consume, and that they not rely on unsustainable and unviable systems for their survival. Their thirty years in Central Texas never corrupted them to the point that they insulated themselves from the production and preservation of good food and clean water. Now, as has so often happened, tossed about by the caprices and greed of tyrants and men, they became pilgrims in the land and exiles from their own homes and hearths. This too was hardly without historical precedent.

The flight of the Vallenses from Texas to parts north is now the stuff of lore and legend. For months they struggled against the harsh terrain, the brutal weather, and their own natural desires for home and hearth; and, for the most part, they overcame. The Vallensian pilgrimage became the largest mass migration of a nation of people since the collapse. Viewed historically, however, the pilgrimage would have to be considered almost commonplace.

There were losses along the way. The pain and suffering and toil of migration took its toll among the Vallenses. Many of the *oldlings* died along the way, and were buried in graves stretching from Texas into Missouri. There were attacks by bandits and raids by thieves, but the Vallenses were a resilient

327

people, and they were looking for a peaceful place to call their temporary home. Unhappily, when God sends a people into exile for His own purposes, things often get worse long before they get better.

In January following the exodus of the Vallenses from Texas, the now 20,000 pilgrims were surrounded by military forces operating under the auspices of the de-facto "King" of the North. Their militia escort had been forced to turn back weeks earlier due to dwindling supplies and other necessities. After failing to convince the Vallenses to stop or turn back, the militia regretfully informed the Elders that they must return to Texas.

General Amos DuPlantis, a former National Guard officer based at Fort Leonard Wood in Missouri, after having seized power in the vacuum created by the collapse, had declared himself the military leader of the North States. Suspicious of the peaceful claims and aims of the Vallenses, General DuPlantis ordered the Vallenses to be driven into a massive work and internment camp located southwest of what was once Springfield, Missouri.

The Vallenses, unable, unprepared, and unwilling to fight, were herded wholesale into a massive "resettlement" work camp for refugees and potential subversives, and once again their hearts were humbled and their future looked bleak.

Tired and cold and decimated from four months of hard travel, the Vallenses were forced to wait in insufferable lines in the freezing weather of winter, in order to be processed into the camp.

Mr. Byler the *oldling* Cobbler, one of the few Vallenses old enough and historically literate enough to understand the true meaning of the words, looked up before walking through the gates of the camp and his fading eyes fell upon the ironic sign there posted:

"WORK WILL SET YOU FREE."

The adventure had just begun...

Addendum
Jonathan's Letter

TO

HIS GREAT MAJESTY

RICHARD the FIRST,

KING of the SOUTH STATES

Sir,

At the hazard of relating events and history that are already well known to the King, it is necessary that I provide you with a brief (or as brief as will suffice) summary of the recent history of our people and our lands before and after the collapse of the United States of America only twenty years ago.

In the intervening decades, despite hardships and difficulties—not unlike those faced by others that survived the upheavals that followed the collapse and dissolution of America and the industrialized civilization throughout the world—our people have not only survived but have thrived in what was once considered the inhospitable land and climate of Central Texas. For this reason, it pains me to say that our land is currently and unhappily under the thumb of the Kingdom of Aztlan and his puppet, the Duke of El Paso.

The world knows of the continuing miracle of our preservation and success, of the growth of what was once a nominal and largely unheard of sect into a mini nation-state of many thousands of souls, and of the proliferation of Vallensian colonies in Texas and elsewhere in North America. Prior to our lands coming under the pretended civil control of the Kingdom of Aztlan, we were sought out, and appealed to, by virtually every ruler and nation in North America, *your own nation not excepted*, to remove ourselves from Texas and to relocate to their countries. They valued our wisdom and hoped that, with our help, they too could bring the wilds of their own lands, now uncultivated and unproductive due to massive depopulation and a lack of expertise required to survive in the current climate, under that benevolent dominion and tillage for which our people are now universally famous. Notwithstanding the numerous generous offers—including that most graciously made to us by your own respected predecessor—we have chosen to remain in our own lands, believing that God Almighty has given these plains and hills unto us in order to magnify His own glory in the taming of such a supposedly inhospitable place even in this difficult time. This is our home.

Our people have overcome so many adversities, as well as the attacks and genocidal intentions of our enemies; and, having endured it all, we again stand in peril of the loss of our lives and lands.

We find ourselves, as a peaceful and passive people, under the threat of annihilation and genocide by the treacherous King of Aztlan, who—despite our peaceful ways and productive lives—desires to bring us into subjection to his own mind and sovereignty (via his pestilent hirelings). He aims to impose upon us his oppressive military tyranny, as well as his own religion—one that is abhorrent to our people and inherently contrary to our own.

We came into this land over 30 years ago, separating ourselves from the Kingdoms of This World, in order to live our lives peaceably, producing our living from the land by the sweat of our own brow. By choosing this simple way of life, we were no burden to any man or government. We lived and worked with the intention of being a blessing to those 'round about by making our poor desert rangeland good and productive soil, and by being an example of good stewardship and responsibility to the people who then lived in the cities and towns around us. This we did diligently, obeying all of the rules and requirements of men and magistrates that were not specifically contrary to the commandments of our God. Our own countrymen that have relocated into Your Grace's country may bear you witness that our conduct has always been pure and holy and that we in no way have tried to gather unto ourselves power, prestige, or position. We have not, heretofore, born arms against the King of Aztlan; rather, we have submitted ourselves (as much as we are able)—according to the commandments of our God—to those civil magistrates with whom God has seen fit to burden us.

During our first ten years on the land (the decade before the collapse), we worked tirelessly, and had managed to build our infrastructure—constructing barns and out-buildings, and working to make productive soil out of what was once marginal range land. We captured rainwater by building ponds, tanks, and cisterns. As much as we could, we relied on our own productivity and the improvement of our lands in order to provide the basic life necessities for ourselves. We weaned ourselves from the common culture of consumption, and, in effect, created a viable, alternative society—one based on production, rather than consumption. During this time, we devoted much of our own precious time and resources to teaching others to do as we did, and actively participated in helping others to learn to survive and thrive in the difficult times that were certain to follow.

When the collapse came, we were not taken by surprise, as most people were; and though we had no way of knowing exactly when that collapse would come, we were absolutely certain that it *would* come and therefore we had prepared diligently for it.

Following the initial maelstrom of violence that accompanied the collapse of the system of consumer supply, there were uncountable disasters, systemic failures, and civil wars leading up to the inevitable dissolution of the civil governments based on that system, and a restructuring of the global political landscape. In the aftermath, many disparate fiefdoms arose, each vying for civil power and authority in the vacuum that resulted from the collapse. We took no part in that struggle for power and in no way sought to gain from the global demise.

The tragic die-off and depopulation of the continent; the end of the availability and ubiquity of inexpensive electrical power; the re-localization of just about every resource; and the subsequent restructuring of society along the lines and model of medieval Europe—all of these factors brought about a 'New World Order', only it was a world order modeled after the monarchial system that has reigned among men for most of history.

Although we were not untouched by the global tragedy, and have suffered greatly, we praise our God that we were protected from the bulk of the violence, anarchy, and bloodshed that destroyed much of the former country in the aftermath of the collapse.

The primary area in which we were correct concerning the manner of the collapse was in our prediction that there would be a loss of power on the global scale, rendering most "modern" technology unusable. The massive loss of life and infrastructure brought about by the collapse (or rather, the inevitable destruction that followed) was beyond what most people imagined. I praise God for sparing us from the worst of it, protecting us via our remote and seemingly unattractive location, our predilection for preparedness and sustainability, along with the many other deliverances we experienced via Divine intervention.

As we had rejected most modern technologies long before the collapse—deeming them detrimental to our safety, our security, our peace, and the simplicity of our lifestyle—we had many advantages in the very hard years that would come.

After a year or so had passed from the worst events of the collapse, many cliques, sects, and entities started vying for power. Our own region first fell under the pretended authority of the first Kingdom of Mexico, a realm hastily thrown together by criminal political and military groups south of the former border, in an attempt to fill the vacuum of power left by the dissolution of the government of the United States.

Our lands were in the far northeastern region of this dominion; thus, owing to difficult travel conditions, we were mostly left to ourselves during the few years of this period.

Moral judgments aside, the first King of Mexico did us little real harm—though I am certain he would have consumed us and/or enslaved us for our productive capability had he been able or permitted to do so by God.

Shortly after, the power of the King of Mexico waned due to the over-extension and over-reaching of his grasp. He was unable to control his northern reaches (especially the drug cartels and criminal enterprises) any better than the nation of Mexico had done prior to the collapse. Thus, when he had run out of ammunition for his guns—and when most of the more productive citizens had been killed or had fled from his poor management and insatiable greed—the King of Mexico was overthrown by the citizenry of his own realm. The new power vacuum didn't remain for long and, within a year, the people of Northern Mexico (the former border states) found themselves overwhelmed by the onrushing invader from the West.

The King of Aztlan—whose power was constituted mainly of the heavily armed drug gangs once at war with one another along the border between America and Mexico—sensed the weakness of his own kinsmen within the first Kingdom of Mexico. Upon the fall of the King of Mexico, he swiftly moved his armies westward from what was left of California and, through murder and violence, absorbed the northern portion of the Kingdom of Mexico into his own Kingdom. Regardless of what Aztlan has claimed, the King was only able to maintain any real control of the former border regions from California to as far as El Paso in Texas, including the southern Rocky Mountain areas in the former New Mexico that he had first conquered with his initial northward push during the early days of the collapse.

On the foothills of the Sangre de Christo mountains (in a place once known as Taos, New Mexico), Aztlan constructed their new capitol which they named New Rome.

The collapse marked the end of more than just the industrial, digital, and consumer revolutions. The drug revolution died with it too. This, in my view, was a foregone conclusion, given some very important and inescapable facts:

The population of North America—according to rather conservative estimates—was reduced by almost 90%, thereby destroying the primary market for illicit drugs. Admittedly, these numbers are estimates, since we have very little information from any of the areas in the northern regions of North America.

There was no coherent, recognizable, accepted currency for many years that followed. Even corrupt farmers were unwilling to dedicate hundreds of acres to drug production when most of the people were starving, and when there was no easy and transferrable means of exchange.

In the absence of the soul-deadening comforts, artificially created and sustained by the former social, cultural, economic, and financial system, very few people who survived were tempted to use drugs. Moreover, former drug users were ill-prepared for the new hardships, and they rarely survived. Thus, the problem took care of itself.

The collapse of the former, rather lucrative, means of support for the Kingdom of Aztlan meant that evil had to seek other financial opportunities. Kings and nations generally resolve to follow one of two policies as it pertains to feeding and supplying the people:

Supporting and protecting the productive capabilities of the people, encouraging them and incentivizing them to work hard and be productive, or,

Reliance on consumption, specialization, aggression, tyranny, and military conquest in order to maintain and expand the Kingdom.

Every nation-state—whether its citizens realize it or not—travels down one of these two paths. While it is obvious that your own highness has chosen the former and most godly route, the King of Aztlan has openly chosen the latter.

We have not accepted this usurpation, though we are officially under his dominion. Our lands were our own and were worked and improved by our own hands long before any usurpers came to claim divine right over our soil.

As Your Highness knows, we have been courted by many monarchs because of the inherent value that is annexed to our right management and benevolent dominion of our soil. What, then, can be the reason that the King of Aztlan and his wicked magistrate the Duke of El Paso, despite all of the benefits he, his fiefdom, and his people would enjoy by dealing benevolently with us, have determined to destroy us unless we succumb to his rule?

Why does he deal harshly with us, when we seek nothing but peace, and—if left in peace—we might help feed his people and help his Kingdom to prosper? Is it not that the King of Aztlan and his compatriot, the Duke of El Paso, seek to pacify and homogenize the entire rightful Republic of Texas in order to use it as a launching pad and base for the invasion of your own realms? If my assumption is incorrect, what other benefit could there possibly be to this usurper King?

Would your own highness waste resources and manpower to subjugate or obliterate a peaceful and productive people in your own realm? Of course not!

The belligerent actions of the King of Aztlan only make sense if it is his intention to unite himself with his co-religionists in Louisiana to move militarily against a more profitable foe. It is our belief that our destruction or subjugation is only an intermediate step by the King of Aztlan in his overall plan to make war against your own Kingdom—a fact your highness ought to urgently consider.

Our people, who are ever grateful to Your Highness for any benevolence shown to us, are not willing to make war against the King of Aztlan, although many would have us do so. We are peace lovers and we believe in eschewing all violence. We believe that the 'sword of just defense' lies in the hand of legitimate civil magistrates, and, before God, we call upon those magistrates to do what is right—to protect the innocent and punish all evildoers.

While we do rely on Providence and the goodness and mercy of Almighty God to defend and protect us, we appeal to you, His servant, that you might be a sword and a scourge in the hand of the Mighty King of Kings, to protect His beloved.

Help us.

I am your obedient servant,

Jonathan Wall - Elder and Pastor among the Vallenses

Make sure to be looking for Book Two of The Last Pilgrims saga...

Cold Harbor, by Michael Bunker

http://facebook.com/ coldharborbook

Coming Soon!

A Must Read Non-Fiction book by Michael Bunker:

Surviving Off Off-Grid: Decolonizing the Industrial Mind

ISBN: 0615447902

Western Society is in confusion, the industrial world is teetering on collapse, and it looks like things could get worse. Agrarian Blogger, historian, and "plain" preacher Michael Bunker has been living off of the grid for many years, and he has some advice for those living in the industrial/consumerist economy... living an off off-grid life is achievable. It has been done for thousands of years, and it can be done today...

It is quite possible that many people who have relied on a failing system for their means of survival will very soon find that they have made a mistake of historic proportions. Historic, because every major "classical" culture went down the same road our society is on today. This book is about the lessons we should have learned, and...

what you can do to survive, and what history tells us must come next.

An excerpt from one of the many 5 star reviews of Surviving Off Off-Grid:

From the Granny Miller blog
 (http://homesteadgardenandpantry.com)
            written by Richard Grossman –

      "This book is not an apologia for Mr. Bunker's theology (though it informs him and is found throughout the book). This work is otherwise hard to categorize. It is part history, part cultural criticism, with some biography. It is explicitly not another
338

"how to" book, but the intelligent reader will extract many practical ideas. The best way I can characterize this book, is that it is about mindset. Mindset is what lets the soldier, policeman or armed citizen win a fight. Mindset is the most important difference between the dead and the survivors in any crisis. Mr. Bunker's thesis is that industrialism and urbanity have "colonized" the human mind in 21stCentury America, and he has set out to de-colonize it. This de-colonizing will create a mindset that will allow families to thrive in what may become an increasingly difficult future.

While dealing with the lofty subject of human thought, this book is anything but academic. The style is very readable and conversational. The prepper or survivalist will find some serious tests to determine just how prepared he really is (starting with some discussion about what the word "Survival" really means). A person who has never thought deeply about how our nation devolved into the present mess will hopefully read this as a needed alarm call. The homesteader or small farmer of any level of experience will find keys to better his endeavors by thinking in new ways.

While I am not an advocate of agrarian separatism, I believe Mr. Bunker may be one of the few people who could write this book. His separatism gives him a perspective of distance from the "grid" (which is much more than mere electric power, including debt and wage slavery, and the omnipresent corporate/government alliance)."

Facebook and Twitter

If you were benefited by this book, visit Michael Bunker on Facebook:

http://facebook.com/michaelbunker

Michael's Twitter:

http://twitter.com/mbunker (@mbunker)

Other Books by Michael Bunker:

<u>Surviving Off Off-Grid</u>, by Michael Bunker (2011). ISBN 9780615447902

<u>Modern Religious Idols</u>, by Michael Bunker (2011). ISBN 9780615498317

<u>Swarms of Locusts: The Jesuit Attack on the Faith</u>, by Michael Bunker (2002). ISBN 0595252974

Michael Bunker constrains most of his communication to "snail mail" (traditional post). Please write him a letter if you have questions, comments, or suggestions. Michael does keep a very small, very intimate email alert list. To receive Michael Bunker's e-mail alerts, which are rare but do include notifications when new sermons or podcasts are posted, and updates on Michael's ministry, ministry trips, etc., please send an e-mail to:

editor@lazarusunbound.com

To listen to the Michael Bunker Radio Show please go to:
www.blogtalkradio.com/michaelbunker.

You can subscribe to Michael's show on iTunes.com

CPSIA information can be obtained at www.ICGtesting.com
Printed in the USA
LVOW091626200712

290925LV00009B/62/P